Advance Pr...
BLACK

"Leah Raeder crafted a darkly delicate yet twistedly honest exploration of self-truth when she penned *Black Iris*. Each page had me racing toward the end."

—Gail McHugh,
New York Times bestselling author of the Collide series

"Fearless, inspiring, and a story that does more than just keep you enthralled. It holds you by the damn throat."

—Penelope Douglas,
New York Times bestselling author of *Bully*

"Erotic, poetic, heartbreaking, captivating, and full of mind-blowing twists and turns; *Black Iris* is the best book I've read this year. Hands down."

—Mia Asher,
author of *Easy Virtue*

"Raeder masterfully weaves a dark, twisted, dangerously sexy quest for revenge with a raw, honest search for kinship and self-acceptance. *Black Iris* demands your attention, your heart, and an immediate reread."

—Dahlia Adler,
author of *Last Will and Testament*

"Reading *Black Iris* was like being caught up in a fever dream. The lyrical prose and heavy-hitting imagery stole my breath away. The moment I set it down, I wanted to pick it up and start all over again."

—Navessa Allen,
author of *Scandal*

"A suspense novel that looks at the dark depths of the human mind. . . . Nothing short of intoxicating."

—*The Book Geek*

Praise for
UNTEACHABLE

"With an electrifying fusion of forbidden love and vivid writing, the characters glow in Technicolor. Brace yourselves to be catapulted to dizzying levels with evocative language, panty-blazing sex scenes, and emotions so intense they will linger long after the last page steals your heart."

—Pam Godwin,
New York Times bestselling author of *Beneath the Burn*

"*Unteachable* is a lyrical masterpiece with a vivid story line that grabbed me from the very first page. The flawless writing and raw characters are pure perfection, putting it in a class all by itself."

—Brooke Cumberland,
USA Today bestselling author of *Spark*

"Leah Raeder's writing is skillful and stunning. *Unteachable* is one of the most beautifully powerful stories of forbidden love that I have ever read."

—Mia Sheridan,
New York Times bestselling author of *Archer's Voice*

"Edgy and passionate, *Unteachable* shimmers with raw desire. Raeder is a captivating new voice."

—Melody Grace,
New York Times bestselling author of the Beachwood Bay series

ALSO BY LEAH RAEDER

Unteachable

BLACK IRIS

LEAH RAEDER

ATRIA PAPERBACK

NEW YORK   LONDON   TORONTO   SYDNEY   NEW DELHI

ATRIA PAPERBACK
An Imprint of Simon & Schuster, Inc.
1230 Avenue of the Americas
New York, NY 10020

First Atria Paperback edition April 2015

ATRIA PAPERBACK and colophon are trademarks of Simon & Schuster, Inc.

For information about special discounts for bulk purchases, please contact Simon & Schuster Special Sales at 1-866-506-1949 or business@simonandschuster.com.

The Simon & Schuster Speakers Bureau can bring authors to your live event. For more information or to book an event, contact the Simon & Schuster Speakers Bureau at 1-866-248-3049 or visit our website at www.simonspeakers.com.

Interior design by Kyoko Watanabe

Manufactured in the United States of America

10 9 8 7 6 5 4 3 2 1

Library of Congress Cataloging-in-Publication Data
Raeder, Leah.
 Black iris / Leah Raeder. — First Atria Paperback edition.
  pages ; cm
 I. Title.
 PS3618.A35955B58 2015
 813'.6—dc23
                                                2014041873

ISBN 978-1-4767-8642-1
ISBN 978-1-4767-8643-8 (ebook)

For all the girls I've loved

BLACK IRIS

APRIL, LAST YEAR

*A*pril is the cruelest month, T. S. Eliot said, and that's because it kills. It's the month with the highest suicide rate. You'd think December, or even January—the holidays and all that forced cheer and agonized smiling pushing fragile people to the edge—but actually it's spring, when the world wakes from frost-bound sleep and something cruel and final stirs inside those of us who are broken. Like Eliot said: *mixing memory and desire, stirring dull roots with spring rain.* In the deepest throes of depression, when sunlight is anguish and the sky throbs like one big raw migraine and you just want to sleep until you or everything else dies, you're less likely to commit suicide than someone coming *out* of a depressive episode. Drug companies know this. That's why antidepressants have to be marked with the warning MAY CAUSE SUICIDAL THOUGHTS.

Because what brings you back to life also gives you the means to destroy yourself.

———

Flick, flick, flick. The lighter in my hand, the sound of my life grinding into sparks that would never catch, under a salmon-pink dawn in Nowhereville, Illinois. Gravel crunched beneath my shoes, polished like oyster shell from the rain. I stopped at the puddle outside our garage and peered into the oily mirrored water, watching the slow swirl of a gasoline rainbow, the tiny orange tongue of fire licking shadows from my face until they washed back over and over. An unlit cigarette hung from my lip and my mouth had a weird bleach taste I tried not to think about. I tried not to think about anything that had happened last night. I was eighteen and, according to Mom, "completely out of control," which to anyone else would have meant "a normal teenager." Mom's favorite hobby: projecting her own psych issues onto me.

Very soon I'd be free of her.

From the alley I could see the backyard, the grass jeweled with dew. Mom's garden lined the walk to the porch, hyacinths with their cones of curled blue stars, rosebuds crumpled like flakes of dried blood, everything glazed in clear lacquer and the air musky with the cologne of rain. At six fifteen she'd wake and find my bed empty. But that wasn't the real problem. The real problem was that in about three minutes, something terrible was going to happen. The thing you'll hate me for. The thing that will make me an Unsympathetic Protagonist.

Since the fourth wall is down, let's get one thing straight:

I am not the heroine of this story.

And I'm not trying to be cute. It's the truth. I'm diagnosed borderline and seriously fucked-up. I hold grudges. I bottle my hate until it ferments into poison, and then I get high off the fumes. I'm completely dysfunctional and that's the way I like it, so don't expect a character arc where I finally find Redemption, Growth, and Change, or learn How to Forgive Myself and Others.

Fuck forgiveness.

Oh, and I'm a writer. Which is worse than all the rest put together.

Open sesame, I texted my brother.

I don't know how I didn't hear it. It was quiet, the crickets creaking like a rusty seesaw, but that other sound must have been there, scratching softly at my brain. I crept into the backyard through the maze of Mom's thorns.

The house was dark, Donnie's curtains closed. *Wake up fuckface*, I texted, punctuating with a smiley. Six twelve a.m. Three minutes until Medusa's alarm went off. Donnie always slept with his phone under his pillow, which was probably slowly giving him cancer. He should've been up by now. *Mom's gonna kill me*, I wrote. *Do you want to be an only child?*

Six thirteen.

Dammit. I had to beat that alarm.

I bolted across the lawn, kicking pearls of dew loose from the grass. A thorn snagged my ankle but I wouldn't notice the blood till much later, in the hospital. My socks instantly went damp. It wasn't until I'd reached the porch that I saw the other tracks, paralleling mine.

A chill swept up my back. I touched the kitchen doorknob. Unlocked.

I didn't open it. That coldness wove around my spine, thickening, binding. Someone was awake. Someone had come downstairs, crossed the yard before me.

I turned.

She was in the garage, at the window. I knew my mother's silhouette from long years of it slipping into doorways, catching us horsing around when we should've been asleep, catching me when I snuck in alone after midnight, my body weary and ancient with all that had been done to it. I knew the high set of those shoulders, that neck rigid with contempt. The closed mouth carved tight into her elegant Gorgon skull. She'd stand there without saying a word. Her silence was the kind that compelled you to fill it with all your wrongs. I could never see her eyes but I knew they burned ice-wraith blue, and now I felt them through the dusty window pane, felt the stare that could turn me to stone.

I removed the lighter slowly from my pocket. Flicked it once with exaggerated languor. Lit up. Took a long, luxuriously filthy drag, meeting her stare. The inside of my body felt carbon-coated, black and grimy. Not the soft pink vulnerable thing I really was.

Okay, bitch. Your move.

She just stood there.

Those moments counted. Those moments when I faced her, eating fire and breathing smoke, telling myself I was hard, that I could crush her and this whole world in my hands. Telling myself she couldn't hurt me. No one could hurt me anymore.

Those moments could have saved us.

By the time I reached the end of the cigarette the sun had torn a red gash at the horizon, and I saw that Mom was unsteady on her feet, swaying. And finally I realized what that rhythmic sound was beneath the crickets. I knew it from climbing up into the garage rafters with my brother to smoke a J, the beams creaking with our weight. Wood, under strain.

I dropped my cigarette in the grass.

In some deep part of me, I already knew. I crossed the lawn, noticing the white square taped to the side door only when I touched the knob. A name scrawled across the paper in her bold, slashing handwriting.

Delaney.

How had she known it would be me?

I ignored the note. I was trying to turn the doorknob and failing. Locked.

"Mom," I said, and rattled the door, then again, louder, "Mom."

She swayed dreamily.

A light flipped on inside the house, a yellow frame falling over me. I braced both hands on the knob and kicked. Everything stretched away like the reflection in a car mirror.

My mind floated above my head, looking down at my body: Laney Keating, her hair matted, a black wash of mascara running down her cheeks, her mouth still bitter from the blowjob, throttling the garage door and screaming her mother's name. I watched her from a faraway place. She gave up kicking and punched straight through the window in a brilliant starburst of glass. I felt the heat shoot up my arm like a drug, saw the redness streaking over my skin, but didn't quite connect it to me, to the girl crawling in over those jagged glass teeth, tumbling to the floor, scrambling up and screaming as she grabbed her mother's legs and uselessly lifted the limp, hanging body. My mind was still outside, staring at my name on the suicide note. All I could think was, How did she know I'd find her? How did she know it would be me?

———

I don't remember much else because I blacked out thirty seconds later. Dad had seen me from the house and dragged me onto the lawn, then Mom, laying us side by side. I was unconscious but somehow I can picture it. Grass curling over bone-white skin, tracing horsetails of dew, tiny clear beads that reflect an entire world full of stars and flowers and our pale bodies, everything she'd left behind. My blood mixed with the dew and turned pink. The glass would leave scars on my right hand like the ghost of a cobweb, which is what scars are: a haunting of the skin.

At the funeral Dad said he thought she'd killed us both. He'd been a heartbeat from getting his semiautomatic and joining us when he realized I had a pulse.

This might sound fucked-up, but the part that really upset me wasn't the suicide. That had been a long time coming. What disturbed me was that she knew I'd find her first.

I am my mother's daughter.

I know what it feels like to plan something that will destroy you, to be so fucking sure you want it that you arrange everything perfectly, prune the roses while you debate the merits of hanging yourself with nylon rope versus an appliance cord, serve your children baked ziti while your suicide note lies in a desk drawer like a cruel bird of prey waiting to unfold its wings until, one morning when the world is diamond-strung with rain and your daughter is coming home from another night of ruining herself (because you were never there for her, you were never there), you get up before everyone else and calmly step into the garage, and that noose, and eternity.

She'd planned it for years. Knew it was coming and kept tending that garden. Those roses she would never see bloom, the irises and peonies, the daughter and son, all of us left behind to flower, somehow, without her.

Well, I did. I bloomed into the dark thing she made me.

I am a creature with a vast capacity for patience, and for violence. For watching. For waiting. For taking the moment only when it is perfect and sure. I'm a hunter like my mother, patient and watchful and still, my fangs full of black venom. There is a terrible thing tucked inside me raring to lunge forth into the light. And I'm just waiting for that perfect moment. Just waiting. Just waiting.

JULY, LAST YEAR

I went to parties that summer. Every party within twenty miles. I was supposed to be prepping for college, getting a head start on my reading. Instead I got a head start on getting wasted.

Donnie came with me sometimes, sitting in the car while I went into the bedrooms of boys I barely knew. I took my clothes off and let the low lamplight paint me honey gold, my slender dragonfly limbs and iridescent skin like the body of a stranger, impossibly light, and I let them touch me while I swallowed pills and snorted powders, clogged my veins with chemicals. I don't know if I was trying to numb myself or to feel something through the numbness. Maybe both. Sometimes you feel things so much, so intensely, it becomes a new kind of numbness, the oblivion of overstimulation. I don't remember their names. It was easier to remember which ones I hadn't fucked. They were a blur of lean abs, sweat-rimed skin, the satin smoothness of hard dicks. My mouth was always slick with peppermint gloss. It made them tingle, they said. Funny that a girl like me would be so good at oral. But we are, you know. Good with our mouths. Janelle—my best and last friend senior year—stopped hanging out with me, claiming she wanted to spend time with her boyfriend before college. Really she just didn't want to be branded a whore by proxy.

Nothing like being slut-shamed by your so-called best friend.

I developed other skills in addition to giving legendary head: shoplifting, arson, vandalism. I got arrested with $437 worth of makeup and perfume stuffed into my underwear and bra. I pushed an old washing machine off an overpass and couldn't get the sound of that spectacular smash out of my head. My body felt like a heap of cheap plastic and glass, and I wanted to drop it off the highest point I could get to on oxy and X. Split every bad atom inside me. Get this wrongness out. One night I totaled Mom's car on a median and woke up in the ER with a concussion and my very first DUI. My BAC was under 0.08 percent and my lawyer said the magic words "mother's death" so I got off easy. Before he took me home, Dad sat at the wheel of the truck, motionless. In the hazy white light he looked as used and spent as me, his skin draping over his bones like a worn-out suit of himself. I thought he was going to cry and my throat thickened, the hot stitch behind my eyes loosening, but then he said, "You're a walking time bomb."

He was right. Mom was wrong. I was a precision-engineered explosive, in perfect control of my own self-destruction.

Later that week Dad said he wanted me out when college started. I was a bad influence on Donnie.

Just like my dead bitch of a mother.

———

Donnie slumped on the futon in my room, watching me try on dresses and discard them. There's nothing between my brother and me, no secrets, no suppressed incestuous subtext. He's two years younger and we know everything about each other. I've seen his dick, and it was like looking at an anatomical drawing. No Lannister shit.

"The black one," he said.

"I wore that at the funeral."

Donnie sighed. His eyes had that faraway fog that came with being really sad, or really high. I flopped onto the futon beside him. He'd been playing "The Mother We Share" on repeat for an hour, so I knew he was obsessing again, about her, and about me leaving. Donovan Keating looks like me: rangy and raven-haired, his nose dusted with sandy freckles, his eyes a mercurial mix of aqua and teal like that sea shade that eats away at old pennies. We both have the same coolness, the same ocean calm, but he's the sweet boy with a chick-magnet Tumblr and I'm the bad girl with a handgun for a heart. He smiles and panties melt. I don't smile. When I show teeth, it's to bite.

"I wish we were somewhere else," I said, laying my skull on his shoulder.

"Where?"

"Somewhere happy."

His arm curled around me. "I'm happy anywhere you are, Rainbow Brite."

Yes, I have an ironic eighties nickname. No, I was not even alive in the eighties.

"It'll be different when college starts," I said. "I'll miss you. You'll miss me. We'll do drugs to compensate."

"We already do."

"I'll miss you," I said more seriously. "So much. You're all I have."

We were quiet awhile. We were both thinking about her.

I stood, dragging a dress with my toe.

"I wish I was like you," Donnie said.

"Like what?"

"Free. You can just let it all go."

He may know me better than anyone, but he doesn't know everything. I never let go.

Dad was asleep in front of the TV, so we took his truck.

Out in the July night I threw my head back and drank a lung-ful of oxygen so rich with chlorophyll it was like wine. Every lawn was uniform green, layered with sod. This is the suburbs: they tear down nature, then you have to go to Home Depot to buy it back.

Interstate 88 ran through a prairie sea beneath an ocean of stars. The faint white shadow of the Milky Way lay like a ghostly finger across the night, holding in a secret. I leaned back while Donnie drove, my arm hooked out the window, the wind in my hair, my heart dilating as widely as the sky. Melancholy does that—opens you up to make space for more of itself.

City lights rose on the horizon, a twinkling zodiac, lifting higher and higher and sprawling to either side until we were in Chicago proper. We sat at red lights with no other cars in sight, just a homeless man curled up beside a shopping cart, two girls smoking below a bar sign that lit them like aquarium fish. They were ghosts, gone when you looked back. Then we were downtown, skyscrapers vaulting around us, and if I let my eyes unfocus it became a forest of chrome and glass, the trunks of massive trees quilted with fireflies. That big-city scent of gasoline and warm asphalt smelled like home.

The party was in Lincoln Park, on a leaf-canopied street lined with greystones and slick cars. It was one of our favor-ite haunts—Donnie, budding architect, would photograph houses while I made up stories about the people inside. I'm morbid, so they were bad people. Sex traffickers. Animal por-nographers. MFA grads. Now I was going into one of those houses, alone. Donnie fidgeted as I unbuckled my seatbelt.

"You don't have to do this, Lane."

"It's my last chance before classes start."

He pushed a lock of hair across his forehead one way, then the other.

"It'll be fine," I said. "He'll never see me."

"I could go with—"

"You're underage."

"Then why don't we go back home?"

"Because I can't live like this." The words shot out like shrapnel. "I have to get back to normal. Okay?"

"You are. You're the most normal person I know."

My heart swelled. Donnie doesn't know everything, but he knows who I want to be. He believes I can still be that person. Even if I don't.

We hugged. I slid out of the car.

"Be careful," he said.

"Always."

I punched in the code at the gate.

The house was massive and bearded with ivy, squares of buttery light falling onto the garden below. Smoke rose in lazy spirals from silhouettes on balconies. I walked through the front door into a dull roar that washed over me without sinking in. I'd taken a couple oxycodone on the drive and my skin was pleasantly woolly, every sensation softened.

A girl wearing a tight smile and an even tighter Phi Upsilon Alpha tee waved me over. "Welcome to the Summer Mixer. I don't think we've met."

"I'm rushing this year. Just wanted to check stuff out."

"Invitation?"

"My mom's an alumna. Caitlin Keating."

But now she's dead.

"Oh, so you're family. Fabulous. Drop your keys in the bowl if you drove. It's mostly sophs on the first floor, upperclassmen upstairs. I'm Mal."

"Laney."

"Great to meet you, Laney. Stay law-abiding, and have fun."

Those are mutually exclusive, I thought.

I began to move past her and she touched my elbow.

"You here alone?"

"Yeah."

She scanned me again, sharper. I'm a whopping five-foot-one, ninety pounds soaking wet, wide-eyed as those dolls that blink creepily on their own. Classic Dickensian waif.

"You look like the girl next door," she said with a note of pity. "Don't go upstairs."

As soon as her attention shifted, I headed for the staircase.

The second floor was pure raunch: strip poker, Jell-O wrestling, two girls Frenching messily while the crowd (male) whooped. Flyers littered the halls, advertising a local club. 80s NIGHT WITH DJ APOLLO. I wandered around, listening, watching, absorbing, until a beefy guy cornered me and offered a red cup. I refused. Never take drinks from strangers.

I could sense *him*.

At every blond head my spine went straight and tight as a cracked whip. His presence was in the air, gamy, meaty, an electrochemical clue that made my skin prickle. I eavesdropped on conversations, hearing his name in slurred syllables. I felt the oily slide of his cologne over my skin. I felt his pheromones seeping into me, making every sensitive part of me harden and buzz.

I was hunting.

Gold flashed in the corner of my eye and flickered out of sight. I'd seen it before. I tracked it through sweaty skin and clouds of perfume to a closing bathroom door. There was an empty room opposite and I leaned in the dark doorway. My heart pumped liquid nitrogen, chilling me to the core.

I held my phone at eye level.

Breathe. Wait.

The bathroom door opened.

Now.

I tapped CAPTURE when a girl stepped out and her head snapped straight to me.

Our eyes locked. Blue, but not like mine. Bleached-out blue. Strapless black dress, bare skin and tattoos. Totally unlike the sorority sisters. She wore an oddly chagrined expression, as if I'd caught *her* doing something wrong. Neither of us moved. One beat, two, three.

She turned and left.

I sank to the floor, cradling my phone. My limbs were watery and weak. Not him. Not him.

"You look lost."

It was the beefy guy who'd tried to give me beer. He stood a few feet away, sipping.

" 'Not all those who wander are lost,' " I muttered.

"Tolkien."

I'd already dismissed him, seeing only a fleshy traffic cone to veer around, but now I looked again. Husky guy in a polo. Light beard, bland bologna-pink face. Standard-issue bro.

"Have you read the books?" he said.

"No, I just memorize quotes to impress neckbeards."

He blinked.

"Bye," I said, standing.

"Who's your favorite author?"

Nope.

"I'm Josh."

Almost to the stairs.

"Josh Winters. I'm a junior."

First step.

"Comp sci major. I read epic fantasy and I play MMOs and I don't know why I'm telling you this. But I've never met a girl who quotes Tolkien and I just want to know your name."

"Laney," I blurted in exasperation.

"Can I get you a drink?"

"No."

"I'm sorry if I offended you. You're just—you're beautiful," he said, and it became excruciatingly obvious how desperate he was. I don't have illusions about my looks. I'm only slightly pretty in a decaying, feral way, my hair a little ragged, my makeup a little sloppy, my gaze a little too piercing and direct. What guys are attracted to is the sluttiness—the give-no-fuck way I carry myself, the mouth that knows how to suck a dick.

"Want to go outside?" he said. "It's quieter."

"No."

"Okay. We can talk here. Or wherever you want."

I stared at him silently.

"What are you into?" he said.

"Revenge."

"Is that a TV show?"

I said nothing.

"How about books? Music? What do you do for fun?"

"I don't have fun."

"Then what do you do at parties?"

"Get high enough to fuck."

He started to smile, hesitantly. "Is that a joke?"

Back to the stairs.

"You're better than me," he called, and dammit, I paused. "You don't care about climbing the social ladder. About playing the game. That takes guts. I wish I could be that way. I wish I didn't care so much what people think of me."

Great. One of those guys who spill all their insecurities to any girl who doesn't reject them firmly enough.

"Sometimes I think I'm just not cut out for this," he went on. "I don't memorize pickup lines. I don't know how to talk about anything except books and games, and then I don't know how to stop talking."

"Maybe that's your pickup line."

"It's a pretty bad one."

"It got me to stop."

He smiled, a tremulous, sincere smile. He was really trying.

"Look, you seem nice, Josh, but you don't want to know me."

"Give yourself some credit. You're smart, and you read, and you don't care what anyone thinks. I would love to know you."

It was his voice that did it, I think. Patient, kind. One of the good-natured sheep.

"Okay," I said. "So, do you want to fuck?"

His face was priceless.

Josh didn't move until I went up and took his big sweaty hand. Then he looked at mine with incredulity and enfolded it gently, as if afraid he might crush me, or that I'd disappear.

Next floor up. His room. Bookshelves filled end-to-end, titles I'd have loved to browse. Rumpled bed. A kite of violet moonlight slanting across the floor. My heart skittered.

You're in control, I told myself.

He led me in shyly, pawing at my dress and hair for a while until I took his face in my hands and kissed him. I willed myself to get aroused but couldn't focus. My gaze drifted to the window, to the city lights scattered like stardust across the sky, and I imagined myself as a constellation of cells, each light-years apart. What happened to my flesh took eons to reach my brain. However solid I seemed, inside I was vast spaces of dark energy and vacuum. Josh pressed me to the wall and thrust his beery tongue into my mouth and I thought, Just get to the point. I guided him to the hem of my dress, feeling nothing. Raised my arms and let it fall like a chrysalis, and my arms kept wanting to rise, like wings.

"You are so beautiful, Laney."

I kissed him to shut him up.

God, I was high. So close to that numb semiconsciousness

I craved. The place I imagined Mom had been when she was tying the noose. If she hadn't been such a prude, she could've dosed herself with little pieces of oblivion, like me.

If she'd been more like me, she'd still be alive.

Josh stripped down to his boxers, his erection poking out. I ran my fingertips lightly over the head and he shuddered.

"Get a condom," I said.

He lowered me to a bed that smelled of sun and grass and lost summers. My head was a million miles away from this. I was thinking about the old wood chipper rusting in our garage, wondering how it'd feel if I stuck an arm inside. If the bones would snap like dry wood, skin tearing, muscle fraying, a rag doll ripping apart. Mom chose the coward's way out. I'd have done it as messily as I could, made myself really *feel* something, because why not? If you know you're going to die, what's left to fear?

That's the thing. Maybe we're not really afraid of pain. Maybe we're afraid of how much we might like it.

Josh kissed the inside of my thigh and I stopped him. "Put a condom on."

"I want to make you come first."

"I can't even feel my legs."

His hand slid into my panties, his fingers doing something I couldn't figure out. "This doesn't feel good?"

"It doesn't feel like anything."

He sagged against me, cratering the bed.

"You can fuck me," I said matter-of-factly. "It's okay."

"This feels wrong. You're not into it."

"Like it matters."

"It does to me." He took a deep breath. "Can I just hold you for a while?"

Wow.

His arms circled me and I pressed my palms to the moon-painted sheet. My chest moved with each breath but I had no sensation of actually breathing, as if it were someone else's body. Half my life seems to have happened to someone else's body. This phenomenon has a name. I told Mom about it once, and before I even finished describing it she said *depersonalization.*

Sometimes I feel like a deperson.

"You seem so sad," Josh said.

Funny, how they mistake emptiness for sadness.

I lay quietly. After a few minutes we sat up and he put the dress back on me. I let him do it, and when he was done I kissed his cheek, picked up my bag, and left.

————

My mother used to say there are two kinds of people in this world:

Those who want, and those who take.

Most of us are sheep who spend our lives in want. We follow the path worn smooth and velvety from the hooves before us. There's no need for leashes or fences—we call those things law and morality. Man is the only animal that can reason and all he does with reason is shackle himself. We eat what we're fed and we fuck what we can't outrun and it's never what we dream about but it dulls the screaming edge of desire just enough. Enough so we keep our heads down, our eyes on the ground. Our fetters are fashioned from conformity and fear.

But sometimes an animal can't be contained. Sometimes a head lifts from the herd and a wolfish intelligence kindles, the nostrils flaring, the eyes catching sickles of moonlight and a hot, earthy breath clotting the cold air, and someone realizes there's really nothing stopping us from taking whatever we want.

And everything is prey.

On the street I lit a cigarette and leaned against the iron fence, watching my smoke fly away. The wind shook the trees softly, the leaves shivering, a sound like dry rain. The heart of the city felt like the middle of a wilderness. No one but Donnie knew I was here. I could disappear into the night, dragging a carcass behind me.

I could disappear forever.

Something pale shifted in the shadows below a tree, and I tensed.

"I'm not sure why I still go to these things," a male voice said. He stepped into a ring of warm streetlight. The paleness was his shirt; his skin was dusky bronze. "It's a meat market in there."

"Pretty sure meat has a higher IQ," I said.

He propped himself against the fence a few feet away, smiling. I couldn't make out much save a shock of white teeth, his face all hard planes of shadow fitting together in sharp chiaroscuro. Music swelled from the house and cut off abruptly at a door slam.

"Waiting for someone?" he said.

"About to leave."

"Not into Greek life?"

"Not into human connections."

His head tilted curiously. "So why come?"

"To skulk around in the shadows outside. Like you."

Soft laugh. "Touché. But it's more hiding than skulking."

I almost asked, *What could a frat boy be hiding from?*, but that would go against my human connection rule.

"Did you find him?" the guy said.

I froze with the cigarette halfway to my mouth, a corkscrew of smoke twisting slowly above my hand. "Who?"

"The person you were looking for."

Before I could respond, the gate banged open and a golden whirlwind swept between us, spinning around in the light.

"I swear to fucking God," the girl said in a low, accented voice, "you are a total shit for leaving me with those—" She noticed me then and laughed, so suddenly I jumped. It was the girl from the bathroom. The one I'd photographed. Of course. "She's here. Good. Did you find out why she's stalking me?"

"We were just getting to that," the guy said.

"I wasn't stalking you," I muttered, trying not to sound sheepish. "I thought you were someone else."

"How insulting. I'm incredibly stalkable." She snapped her purse open and pulled out a pack of cigarettes. "Got a light?"

It was an Australian accent, a mischievous twang in the vowels. That same mischief was in her face, in the curve at one corner of her mouth, the slyness in her heavy-lidded eyes. I handed her my lighter and she studied me, the flame splashing her face with amber, giving her a diabolical look.

"So." She exhaled. "Invite her yet?"

"I don't even know her name," the guy said.

"You're crap at picking up girls, Armin."

"That's why I leave it to you."

Aussie girl smirked. She wore that strapless black dress like a weapon, lithe and sleek, femme fatale–ish. The tats sleeving her slender arms soaked up the light. I still couldn't get a good look at the guy.

"The bloke with no discernible social skills is Armin," she said. "I'm Blythe. We're getting the fuck out of here. Want to come?"

"Where are you going?"

"Umbra."

The club from the flyer. "I'm not twenty-one."

"Maybe this isn't a great idea, Blythe," Armin said.

"Oh, piss off." She flicked her cigarette away in a pinwheel of sparks. "I was clubbing at fourteen, and look how I turned out."

"That's exactly my point."

Blythe laughed, so infectiously I did, too. She turned that incandescent smile on me. "Get a good photo?"

Blush. "I didn't look."

"Give me your mobile."

I gave it to her. She seemed like the kind of girl it was pointless to say no to.

She laughed again when she saw her pic. When she showed Armin I caught a better glimpse of him: the lean lines of his face, the smokiness around his eyes, as if smudged with coal dust. His hair was a rich brown streaked with rust. Latino, maybe, or Middle Eastern. As Janelle would have said: fuckhot. The two of them bent their heads together, and I realized they must be a couple.

"I look wretched," Blythe said. "You got me without my mask on."

" 'I like a look of agony, because I know it's true.' "

Yes, Laney. Totally fucking nerd out on them.

But she surprised me. "Emily Dickinson. The woman in white."

"English majors," Armin groaned.

"The plot thickens." Blythe returned my phone. She was looking at me differently now. "You know poetry."

"A little."

"A little is dangerous enough." She shot Armin an arch glance. "He only reads textbooks and image memes."

"Not true. I read your stuff."

"It's crap anyway."

"Oh, the false modesty. Blythe's good, and she knows it. Don't compliment her, though. Goes straight to her head."

"He thinks I'm egotistical."

"It's called pathological narcissism."

"They don't even have a clinical term yet for what's wrong with him. What about you, English major? You write?"

I was trying to follow their rapid-fire banter. "Sort of."

"Sort of how?"

"I'm working on a novel, but it's terrible."

Blythe laughed. "A girl after my own heart. What's your name?"

"Laney."

"Well, Laney, terrible novelist," she said, hooking one arm through mine and the other through Armin's, "you are cordially invited to join a bloody know-it-all and a pathological narcissist at Umbra tonight."

"I'll keep you away from bad influences," Armin said.

"He means me."

"She knows, Blythe." He eyed me over her head. "Coming?"

As if that was even a question. These were the smart, charmingly weird people I'd dreamed of meeting my whole life. Dad said college would be different, but adults just tell you that so you don't kill yourself. *It gets better* is the biggest lie they've sold to our generation, unless *it* means the meds. But here were a girl and boy too brainy and bizarre to fit in with the red-cup-and-condom crowd, and already I was half in love with them both.

These were the people I'd been waiting for.

How could I say anything but "Yes"?

———

I sat between them in the cab, though Blythe was the natural center of everything. Listening to her banter with Armin was like standing between two ballet dancers in a gunfight. They circled each other elegantly, feinting, pirouetting, setting up the fatal shot, and Blythe was usually the one to fire it point-blank to Armin's chest. He accepted his wounds with a gentleman's grace, and the dance resumed. I sank into the seat and let their voices hum on my skin. Ribbons of light threaded through the streets, cars flowing like pulses of illuminated blood into the city's steel heart. When we crossed the river Blythe grabbed my elbow and made me look: the water was a thick black stroke of ink speckled with gold flakes and silver chips, the shattered reflections of a thousand bright windows, shimmering. Her eyes sparkled the same way, filled with a thousand tiny lights.

"You're not looking," she said.

But I was.

Armin nudged my knee. "So who were you hunting, detective?"

If I wasn't still so high, I might've reacted more viscerally. Instead I felt it in a scientific way, his touch like an electromagnetic pulse, disturbing something in me at a particle level.

"Nobody."

"You took my picture," Blythe said.

"Wrong person."

"Who's the right person?" Armin said.

"Nobody."

They both laughed.

"How fun," Blythe said. "I love a game."

"It's not a game," I said.

"Oh, but you're wrong." Armin spoke to me, but he was looking at Blythe. "Everything is a game to her."

For the first time she didn't have a witty comeback. She just stared at him, eyes glittering, and somehow I knew he'd fired the lethal shot that round.

We cruised through dead streets where neon perfused the air like colored smoke. Traffic lights blinked on and off, emerald and citrine and ruby splitting in dazzling shards across our faces.

"So you guys are Greek?" I said to break the silence.

"I'm a Pi Tau alumnus," Armin said. "But those days are behind me."

"I'm Australian," Blythe said. "We don't pay for friends."

Armin leaned into me and stage-whispered, "Her culture is far more advanced. They wrestle crocodiles."

"Please. You Yanks are the worst. My first week here, I was propositioned by a porn director."

"It was not porn," Armin said, laughing.

"It totally was."

"This guy was casting students for an 'erotic art film,'" he explained. "It was tasteful."

"Art film, my arse. Like, literally."

"Blythe has little appreciation for cinema nouveau. I had to bail her out of jail. She was almost deported."

"What happened?" I said.

"Caught this perv filming my bum and smashed his camera. Should've been his face."

"She's a hands-on problem-solver," Armin said.

"Pervo kept talking about my 'star quality.' FYI, Laney, that is a euphemism for fanny."

"What she's failing to mention," Armin said, "is she tried to negotiate a higher rate. He didn't have the budget. Only then did she break his camera."

Blythe eyed him coolly. "But enough of my misadventures. Let's regale her with the enchanting tale of Armin buying Australian porn."

"It was ironic," he protested. "I didn't think you were actually in it."

I started giggling. Legit giggling.

"Holy shit." Blythe touched my chin, turning my face. "Look at her eyes. She's high as a fucking kite."

"No drugs," the cabbie barked. "You leave."

"Relax, mate. We don't have any drugs." She leaned closer. "They're all in your bloodstream, aren't they?" Her breath was warm on the side of my neck. "I'd have to be a vampire to get them out."

"Blythe," Armin said, suddenly stern.

"Christ. Everyone's a judge." She pulled away.

Another charged, tense silence. There was something I wasn't getting about the two of them. Some subtext. I moved my bag to my thigh, brushing Blythe's leg. She glanced at me, at my curled hand, and her eyes lit up. No one saw her take the pills, not even Armin. *Good girl*, she mouthed.

If you're keeping score, that's the first time I sided with her against him.

Then the driver turned and there, tucked between highrises, was an enormous mansion like something out of Poe. All black granite and gables, brimming with ominousness. The marquee read UMBRA. Behind it the logo glowed, a circle of shadow slipping over a white sun.

Armin paid the driver and popped his door. So did Blythe, and I froze when they both offered hands. Choose a side. Make a statement. High school all over again. I took Armin's and got out quickly. Blythe's gaze followed us, and something snagged behind my ribs, a fine, sharp wire catching hold. Of what, I didn't yet know. I just felt the catch.

We entered through a side door and followed concrete hallways until we emerged into a haze of noise and sweat, cool and murky, subterranean. The foyer was a massive marble-floored space carved up by stone arches. The air thrummed with voices, cologne and liquor and dry ice mingling in a heady scent. An electric chandelier hung overhead; the wrought-iron torch sconces were stuffed with glow sticks. Music came in tidal waves, swelling and ebbing.

"What do you think?" Armin said.

"Pretty sweet."

"And the best thing," Blythe said, turning and spreading her arms, "is that we're fucking gods here." Her eyes flashed at me. "Welcome to the underworld, Persephone."

I shivered.

Armin cupped my elbow and guided me toward a spiral staircase. This time the oxy didn't stop the burst of static at his touch. We lost Blythe on the stairs, and when I looked back for her he said, "She does her own thing."

We stepped onto a catwalk above the dance floor. Crimson lasers swept over the crowd, oscillating, hypnotic, bass pumping so thickly from every direction it felt as if we were inside a heart, the dense sea of bodies rolling like one muscle, beating with one pulse. Lasers caught split-second cameos: a head thrown back, a hand reaching for someone. Abandon and desire.

We stood at the railing, our shoulders pressed together.

"Are you guys still in college?" I had to half yell to be heard.

"She's an undergrad. I'm working on my master's."

"In what?"

"Clinical psych."

I imitated his groan from earlier. "Psych major."

Armin smiled, a perfect crescent of porcelain. The man had fucking dimples. Ridiculous. "Not a fan?"

"Doctors fuck your head up more than it already was."

"That's a somewhat biased view."

"I'm somewhat biased."

"Why is that?"

Nice try, doc. You're not getting into the Chamber of Secrets that easily.

We gazed down at the dance floor. "Cold Dust Girl" by Hey Champ came on and I spotted Blythe right away, dancing alone. It was as if a spotlight shone on her, face upturned, eyes closed, swaying in slow motion while the world around her was choppy and frantic. Her hair lifted and caught the light, floating in frozen veils of gold.

"How long have you been with her?" I said.

"We're just friends."

"She's not your girlfriend?"

"No."

I waited a beat. "Do you like girls?"

Armin winced, his eyes crinkling.

"It's just, you're ridiculously hot, and you have a ridiculously hot girlfriend who's not your girlfriend, so—"

"I like girls. But I'm not with anyone right now." He seemed amused. "What about you?"

"What about me?"

"Do you like girls?"

I raised my eyebrows. "Does it look like I do?"

"You can't tell by looking."

"Then how can you tell?"

"Girls who like each other have a different energy. More intense. Furtive. They're part of a secret world. They speak in code, like spies. Everything has a hidden meaning."

"You sound like an expert," I said, laughing.

"You sound evasive."

"Like a spy?"

"You tell me."

That wire inside me gave a little twang, as if he'd plucked it. I turned away. Wrapped my palms around the railing, soaking up the coolness of the steel. But my mind hung on the warmth of his arm and the smell of pine needles, clean and spicy and green, reminding me of Christmas.

"Why aren't you two together?" I said.

"Stick around and you'll see."

"Does she turn into a pumpkin at midnight?"

"Something like that."

"So this is what you do," I said in a too-casual voice. "You bring an underage girl to a club. Your wingman—wing-girl, whatever—conveniently wanders off. Next you'll buy me a drink, help me into a cab—"

"I don't take advantage of girls, Laney."

"You wouldn't be taking advantage."

I'd said it in my devil-may-care way, but the words shaved sparks from the friction between us. Our eyes met. Red light traced the bold line of his brow, the striking angularity of his face. The stubble shading his jaw glimmered like iron filings. He looked at me in a way that felt like being touched, like a blind man seeing with his fingers, mapping my bones and skin in his mind. I felt weirdly exposed. *Seen.*

"It's not what you think," he said.

"What do I think?"

"I'm not that good. I can't read minds."

Then read my body, I thought, but he only smiled.

"Tell me something." He leaned closer, his voice raspy at the edges, charred. "If you hate human connection so much, why come with us?"

Because I don't hate it. I hate how much I need it.

Because you're the ones I was waiting for.

Because you smell like prey.

"Read any Kafka?" I said.

"Guy turns into a giant bug?"

"Right. *The Metamorphosis.* He wrote a bunch of other stuff. Vignettes, really. Just descriptions of feelings." I sketched the golden arcs of Blythe's hair with my finger. "There's a story where this man calls for his horse to be saddled one night. He hears a trumpet blowing in the distance, but nobody else can hear it. The servants don't understand his urgency. They ask, 'Where are you going?' And the man just says, 'Away from here.'" I looked up at Armin. We were closer than I thought.

"He has no supplies, no map. The servants warn him but it doesn't matter. Every time they ask where he's headed, he says, 'Always away from here. It's the only way can I reach my destination.'"

"Sounds like suicide."

"That's one way to see it. Suicide isn't really about death, though. It's about change. Release."

"Release from life is a permanent change."

"Sometimes all you know about where you're going is that it's away from where you are."

Armin leaned on an elbow. "It's you. You're the rider, flirting with annihilation. Venturing into the night with strangers. Trying to find yourself by losing yourself completely."

I liked that. But I didn't tell him.

"You're one of those scorched-earth types," he said. "Burn it all to the ground and start over."

"You've got to die to be reborn."

"Like the phoenix." He tapped his fingers on the railing. "Seems a bit masochistic."

"I'm a bit masochistic."

"Why?"

"If I'm going to feel bad all the time, I might as well enjoy it."

"You don't have to feel bad, Laney."

"Let me guess. Your solution is to throw pills at people and call them cured."

He lifted an eyebrow. "I can't even prescribe."

"Doesn't matter. You're a doctor. Or will be. Someday you'll realize you can't fix anyone, only dull the pain."

He didn't respond for a minute. Then he said, "Is someone in your family mentally ill?"

I looked away.

"I won't pry. You don't have to answer. It runs in my family, too."

"I don't care what runs in your family."

Armin fell silent and I stood there with an anger churning in me, like the bass grinding deep in my bones, rising, bubbling up into a fever in my blood.

"You think you know me after an hour," I said. "You think a few psych classes means you know shit about real life."

"I don't—"

"That's right. You don't." I flicked him a cold glance. "Look at you. You're a walking Abercrombie ad. We are not even on the same planet."

"You're angry."

"Wow. You really are good."

"And guarded. You've been hurt, but you still crave connection. Understanding. So you throw yourself into risk in a calculated way. You're a paradox: a careful daredevil."

The *devil* made me shiver. I hated that he had my number so fast.

"Spare me the Psych 101," I said. "You know who else is good at reading obvious clues? Con men."

"It's intuition. I didn't learn it in school. I learned it from watching people. From listening."

"Yeah, well, listen to this. Whatever you think you know about me, you don't. You don't really care, and you can't fix me."

"What makes you think I want to?"

My mouth dropped.

He smiled, lessening the sting. "Nothing personal, but I have selfish motivations of my own. I'm not obligated to fix everyone." His gaze drifted to the dance floor. "Most of us can't even fix ourselves. We're all saddling horses in the night, trying to outrun the darkness."

Armin was not what I expected.

In a typical college romance novel, he'd be a gorgeous but

troubled sex god who'd cure all my deep-seated psych issues with a good hard fuck. I'd smell his misogyny and abusive tendencies from miles off but my brain would turn to hormone soup because abs. That's the formula. Broken girl + bad boy = sexual healing. All you need to fix that tragic past is a six-pack. More problems? Add abs.

It's Magic Dick Lit.

But this was no bad boy. This was a boy who'd rather get into my head than my pants.

Most of the time romance isn't even about love, anyway. It's about escape. Fantasy. Salvation from the mundane. Save me from boredom, from exhaustion, from my undersexed body, from microwave dinners and reality TV, from going to bed alone or with a vibrator or a cat. Save me from my desperately ordinary life.

We're all Kafka's rider, trying to get away from ourselves.

Maybe I'm a little bitter.

And maybe this isn't your typical college romance novel.

The DJ segued into a down-tempo track. Blythe had stopped dancing and was staring into the distance, waiting. A guy snaked through the crowd toward her, a hunk of silk and gel and gym-molded muscle, more product than person. She pivoted on her heel, the guy trailing in her wake. Before they disappeared she glanced straight up at us. Her face was cool and blank. In that moment I knew we were the same, me and her. Hunters.

"That's why we're just friends," Armin said, so softly I barely heard. "She can't fall in love, and I can't fall out."

———

We hit the dance floor after Blythe left. Armin filled in for the DJ and I joined him in the booth. "What do you want to hear?" he said, and I remembered Donnie at home and asked for "All I Need Is a Miracle." Our song. Armin let me do the crossfade, which felt amazing, my hands gliding over the starship controls of the mixer and filling the cosmos with sound, giving life to three hundred pounding hearts. His hand floated over mine, then pulled away. He played "Don't Lose My Number" by Phil Collins and I thought of my half-assed garage band with Donnie, crooning eighties covers on Dad's karaoke machine, our hair teased out with mousse. Armin caught me lip-syncing and grinned. Despite my best intentions, I was enjoying this. Too loud to talk. We spoke through songs. Me: "Everything She Wants." Him: "Invisible Touch." Me: "What Have I Done to Deserve This." He laughed at that, a beautiful laugh, really, his teeth gleaming opal behind those dusty-rose lips, and I wondered what it would be like to kiss him. If I would feel anything, or if it would be vacuum and void like it always was.

The original DJ came back and we stepped down, bouncing on our toes, energized.

"Impressive," Armin said in my ear, and my spine lit up like a strand of Christmas lights. "You know your eighties."

"Me and my brother are total eighties nerds."

"Younger brother?"

"Yeah."

We waded through the crowd to the bar, where he ordered two Sprites. "I have a younger sister."

"Is that why you decided to be my white knight?"

His shoulders stiffened. He wore a dress shirt with the sleeves rolled up and faded, form-fitting jeans. When he frowned his eyes nearly closed, his eyelashes so long and kohl-black they seemed almost feminine.

God. I'm describing a man's eyelashes. Fucking shoot me.

"How was I white-knighting?" he said.

"Come on. Blythe stalked *me*. I caught her in the bathroom. You guys were watching out for the dumb pledge."

"She has a thing for lost girls." He handed me a tumbler. "Were we that obvious?"

"She looked super guilty when I caught her."

"Her face doesn't hide anything."

I looked down into my glass, thinking, Perfect.

"It was her idea. Like I said, I don't harbor delusions of being anyone's savior."

"Whatever. It was nice."

His eyes did that crinkling thing again. "You don't like saying thank you, do you?"

"I don't want to get a reputation."

"For what?"

"Being human."

He laughed and took a swallow of his drink. I set mine on the bar. When he raised an eyebrow I said, "I don't take drinks from strangers."

"Are we still strangers?"

I averted my eyes, my face inexplicably hot. "Or from doctors."

"Fair enough. You've made your hatred clear."

"I don't hate you. I can't hate a man who shamelessly loves the eighties."

"So what did you give her?"

This guy was good. Lull me into camaraderie, then cobra strike. "What?"

"Don't play coy. What was it?"

"I don't know what you're talking about."

"I'm talking about the pills you gave Blythe in the cab."

I shrugged one shoulder. "Just some oxy."

Armin sighed.

"Hey, *she* wanted it—"

"You hate meds, but you're a pillhead. I should've known."

"Dude." I gripped the counter. "Don't judge me. You don't know the kind of shit I have to deal with. Look, I kept my grades up and got into CU. I'm fine."

"That doesn't mean you're fine."

"It means I'm a high-functioning addict."

Surprisingly, he shrugged, too. "Okay. Honesty. Points for that."

"Don't patronize me. I don't need your approval."

"I'm not giving it. I've just seen too many people ruin their lives with drugs."

"Like your sister."

"Like my sister." His gaze turned shrewd. "How'd you guess?"

"I watch and listen, too."

"You have a good sense of people."

But I didn't. My mother had a good sense of people. *We're all bad,* she'd said. *The only thing we're good at is hiding it.*

Someone bumped into me from behind, and Armin slung an arm around my shoulders protectively. Whoever it was mumbled an apology, but neither of us were paying attention. I was staring at that rose-lipped mouth, then up into his eyes, a clear reddish-brown like carnelian, speckled with tiny flaws of amber and copper where the light caught.

Fuck. They're brown. His eyes are fucking brown, okay? Stop being a terrible writer, Laney.

"Want to get out of here?" he said.

"Yes."

God, yes.

––––––––

Downtown was eerily beautiful at night. In the hot spill of cider streetlight, the asphalt glittered as if coated with crushed diamond. We crossed wide, wind-haunted streets that were almost postapocalyptic: no cars, no people, perfect stillness, and the shop signs—TRY OUR NEW, TWO FOR ONE—somehow portentous. "Try our new Prozac milkshake," I said. "Two lobotomies for the price of one."

Armin shook his head. "Ghoulish."

We walked for miles. It was after three but before dawn, that timeless, silky stretch of night that feels as if it'll run on forever. My feet were numb and my fingertips buzzed with blood. I felt immortal. We found the plaza where a giant steel sculpture crouched, the Picasso, that weird chimera with its long baboon face and arching wings and stick ribs, and I climbed up for a pic. Armin gave me a hand, and when I braced myself on his shoulders I felt the heat of his body through his thin shirt. My fingers curled in the linen.

A breeze wafted off the lake, water-cool. "Where are we?"

"Almost to the beach."

I hopped down and he caught me, even though I didn't need it. Our hands joined for a second.

The skyscrapers fell away, stone wings unfolding and exposing the dark blue heart of the lake. There were cars on Lake Shore Drive, but when we crossed it felt like the waking world behind us winked out. The sand had a lunar glow, like moondust. I kicked off my shoes and let my feet sink in. The top layer was still warm, but when I dug deeper I hit a colder reservoir. Where the lake lapped the shore the smell of wet sand and algae was dizzying.

"Come on, Eileen," Armin sang out.

"Can we even be here?"

"Nothing's gonna stop us now."

"What about the cops?"

"I'll run. I'll run so far away. With or without you."

"Stop making bad song jokes."

"Stop laughing at them."

His voice was doing something to me. A hot coal lay low in my belly, and every time he spoke it flared. "This will never work," I said. "You and me."

"Why not?"

"Because you're an East End boy, and I'm a West End girl."

I could see that big damn smile in the dimness. He kicked his shoes off, moving toward me. His shirt and eyes were ghostly blurs. I smelled wintergreen on his breath.

"But I'm the king of wishful thinking."

"Armin, shut up and kiss me."

He leaned in and I reached for his face. Stubble tickled my skin. His breath warmed my palm and lit a nerve all the way up my inner arm to my spine. It shrieked through me like a firework, ending with a bright pop in my brain. My eyelids fluttered closed, my belly tightening and mouth opening, and the kiss felt so imminent I gave a start when it didn't happen.

"Don't you want to?" I whispered.

His hands settled against my face. "That's not why we're here."

The words were a denial, but his hands wouldn't move and we shared the same hot breath. My heart flung itself fiercely at my ribs, as if it could close the space between us.

"I don't believe you."

He brushed my bare arm, teasing out a shiver.

"Come on," he said.

I followed him to the shoreline. There was a rock-walled harbor to one side, the water slapping gently against fiberglass hulls, a sound like something breaking delicately, prettily. We sat in a hollowed-out dune and leaned on our elbows, hidden from the street. My bare toes spread against the horizon. The sky switched on, heating up to a vibrant indigo.

"This is my 'away from here,'" Armin said. His voice sounded like sand flowing through glass, at once grainy and smooth.

I was going to tell him he was wrong. Away from here isn't a place, it's a state, inside you. It's escape velocity. It's losing yourself, anywhere. But then I thought, Maybe *I'm* wrong. Maybe this isn't a *where* at all.

"What about the club?"

"That's Blythe's. This is different. This is mine."

But you brought me here, I thought. "How'd you become a DJ?"

"Questioning my skills?"

"No, just curious."

"I know somebody." His eyes danced away. "This world is run by people who know somebody. You scratch my back, I scratch yours."

I sketched a pattern in the sand, a dark disc eating a light one, the Umbra logo, then smeared it out. "You take my eye, I take yours."

"Are you always this morbid?"

"Is it at all endearing?"

He laughed.

"So why'd you guys adopt me?" I said.

"I don't pretend to understand Blythe's motives. I've known her for three years and she's still an enigma. Either she has some brilliant master plan I haven't figured out yet, or she's totally irrational. But I went along because I couldn't take my eyes off you."

My heart gave a small hiccup.

"You're not like them, Laney. I saw it the second you arrived. You didn't belong there."

"Where do I belong?"

"On a rocky cliff above a tempestuous sea. With the salt breeze whipping through your hair, and a house burning behind you."

I had to smile. "Maybe you're not so bad at the whole head-shrinking thing."

"Maybe we're more alike than you think." When he spoke I was aware of the way his lips moved over his teeth, enunciating words so meticulously. Little things like that tell you everything about a person. "It's almost time."

"For what?"

"What I wanted to show you."

We both lay back in the sand, and the drain of the long night and the last dregs of my high hit at the same moment, making me immensely weary. My eyes drifted closed. When I jerked awake it felt like hours had passed. I'm not sure how long I flickered back and forth between states of consciousness before Armin touched my shoulder. I sat up, disoriented. The sky looked like layered sherbet, creamy peach melting into raspberry and blueberry, shading the world in soft, milky tones. The sun was an eye-smarting bead of white light trembling at the horizon. A woman jogged barefoot along the tide line, sand sticking to her shining brown shins. I felt like I'd woken up in another universe.

"Where am I?" I said blearily.

Armin's voice floated to me like a breath of morning mist. "Away."

I slept on the Metra, asking the guy across the aisle to wake me at Naperville. The town air was drowsy and sweet after the city. I walked home half-asleep on my feet, a zombie in Wonderland, taking off my shoes to tread barefoot on lush store-bought lawns. Armin and Blythe and Umbra seemed like a bizarre, fading dream. I unlocked the front door and headed for the stairs.

Dad was in the kitchen, sitting with his coffee and tablet. Neither of us spoke. He cleared his throat, then looked down.

When I paused at the top landing I could see the bald spot on his head. It seemed so vulnerable, so babyish. It made something sad twist inside me. His gaze remained fixed on the whorls in the wood grain.

I locked my bedroom door. Pulled my dress over my head, tossed my shoes into a corner. Slipped the small silver key from my purse and stepped into my closet.

Upside to having a brother obsessed with architecture: he will help you build a concealed door in the crawl space between your rooms.

I shut the closet, sealing myself in darkness.

I could find the lock by touch. I knew the furry splintered surfaces like my own heart, the taste of sawdust and wool and time. The smothering heat like a human hand over my mouth. I knelt gingerly and felt for the portable light.

Flick.

The space was about the size of a car interior, a rectangle of cinderblocks and plywood.

And every square inch of it was covered with *him*.

His face, printed from Facebook and newspaper articles. *Rising star. The boy with the golden touch. [Scratched out] carries Redhawks to state championship.* His transcript. Schedule from senior year. Bills and bank statements sent to his parents. His daily routines, traced on maps. A massive dossier.

I picked up a pen and crossed PI/PHI SUMMER MIXER off the July calendar.

He was going to Colorado for the first half of August—I had a copy of his hotel reservation and hiking itinerary—then no data until classes started in September. I wouldn't see him till school began.

But that was okay. Like my mother, I was nothing if not patient.

I plugged my phone into my laptop and copied the photos

I'd taken at Umbra. Strange, twisting staircases and labyrinthine hallways. Places to get lost. Places to be among hundreds of people without being seen.

I paused at the pic of Blythe.

She was wrong about looking wretched. She had an unreal beauty. I'd caught her with a curiously wry expression, mouth half-open, brow furrowed. Her canine teeth were longer than the others and it made her slightly impish. Vulpine jaw, the sort of absurd cheekbones only mannequins possessed. Her eyes had a look of lazy cunning and were the blue of ice on a winter creek, shot through with frost, arrestingly pale. I brushed a finger over her cheek.

Something thumped in my bedroom.

I shut everything down and backed out of the crawl space, locking it behind me.

Donnie lay in fetal position on my futon. I hadn't even noticed him when I came in. He'd kicked my desk when he tossed. I sat beside him.

"Laney?" he murmured.

I nudged him over and wrapped an arm around his waist. I still had only my underwear and bra on, but this is my baby brother, for fuck's sake. He's like my kid. The way I love him is the way you're supposed to love your children. The way Mom never did.

"What happened?" he said.

"Nothing yet. Just surveillance."

Donnie let out a long sigh. There was no mistaking the relief in it.

"It's okay," I whispered. "Everything's going to be okay."

He sighed again, shuddering, and the breaths after that were ragged and I knew he was crying and my arms tightened around him so hard it hurt us both, but I couldn't stop.

"I wasn't sure you'd come back," he said.

"I will always come back to you." My voice was fierce. I rocked him, waiting for his tears to end, for mine to start. "I'm not her. I won't leave you. I promise."

It became a sort of lullaby, me telling him it was okay, that we were both okay and I would never leave and someday, soon, everything would be better.

Someday I would make everything right.

AUGUST, LAST YEAR

Blythe blew a stream of smoke in my face. "That bloke with the arms is looking at you."

We stood outside Umbra on a simmering summer night, the concrete still soaked with heat. Her hair was wild and wind-tossed, curling over her bare shoulders, shining like spun gold in the streetlight. I studied her tattoos. Watercolor style, cyan and magenta and canary washing down her skin as if a painter would come back any moment to finish. On one shoulder, a skull leaked rainbow acid. On the other was a lily that was sometimes a flower and sometimes a girl's lush pink mouth. Images from her poems. Half-melted, dreamlike.

I'd read every one. Some I could recite by heart. "Neon Narcissus." "Wide Blue Nothing."

I was becoming sort of an expert on Blythe McKinley.

"He's looking at you," I told her. "Don't lie to make me feel better."

She smiled, all sun-kissed blondness. Next to her I felt like Wednesday Addams. "I'm constitutionally incapable of lying."

"Also a lie. Remember the guy at the theater who asked for your number, and you gave him mine?" I counted off my fingers. "And you told that cabbie you were married. And the guy on the L that you're gay. And yesterday, the dude in the suit—"

"Okay, okay. Let's not get Kafkaesque with the accusations."

"We're the sun and moon, Blythe."

"What does that mean?"

"I turn invisible when you're out."

She laughed and swirled a finger in my hair, resting her hand against my face. Personal boundaries meant nothing to her. "Don't be fucking ridiculous."

"I'm never ridiculous."

"Except when you're ridiculous." There was fondness in her expression, and it made me warm. "I don't blow smoke up people's arses. If something's shit, I call it shit."

"Australia's national poet, ladies and gentlemen."

"Oh, fuck off. You really think I'd lie to you?"

"That's what friends do."

"I'm not that kind of friend." Her hand trailed to my jaw, her fingers soft. "You can't even see it. You have the most perfect little doll's face."

A charge prickled over my skin, turning every nerve up to full brightness. I pulled away.

"Seriously," I muttered. "I don't want some skeezy dude."

"I'm trying to get you laid, not bloody married."

"Not interested."

"You're a teenage girl. Your libido could solve the global energy crisis." She grazed my elbow with a fingernail, and I jumped. "See? Way too tense."

"I'm fine."

"Two Xanax deep and still grinding your teeth."

"So you're a doctor now, too?"

Her eyes narrowed. "You're always defensive when you're hiding something. I'll figure it out."

God, wasn't it obvious?

Arms McStud and his buddies were still watching us. One licked a finger and ran it over his crotch.

Blythe exhaled in their direction. "That's about as sexy as a dog licking its balls."

They broke into lupine grins. McStud threw his head back and howled.

"And you want to hook me up with *that*," I said.

"No." She ground her cigarette in the ash can. "I want to fuck with the male gaze."

"Blythe, don't do something crazy."

"Are you in?"

"God. Okay. Yes."

She flung an arm around my shoulders and before I could react, she bit my earlobe, hard. It took all my self-control not to yelp. The guys fell silent. I couldn't move. Teeth touching tender flesh. Hot breath melting my spine into mercury. Sensory overload. Finally she pulled away and the guys started catcalling again, but this time it was stuff like *So fucking hot* and *Now make out.*

Blythe walked us to the door. Her face was pure smugness.

"You could've warned me," I said, a little breathily.

"It's no fun that way."

She didn't let go till we reached the bar, and when her arm dropped I felt a pang of loss and thought, Careful.

I'd been to Umbra almost every night since July. By now it was home. Tonight Armin deejayed in the underground room, the Oubliette. Each wing had its own theme: the Oubliette was a dungeon full of dry ice and filthy raw electro-house, while the Aerie on the top floor was high and open, percolating with sugary pop. Blythe liked the main room, the Cathedral, best, because that was where you went to be seen.

"Sex on the Beach, please," she told the bartender. My favorite.

He eyed me dubiously while he fixed her drink. I clasped her hand, passing her an oxy. We both tucked our hair back and tongued the pills from our palms in perfect sync. The simplest way to not get caught doing a bad thing is to do it in front of everyone. Because most people are good—or scared, which is the same thing, functionally—and good people associate badness with guilt. Skulking, hiding. Lurking in the dark. They assume you feel their shame, that you'll try to hide your sins. They try to catch you in the shadows. No one looks for badness in the light.

The bartender nudged a glass across the counter.

"Cheers," Blythe said, tipping her head back. Her mouth was a ruby kiss through the sunset colors of the drink. When she gave me the glass I turned it till the imprint of her lip balm faced me.

She watched me drink. Her gaze touched my throat like fingertips.

Afterward we wandered through the club. Blythe was restless, never stopping to dance or banter with the guys who hit on her. We crossed the Cathedral twice before heading downstairs. The oxy had started to kick in, blurring the edges off everything. No more hard surfaces. My feet didn't hit the steps but touched down in soft white cloud, and that cool numbness twined around my legs, inscribing my veins with frost.

Blythe stopped suddenly in the middle of the stairway. People forked around us.

"When are you going to let me read your book?" she said.

This conversation again.

"I told you, it's not that good."

She came back up the steps, looming. "And I told you, that shit needs to breathe. If you keep it locked inside, it'll rot. It'll become so insular and personal it won't mean anything to anyone but you."

"It's already too personal."

"All the more reason to let it out."

"It's stupid teenage diary bullshit, Blythe."

"Keats died at twenty-five. Shelley was twenty-nine. Byron, thirty-six. Their stupid teenage diary bullshit is now considered high art."

"I'm not Lord fucking Byron."

"You're a terrible judge of your own work, like every writer who's worth a shit."

I looked up at the ceiling. "You're going to ruin it. Just let it go."

"Ruin what?"

"The mystery. Before you know someone, you build them up in your head."

She winced. She actually looked hurt. "You think I don't know you. That I've got some fantasy in my head. Laney Keating, tortured artist, undiscovered genius."

"That's not what I—"

"How do you think I see you, then?"

Perfect little doll's face. "I think we all have illusions about each other."

"Christ, this pompous crap sounds like Armin."

It was true. And I could feel everything careening in the wrong direction, so I blurted, "Fine. You can read it. But only if you swear not to show him."

The sparkle instantly returned to her eyes. She smiled, and I could imagine the proverbial bird feathers between her teeth.

"I knew I'd wear you down. Deal."

"You manipulative bitch," I said.

"A bitch is a woman who gets what she wants."

"Then you are the biggest bitch ever. And you *swear* you won't show him."

She laughed.

"I'm serious, Blythe."

"I'm sure you are."

I grabbed her shoulder. Her inked skin was soft. "Donnie's

the only one who's read it. I don't want anyone else to see. Only you."

She peered into my face. Too close. Her eyes were so pale and clear the light went straight through, flashing off the silvery backs like a mirror. The sudden intensity unnerved me.

"When will you really trust me?" Her breath was sweet, orange spiked with vodka. "Is there a secret test?"

Not for you, I thought. Never for you.

I opened my mouth and someone staggered into me, spinning me half around.

Some club guy. I didn't recognize him, but I sensed Blythe tensing.

"Watch your fucking step, mate."

He shot me a smile. It was Arms McStud, beer bottle in one hand.

"Sorry there. I was distracted by your friend." His real focus was on Blythe. "You ladies like a drink?"

"We're good," I said.

He kept smiling, as if I'd said something cute. "How about a dance?"

"We're good," I repeated, firmer.

The guy looked at me, his smile snapping flat like a jackknife. "Ugly Friend can wait until the tens are done talking."

It struck somewhere in my solar plexus. Welcome back to high school, Laney.

Blythe stared at him icily. "You've got five seconds to get the fuck out of my face."

The smile returned. He looked at her, then me, disbelieving.

"Four," Blythe said.

"Hey." The guy elbowed me aside, towering over us. "Let's try this again. I'm—"

"Tired of counting," Blythe said, and shoved a palm into his thick chest.

He lost his balance, tripping on a step and sitting down hard. His beer tipped into his lap and foamed over his jeans. His face went red as raw meat.

He stared balefully up at us both. Settled on Blythe.

"You slut."

I knew it was coming, and still I flinched. She didn't.

McStud pulled himself up with one arm, giving us a good view of roid bulge laced with veins. His T-shirt looked painted on, tight as skin. "You're going to regret that, slut."

My jaw clenched. "Stop talking."

He ignored me. He was locked in some eye duel with Blythe, both of them wearing the same grim, avid expression, alpha versus alpha. A crazed energy crackled between them, almost sexual. With plunging dismay I realized I could envision her fucking this guy. This stone-dumb sexist piece of shit.

"I know you," McStud said. "You're the Aussie whore they pass around. Any dick here you haven't sucked yet?"

"Just yours."

He laughed. Music throbbed below us, a deep dull ache.

"Let me buy you a drink," he said incongruously, switching the charm back on. Typical pickup tactic: neg the girl, then woo her.

Blythe smiled her heartbreaker smile. "You're not great at reading the situation, mate. Here's a little hint: fuck off."

The charm dissolved. He glanced at me again, seemed to see me for the first time. I mentally cringed in anticipation of what came next. When a girl doesn't fall to pieces over some pheromone-drenched caveman, she's one of two things. She's either ugly like me, or—

"Not worth it," he said. "Couple of dykes."

All I saw was the blood. I didn't even see Blythe hit him. Just a brilliant bouquet of liquid red petals bursting in his face.

People surged around us, yelling, grabbing, stopping the

fight, and in the chaos I got pushed to the back of the crowd. Someone had Blythe by the elbows, holding her while she writhed like a wildcat. They lifted McStud to his feet as he spouted off about suing the club and the drunk slut for all they were worth. Blythe didn't flinch. In her eyes I caught a maniacal glint of delight.

"You stupid cunt," she crowed at him. "You can't slut-shame me if I love being a slut."

Two minutes later, bouncers dumped us all on the street.

———

By the time McStud ducked into a cab with one last Cro-Magnon glower, all the fight had drained from Blythe. We sat on a curb in a pool of warm whiskey streetlight, heads hanging, hair tumbling over our knees. Blythe flipped her cigarette box end over end. Nervous habit.

"Armin's going to kill me," she said.

I held out my hand for a cig.

We lit up, sent smoke spiraling into the light. A police siren wailed far away, keening and lonely, melancholy.

"Why'd you hit that guy?" I said.

"Because he's a fucking useless prick."

I raised an eyebrow. She raised one back.

"And it improved his face."

We started giggling.

"It's not funny," I said. "They'll ban us for life. They'll deport you."

"So stop laughing, you lunatic."

"I can't if you won't."

This made her laugh harder. She tried to take a drag and smeared blood on her lip.

"You're bleeding," I said, alarmed.

"It's mostly his." She scrubbed her hand over her mouth,

spreading that rusty redness, then smiled, more of a leer. "Am I still pretty, Laney?"

God, yes. "You look feral."

Blythe threw her head back, roared hoarsely at the sky. Sweat glazed her neck, freckled with stray glitter from the club, like stardust.

"Why'd you hit him, really?"

She scraped her cigarette on the pavement, painting a trail of sparks. "Because he deserved it. Because of how he treated you."

"Not because of that slut stuff?"

"A girl who likes sex is a slut. A guy who likes sex is a stud." Blythe crushed her cig messily, a confetti of ash and ember spraying up over her hand. "Double standard crap. I'm doing my part to spread feminist enlightenment."

"One broken nose at a time."

We laughed. But I thought, You hit him when he called us something else.

I flicked a pebble into a sewer grate.

"Don't let them scare you off," she said.

"Who?"

"Blokes like that. They think they're entitled to my attention because God gave them a dick and the world owes them beautiful women to put it in. They feel threatened by you."

My heart quickened. "Why?"

"Because they don't understand us." She squinted into the streetlight. "You and I may as well be speaking our own language. You're the only one I can really talk to about anything. About everything."

The blood on her mouth looked like smudged lipstick. On me it would've been deranged, but on her it was weirdly beautiful. Even sitting still she was a hurricane. Always going two hundred miles an hour, so gorgeous in that haphazard, unwound way, the kind that pulled you in and then shredded you up.

"Want to know the truth?" I said. "I've been dying to show you my book. But I'm terrified, too, because then you'll really know me." I looked at my hands, my fingers ticking nervously. "I hide myself in my words. There's a cipher, and one half is in my writing and the other half is in me, and if you have them both then you'll understand everything. Strangers think it's just a story, but you'll know what's real. You'll know who I really am."

She gave me a sidelong glance.

"Does that sound crazy?" I said.

"It sounds exactly like me. I have a confession, too. Armin hasn't read my new stuff. Only you have."

"How come?"

"He wouldn't understand."

"He's actually pretty insightful."

"Then maybe I don't want him to understand."

I swallowed. Why? I thought, but I already knew.

Blythe dug into her purse for a tissue. Dabbed her bloody knuckles, wiped her mouth ineffectually.

"You're just making it worse." I touched her wrist. "Here."

I got it all except one stubborn spot. She smiled faintly and I decided, Fuck it. Licked my thumb and swabbed the blood from the corner of her mouth, pulling her lower lip open. My hand shook.

She stared me straight in the eyes. I couldn't meet that stare.

"You're falling for him, aren't you?" she said.

"Who?"

"Armin."

I almost fell over. "Are you crazy?"

"You've been twitchy all week. Whenever I bring it up, you dodge the question."

"I've actually been happy all week."

"Then why do you look electrocuted when anyone touches you?"

Not anyone.

"Don't lie to me, Laney. If my best friends are falling for each other, I have a right to know."

"Can we stop talking about—" I began, then blinked. "Wait, what?"

Blythe sighed at the sky. "Christ. My life is a young adult novel."

"Did you just say I'm one of your best friends?"

"You *are* my best friend, you twit."

The planet tilted. Gravity shift. My limbs went ridiculously light, my body made of papier-mâché.

"Don't look so shocked," Blythe said. "It's no big—"

I grasped her hand. "You're my best friend, too."

I thought she'd brush it off the way she usually did when things got serious, but she squeezed back, hard. It felt so good. So right. The whole summer was inside of us.

"Ever get déjà vu about people?" she said. "Like you've met them before, somewhere. Maybe in another life."

"Yes."

"It's fucking weird."

"It's not. I feel like I've always known you, Blythe."

That trademark smirk slanted over her mouth. "Maybe we were literary giants once. Grandiose and tragic, snuffed out before our time."

"Like Scott and Zelda."

"The Fitzgeralds. Bloody brilliant. Though if I end up in a sanatorium, it's your fault."

"What if I'm the crazy one?"

She gave me a droll, knowing look.

"I'll never be as good as F. Scott anyway," I said.

"Rubbish. You're halfway there. You're a self-loathing alcoholic. Now you just need money and talent."

I shoved her away. "I'm never showing you anything," I said, laughing.

Blythe threw an arm around my neck. "You will. Someday you'll show me everything."

Her face was closer than I realized, her breath warm on my ear. Her expression was gleefully devious but as I looked at her it cleared, steadied, and she returned my gaze a moment too long. My breathing felt strangely pronounced, as if it filled my whole body rather than my lungs.

I broke eye contact.

"Hey." She touched my knee, her voice lower now. "No matter what happens between you and Armin, I'm your friend. You don't have to hide anything from me."

God, how did she not see it?

"Nothing's going on with me and him."

"Right. That's why you tell me to fuck off whenever I mention some bloke."

"Maybe I don't want some bloke," I said impulsively. "Maybe I just want you."

It was like I'd fired a gun. She suddenly looked at me. Really looked.

Everything went off balance again. Lights veered one way, sounds the other. My heart spun in my chest like a toy top. Her eyes danced back and forth, searching mine, her eyelashes glimmering and her mouth so red and soft-looking and sweet and without thinking I leaned in and she did, too, all the blood in me flooding my skull, ringing, roaring, leaving my hands tingling and hollow. Her face tilted toward mine. I mirrored it, started to close my eyes.

"Blythe?"

Armin's voice.

We both whirled around. A silhouette stood against the streetlight.

Blythe rose, smoothing her dress.

"I cannot believe you did this again," Armin said, approaching.

"He started it."

"You can't get yourself arrested. You'll lose your visa. I shouldn't even need to tell you this."

"Welcome to tonight's program, Armin. I know you're just tuning in, but perhaps show some fucking concern whether we're okay."

"I'm sorry. I know you can handle yourself. I thought—" He sighed. "Are you okay?"

"Peachy. How about you, Lane?"

"I'm fine."

"Great. Since we're all unmolested, please continue the lecture."

Armin grimaced, suppressing frustration. "I'm not lecturing. I'm reminding you how dangerous it is to act like this."

"Like myself?"

"Blythe."

"What, then? Should I have let him shove her around? Maybe feel her up a bit?" Her tone was mocking, but a thread of tension ran along her jaw.

"You should have called security, not punched him in the face."

"You weren't there."

"I don't need to see you proving your alphaness to know what happened. You can't take these risks, Blythe."

"No, what I can't do is just watch while some arsehole insults your girlfriend."

Her shout echoed down the empty street. Armin stared at her, startled.

"It's okay," I said, moving midway between them. "He won't press charges. He's underage. They told him not to come back."

Armin's face tightened. "Don't get caught up in this, Laney."

"Caught up in what?" Blythe said. No answer. "Right. Nothing. Perhaps we should have a frank conversation about this incredibly tense nothing between us."

My heart jolted.

Armin touched her shoulder and she glared at him. Neither spoke, but the look between them conveyed things I couldn't intuit. His touch was some kind of salve that soothed her.

"I'm sorry," he said. "You're right. I wasn't there."

"Yeah, well, not like I ever go off half-cocked and make you clean up my messes."

He finally smiled. "Because who could put up with that for three years?"

"Probably someone with undiagnosed psych issues."

"If only we knew a competent doctor."

"There's always your dad."

"Low blow," Armin said, laughing.

Argument over. That easily they were friends again. So knowing, so natural. I felt like I had begun to disappear.

"Got him good, though," Blythe said, brandishing her knuckles.

Armin asked if she wanted to go to the ER, which she took as an insult to her Aussie fortitude. They joked around. I shrank back, wondering if they'd even notice if I left.

"Come here, you."

Blythe stood with a hand outstretched to me. Armin's head tilted, and though I couldn't see his face in the dark I sensed his pensiveness.

"I'll get the car," he said.

Reluctantly I went to her, my limbs wired all weird, jittery.

I was too nervous to take her hand, so she put it on my bare arm, which was worse. Her face was full of curiosity, mischief, and something nameless but intent, something between fear and thrill. Exhilaration, maybe. It did crazy things to my heart. I looked away self-consciously and she yanked me into a hug, a shock of unexpected warmth. We'd never hugged before. She was surprisingly slight, sparrow-boned. I'd been thinking of her as half god, someone whose pedestal I could barely brush with my fingertips, but really she was just a girl, like me. Her heart beat too fast and her hair was tangled and when my cheek grazed hers I held it there. My arms coiled tighter.

Mine, I thought. Mine.

We pulled apart and fell into step behind Armin without a word. When we passed into a halo of streetlight she took my hand, and she didn't let go till we reached the car.

One August night I sat in the crawl space in my underwear, watching a spider scurry over a map of Chicago. When I couldn't sleep, which was often, I came here. To see his face. To remind myself why I was alive. To become still.

There were new pictures now.

Armin was easy: his family had money, and people with money dropped more bread crumbs. He was twenty-three, born in St. Louis. His parents were liberal, loaded Persian immigrants. Dad was the shrink; Mom, a professional volunteer. They lived on a palatial estate somewhere in southern Illinois and did outreach work for trailer trash. How philanthropic. Apparently the philanthropy didn't work for Armin's sister, who had been in rehab twice. Armin was the good apple. Psych major. Swim team. Pi Tau big shot. Honors and scholarships. Tidy, precise, methodical. That type of perfection was usually brittle. Easy to crack.

Blythe was tougher. She was twenty-one, born in Melbourne. She'd come here three years ago on a student visa. Scant online presence under her real name. Social media was her weakness. Once I linked certain usernames to her—*archer, artemis, moonhunter*, references from her poetry—I found accounts crammed with photos: wild after-hours parties at Umbra, drunken adventures with Armin, even old shots from Australia, the colors eye-wateringly vivid, sun-blasted white sand and heartbreak-blue sky. Her father, burly and ruddy-faced, one leg propped on a sailboat. The two of them grinning into the merciless sun. None of her mom. "Artemis" explained Armin's stage name: DJ Apollo.

Artemis and Apollo. The huntress and the healer, twin gods of the moon and sun.

Some photos were hard to look at. The two of them together. His arms around her waist. Her neck thrown back, one hand on his thigh.

I hit PRINT. Beneath his too-perfect face I wrote BOYFRIEND in Sharpie and circled it over and over until the paper started to disintegrate. Blythe, again, was tougher. I hesitated with the marker and finally wrote BEST FRIEND. Her current roommate was leaving when fall semester started. She was broke and anxious to find a replacement. What serendipity: an empty room just when I'd need one.

Right after I canceled my dorm reservation.

I leaned back, my hair twisting across my face. It was so fucking hot in here. The sweat made me feel stripped down, distilled to my essence.

I was obsessed with *him*. I had to be. But now I was becoming obsessed with *them*, too. I knew their birthdays by heart (mistake to let me hold your purse while you took a piss, Blythe). I knew their college schedules (mistake to let me charge your phone while you deejayed, Armin). I even knew their horoscopes—I was ravenous for any clue to who they were, what motivated them. Armin was a Gemini, quick-witted and silver-tongued. Blythe was a Sagittarius, fiery and brutally blunt.

If you haven't already guessed, I'm a Scorpio.

The spider crawled onto my big toe and perched there. I poked it with a fingertip and it climbed on, and I brought the finger to my face. They're so weird-looking up close, those miniature clockwork bodies, eyelash legs joined to the onyx carapace, like a piece of living jewelry. And they go about their lives in total silence, spinning sticky glass through the air that you never see until you're caught in it.

I opened my mouth and put the finger inside, my lips sealing.

Swallowing is something you do thousands of times a day and rarely think about until there's a spider in your mouth. Then you're intensely aware of the saliva pooling beneath your tongue, the shallow arch of your palate, the jaw that aches to crush and grind. You're just a weird-looking little clockwork contraption, too. We're all machines made of skin and bone, breathing and eating and fucking, shitting and bleeding and dying. Machines break every day. There are billions more where they came from.

I opened my mouth again and withdrew my finger. The spider looked at me impassively.

I shuddered and set it free.

———

That summer, we were gods.

Blythe showed me how to control men. No more Ugly Friend. We were sky high and ice cold, pure untouchable sex in fuck-you heels and scarlet lips, our hands all over each other, driving boys crazy. Driving ourselves crazy. I'd never be beautiful like her, but the glamour of her aura transformed me from Wednesday to Morticia and somehow I became darkly alluring, enigmatic. I learned to read her so well she didn't have to speak. The flick of her eyes, the tightening of her jaw indicated *no*. Girls like us did not accept the first slobbering puppies who tumbled at our feet. We made them wait. We touched each other and laughed. We called them to us with our eyes. When she put her lips on my ear they noticed, and wanted us. I wanted us. Night after night I watched her go home with different boys, never the same one twice, and that taut wire inside me stretched finer and finer until it felt sharp as a garrote. I wanted to ask her to stay, but I couldn't loose the words from my throat. I slammed cab doors behind her and that moment right before the car pulled away, when we glanced at each other through the glass, felt sharper, keener, every time.

I never went home with any of those boys. I was fixated on one.

The first time I kissed Armin, it was in the DJ booth in front of the entire dance floor. I brought him Red Bull in a cup and laughed at the face he made when he gulped it down. He let me play an eighties set on my own, and even though the beatmatching software did most of the work I felt an animal power, my hands moving over the faders in slow arcs, watching the bodies on the floor respond, their blood white-hot, their breathing heavy. It felt sexual—that touch and response, a warm tension building in my belly and the backs of my legs. Their bodies flowed seamlessly from track to track. Their energy fed me and my heart thickened and trembled, ready to burst. When Armin touched my shoulder and leaned in to say something I leaned in, too, and kissed him. It was spontaneous, quick. I pulled away, wincing with sudden shyness, and he looked at me and reached for my face and that was when we really kissed. I had to stand on tiptoes but felt like I just kept rising, my eyes closed, my body made only of sweat and breath and light. He tasted like bitter citrus and he kissed me the way he did everything, with elegant precision. The crisp winter smell of him filled my skull. I wanted to feel all of his body against mine, rawness and rough stubble and his tongue in my mouth, but he broke away and we stared at each other as the crowd danced on, their hearts beating in wild time with ours.

Nothing was different after that. It was still the three of us, always.

At stores Blythe and I modeled clothes for Armin and he flashed his glossy AmEx at the register. He had a sterling silver money clip with two discs embossed on it, like an eclipse. The Umbra logo. Blythe refused his gifts; I didn't. He loved seeing me in things he'd bought. I loved it, too. I learned to read him just as well, which dresses made his eyes go soft and gauzy. Blythe would always be prettier than me but I had something she never would: vulnerability. When I slipped into girlish frilly things and donned my solemn, wide-eyed pout, Armin looked at me as if nothing else existed. When his back was turned Blythe and I slipped into dressing rooms together and stuffed trinkets beneath our clothes: tubes of gaudy lipstick, garish charm bracelets. The tackier and costlier, the better. We didn't even want them. In the cab on the way home we'd toss them out the windows, laughing. Armin bought me everything I wanted and Blythe destroyed everything I wanted to destroy.

The second time I kissed Armin, on the spiral staircase, I had one hand behind my back, my fingers knit with Blythe's. When I told them my dorm assignment fell through, Armin was the first to suggest I become Blythe's roommate. Donnie scored some X from my dealer back home and I offered it to my new friends, and Armin refused but Blythe, of course, didn't. Armin wouldn't leave our sides that night. He was worried someone would take advantage, not realizing we were the predators. He slow-danced with me up in the Aerie, my cheek against his chest, a disco ball spinning out a field of stars. I breathed in his pine scent and ran a hand over the thick ropes of muscle in his back while Blythe sat in the lounge, watching us. That night I caught them arguing. They thought I was in the bathroom but I was standing behind a tall couple, listening. Blythe's unmistakable accent cut through the crowd, saying *It's not the same* and *You can't punish me forever.* Armin's mellow voice was lost, but when I stepped out I saw her hand on his chest, knotted in his shirt. He backed away from her and they became all smiles. The X smoothed the abrasions over, and later Armin watched me dance with Blythe, her body light against mine, her hand curled softly at the nape of my neck. When we stepped apart I stood in the silhouette of her smell, a sweet girl musk, blackberry and vanilla, and I felt dizzy and buoyant like something in me was rising and rising, endlessly. All I wanted to do was follow it higher.

Dawn broke as we walked to the beach. I lay in the sand between them, our arms linked.

"I love you guys," I said, then felt dumb and cliché, so I added, "I really do."

Blythe laughed. "You are fucking high."

"Yeah, but I mean it."

I rolled my legs, relishing the prickle of sand against my calves, and the hot pink tongue of the sun lolling over the water, and their skin, so different, Blythe's silky and cool and Armin's coarse and warm. Everything was so *real.* As if the life I normally lived was a pale ghost of this one, washed out and numb.

"Delaney," Armin said, his hand moving over mine, to my dress, my thigh. "You make me feel so alive. What have you done to me?"

"I put a spell on you," I whispered.

He leaned in. My breathing was out of control, but not for the reason you think. Because while he was focused on me, Blythe had brought my hand to her mouth, her lips brushing my palm, her breath tracing the saliva she left there, and I felt an insane thing surging in me, an upward twisting, all of myself winding with an awful torque that needed immediate release. I kissed Armin, hard, my teeth catching on his lower lip. He kissed me back and pushed me down into the sand. Gold dust rained out of his clothes. The long, hard thigh sliding between mine made me gasp, and he kissed my throat, the delicate swoop of my collarbones, while Blythe's breath beat like a slow, airy heart against my palm.

That summer it was the three of us. Always, always, always.

Things feel eternal and timeless on X. Seconds or centuries later we lay sprawled in the sand, my legs tangled with his, my arms around her waist, my eyes closed and the sun gilding my body and the whole world golden, bright, and warm.

MARCH, THIS YEAR

I'm a middle-aged man with an unhealthy attraction to pre-pubescent girls," Professor Frawley said.

That got everyone's attention. Everyone's but mine.

I let my eyes wander to the windows. Top floor, ten stories above the city, with a view of frozen blue curving along the electric spine of Lake Shore Drive. The sun was falling, making flame-colored creases on the ice. *From what I've tasted of desire*, I thought, *I hold with those who favor fire.* From up here the tiny headlights looked like nerve impulses, a million neurons firing into the darkness.

Advanced Fiction Writing was a semester-long advertisement for Ian Frawley's shitty novel. Apparently a lot of failed novelists became writing teachers, or writing teachers failed at becoming novelists. Chicken or the egg. We mostly discussed the themes of Frawley's book—white middle-class academic suffers midlife crisis, has affairs with younger women (which Blythe would've undoubtedly called "Updike-wannabe sexist crap")—then, occasionally, our own work. I was writing a novel called *Black Iris*, about a woman who kills herself and leaves a note for her teenage daughter, and how the daughter carries the note around without ever having read it.

"Why doesn't she read it?" Frawley had asked, intrigued.

I could only shake my head.

"Work on motivation," he said. "Behavior is deterministic. There's always a cause."

Prick, I'd thought. But he was right.

Now Frawley leaned against his desk, his trim, svelte frame clad in an Italian suit. Early forties, married, but with a foxish Petyr Baelish smile that said he slept with his students, the younger the better.

"I've got a plan," he continued. "I've rented a room from a widow and her twelve-year-old daughter. The mother is interested in me, but it's the girl I want. I live with them for months. I insinuate myself into their lives, earn their trust, their adoration. They both fall in love with me. But I'm only in love with one of them. When the opportunity arises, I remove the mother from the picture. Now it's just me and the girl. What is age but a number? I take her on a road trip, a tour of the finest roadside diners and motels America has to offer. I buy her anything her heart desires. We make love. We're crazy about each other, and it doesn't matter that I'm three times her age. It doesn't matter what anyone else thinks."

The class watched him nervously, some of them evidently finding *Lolita* more true crime than fiction.

"She initiated sex the first time. She wasn't a virgin. She enjoys making love, though maybe not as much as comic books and candy. If I have to trade her toys for sex, well, it's no different from most marriages." Uneasy titters from the class. "And if she calls me a brute and an ape, well, I'm tall, dark, and handsome, though unfortunately rather hirsute. Sometimes she cries herself to sleep because she misses her dead mother. It's not that I'm afraid she'll run away. Why would she run? We're in love. It's just that she's a young girl, and young girls play games. She teases me and says she'll tell the police what I've done, so I tease back and threaten to dump her in a home for wayward children. No more toys or candy. How would you like that, Dolly? Isn't it better to be with me, to see this beautiful country together? Why must we fight when we love each other so?"

Frawley laced his hands behind his head, raising his eyebrows.

"What do you think, class?" he said. "Are my young paramour and I in love?"

An instant chorus of *no, sicko, pedophile*, etc. Frawley smiled, patronizing.

"Yes, yes. Good. What else am I? Think about it in a literary context."

Villain, antihero, antagonist, etc.

He kept smiling, waiting for the right answer. Grudgingly I raised my voice.

"Unreliable narrator," I said.

Frawley smacked his hands together. "Bingo."

Everyone looked at me.

"Very good, Ms. Keating." The professor paced, his voice looping around me. "I haven't told you the whole story. But you can tell from clues I've dropped that something isn't right. I'm withholding information. I want you to believe a lie."

He stopped somewhere behind my desk. I didn't turn.

"A novel with an unreliable narrator is really two stories in one. There's what the narrator tells us, and there's the truth. Sometimes they overlap. Sometimes one illuminates the other. Nabokov's *Lolita* is the example par excellence: Humbert Humbert is so blind with lust and self-justification that he ignores his young victim's suffering. Desire can be a powerful obfuscating force.

"In the Romantic era, writers would often conflate desire with the concept of the muse. 'Divine inspiration,' in the form of a beautiful woman in a toga with one breast bared, or whatever. Robert Graves envisioned the muse as a woman inhabited by the spirit of a goddess. To love her was to be inspired. To want her was the genesis of art. It blurred the lines between lust and inspiration in a way we've always intuitively known they should be blurred, because desire underlies every act of creation. Yes, boys and girls, we're talking about sex."

My phone vibrated against my thigh, and I jumped.

"A writer does her best writing when she's driven by desire. This is why romance is the most popular category in fiction, in the entire literary canon. It's all romance. They were all writing about it, in one way or another. The great works of art, the religious ecstasies—it's libido, transmuted to something socially acceptable. Why it was socially acceptable to talk about your passion for God but not a fellow human being is an interesting question. Anyway, in this sense, unreliable narration may be trying to tell us about a desire that can't be expressed directly, but must be distorted, obscured. Perhaps it's something the narrator doesn't fully comprehend. Or perhaps it's something she understands, but doesn't yet accept. Ms. Keating, what's in your head right now?"

Bastard. He'd tricked me into letting my mind drift.

"I don't know."

"You do know. Close your eyes. What do you see?"

My head was in a million pieces, in memories, in a moonlit hallway shoved up against a door, in a room where candles threw three shadows against the wall, in a catacomb beneath Umbra where you could scream your heart out without being heard.

"Nothing."

"You didn't close your eyes."

I humored him, if only to get this over with.

"Please. Indulge us."

This dickbag. I didn't want to tell him I'd spent most of his stupid class fantasizing about skin. Skin against my hands, my mouth. Heat. The sun burning through my eyelids, kindling the blood. A fist curled in the sand. All the grains running out, escaping. I kept curling it tighter, trying not to let go, but I couldn't. I couldn't hold on.

My eyes opened. The room was dazzlingly bright. I'd said all of that aloud.

"Interesting." Frawley cocked an eyebrow. "Loss of love is an eternal theme. You may want to explore its subtleties in your work, Ms. Keating. Mr. Teitsch."

He moved away, leaving me shivering and forgotten in the light.

"Close your eyes, Mr. Teitsch."

My hands perched on my knees, crooked as claws.

The phone.

One notification: photo with text message. As I looked at it the rest of the room dimmed out like in a movie, a vignette fading in around the screen.

The photo wasn't the shock. It was tamer than I'd expected. But I could not take my eyes from the words.

My mind was consumed with a single thought.

Run.

At the end of class I darted out the door, sprinting by the time I reached the elevators. I ducked into the stairwell, skipped down three steps at a time in a vaguely guided fall. On the ground floor I hurtled into winter air and ran flat-out along the black granite beach, across the commons where the grass was dull silver and dead gold, up the bridge over Lake Shore Drive and down into the city, banging people's elbows and hips in my haste and never looking back. It began to rain. My soles slipped on slick asphalt. My lungs burned like an internal combustion engine. At the Red Line station I cut ahead of someone and jumped a turnstile. Shouts rose behind me. I rammed through the crowd on the platform, searching.

Grabbed a blonde's shoulder and spun her around: a stranger. Every face was wrong. Too late.

At the railing a girl stared down into the street, watching rain fall on the red and black lacquer of Chinatown, the twin pagodas in the distance. She wore a beanie, so I'd missed her at first, but I knew the sun-gold hair framing that face.

I walked up as a train arrived and she didn't turn around. She'd been standing there awhile, letting them pass.

My body felt like a burned candle wick. I'd spent myself on the mile run. Speech was too difficult. I waited until the L left and touched her coat sleeve.

We hadn't seen each other in three months. Three months, one week, and four days, to be precise. I could tell you the hour and minute, too. When she turned we both stood there, speechless. This face. *Missing someone is the whetstone that sharpens want*, Mom said once. If it was true, then all that was left of my heart was an edge looping in on itself like a Möbius strip, slicing me up inside.

I breathed her name.

Blythe pulled out her earbuds and touched my cheek with cold fingers. "Are you really here?"

The edged thing that occupied my chest gave a sharp twist.

"We have to talk," I said. "It's an emergency."

Despite this, neither of us moved. I couldn't look away from her face. Mist lay on her skin in a gossamer film. She looked fey, unreal.

"Come on, then." She slung her bag over a shoulder, visibly braced herself. One glance at me then no more. "And hide your face."

I took a Blackhawks cap from my bag and drew it low over my eyes.

We walked through the red arch that said WELCOME TO CHINATOWN, crossing wet blacktop scribbled with neon like leaking paint. Rain hovered midair in a diamond-flecked veil. We lit cigarettes simultaneously and both of us laughed, soft, more like sighs. Behind us the trails of our breath and smoke braided into a double helix.

Blythe picked a restaurant at random and we sat in a vinyl booth under a paper lantern, awkwardly staring at each other's hands on the tabletop. I stripped off my soaked coat and cap and started shivering. She ordered something, asked where the restrooms were. The server watched us walk in together.

I locked the door. When I turned she took me in her arms. My eyes shut.

For a long time we didn't speak. We held fiercely, ribs touching, her heart beating against my breasts, every breath she took echoed by my body. Always falling into each other's rhythm. I buried my face in her hair and inhaled that dark berry scent, my mind blanking except for her. My shirt was damp, my hair stringy with rain. I didn't care. I didn't care about anything.

"God, you smell good," she said.

"Liar. I'm sweaty. I ran all the way here."

"I never lie." She pulled back, put her hands to either side of my face. "Your eyelashes are wet. Like little black petals."

I lowered them and she pressed her mouth to my eyelids, one after the other.

"I've missed you so much," I said.

Her hands trembled, touching the tiny gold cross at my throat. "I haven't missed you at all. It's just that there's no color in the world anymore, and every sound is the buzzing of flies, and everything tastes like dust."

Oh, this was dangerous.

I wrenched away and paced the bathroom. Sickly white fluorescence on bone-colored tile. The odor of ammonia and grease. I breathed deep, filling my senses, pushing her out.

"Sweet girl," she whispered.

I dug my phone out of my pocket. Returned to her and drove her up against the door. Not sweet now, our old vicious selves returning.

Her eyes bounced rapidly between mine and the screen. Then lingered on the screen. Then returned to me, slower.

"Who sent this?"

"I don't know." I slammed my phone against the door, not caring if it cracked. It slipped and spun across the floor, faceup, the damning photo blazing. The three of us, seen grainily through an apartment window. My shirt was off. Just a black bra and their hands on my skin. His hands, and hers. The bloodied shirt wasn't even in the frame but it didn't matter. The words said it all.

I SAW YOU.

My hands knotted in Blythe's hoodie, nails meeting flesh. "I don't fucking know who. But someone saw us. *And they know.*"

SEPTEMBER, LAST YEAR

The mattress was the last thing left. I was about ready to collapse atop it, but Blythe kicked my ankle and said, "Not yet, lazybones."

My entire life fit into the bed of Dad's truck. Kind of crazy that you could pack it up and drive for an hour and become part of a new universe. It was the last weekend before college began, autumn stealing in, wrapping the edges of leaves with gold foil, cranking up the blue in the sky till it reached that agonizingly pure shade that hit you square in the gut like a fist. I sat on the tailgate in the shade of an elm, sunlight lacing through the leaves and laying a filigree of fire over my skin.

"Got a smoke?" Blythe said, joining me.

I gave her my pack.

"There's only one left."

"All yours."

She lit up and took a drag, then gave it to me.

The radio was on in the truck, playing Lorde's "400 Lux," the backbeat slow and boomy like the last languid pulses of summer. I laid my head on the mattress, drumming one foot on the tailgate. Blythe snapped her fingers with the snare and we kept time together perfectly. In moments like this I could forget I ever had a past life. There was just now, blue sky, warm asphalt, our skinny colt legs in cutoffs, me and my best friend. I'd worried about moving to Chicago because the more people there were around me, the more alone I felt. Little wolf in a big wood. With her, though, I was never a nobody. She scorned the hangers-on who mooned after her and instead got into poetry-quoting matches with me, asked my opinion on a work in progress, listened to me angst about my writing. We'd stay up late drinking coffee and smoking and talking. We could talk forever. I traded the cigarette back after each drag and during the bridge she caught my hand and said, "I'm glad you're here," and my heart felt so large and light I could let go and watch it shoot up into the leaves like a balloon.

"Look what the cat dragged in," an unfamiliar voice said.

Someone stood in front of the tailgate.

"Holy fucking shit." Blythe jumped down and tossed the cig, though we'd only finished half. "What are you doing here?"

"Nice to see you, too, slut."

They flung their arms around each other. It took a moment before I saw the new girl clearly: tall and tawny-skinned, a mane of sable hair raveling around her shoulders. She wore a tennis skirt and tank like a ball gown. Blythe could be cocky, but this girl was operating on a whole other level. She exuded majesty as if her every step fell on red velvet. Her big, dark eyes made me feel infinitely small.

I instantly knew who she was.

"When did you get here?" Blythe said, still hugging her. The girl's eyes stayed on me.

"Drove up this morning."

"He didn't tell me you were coming."

The girl smiled indulgently.

"He doesn't know," Blythe said. "Christ. He's gonna freak."

"Is he here?"

"Yeah, upstairs. We're moving in—" She finally remembered me, and yanked my arm. "Get over here, you misanthrope. This is my roommate, Laney. Laney, this is Armin's sister, Hiyam."

Cue dramatic organ music.

"Nice to meet you," I said.

"Likewise." Her eyes narrowed in cool amusement. She raised her face to the sun, breathed in deeply, then looked back at us. "I'm dying for a cigarette, bitches."

———

After the squealing (Hiyam) and the sighing (Armin) and the private talk (Blythe and I pressed our ears to the bedroom door but only heard her whine "Armin-*joon*" over and over), I finally had my own room in my very first apartment. Our place stood at the top of four steep flights like something out of Edward Gorey (L *is for Laney, who fell down the stairs*), in a neighborhood that pretended not to be Humboldt Park, but basically was. Armin called it the kind of place where you could play "Firecracker or Gunshot?" on a summer night. Blythe called it "an authentic American experience" and refused to let Armin buy us anything, including a nicer neighborhood.

"Don't let anyone own you," she said, "and don't be owned by anything."

"And try not to get shot," Armin said.

Blythe rolled her eyes. "Drama queen."

She disappeared with Hiyam on a cigarette run. Donnie had come with me, and we helped Armin clean the apartment. My brother and I spent half the time horseplaying while Armin grew increasingly withdrawn. When I walked into the bathroom he was kneeling on the tile, forehead and arm propped on the sink. He'd stripped down to his undershirt, a fine rime of sweat glazing his skin, buffing it like bronze. Sweat turned his scent into the aroma of wet cedar chips. I drank the air, mesmerized.

"So why's your sister here?" I said.

"She deferred college for a year."

"Because of rehab?"

"Yes."

"Is she going to live with you?"

His shoulders heaved. "We haven't worked that out yet."

I put a hand on his back, lightly. The hard curves of muscle made me want to press tighter, to follow them as they spun around his bones. Boys are so beautiful when they don't realize how powerful they are. When they hold it with quiet grace, oblivious to how easily they could rip the world apart. Once, in one of her Byronic fits, my mother said she wished I'd been born a boy. *You're like me,* she said. *Hunter. Taker. This life will be a cage for you.* I didn't understand until I got older. Then I wished it, too. Every fucking night.

Armin tilted his face upward. "Laney."

"Yeah?"

"No pills around her. Please."

"I won't."

"Promise me."

I took my hand away. "I said I won't."

"I'm not trying to be a dick. She's my—"

"I know. I have a brother, Armin. I would kill you if you ever put him in danger."

He stared up at me with those dark doe eyes. "You should stop, too."

"I can handle it. I'm sorry your sister can't."

I made for the door and Armin stood, reaching past me, swinging it shut. His arm hung over my shoulder, his heat enveloping me without touching.

We didn't move or speak. Only breathed, slow and deep.

Every tendon tensed and drew my skin so taut the pressure of air against it was agony. A body has a way of wanting to be touched so badly that the touch itself will hurt, but so will remaining untouched. Nothing helps.

"Don't lead me on again," I said, turning. "Don't touch me if you're not going to fuck me."

He pushed me against the door, his mouth coming down on mine.

I had nothing to hold on to but him. He lifted me beneath the knees and his skin was like hot metal, sticking to me, searing. I'd kissed him dozens of times but this time was different. This time led to something irrevocable. My fingers curled in his hair and kept curling till he groaned and bit my lip. I tasted salty tin and laughed. He silenced me with another kiss. This one was less vicious but more intense, too intense, his tongue finding mine again and again, his torso coiling against me, snakelike. My legs tightened around him. I was wet as fuck. I was coming apart. I had kissed boys, fucked them, taken them into my mouth, given my body up to everything they could do to it, and it hadn't felt like this. It hadn't felt like anything. Every time I tried to get space and regain control Armin filled it effortlessly, driving me back until I was walled in on every side, nowhere to go but into this heat, this blazing white-hot oblivion.

A door slammed and girlish laughter spilled through the apartment.

I pressed my cheek to Armin's, breathing hard.

"We'll finish this later," he said, his voice raspier than usual.

Then the party began. We ordered pizza and mixed cheapo cocktails of Bacardi and Fresca, which Hiyam said was "so college." We limited ourselves to one drink out of respect for her sobriety but that was enough to make Donnie flushed and bright-eyed. When Armin turned up the music, Donnie danced. My shy little brother who hid in his hoodies like a turtle in its shell. Blythe whispered something in Donnie's ear, and his flush deepened, and the two of them pressed close, her hands sliding over his hips.

I looked away.

Hiyam blew a smoke ring and said, "Your brother is so hard for her."

My brain smoldered. People moved around me, talking and laughing while I sank into the couch, chain-smoking, lost in my own head. Shadows tilted across the room, folding up the light into little squares, sealing us in dark envelopes.

"Laney. Come here."

Blythe peered at me from a doorway, looking like she was up to no good.

I met her in the kitchen. She had the bottle of Bacardi and one glass.

"Bottoms up," she said, handing it to me.

Her eyes were already shiny. I shook my head, but swallowed it in one gulp. The stuff was like warm acid.

She poured another finger.

"You're bad," I said softly.

"So are you."

I smelled the alcohol on her breath, razor sharp. She downed it and set the glass on the counter a little too loudly, and I filled it again.

"Be normal out there," she said. "Armin'll kill us if we're fucked-up around Hiyam."

"I fake normal every day of my life."

Her face grew solemn. I drained the glass and set it down soundlessly.

"This is sad," she said.

"I know. I hate Bacardi."

"*This* is sad, you twat. That we need to get fucked-up just to be normal."

"Sarah McLachlan commercials about homeless puppies are sad. This is reality."

Blythe gave me her thousand-lumen smile. "Little Laney. My ball of bloody sunshine."

I looked down at the counter, thinking, Call me more things. Call me yours.

"I'm glad you brought Donnie," she said. "I've been dying to meet him."

"How come?"

"To figure you out, mystery girl. How are you so tiny when he's so tall?"

"He got all the height genes."

"What'd you get?"

"All the crazy."

She laughed. "And all the cuteness."

God. Maybe I wasn't ready. Change the subject. "Be honest. Were you this messed up before you met me?"

"You think this is messed up?" She leaned on a palm. "I used to drink every night till I blacked out. Couldn't go to bed sober. And you know Armin, Mr. Straight Edge. Never let me enjoy it."

"Why'd you drink?"

"To slow down."

"Slow what?"

Her eyes flicked to one side. "There's something inside me that spins too fast. Sometimes it makes me crazy."

I knew what she meant. Mom used to hide empty wine bottles in the garage. She'd get up early after passing out drunk on the couch, dispose of the evidence before Dad saw. When she didn't drink she'd be up all night, doing things. Once when I was little I dreamed I lived in a house made of cake, the walls painted with frosting, and when I woke at dawn I found her pulling cupcakes from the oven. The kitchen table was covered with them.

Hundreds. Carrot and gingerbread and black currant. *Delaney*, she'd said, laughing, *you're dreaming*. But I knew I wasn't.

I felt uneasy. "Is that why you get high with me?"

"You're different." Blythe peered up at the light, the sunset tint bleeding through the old Tiffany-style shade. "It's different with you. I feel—never mind, this is silly."

"Come on. What?"

She didn't quite look at me. "You're so fucking intense. When I'm around you everything is amplified, acute. You've infected me with it. Today I got off the train early and walked home, tasted the autumn air in my mouth. Watched leaves blowing out of the trees. Felt the skeleton inside my skin, this part of me I can't see that will remain when I die, outlast me. Everything was bloody poetry. I need to numb myself a little or I'll go mad."

My heart beat too fast. "I don't want to make you crazy."

"Bit late for that," she said wryly, but her pulse thrummed in her throat, quick and hard.

"This is dangerous. Me and you. We're pulling each other over the edge."

"Let go, Laney. Falling feels amazing."

"Right until you hit the ground."

She jumped onto the counter and tilted her head back. She was every bit Artemis tonight, wild-eyed and tangle-haired like she'd just stalked out of the woods from a kill. Her tattoos were painted on with blood and rainwater.

"Come up here."

I boosted myself beside her, shakily.

"Feel how high we are. Wouldn't it be lovely to fall?"

What did she really mean? "We should stop, Blythe."

"Should, should. 'I should wear tiger pants, I should have an affair.'"

" 'We should meet in another life, we should meet in air, me and you.' "

She gave me a sly half smile.

"Plath was crazy, you know," I said.

"In a beautiful way."

"Like you."

Blythe only laughed again. God, that laugh did something to me. "You've got to admire her balls. Stuck her head in an oven. Biggest feminist fuck-you ever. Fuck domesticity, fuck depression, fuck everything they thought about her."

"That's how you make me feel."

"Like you want to stick your head in an oven?"

"Like I don't care what anyone thinks. Like I'm crazy, in a beautiful way."

Know what else is crazy? That was the first time I said I loved someone.

Blythe leaned so close I could see every flyaway wisp of hair gilded by the kitchen light, every throb of blood along her jaw. The golden swan arch of her throat daring me to kiss or cut it. She laid a hand against my cheek, cool skin to warm, and said, "Look at you. You're a crier when you're drunk."

"I'm not crying."

"What's this, then?" Her thumb brushed a tear.

"Falling."

She watched my mouth as I spoke, then raised her eyes to mine. "You're so pretty, Laney."

"I'm really not," I said, lowering my face, and she lifted it and leaned closer and kissed me. Just once. She caught my bottom lip and held it, lightly, so light it seemed the breath I exhaled against her mouth could break this. We were perfectly still, nothing moving but the air between us and the blood crashing through our veins. Then both of her hands were on my face and she was holding me there, kissing me for real. Still slow and soft, like an echo of something that had already happened, or was about to. My eyes were slightly open but all I saw was a twinkling haze, tears dotting my eyelashes like the city skyline at dusk. When I'd kissed Armin, it was fire. Something visceral happened at the deepest cellular level of me. I'd felt it low in my belly, hard and tight, animal, unreckonable. But when I kissed Blythe it was all air. High in my chest, a rising lightness, an evanescence, all the dark, heavy things in me breaking up and scattering like dandelion seeds. *Things fall apart*, I thought. *The center cannot hold.* It was happening, finally, finally. I cupped the back of her head, combed my fingers through her hair. Tried to match her lightness but it wasn't light anymore. My tongue grazed her teeth and I tasted rum and vanilla and something that was just her, something I couldn't get enough of. I couldn't stop. We hopped off the counter and she pressed me to it, pinning me there. We kissed like we were coming up from some cold depth and the only air was in each other's lungs. Pure oxygen. Tingling spread through me until every atom buzzed, shimmering, scintillating, the way you come back to life at the water's surface and every cell blazes with that first fiery-sweet breath, and I was just a billion tiny points of light condensing into heat and skin for a moment, for this kiss.

Blythe broke away suddenly and I made a sound against her mouth, half a cry.

"Where are you two?" Armin called, and we jumped apart, grabbing the bottle and glass, and sang in unison, "Coming."

I stared at her. That moment when the spell breaks, the madness clears. Then we started giggling wildly. We were drunk. On cheap rum and each other. We hid the bottle and almost broke the glass and had to lean together for balance. She looked into my face, her eyes electric. "Keep it together, you bloody lightweight," she said, and I wanted to kiss her again. But she pulled me by the hand into the living room and everyone was there, watching. What had really changed? Nothing. I felt the same about her as I always had. I lit a cigarette and blew smoke like a cloud of frost, gave them my bitchiest *what are you looking at* look. Just normal Laney. When I kissed Armin later he frowned at the taste of rum. "It's from Blythe," I said, and laughed. He didn't get the joke.

That evening Hiyam decided to paint my room. We all went down to the basement to scrounge for spare cans, but found only cobwebs and a giant centipede. Hiyam screamed *Oh my god kill it* and Blythe scoffed *Don't be a softcock* and Donnie stomped on it. Hiyam attached herself to my brother, her new hero. We split up to search. I wandered off alone, my head a whirlwind. I couldn't think straight. Couldn't stop replaying the memory of his kiss, and hers. Getting drunk: mistake. Letting my guard down: mistake. Losing control: mistake mistake mistake. I was bent over a dust-caked crate of vinyl records, touching my mouth softly, remembering, when hands slipped around my waist.

I closed my eyes. "They're right there."

"I can't get you out of my head," Armin said.

We were hidden behind an old washing machine piled with boxes, but I could hear them—Donnie and Hiyam murmuring, and Blythe's explosive laugh, like a firework, a gorgeous shriek bursting and dissolving into sparkling peals.

"Good," I said. "Suffer a little."

His arms flexed, pulling me closer. "You're cruel to me, and I think you like it."

"You should talk."

"Do you know how much I care about you, Laney?"

"God, don't."

"Don't what?"

"You're just going to tell me to stop getting high. Or drunk. Whatever the doctor orders."

"Wrong. I'm going to tell you I want you. With me, in this moment. Completely."

He pressed his mouth to my neck. It felt like a hot blade going in, a liquid stab of heat straight to the brain stem. I tilted my head away, my hair tumbling into my face. Armin kissed the cords of my throat, his hands sculpting over my collarbone, my breasts, pulling me back against the hard ridge in his jeans. My palms thumped onto the washing machine, my shirt riding up and my belly touching cool steel. His mouth was right against the carotid, that thick thread of blood that supplies the brain. In a hanging the carotids are usually compressed, causing unconsciousness in a matter of seconds. It's more common with women. Our necks are thinner. I was dizzy, still drunk, but when his knee nudged my legs apart I said, "Don't stop, don't stop," and when his leg pressed between mine I quit using words. I made some kind of animal noise that meant *more*. There was only the color white in my head, an amalgamation of all colors, all senses. White is the color you see right before that final blackness. It's possible to survive a hanging, but for the brain to be so blood-starved you're nothing but a vegetable.

"Laney," Armin murmured, "come back to me."

He turned my face to one side and kissed me and I bit him, hard. Hot gush of sugar and iron in my mouth. His arms tightened, one hand slipping inside my jeans, between my legs, and at that point there was not much human left in me. Crazed fantasies filled my head: him tearing my pants off, spreading my thighs and fucking me right there in that damp darkness. And Blythe lifting my face to the sunset lamp, the soft collision of her mouth and mine. And a pillow beneath my knees, a sweaty muscled abdomen rippling above me. Desire mixed with memory. I was all want, nothing but a hunger with a mouth. I could have taken him right then. I wanted to. I wanted to be fucked like I hadn't been in so, so long. My head was a cyclone of fire and if I weren't so drunk I might have screamed, the way Hiyam screamed when she saw something horrible. I was the horrible thing. Locked in here alone in the cage of my skull, with these claws for thoughts and all this red, wet want. I leaned into Armin's hand, the hard finger grinding against my panties. My thoughts split in a million directions. Closing my eyes only made it more disorienting, so I opened them and I guess I already sort of knew what I'd see.

Vaguely I remembered someone calling *We found it, come on, Laney*, and footsteps receding, yet Blythe stood less than a dozen feet away, her mouth hanging open. It wasn't her face—it was the look in her eyes that stabbed straight through me. Hurt, but a knowing, unsurprised hurt. Like this was something she knew was coming but thought she could hold off a little longer.

Armin hadn't seen her. His head was bowed over my shoulder, his hand moving agonizingly, sweetly, right against the poison in me. I let myself gasp once, loud enough to be sure Blythe heard.

She turned and walked away.

———

I was the last one upstairs. Everyone was in my room. The music was loud, their voices louder. I went to the kitchen and turned on the cold water and splashed it into my face.

There is a goal, I thought. Remember that. This is a means to an end.

They are a means to an end.

My skin pinkened, then paled in the water. I willed the numbness to seep through to my core.

I didn't hear anyone behind me but when those hands slipped around my waist again I eased into them, sighing. Even when I realized the difference I didn't stop. I knew their skin so well. His was coarse like the head of a match. Hers was just soft, pure fucking softness, like air blowing over silk, the barest glide against mine. One hand slipped under my shirt and cupped a breast. I stiffened the way you do in electrocution, the inside of your body roiling and manic, the outside paralyzed.

"Did he get you off?" Blythe breathed against my ear.

"No."

Her hand tightened on my breast and my teeth clamped so hard it felt like they sparked.

"Too bad. I would have."

She pulled away and I turned with her. Caught skin, clung with my nails. I raked the inside of her forearm as hard as I could, gloriously savage, uncaring, and we stood there inches apart, our teeth bared and our hair scattered across our faces. Three ragged strands of rubies welled up from her skin. The air had that impeccable stillness that comes right before lightning.

"Did I hurt you?" I said, my voice guttural.

"Like you wouldn't believe."

We weren't talking about blood and skin.

"I never meant for this to happen, Blythe."

"How long do you want to keep pretending?"

"Pretending what?"

"That we're just friends."

My heart shot into my throat. "I never pretended."

"I knew you didn't mean what you said that night. You're just another straight girl messing around."

"I meant it. But there's a reason I'm so cautious."

"You want to have your cake and eat it, too."

"I want you."

Her eyes were cold. "What you want is in the other room with your come all over his hands."

"What the fuck is going on?" Hiyam said from the doorway.

I jumped back, my nerves so charged with crazed electricity it would've taken nothing to let go. I wanted to. I wanted Blythe's skin under my nails, her mouth under mine, the two of us tearing each other apart. She didn't even glance at Hiyam. Only me. No heat in her face, no fury. Sheer ice. Blood crawled down her arm and pattered on the floor.

I couldn't say it. What I really wanted. Not here, not like this.

Coward. Scared little girl.

I turned and walked away.

———

That night, and for weeks afterward, we barely saw each other. Barely spoke. We lived together like ghosts, seeing only closing doors, mysteriously moved objects. In the mornings the bathroom mirror was steamy and I looked for a message. *I'm sorry. I miss you.* Nothing. I wrote a line from Plath—*I am not cruel, only truthful*—then smeared it out. Days flickered past, slowly shading into silver and gray like someone going over the world with a graphite pencil. New classes and new faces filled my head. I read books on trains that smelled like cold aluminum and newsprint, intentionally missing my stop, taking them to the end of the line and switching at the terminus to take them all the way back. On the nights Armin deejayed Blythe was never at Umbra. I walked through the crowd alone, feeling halved, my whole side one raw wound. Even Armin with his syrup-slow kisses didn't make that ache stop. Only pills. Lots and lots of them. Late at night when her door slammed I crept to the laundry basket and picked up her cardigan, crushing it to my face. Still warm. Voices behind the door, hers and a boy's, low and muted. Always a different one. Always. I breathed in the smell of blackberries. Bit the wool, shredded it with my nails. Left it looking like a cat had destroyed it. She never said a word.

Girls love each other like animals. There is something ferocious and unself-conscious about it. We don't guard ourselves like we do with boys. No one trains us to shield our hearts from each other. With girls, it's total vulnerability from the beginning. Our skin is bare and soft. We love with claws and teeth and the blood is just proof of how much. It's feral.

And it's relentless.

MARCH, THIS YEAR

Seventeen steps. Exactly seventeen steps from elevator to apartment. Down the concrete hall, past steel doors to a bare bulb in a wire prison, a shriek of light in my eyes. I stared until my retinas burned white, blind. Pulled at the chain around my neck till it cut off circulation for a second. I don't know how many times I walked those seventeen steps there and back like a caged wolf, lean and vicious, ready to snap.

The elevator opened and a woman stepped out. I watched her walk fast to her door.

I may have snarled.

It was late when the elevator chimed again and this time I was waiting in front of it.

Armin raised his head from his phone and startled.

"Jesus, Lane. I've been calling you all night."

"Don't talk. Unlock your door."

"Blythe said—"

I stuck a hand inside his coat and grabbed a fistful of silk shirt, twisting. "Unlock. Your. Door."

He put the phone away. Watched me with wary eyes. We went into the apartment together. I closed the door behind us, slamming the dead bolt.

"Laney—"

"Is Hiyam here?"

"Are you okay? What's going on? Why didn't you—"

I slapped a palm on the kitchen island. "We are being blackmailed. Is your sister here?"

Armin ran a hand through his hair, quick and nervous. "No. She's not." Ran it through again. "What do you mean, 'blackmailed'?"

I showed him my phone.

All the lights were off, but through the windows the gold haze from a hundred skyscrapers tinted everything sepia, like an old photo. I watched Armin's face, lit eerily from below. His eyes moved over the screen.

"Who sent this?"

I leaned against the counter, suddenly exhausted. I hadn't eaten today and my throat felt coated with ash. I was all smoke and bone, skinny, shivering. Worn down. Unwell. Hatred is a poison and you cannot carry it inside your skin without getting sick, too.

"Laney?"

"I googled it. No records. Probably a burner phone."

"Burner phone."

"Yeah."

He smiled uncertainly. "Listen to what you're saying."

"What, it's paranoid?"

"You're jumping to—"

"We had burners. Someone else does, too. Armin, they're not fucking around. *They know.*"

He put my phone down and walked to the end of the kitchen. Then back. Then away again, combing his hands through his hair. Blythe had been a tornado of energy and fury, desperate to do something, anything. Armin always circled the problem first. Analyzed it from 360 degrees. Careful, considerate boy. So careful with everything. With me.

"Okay," he said after a while. "Okay."

Only my eyes moved, following him.

"This photo was shot—" He glanced at the screen. "That's her kitchen. This is from the south. What's south of her building?"

"Empty lot, then another building."

"Maybe one of the tenants—"

"That building's only three stories. This angle is from straight across."

Our eyes met.

"The roof," we said simultaneously.

Someone had climbed onto the roof of the adjacent building. Waited for us.

Armin began pacing again.

"Okay. Let's assume this is . . . a threat. How did they follow us? We were fast and clean. Unless Donnie—"

"They didn't follow us."

Shadow. Light. Shadow.

"Someone was already up there," I said. "They knew where to go, where to look. Where to see *us*."

The three of us. Together. Like always.

"*I saw you*." Armin's throat rippled with a swallow. "It's not even about him. They don't care about revenge. They care about hurting us."

Come on, I thought. You're so close.

"This is someone who knew what we were planning that night," he said. "Someone who was waiting."

"Just say it."

He stopped pacing, that handsome profile in silhouette. "It's one of us, Laney. One of us turned."

OCTOBER, LAST YEAR

On Homecoming Day the air had a sweet dry tang of rust, like old blood. Corgan University sat on the edge of Lake Michigan, a sprawling ivory palace we'd nicknamed Hogwarts, perching atop shelves of cracked granite as if part of the city had broken off centuries ago and crumbled into the lake. I liked the sense of being surrounded by massive, ruined things. Hiyam and I wove arm-in-arm through tailgate partiers, our hair wind-tossed, sunglasses flashing. My body was wired. I could navigate by feel, follow the electric crackle that leaped from body to body and skittered over gravel and snapped in blue arcs at the corner of my eye.

Hunting always brings me to life.

"You don't have to babysit me," Hiyam said for the umpteenth time. "I won't get fucked-up."

"I'm not your babysitter," I said.

I was basically her babysitter.

She'd moved in with Armin, so her sobriety was everyone's problem now. It takes a village to keep someone out of rehab. At first Armin was nervous about letting his newly detoxed sister hang out with his habitually toxed girlfriend, but Hiyam policed herself pretty well, and it wasn't exactly clear I was Armin's girlfriend, anyway. This ambiguity became poignant when we'd make out for half an hour until he'd grab my wrist, removing my hand from the erection in his jeans. I'd be so pissed I'd hit him. "If you don't want to fuck me, fine, but stop leading me on." He'd pin my wrist to the couch, his body over mine. "I want you so much I can't think," he'd growl. Which led in circles. "Then why are we still talking?" I'd say, and he'd say, "It's complicated," and I'd guess that *complicated* meant Blythe.

Blythe fucking McKinley. She was always there with us. Between us. Part of us.

"It's not that you're boring," Hiyam was saying now. Hiyam had a way of making everything sound like a backhanded compliment. "It's just that I'm an adult."

"Eighteen is not an adult."

"Legally it is."

"Legally you could join the Marines or have a kid. If you think you're ready for that, you're nuts."

"I've done *actual* adult shit."

"Doing adult shit doesn't make you an adult."

The sunglasses swiveled to me. "You remind me of someone."

Before he enlisted me as babysitter, Armin had warned me about Hiyam. "Keep her away from drugs, and from girls her own age. She has a habit of abusing both."

"I'm a girl her own age."

He'd frowned, reconsidering.

"Look, I'll handle her," I'd said breezily. "If I can keep Blythe from jumping off a rooftop on X, I won't let your sister walk all over me."

It hadn't even occurred to me what he was doing. Why he paired us together. Well played, doctor.

"Heads up, *Princess Diaries*," I said now, steering Hiyam away from a group of sloshed frat boys. She wore skintight jeans and a cling-film T-shirt, white leather boots, gold hoop earrings. She looked twenty-eight, not eighteen. The frat boys hooted.

"That's her shirt," she said, ignoring them.

"What?"

"You're wearing Blythe's shirt. I bought it for her."

"I'm borrowing it."

"I thought you two weren't on speaking terms."

Shrug.

"Then why are you wearing her shirt?"

"So she can't."

"How petty." Her eyes narrowed. "Did something scratch you?"

I pulled the collar higher, not answering.

We bought canned drinks and headed for the stage, passing various club tables: frats and sororities, activism, geekery, all the stuff that's supposed to make college the Time of Your Life™. Of course Hiyam dawdled near the giant rainbow flag staffed by a boy band of Adonises (mostly in vanilla flavor), their smiles gleaming violently in the sun. PRIDE, the banner said. Like that wasn't obvious from the gaggle of sorority bimbos fawning all over them. If they fawned any harder, they'd leave a stain.

"People are so tolerant here," Hiyam said.

"Yeah, it's so tolerant for straight white girls to lust after hot, unavailable white boys."

She finally cracked a smile. "Such a bitch, Keating. I like it."

Up onstage Armin spun AWOLNATION for the crowd, his long, lean torso in a V-neck, a beanie slouching on the back of his skull. Those lithe hands moved over the mixer with confidence and finesse. The same way he touched me. He knew how to make me crazy, his thumb gliding down my throat and between my breasts, pausing over my heart. His fingers could span my entire rib cage. I felt hot. I took my shades off—and spotted the golden-haired girl onstage, watching me.

Blythe and I eyed each other coolly. That almost-smile curved at the edges of her mouth.

Armin was midset but when I climbed up he kissed me in front of everyone, lifting my face until I stood on tiptoe. His skin was sun-warm and his lips tasted like beeswax balm. I closed my eyes and dissolved into heat and honey. People whistled. Armin let go and my heart seemed to hang in place, stuck in midair. It made feeble little flutters, like a pinned butterfly.

"If you're done sucking each other's faces off," Hiyam said, "I'm thirsty."

"Be good," Armin said in my ear.

"If I'm not, you won't know."

He ran a thumb over my bottom lip. There was a faint ember-like light in his eyes. I'd seen it before. I knew what it led to.

Today I would take it there, one way or another.

I carried our drinks to the rear of the stage. Blythe passed me cups without speaking. When our hands brushed I yanked mine back as if I'd been burned.

"Oh, the tension," Hiyam said. "I'm tingling."

I poured, and Blythe pulled out a pint of Seagram's and spiked the cups.

"That is so college," Hiyam said.

I handed her a virgin soda. "Don't touch Armin's. It's Red Bull."

"Like I want that nasty shit."

"I mean it."

She looked at me as if a dog had just spoken to her.

The three of us sat on a road crate, me in the middle. The air was so saturated with bass every breath felt thick, thrumming in my lungs. It wasn't quite like Umbra but something untamed worked its way through the crowd, stretching the skin of the bodies it entered, dilating nostrils, glazing eyes. That wolfishness.

Blythe looked at the cup in my hand.

"Guess we're sharing," I said.

"Guess so."

She drank and then I did. Hiyam peered at us over the top of her sunglasses. "Wait, when did this happen?"

"When did what?" I said.

"You skanks were fighting over who gets to fuck my brother." Her eyes widened at the cup. "Oh my god. Is that a metaphor?"

"No," I said, at the same moment Blythe said, "Yes. It's a love triangle."

I glared at her. "It is not a love triangle."

"Except when it's a love triangle."

Hiyam's eyes darted between us, intrigued.

"Seriously, Hiyam," I said. "We worked it out. Our friendship is worth more than some guy. No offense to your brother."

"Besides, who could stay mad at this face?" Blythe said, pinching my cheek.

I could've bitten her.

"Armin-*joon*," Hiyam sang, sliding off the crate with his drink. "Your harem is getting along. It's boring."

I started to follow, but Blythe's hand dropped to my shoulder.

"Stay awhile," she said.

That hand was a magnet, the iron in my blood and marrow snapping to it. I settled back and watched Hiyam curling around her brother, serpentine.

"Nice lampshading," I said to Blythe.

"If it's right there, you've got to say something."

"Apparently you've got to say everything."

"That's the beauty of it. Tell them all your secrets, and they'll never believe you. They'll think you're hiding the truth."

"Yeah, well, warn me before your supervillain reveal speech."

Her hand grazed my thigh, just past the hem of my shorts. My teeth clicked together.

"It looks good on you," she said.

"What?"

"My shirt."

Hiyam was messing with Armin's phone. Reading our texts, probably. He'd tell me he couldn't sleep and was walking along the beach, thinking about me, thrusting his fingers into the sand and letting it slip away, over and over. I'd tell him I couldn't sleep and was jacking off, thrusting my fingers into—

Blythe nudged my knee. "Where are you?"

Wind lashed our hair across our faces. Her hoodie was unzipped, a long blond lock twisting across her collarbone, this way and then that, like something alive, touching her.

"I'm right here," I said.

"A thousand light-years away."

Something soft unfurled inside me, a small tenderness. It was agony sometimes, being near her.

"You're shivering." She shrugged off her hoodie and laid it in my lap, got up to go.

I caught her wrist. Couldn't help myself. "Want me out of your shirt?"

Blythe laughed, low in her throat. Then she was gone, jumping down into the crowd. I slipped into her hoodie and pressed the sleeve to my cheek. Still warm.

Something caught my eye. Hiyam taking a cup from Armin, raising it to her mouth.

I moved without thinking. Launched myself forward, my shoulder connecting with her back. An arc of bright wetness sliced through the air, a liquid pinwheel of light. Then it was all over Hiyam, and Hiyam was screaming, and Armin was pushing the two of us apart, saying, "There's a sweater in my car, go to my car." Hiyam's soaked shirt painted her breasts in a clear glaze, her nipples hard.

We walked to his car without speaking. Her silence was volcanic.

When we passed the frat boy gauntlet the second time, she wasn't so cocky. She hugged her arms to her chest.

"Show us your tits," a frat boy yelled.

"Show us yours," she muttered.

They kept yelling. I reluctantly offered her Blythe's hoodie, but she refused.

"I'm sorry," I ventured. "I'm such a klutz."

"Just don't talk."

While she rummaged in Armin's Range Rover I wrapped my arms around myself. If I breathed deeply, I could still smell blackberries.

"I don't get it." Hiyam had frozen with her ass in the air like some porn pose, but for once, I think, she was oblivious of her sexuality. "What the fuck does he see in you?"

"Look, I know you're mad—"

She wheeled on me. "You don't know shit. You're just another junkie he thinks he can save. Did he give you the 'only you can save yourself' speech yet? Because it's bullshit. He says that and then rescues strays anyway. Why do you think he's still obsessed with Blythe?"

My throat went tight. "Obsessed?"

"Wake the fuck up, Keating. My brother likes you broken. That's the only thing you do better than her."

I stared at her for a long time, not blinking. In the raw wind my eyes went glassy, which gave the intended effect.

"God." She slammed the car door. "Forget it."

But I didn't. I never forget.

We passed Blythe on the way back. She sat on the hood

of someone's car like a pin-up, bare legs crossed. Two bros in polos and boat shoes hovered near. Meaty, sweaty, crude. Beneath her. Beneath *me*. They couldn't quote poetry, couldn't read the nuance in the subtlest flicker of her expression. They were just big, and dumb, and hard.

I looked away, grinding my teeth.

The afternoon whirled through my head. Turquoise sky, clouds shifting across it like the silver powder in an Etch A Sketch, drawing and erasing itself over and over. Touchdown. The lot erupted into a frenzy. Armin took a break and spent it kissing me in his car. I closed my eyes and imagined Blythe walking by, seeing us. After his set we sat on the rocks at the edge of the lake and I made him drink a beer, laughing when that handsome face contorted at the taste. In retaliation he made me kiss him. He kept touching me everywhere, held me down on a flat stone and kissed my throat and said, "I just want to feel you," as if I were some strange new thing that befuddled and amazed him. The colors of the day deepened like a bruise. I avoided the football game, the name that made my blood blacken, until people tossed their hats up against the pale vapor of the stadium lights, shook bottles of beer and sprayed foam into the air. We won. For a moment we were all alive and invincible, immortal. We won.

Our victory song was "The Baddest Man Alive" by the Black Keys and I almost choked. Irony, you bitch.

We broke the stage down under the moonrise, our shadows long and sharp like storybook monsters. Hiyam fell asleep in Armin's backseat. Blythe left with a look that wrecked my heart a little. Don't go, I thought, letting her go. I sat on an amp and watched the sea of red taillights leaving the lot.

Armin came over and nestled between my knees. "Hi."

"Hi."

"Hi," he said again.

I tried not to smile. "What?"

His hands brushed the small of my back. "You."

A sound tech loaded equipment into a van. We were alone onstage, spotlit in a hot white disc. I imagined a dark circle eclipsing it.

"There's something I've been meaning to tell you." His eyes shone with all the colors of autumn, rich oxblood seeping into the deep russet of October soil. "But I could never find the right time. Or the right words."

"Please don't say some cheesy romance-novel shit, Armin."

He grinned. I touched his face.

"Seriously. Let's not say things. Let's just be."

"I can't help it." He let me trace his stubbled jaw and the bed of his lips as he spoke. "When I'm around you, I feel like a different person. More electric, more alive. Like I'm high."

"I thought you never got high before."

"I don't need to. I have you."

"What did I just say about cheesy romance-novel shit?"

"Deal with it, Miss Novelist."

He put his face to my neck and inhaled, rubbed his stubble over my skin like a big cat. Then he looked at me spacily, pupils dilated.

"*Are* you high?" I said, laughing.

"You smell like her."

Lightning strike to the heart.

"Like her," I repeated.

He frowned, hearing it.

"Like her. God, Armin. Is there something going on with you and Blythe?"

"Is there something going on with *you* and Blythe?"

I gaped.

"I'm not blind, Laney."

"Unbelievable." My hand was on his shirt and I made it into a fist. "I've been throwing myself at you shamelessly and this is what you're worried about."

"I believe you want this. That you want me. But there's something off. You're so closed up."

A tendon tightened along my jaw. It felt like barbed wire. "It's hard for me to be vulnerable, okay?"

"Did something happen? With another guy?"

"You're going to ruin tonight if you keep talking like this."

"I want to understand you."

"No you don't." I pulled him closer, my thighs to either side of his waist. "You want to fuck me."

When he spoke it was breathy. "You worry me sometimes. This all feels so . . ."

He trailed off and I said, "So what?"

"Calculated."

It's surreal, watching the prey become aware of you.

"What do you mean?" I said.

"Like you want to fuck me just to get something out of me."

"Oh my god. If you think I'm some gold-digging—"

"Not money. Nothing that simple." Armin touched my cheek, his eyes sad. "Your heart isn't in this. You're going through the motions with me. I know it, and I can't stop wanting you."

I smiled bitterly. "You're not supposed to see the puppet strings."

"What?"

"Of course I'm manipulating you. I'm messed up. I don't know how to do the emotional intimacy thing."

"You do it with Blythe."

I was spared from response by a burst of sound behind us. A door opened, voices carrying across the pavement. Armin's gaze didn't waver.

"I am falling in love with you, Laney Keating."

"Don't say that."

"It's true."

"Don't say it," I said miserably, looking away.

"Why?"

Falling for someone is like pulling a loose thread. It happens stitch by stitch. You feel whole most of the time even while the seams pop, the knots loosen, everything that holds you together coming undone. It feels incredible, this opening of yourself to the world. Not like the unraveling it is. Only afterward do you glance down at the tangle of string around your feet that used to be a person who was whole and self-contained and realize that love is not a thing that we create. It's an undoing.

"Because you deserve better," I whispered.

In the near distance silhouettes moved against the light, all strut and swagger. Armin touched my face with gentle restraint. So respectful of my boundaries. Of the edges of my craziness.

"You don't have to manipulate me," he said. "I won't lose interest simply because it's difficult for you to open up."

"Maybe you should." What the hell was wrong with my throat? All gnarled and dry, words coming out like splinters. "Maybe you should go now, before I do something horrible to you."

"The worst thing you could do is break my heart."

I'm going to, I said, but it caught in my windpipe, a tissue snagging on those splinters, tearing into a hundred shreds and leaving my mouth as dust.

Someone laughed. We both turned.

A group of guys passed us. Greek marble torsos, chiseled ivory teeth. Hair still wet from the locker room shower. They were only visible for a moment in the pool of light but that moment hung and dragged like a glitch. The one in the middle was blond, broad-shouldered, strolling with a viper's sinister grace. Mr. I Have the Whole World on the End of My Dick. Breathing the same air I did.

When you are this close, this fucking close to everything that gives meaning and purpose to your sad little life, it's hard not to feel awe. To feel the threads of fate pulling tight and neat around your throat. So tight you can't breathe.

I couldn't breathe.

"Laney?" Armin said.

The viper was laughing. His phone at his ear, his male-model face split with a glow-in-the-dark smile.

I slid off the amp and stumbled. My head tilted heavily and if Armin wasn't there I might have fallen.

"Laney, what's wrong?"

I felt fuzzy at the edges, partially erased. "I'm going to be sick."

"Are you on something?"

I shook my head. The group passed into shadow again, dissolving into the night.

Armin stared after them. "Who was that?"

Well, that's easy.

That is the boy who ruined my life.

That is the boy I am going to kill.

FEBRUARY, LAST YEAR

The clearest sign of coming catastrophe is when all the bad shit in your life suddenly stops. You're entering the eye of the shitstorm.

On a winter morning in my senior year, my breath a wake of white smoke, my skin narco-numb from cold (also, narcotics), I walked into a high school that had miraculously forgotten I existed.

My hair was growing out after the tragic pixie cut I got over break, shaggy now, almost cute, but the other day Brandt Zoeller had made a V with his fingers and stuck his tongue between them, so it wasn't grown out enough. When I passed him—his whole entourage at his locker, the jock reek and Axe body spray enough parts-per-million to make me hurl—he didn't say a word. None of them did. Their silence sent my hackles up, the way you miss an irritating noise in the first edgy minutes of quiet. You become so accustomed to being bothered that *not* being bothered is alarming. Inertia is the most comfortable state for all things, including pain.

Zoeller watched me with those unblinking reptile-green eyes. Aside from the creeper stare, he was absurdly attractive. Another truism: the hotter they are, the better odds they're an asshole. Romance novels at least get that right.

I felt his gaze trail me down the hall.

In English we were doing a poetry unit, and I was sitting in the last row, ankles crossed, staring out at a field of frosted grass glistening like tinsel, the sky a crumpled sheet of silver tissue paper, the world all wrapped up in ice and waiting for spring to tear it open when I heard the words that peppered my gauzy consciousness like 9 mm rounds.

"The love poetry of Sappho."

I hunched inside my hoodie. Jesus, I prayed. Please don't ask someone to read.

Mrs. Thomlin recited a poem, blessedly short—"Awed by her splendor"—and moved on to Browning.

It wasn't until second period that I realized it was Valentine's Day. There'd been hearts on everything for weeks. February is one long trailer for this fucking Hallmark holiday. They were milking it: buy your sweetie a box of chocolates, roses, or a special (PG-13) message you could read over the PA. Because this was high school, bastion of brain-dead pop culture parrots, most of the "special messages" were song lyrics. One girl had a sense of humor and dedicated a Bieber quote to her bestie. "Carpet munchers," a boy said in the hall, and his friends snickered.

I darted into the bathroom.

A handful of preppy girls flounced out, ignoring me. I turned on the cold water and doused my face. When my eyes opened, Kelsey Klein stood beside me at the sink.

I swallowed the first spike of an impending heart attack. Of course I was standing there looking like a drowned kitten when Kelsey showed up. Of fucking course. She slicked strawberry gloss on her lips, blew herself an air kiss, and glanced over.

"Hey, Delaney."

My eyes bounced from her to my reflection, confirming it was actually me. Kelsey said hello to me. Kelsey did not freak out and run. Kelsey, who'd read the fucking poem I left (idiot,

idiot) in her locker (moron) before Christmas, and signed (dumbass) with an *L*, which Zoeller somehow knew about because Zoeller knew everything, and which he'd quote to me sometimes, taunting.

"Hey," I croaked.

Smooth, killer. Real.

Kelsey smiled. A lopsided one that made her left eye squint—just the left. Her genuine smile, the one she gave when she didn't care how photogenic she looked. She tilted an apple cheek upward and made it a wink, a secret between me and her, conspiratorial. "Happy Valentine's Day," she said.

When the door closed behind her all I could think was, *Awed by her splendor.*

I met Donnie at our usual rendezvous point by the water fountains.

"You all right, Lane?"

I shrugged, faking nonchalance. It's strange being the big sister when you're half the size of your little brother.

"Zoeller bothering you?"

"No. That's the weird thing. He's totally ignoring me."

Two sophomores passed, and one said coyly, "Hey, Donnie."

Donnie smiled down at his shoes. They giggled as if he'd said something outrageous.

"I do not understand girls," I said.

"Aren't you one?"

I shrugged. I'd never felt like it. Never felt like anything, really. Girl, boy, whatever. Nothing quite fit. That's what Zoeller and his mouth-breathing minions never got: I didn't cut my hair because I wanted to look like a boy. I cut it because I didn't feel like a girl.

I shoved my fists into my hoodie. "Going to lunch. See you later."

Donnie touched my arm.

"Happy Valentine's, Rainbow Brite," he said, prodding something into my chest.

It was a Moleskine journal, sleek black leather, the pages crisp and cream white, thirsty for ink. Inside the cover he'd tucked a photo of us at Navy Pier. We sat on the dock, two silhouettes matted against a brilliant blood-orchid sunset, the light peeling away in lush petals and falling into the lake. Mom had taken that photo on one of her rare good days.

I hugged him, letting go of the journal, only the fierceness of my hug suspending it between our ribs. It pulsed there like a shared heart between us.

"Happy Valentine's," I said. I love you more than anything.

Even lunch that day wasn't horrible. Deep dish pizza from Lou Malnati's. I flipped open the Moleskine and pulled out a Pilot rollerball. Nothing beats the purity of that first blank page. *February 14*, I wrote. Then I closed my eyes and absorbed the afterimage. Jock table: thug wannabes, roid-pumped bodies. Stoner table: sleepy smiles; Harlan, the boy I'd lost my virginity to freshman year. Emo/scene table: Donnie's crowd, forward-swept bangs and eyeliner. Nerd/geek table: probably where I should've been if I weren't such a pussy. Then me, a table all to myself, the loser table, while a figure approached—

I opened my eyes.

"Are you Delaney K.?" the boy said. His Adam's apple looked like a chicken trying to peck its way out of his throat.

"Why?"

He shrugged, helpless. Nerd/geek. They don't do well with girls. Another reason why I was one of them.

"Are you Delaney?" he said again. His eyes were desperate.

"Yeah."

He thrust a hand out, almost aggressively. His voice cracked. "Happy Valentine's Day."

A red rose in a clear plastic box, with a card.

What the hell?

I took it because it seemed like the kid would self-destruct if I didn't, and he scuttled away. I scanned the cafeteria. This had to be a prank. Where was Zoeller?

Nowhere. No one was paying attention to me.

I sat there for a good two minutes, debating leaving my tray and the rose and walking out. This had to be a mistake.

At least read the card, Laney. You know you're curious.

Shut up, brain, you asshole. You got me into—

Wait, why are our hands tearing open the envelope?

L,

   I can't stop thinking about you. If you still like me, give me a sign. Come before 5th period, hall 2.

                              Love,

                              K

I read it three times to make sure, then once more, to dull my disbelief. No fucking way. No way. But she'd looked at me in the bathroom, unfazed. Smiled. That smile she didn't give strangers, the natural, imperfect one, the one that fucked me up in the first place, that made me think crazy thoughts like *If I could fall in love with a girl, it'd be her.* Those *ifs* are dangerous. You try them on in your head like dresses, so easy to slide in and out of. *If I kissed girls, I'd kiss her. If we kissed, it'd go like this.* At some point I dropped the *if* like a slip and just wore the feeling, nothing between it and my skin. *When I kiss her. When it happens.* All of it took place in my head, in silence, locked tight in skull bone and the frantic synaptic whispers between neurons, no clues popping out except the passive-aggressive haircut, the incriminating poem.

That's the problem with writers. Too much imagination.

The greater part of me knew it couldn't be real, but the

hopeful part, which is more concentrated and condensed, rich in nine essential delusions, thought: It's not all in your head.

I dropped the rose into my bag, with the Moleskine.

––––––––

Mandatory guidance counseling should be covered by the Geneva Conventions. We're captives, and it's torture.

Mr. Radzen—who said we could call him Jeff or Jay or Radz, but never Mr. Radzen—leaned back and propped his feet on the desk. He was fortyish, ex-jock turned coach, arms still ripped but abs gone soft with beer. His broom-handle mustache was straight out of *Axe Cop*. He drove a 1995 Sunfire (possibly a high school graduation present) and still listened to Pearl Jam.

This was my guidance counselor.

"So, Del."

He hiked his eyebrows in an attempt at flustered charm. Rumor was he'd banged half the cheerleading squad.

"It's Laney."

"Huh? 'It's raining?' Speak up, hon."

"Never mind."

"We both know why we're here, don't we?" A smile spread beneath the mustache, making it quiver, like something furry and possibly alive. Sometimes I thought of the mustache as a separate sentience.

"Why are we here?" I said, refusing to be complicit.

"Our attendance has been a problem, hasn't it?"

Jeff liked to frame everything as if we'd both done it. We'd both skipped school. We'd both failed a drug test. We'd both written a murder/suicide fantasy and handed it in as a creative writing assignment.

"Been missing work?" I said. "Back on the booze, Mr. Radzen?"

He sucked in his cheeks. "Del, honey. Don't jerk me around."

"That's what this whole thing is. One big jerk-off."

"Looks like we're doing better," he said, shuffling papers. "Only one absence this month. That's what I like to see. Improvement."

I hadn't "improved" anything but my ability to hide how fucked-up I was. Here's the therapy transcript from winter break, more or less.

DR. PATEL: Mrs. Keating, I believe your daughter has
    borderline personality disorder.
MOM: Dr. Patel, I believe my daughter has teenage
    hormones.
LANEY: [Stares at the floor silently.]
DR. PATEL: She's suffering from acute dysphoria. I'll prove
    it with my list of irrefutable symptoms.
      1. Unstable and/or intense emotions that are often
    debilitating, especially intense feelings of rejection
    (patient feels targeted by bullies at school, has no
    friends).
      2. Impulsive and/or self-destructive behavior to
    relieve emotional pain (e.g., substance abuse).
      3. Victimhood and fragmented self-image (patient
    says everyone hates her because she is "different" but
    will not explain how).
      4. Vindictiveness, manipulation, dissociation,
    thoughts of self-harm (patient may be a suicide risk).
MOM: You described being a teenager. Being a teenager is
    not a personality disorder.
DR. PATEL: I understand your skepticism, but—
MOM: I brought her in for cognitive therapy. She simply
    needs someone to talk to.

LANEY: [But not you, Mom.]

DR. PATEL: Yes, and we'll do that, but in the meantime I would like to start her on an anti-anxiety medication—

MOM: I don't want that shit in my body. Her body.

EVERYONE: [Awkwardly ignores the Freudian slip.]

LANEY: I'm willing to try it, Mom. Anything that might help.

And so they gave me free Xanax, which I'd already been abusing for months.

Jeff was droning on about *attainable goals* and *focus* and *strategy* and other coach-speak, so I took an inventory of his desk. Framed photos, not of family but of vehicles: Jeff leaning "sexily" against the Sunfire; Jeff on a schooner; Jeff beneath a fighter jet with his arm around a uniformed airman. A wrestling trophy from the eighties angled to show Captive in Seat (me) Jeff's HONORABLE MENTION. A ceramic trout with a swollen encephalitic head gaped at me, bearing the inscription BIG FISH IN A SMALL POND. I could not tell if it was ironic.

"Hon," Jeff said, "you're not listening."

"Why the hell should I? You never listen to me."

The mustache twitched. It looked like it might run off.

"You don't want to hear my bullshit, I don't want to hear yours." I swung a foot onto his desk, perilously close to BIG FISH. "Spare me your community college psych degree. Why don't we just sit quietly till our time is up?"

The rose had gone to my head. Someone liked me. Finally, someone liked me. An impossible someone, a girl I was crazy about. None of this mattered anymore.

Jeff stood and snapped the blinds closed.

"You're real hot shit, aren't you," he said behind me. "Real hot shit, Miss Princess."

My wolf instincts kicked in. Stay still. Observe.

"You've got authority problems. Okay. Join the club. But that doesn't give you the right to disrespect me, you spoiled bitch."

I raised my eyebrows.

"Take your foot off my goddamn desk."

I did, my heart beating fast.

"Now say, 'I'm sorry for disrespecting you, Jeff.' "

"Fuck you," I said impulsively.

"Now apologize twice."

"I'll run out of here screaming you touched me."

"Go ahead, hon. We're on camera. I'll have you expelled faster than you can say 'false allegations.' "

I sank into the chair.

"Here's my take." A steak-sized palm thumped onto the backrest. "You're a junkie. You throw a few tantrums, get a doc to call you manic-depressive or whatever. He writes you a free pass to the grown-up candy store. Then it's party time."

"No."

"I see a dozen girls like you every day. You just want to get wasted. Look up some symptoms, call yourself some flavor-of-the-month disorder, and bingo. Pillville."

"You're wrong." I took a choppy breath. God, do not cry. "All I do is stay home and sleep."

"Why?"

"I don't know. Aren't you supposed to help me figure that out?"

He came around and leaned on the desk. He seemed more sympathetic now that I was sniveling. "Why'd you do that to your hair? Cut it off like that."

"I don't know."

"You were prettier with it long."

My throat burned. More fuckable, Jeff?

"Are you having an identity crisis?"

Jesus. Everyone with an age that ends in *-teen* is having an identity crisis.

"Look, I don't know much about this homo stuff. There's a group for it, the Rainbow Alliance—"

"Oh my god," I blurted. "I'm not—I'm *not*."

"You can talk to one of your own—"

"*I'm not*."

"Okay, hon. Whatever you say." He flexed his burly arms in a shrug. "Chin up, Delilah. It gets better."

Wow.

I almost burst out laughing. Hid it behind a nose wipe. God. This was pretty on par with the ridiculousness of my life thus far.

You know, though. Delilah was a cunning bitch. She seduced Samson, then cut off his hair for silver. The Philistines gouged his eyes out and enslaved him. So much for strength.

High school had taught me many things, few of them from books. One was this:

Strength is not in the body, it's in the mind. It doesn't lie in flexing your muscles and crushing those who oppose you. It lies in being the last one standing. By any means. At any cost.

———

Third-floor bathroom. Three cigarettes. My nerves were hopeless. I kept touching Kelsey's card in my pocket to reassure myself it was real.

Maybe it wasn't that crazy. Maybe one day you opened your locker and out fluttered a thinly veiled confession from someone you'd never known looked at you that way and your heart tripped and you face-planted straight into love. Maybe people could fall in love without an identity crisis, without snickers and sly-dog looks in the hall. Just the right words at the right moment.

Maybe I would go crazy if I didn't find out why she sent the damn rose.

Hall 2 looked like a hospital, that long winter light giving everything a cold, disinfected glaze. My hands were pale and flimsy as paper. I wished I'd saved my morning Xanax.

I timed it so I walked up during the period change, just as Kelsey slammed her locker closed. But she pivoted fast and caught me with a hand in my bag, my mouth agape.

"Jeez," she gasped. "You scared me."

"Sorry." I couldn't move.

Kelsey laughed, eyes flicking to one side, flirty. "No, it's okay. Hey again."

"Hi."

My heart was machine-gunning inside my chest, ribs snapping, bone chips flying. We looked at each other. She was flushed as if drunk. It gave me courage.

"I got your card," I said.

Then the rose was out. Her fingers wrapped around the box and froze. We were both touching but not quite holding it, balancing it fragilely in midair. Kids flooded around us, all reckless voices and sneaker squeaks crashing against the softness of this moment.

"I just, I wanted—" Inhale, rush it out. "I can't stop thinking about you, either. I'm crazy about you. I have been for ages."

Her mouth fell. Kids glanced at us. Hot eyes, hissing whispers.

"I can't—" Kelsey started, then swallowed. "I can't take this."

"I'm sorry, I didn't mean to make a big—"

She pushed the box at me. "*I'm* sorry. You're really nice, Delaney, but I'm not . . . like that."

If I have a fatal flaw—besides holding a grudge—it's the need to understand *why*. Why do things work this way. Why does this happen but not that. What's the underlying mechanism, the gears that turn and click into place.

So I said, "But you got the poem."

Kelsey blinked.

"And I saw you this morning. You weren't—I mean, you didn't—"

You didn't freak out that I'm in love with you.

"Oh," she said quietly. "I thought it was from Luke."

Because I'd signed it *L*. Because she only knew me as Delaney. The name on my ID.

Because I was no one to her. It was all in my head.

Across the hall, hyena cackles.

In the YouTube video, which I watched over and over again later, you see me turning in horror-movie slo-mo. No fear or shock on my face. Pavlov trained me well. There's only a slack fatalism. My expression doesn't change as I meet Zoeller's eyes. My expression didn't change later when I watched the views tick up on "DYKE GET'S SHOT DOWN ON VALENTINES!!!!," though my eyelid twitched at the misplaced apostrophe. The rest was a movie, melodrama happening to an actress, all fake. I couldn't look at Kelsey's face. I'd humiliated her. Made my sick obsession common knowledge, made her turn me down in front of everyone.

After I took the rose back, Luke North turned his phone to get the entourage's reaction, their yipping laughter, ugly, throats vein-gnarled, acne blazing. I watched the video over and over until all feeling went away. Until I stopped imagining popping their heads off as if they were Ken dolls. Until my brain stopped churning raw snuff, blood splatters, faces exploding, beating pounding smashing them into nothing. Cutting them up and cramming the pieces back into those long lupine jaws. Choke on it. Choke on it, you fucking dogs.

I watched until I was clean. Dead. Pure.

Zoeller never laughed. He didn't even smile. He stared across the hall at me, calm and unmoved, waiting. Waiting.

———

Somewhere between pill three and pill four, the nausea kicked in. You've got to keep them down, keep that milky venom in your belly until it seeps into the blood, uncoils in a million white silk tendrils and turns to liquid sleep. I dropped off in degrees, my room and the shadows and the song on repeat growing more dreamlike until I wasn't sure it *wasn't* a dream. How sad, to fall asleep and dream yourself exactly where you were. Sleep was supposed to be my away from here. My body had the heavy, meaty feeling it got in REM, limbs thick and sluggish, a weight pressing on my chest that became a creature when my eyes closed. An incubus with Zoeller's face. It vanished as soon as I opened my eyes. Chill, I told myself. Drift. I listened to "Don't Dream It's Over" and wondered how many kids in the eighties killed themselves to this song. Then there was a figure in the doorway and I tried to scream. The figure came toward me, put its hands on me, smothering.

Donnie.

"I'm okay," I said in a strange deep voice.

He picked up bottles from the nightstand, grimacing. His phone appeared in his hand. Reality was skipping a little, frames dropping here and there like a stuttering video.

"Whatareyoudoing?" I said, the syllables a smear.

"Calling 911."

I had enough coordination to knock his phone to the floor. "Don't. I'm okay."

There was water on his face. No, he was crying. Fuck.

"How many did you take?"

If I could just get the wad of wool out of my mouth, I could talk. Except I think the wool was my tongue.

"I'm calling Mom."

"No." I sat up but my skull was a snow globe, whirling white. Back to the pillow. "I'm okay."

"Your pupils are so small."

I closed my eyes. The lids were feverish, glowing. I felt like I could see in X-ray through the universe.

"Don't go to sleep. Laney, please, don't go to sleep."

Donnie crying made me want to cry. "I'll be okay," I said slowly, not slurring. "Two hundred milligrams."

"That's way too much." He touched my face. His hands scorched. "You're so cold."

"Can you just stay here," I said, "till I come down?"

Our fingers laced together.

In "Fever 103°" Plath talks about illness as divinity and right now I was sick and I was divine. *I am too pure for you or anyone*, I thought. *Your body hurts me as the world hurts God.* Later there would be vomit and shredded muscles but for now there was just pure light and no pain. No body. If my heart stopped it would not be the worst thing. As long as they got Donnie out of here, didn't let him see me destruct like this. But I needed him, too. The only one who really cared, who let me do this shit to myself without letting me die. My Holden Caulfield, catching me when I got too close to the cliff's edge.

I dozed in and out, queasy but beautifully empty. In my dreams I stood in a field of falling snow. Flakes collected on my skin, not melting, growing thick and fleecy. When I brushed a finger over my forearm the snow sloughed away and there was nothing beneath but bone.

It was late when I realized I'd been staring at the ceiling for a long time, lucid.

The house had that curled-up feeling, tender and stunned after a day of our abuse. Donnie was asleep on the floor beside the bed. I padded to the landing, my mouth dry, my stomach folding in on itself. My whole body felt like origami, paper-thin and bent a hundred ways. Downstairs was pitch-black save for the bluish bleed of starlight from the kitchen. My parents were talking so quietly I didn't hear them at first.

"Nothing else works." Dad's whisper, flinty, tired.

"Absolutely not." Mom never bothered whispering. Her voice was naturally soft, but in a way that made you listen more intently, strain to hear far-off thunder. "It makes no sense. You want to give her pills to make her stop taking pills. *That's* insanity. They should medicate you."

Shit. They were talking about me.

"Caitlin, refusing to get her the help she needs is tanta-mount to child abuse. We can't do that to her."

"How dare you fucking accuse me of abusing my child."

My heart lurched, hearing her swear at Dad.

"I didn't mean it that way. I meant—you're twisting this around."

"What other way is there to mean it?"

"Honey, your history is tainting the way you see it. She's not the same as you. It won't affect her the same way. And she's a child."

"My child," Mom said again. No mistaking the possessive-ness.

Something flickered in my heart. Something dark.

"I made a concession for the Xanax," she went on. "It's no worse than a few glasses of wine. But I'm not putting her on mood stabilizers. End of discussion."

"You can't make a unilateral decision on this. Not when you're . . ." Dad trailed off.

"Say it. *Say it.*"

"When you're acting unstable, okay? I'm worried about both of you."

Mom laughed. Noises: liquid sloshing, glass clinking. Then a silence that she broke.

"Acting. That's what I do for you, isn't it? I act."

"I think you've had enough to drink."

"Oh, this is rich. She could be lying in a puddle of her own vomit and you're scolding me about the wine." Something clattered, glass on steel. I felt it ring in my teeth. "I can't be angry anymore, or I'm having an 'episode.' I can't be sad or everyone hides the sharp utensils and shoelaces. I can't be fucking human. I have to act 'normal' or you'll have me committed."

"You know I'd never do that, Caitie."

"What is 'normal,' anyway? Is being Mary fucking Poppins normal? Because that's insanity, to me. Anyone who's happy in a world this fucked-up has serious psychological issues." Something clattered again and shattered. She'd hurled a glass into the sink. "You hypocrite. You think I'm crazy because I see things as they are. You'd rather put on Disneyland goggles and watch TV and pretend it's fine. It's not crazy if I see monsters when I live in a fucking nightmare."

When she spoke to Dad like this I felt sorry for him, but I also thought, She understands. It could be me saying those words.

"This isn't the time for philosophical debate," Dad said. "It's late. It's been a long day. We can talk tomorrow."

"I've never felt more awake. Don't you see what they're doing? They want her to be an android. Purge all the faulty human parts, make her a happy little robot. I'd rather she suffered. Suffering is the only honest response to this life."

"This is paranoid and disordered thinking, honey."

"You have a fucking clinical term for everything, don't you?"

Another silence, but in the quiet I heard the pad of foot-steps, back and forth, back and forth, neurotically.

"Caitlin," Dad said. "Go to bed."

"I'm not tired."

"You didn't sleep last night."

"How would you know?" Her voice was bitter. "When was the last time we shared a bed?"

"Honey, look in the mirror. Look at your face. You've barely slept all week."

"I'm not having a fucking episode, Ben. I'm just stressed." A rubbery screech. Then: "She's awake."

Rabbit fear shot through me. I turned but nausea welled and I clutched the railing, tamping my guts down.

Footsteps. That familiar silhouette.

If I stayed still enough, made myself small enough—

"I hear you breathing," she said hoarsely.

I could never hide in my mother's house. When I was little, it was a game. Stalk Mommy. At first my hiding spots were childish: behind a curtain, feet poking out, or beneath a blanket that pulsed with hummingbird breaths. But I got older, and better. I'd slink to the landing and peer through the slats with feline eyes, watch her sprawl on the chaise with a book in a gold disc of sunlight. Her back to me, the pages turning and turning until she'd say, startlingly, *Hello, Delaney.* I'd slink downstairs and circle her, analyze the room like a crime scene investigator. Was it my reflection in a vase? Hidden camera? Did I smell? Finally I relented and asked how she knew. *I always know where you are*, she'd say. Nothing more. Like it was the truth.

"Your father and I," Mom said now, "are discussing whether to medicate you. After your self-medicated overdose."

You should talk about self-medicating, I thought.

"I didn't overdose."

"Do you remember Donovan scrubbing bile out of the carpet? Do you remember me washing it off you in the bathtub?"

I had no idea what she was talking about.

"You could have choked on your own vomit. Died like that."

"Well, I didn't." I stared down at her, glad I couldn't see her face. "Did you call 911?"

"No."

"Are you going to tell Dr. Patel?"

Mom considered. "No."

Thank fucking God. If I got caught in a suicide attempt, it was mandatory hospitalization.

"Okay, well, I'm tired, Mom. We can talk tomorrow. I'm going to bed."

Her hand darted through the railing, snake-quick, seizing my ankle. Her nails bit the skin. "You go when I tell you to go."

I kicked her off and took a step, but I was dizzy and stumbled backward and she was there, catching me. Pinning me to her body. Pointless wrestling for a minute, then I slackened in her arms. Mom was nearly a whole foot taller. It made me feel like a little girl who could never grow up.

"Let go of me," I said.

"Who do you think you are? You're mine. You're mine, Delaney."

"Let go, you psycho drunk."

"I am not drunk."

"Then just psycho." She had me in a headlock. "Mom, you're choking me."

Dad's voice floated up. "Caitlin, let her go."

"I will never let her go," she said, eerily flat.

The hall light switched on and Donnie blinked at us and everyone started talking over each other, Mom's vinegary wine breath on my face. "I will not watch my daughter kill herself in my fucking house," she said, and I snapped back, "Then I'll do it somewhere else," and she said, "Go, then, if that's what you want. Get the fuck out." Dad and Donnie pleaded in the background, *Honey she's a child honey stop* and *Mom please don't do this*, but she was hauling me down the stairs in clothes I didn't remember putting on, a T-shirt and jeans, no bra or socks. The front door opened, icy wind screaming into the foyer. Mom pushed me out. The concrete stung my bare feet, so cold it burned. I turned around timidly.

"Mom?" I said in a small voice.

The door slammed.

I stood there, too shocked to shiver. Muffled shouts from inside. Outside, the quiet closed in, a thick glass case. On display: fucked-up, pathetic, confused little girl.

I sank to the stoop, lost.

Sometime later the door opened. Dad pressed a bundle into my lap: shoes, blanket, phone, keys. "Sit in the car for a while, sweetheart. She'll calm down."

"She's crazy, Dad. Actually crazy."

He didn't reply, but the look in his eyes said *I know*.

I let myself into the garage and climbed into his truck, shaky with cold. Fuck *her* car. God, what was even happening? Maybe this was all an oxy dream. I'd wake with my head propped on the toilet bowl, staring down at my spewed-up rag-doll stuffing.

I turned on my phone.

Before today, I'd had two dozen Facebook friends. Now I had two hundred friend requests.

My stomach caved in.

There were messages on my wall. I tried not to read them but words flickered out at me like adder tongues. *Fag. Nasty. Hot. Support. Pray for you. Does it taste like.* God, just shut up, everyone. I deleted the account. My call log was cluttered with strange numbers. How the hell did they find me? Delete delete delete. One number had texted every hour, on the dot, since three p.m.

We need to talk

It's important

Answer

I can help you

And so on. As I sat there, a new one came in:

I know you're there Laney

I was just freaked-out and angry enough to text back, *Who is this?*

Z

I was still staring at that letter when the phone rang. His number.

I shifted across the icy leather. Pressed my knuckles to my mouth. Shit. Shit, what should I do?

ANSWER.

"What the fuck do you want?"

"Don't hang up." Brandt Zoeller's voice, deep, smooth, with a touch of molasses and whiskey, a dark sweetness. "Let's have a conversation."

"Give me one good reason."

"I got the video taken down."

My heart filled the silence, thudding slow and hard.

"Laney? You still there?"

"Yeah."

"I'll talk. You listen." His voice shifted farther away. I wondered if he was lying down. "It was up for a few hours. It didn't go viral outside school. If it had you'd be a celeb. Nothing gets the Internet justice league's panties in a twist like a fag being bullied."

I said nothing.

"It's gone. If any copies show up, I'll take care of them. But they won't."

"Why did you do it?" I said, hating myself for asking.

Another shift, closer now. "Because you're weak. Because I could."

I hadn't expected cold honesty. It was weirdly refreshing.

"Now you understand," Zoeller said. "I made it happen, and I unmade it."

"Why stop? Why not just keep bullying me until the inevitable suicide? That's your endgame, right?"

"I don't have an endgame. I play for fun."

"Whatever." I slumped in the seat, suddenly weary. "What do you want?"

"I want to get inside that fucked-up head of yours and roll around in the filth, Insaney Laney."

I jerked the phone away and hit END CALL.

Fucking asshole. Troll.

Idiot me, falling for it.

Still getting played. Bullied. Not just by him, but by my own damn mother. Because he was right. I was weak.

I curled up on the truck seat and pulled the blanket over my head. It was a long time before I fell asleep, reciting Eliot. *I said to my soul, be still, and let the dark come upon you.* In the middle of the night I woke with fire knifing up my throat and ran to a bucket to puke, all acid. Amazing that you can hold so much of it inside your body without dissolving. I rinsed my mouth in the laundry sink, laid my cheek on the freezing concrete, passed out. Sometime in the night Mom carried me upstairs. I remember her arms slipping around me and mine helplessly latching onto her neck, her words falling coolly and lightly into my hair like snow. *You frighten me,* she said, or I dreamed it. *You're the only thing that frightens me. Because you're just like me, my little black iris. You're just like me.*

OCTOBER, LAST YEAR

Chicago flashed across the windshield, all gunmetal and dark glass, a cloud-wreathed kingdom blotting out the stars. Hiyam slept in the backseat. I stared at the streets as Armin drove, my neck stiff. I felt sick, snakebitten. It was the first time I'd been that close to Zoeller in six months, and up until half an hour ago I hadn't been entirely sure he was real anymore. Sometimes you obsess about someone so much you start to believe you've invented them. Zoeller was like that, a secret thorn I'd been nursing in my side, almost tenderly, hiding him in myself. Now it was out. Armin had seen him. He'd have questions. I'd answer. We'd do the whole script—*Why are you crying* and *What did he do to you* and *I'm sorry, I'm so sorry*—and it wearied me, thinking of all that came next. Blythe would never be so predictable. She'd seize the moment by the throat, wrangle it still, take it somewhere no one expected.

I touched Armin's hand on the wheel. "I don't want to go home."

Dashboard lights glimmered over his eyelashes. My Midas. My golden boy.

"Take me to the beach."

He seemed like he'd argue, then he flicked the turn signal.

Hiyam didn't wake when we parked. I left Armin at the car and ran for the sand, tore my shoes off, flung them into the night. I was wild, raw. Animal. All these things I had hidden away inside me in neat, sealed, hateful boxes—I was almost ready to open them. Like Pandora.

I went straight for the water.

"Laney," Armin called.

The first step was a razor of cold sliding up my legs. I kept going, wading deeper. Armin's running feet touched down in puffs of sand. The moon slashed a million fine slits in the black silk of the lake. Keep going. Farther. My shorts were soaked when he reached me, grabbed me around the waist, and I cried, "Let me go, let me go."

"I will never let you go."

He pulled me back to the shore, our feet kicking up waves of sand that stuck to my legs and glittered like diamond dust. I dragged him to the ground with me. He propped himself on one palm, panting.

"Talk to me." He cradled my cheek. "What is happening? Why are you crying?"

Right on cue.

I took his hand and moved it to my chest, to Blythe's hoodie, to my breast.

"Don't do this," he said. "Don't shut me out right now."

"I'm not shutting you out. I want to fuck you, Armin."

"That's how you shut me out. You make it physical instead of emotional."

"You still don't get it."

"Then help me understand."

For the craziest moment, I wanted to. I wanted to tell him everything. All I'd done and all I meant to do. But then he said:

"Did you know that guy in the parking lot?"

"I don't want to talk about it."

"You never do." Armin sounded almost angry, for once. "I

know you have trust issues, but you trust Blythe. And she'll hurt you more than I ever will."

I turned my face, crushing it into the sand. "Do we have to talk about her every fucking time we talk?"

"Do we? You tell me."

I rolled away from him and scrambled upright. My calves were spangled with silicon stars, my wet feet caked. Sand clung to my cheek where tears had spiderwebbed over my jaw. Armin stood, a shadow sketched in wisps of moonlight.

"Come home with me," he said.

Finally.

We walked back to the car, silent. It started to rain, crystal streaks flashing like a hidden hand clawing the air, tearing something we couldn't see. We didn't look at each other but the space between us was dense and charged and every time he moved, I felt it. Something in him sizzled and snapped like a live wire. That electricity would find a way out. Find its way into me.

Armin's apartment was on the tenth floor of a high-rise near the lake. We half carried Hiyam through a lobby decked with art deco lamps and slab marble that looked like the cover of an Ayn Rand novel. I walked barefoot, tracking sand over rugs as if I'd just emerged from the sea. I watched Armin put his sister to bed on the couch. She spoke in Persian, whispery and ragged, the words tangling deep in her throat and then unfurling, flowing in startling cadences. He kissed her forehead.

"What did she say?" I asked him in the kitchen.

" 'I was a good girl today. I will be a better sister for you, brother dear.' "

"I want to hear you speak it. Will you say something in Persian?"

He leaned on the counter. I smelled the storm on him. There's a word for that scent, the breathy fragrance that's released when rain soaks soil and floods your sinuses like a drug:

petrichor. *Petros*, stone. *Ichor*, the blood of gods. There was a disturbing loveliness in that image, gods opening their wrists to slake the earth with their quicksilver blood.

Armin cleared his throat.

He spoke softly and rhythmically, reciting. Persian sounds like a harsher French, spilling over the tongue in spools of rustling gossamer until it hits a sudden snag, tears into pretty tatters. I stared at his mouth, his throat, the way it seemed to come from his entire body, not just the head, like English. When he finished he glanced at me, almost shy.

"What does it mean?"

"It's poetry." I must have gaped, because he laughed. "Don't believe everything Blythe says about me."

"You mock us when we nerd out over poetry."

"You mock my major."

"It's not your passion. Not like ours."

"Fair enough." He drummed his fingers on the counter. "English is my first language. I didn't learn Persian till junior high, and I'm barely conversational. Never applied myself. So it's still sort of mystical to me. In English, poetry is words. It's packed with so much meaning, so much dimension—I process it semantically. But in Persian poetry is more like music. My understanding is so limited and childish that I hear it with wonder. I hear it with my heart instead of my mind."

Something was unraveling inside me, and he wasn't even aware of it. He had no idea how he was tearing me apart.

"What was the poem?" I said.

Armin took my hand. "Rumi dreams that love is a garden, like Eden. A dangerous paradise. In the garden he feels pure, dizzying bliss. Intoxication. But he wakes up alone and hungover, and cries out in anguish. A girl answers. She tells him he is not alone. That she will be his garden. The silver moonlight that falls on flowers, the clear water. She'll be his ecstasy. She says, 'I will bring you roses. I, too, have been covered with thorns.'"

In that moment I realized something. My heart was large. There was more love in it than I ever knew.

I stood on tiptoe and he leaned down and we met there in a space dappled with the neon confetti of city lights. We kissed like people resisting the gravity between them, trying to gracefully slow a fall. He brushed his mouth over mine. Our tongues coiled together, holding. Smoke and citrus. He combed a hand through my hair and drew my face closer, my body to his. My bones were gel and my muscle was hard as stone, everything reversed. I wasn't even high. This was all him. Getting to me. Breaking through. I didn't know where or how to touch him. This wasn't the usual rough, heedless rush with a boy—I wanted to make him feel what I was feeling, this undoing. This slow coming apart.

Leather creaked. Hiyam turning over on the couch.

We pulled back, not breaking eye contact. Armin lifted me under the legs and I wrapped myself around him and he carried me toward the bedroom. In his arms I was featherlight, fine and fragile, the girl I never let myself be. He stopped in the hall and hefted me against the brick wall, his hands sliding inside my shorts. Every touch infused me with fire. Our kiss now was hungry, mouths opening wide, teeth clicking, his stubble grinding over my skin. I felt so fucking small. A doll in the hands of this beautiful boy. His hips rolled against me and my head banged on the brick. I let my eyes close, let his mouth move down my neck in a slow slide of lava, let his fingers move beneath my panties, over smooth skin to the edge that made my hands claw, and he stopped there, tracing, making me crazy.

"Tell me again," I said, my voice breaking.

"Tell you what?"

"That I smell like her."

He yanked down the zipper of my hoodie and peeled it off.

I was totally lucid. Every moment. Each step into the bedroom, each tug at his fly rang in my body clear as a bell. The door closed. He laid me down and took off his shirt and removed my shorts and underwear and that was as far as we undressed. Then his lips were on mine again as he reached for the nightstand. He tore a condom wrapper, took his hard dick in his hand. God, this was actually happening. After all his resistance, all my careful, subtle work, here it was. That shock of dawn breaking on a garden you've planted and tended and suddenly it's all in bloom, bursting with colors you'd only seen in your head.

Armin swept a hand through my hair, tilting my face upward. "I'm in love with you."

"No you're not."

"I am, Laney. I have been since that first night."

For a second reality broke into two halves: now, and then. Now was the gentle boy whose brains I wanted to fuck out; then was the monster who'd ground me into nothing, into ash and dried blood. Be here, I told myself. Now. In this moment. "Don't say it. Just fuck me."

"I want to know how you feel."

"I feel like being fucked."

He lowered himself, his weight against my belly, his hardness between my thighs. "Is this all I am to you? A body?"

"That's not fair," I said, breathless. "You're holding back from me, too."

"You know why I am."

I wished I still had the hoodie. Just to hold. I felt naked, but not in a physical way. "Why?"

"It's been between us this whole time." He was looking through me. "I told myself I wouldn't fall for you. Not when I had to share you like this."

"What?"

"Your heart doesn't belong to me."

That heart punched hard. "Who does it belong to?"

"Your pills. That's what really makes you happy."

Relief flooded through me so powerfully I shuddered. "No, that's what makes me normal."

"Are you high right now?"

"God, Armin."

"Are you with me, or somewhere else?"

I raised both hands to his face. "With you. Don't you understand? You're my away from here."

"You're going to break my heart, Laney."

"I know," I said, pulling his face closer. "But I need this. Make me feel normal."

I saw it happen in his eyes, that moment when he let go.

Armin pressed himself to the point where all the ache and need in me converged, and our eyes locked as he pushed inside, so slow, so maddeningly controlled I could've screamed. I'd imagined fucking him a hundred times and nothing had prepared me. When I fucked guys I didn't have this patience. This care. I did it fast and hard before the nausea had time to settle, shrugged off their touches and kisses. It was business, unsentimental and impersonal. Dirty. Smutty. Crude. I didn't know any other way. So I let him fuck me like that for a while, eyes shut, head empty, just feeling. My foot curling in the silk sheet. The long, tigerlike sinews of his body gathering and rippling beneath that burnished bronze skin when he stretched, when he breathed. The rough grain of his skin dragging over mine. He fucked like he kissed, wholly, with all of himself, pushed all the way inside and held there, made me feel how full I was. Made me just *feel*. No room for thought, for that white space between brain and skull where I hovered with my secrets. I wrapped my hands in the milky coolness of the sheet. Every time he pulled out I wanted him back, wanted that fullness that drove me to the edge of annihilation, but the longer it went on the less intense it felt, the white space widening, pulling me out of my skin. I opened my eyes. Looked at the neon sprinkles on the ceiling, the polka dot patterns of rain. Felt Blythe's shirt rustling against my breasts, my head full of the black wine sweetness of her. I thought of Armin fucking her and slammed my hips against his. He took my jaw in one hand, kissed my mouth and my forehead, watched my face as I rode but never quite slipped over the edge. I clawed at his back, clutched his ass. "Harder," I said. "Fuck me harder." I bit his earlobe. Blythe's move. When he screwed his eyes shut and thrust deeper, my body jolting with the power of it, I knew he was fucking her in his head, giving it to me rougher as he tried to push her out, and when I thought about her and her soft mouth and her face between my legs it pushed me over, the tension in me snapping into a million little lashes, a whip cracking in every nerve. Armin felt me come and clenched me so hard I thought he'd break my collarbone. He fucked me deeply, too deeply, making my teeth grit until that final monstrous snap went through his body, too.

Still. Empty. A beautiful purged high. Everything was so small from up here, thirty thousand feet above myself. How strange that this world could cause me so much pain when it was just a tiny sapphire, a speck of blue dust revolving in the sun.

"Did I hurt you?" Armin said in that voice like cinders crumbling.

I shook my head.

He kissed me and I kissed back, my lips swollen, numb. His hands moved over me, spanning the thin flute of my neck, the bird bones of my fingers, marveling at my delicacy. I looked away.

"Are you okay?" he said.

"Yes."

I felt him pull out. Fought the urge to curl into myself, cover up.

"Laney."

His face was soft with bliss, his eyes almost bashful, boyish. It gave me a twist of faint anguish in my chest.

"Are you really okay?"

I kissed him again. He was so warm, his body exuding heat like a furnace, and I wrapped myself around him, shivering.

"Cold?"

"I always am, after."

Armin pulled the sheets over us and we took the rest of our clothes off, pausing to touch each other. First time we were completely naked and it was *after* we'd fucked. My skin against his looked like moonlight on sand. I shivered again but there was a hot glow inside me now, a core of power. I had gained something by doing this, not lost. I had not been diminished.

"I guess it's true," I said, sliding my calf over his leg. His hair prickled against me. "I'm a slut for poetry."

"You've got that backward. You seduced me."

I slid my leg higher along his. Bared my teeth, licked the top ones. Armin laughed.

"Vixen," he said.

I shook my head.

"No? What are you, then?"

"A wolf."

He ran a hand through my hair and pinched my earlobe. "Where did you learn that ear thing?"

No reply.

"The wolf has secrets."

"All wolves do. Think Hiyam heard us?"

Armin groaned, and I laughed.

"If she didn't, I'll make sure she does next time," I said.

His whole frame flexed, pulling me in close and rolling me atop him. My legs spread to either side of his. He was hard again, and he'd taken the condom off, and the bareness of his skin against mine made my breath catch. Nothing between us.

"When is the next time?" he said.

"Right now."

I leaned down to kiss him, but before I reached his mouth he tensed and his muscle kept me from completing the kiss. My hair tumbled around our faces, a cup of dark petals.

"Not tonight," Armin said.

"Why?"

"I see how this goes. We hook up, and I let you in, but you don't do the same for me."

"I'm letting you in, Armin. It just takes time."

"Then I can wait."

He'd locked us together but couldn't stop me from tightening my legs, sliding against that hard dick. "This is how I let you in. I can't do it without this."

"Without sex," he said through his teeth.

"Yes."

I pressed closer and he moaned helplessly. His hands went to the small of my back, resting there with a lightness so gentle it made something shift inside me, a hardness in my chest turning soft. I was ready to fuck him again. I was ready to take him raw, ride him, make him come inside, but that gentleness stopped me. It filled me with guilt.

"You don't trust me, Laney. Even now. I see it in your eyes." His fingers strayed over my face, my neck. Paused there, stroking. "I did hurt you."

"It's an old scratch."

"From where?"

"I don't remember."

For a long time he merely looked up at me and I wondered how transparent I was.

"Stay here tonight," he said. "I'll keep you warm."

He wrapped me in his arms and I burrowed into the sheet. Our clothes were strewn across the bed and I pulled Blythe's shirt to my face, breathed deep, and closed my eyes.

———

When I slipped out of bed, Armin was dead asleep. For a while I stood watching. His torso and one leg lay bare, ivory silk flowing over his body like sculpting clay. In sleep he looked so vulnerable, eyebrows raised, pouting, questioning something in his dreams. The rain had diffused into mist, painting the sheets with slow-moving shadows. I was still naked and grabbed a button-down off the top of his hamper. A scarf of scent twined around me, crushed pinecones, split firewood left out in the rain. The shirt hung nearly to my knees.

I peered into the living room at Hiyam's heaped blankets. Fetched my phone and cigarettes and stepped onto the balcony, sliding the door closed, soundless. Ten stories up I could taste wet concrete. It didn't seem to be raining that hard but in half a minute I'd collected a shell of nacre on my skin, a creamy coating of pearl.

I wasn't expecting an answer, and when she picked up my heart fluttered like paper caught in bike spokes. "Hey," I said into the silence. She exhaled smoke. Then that long, low *hi* that was almost two syllables in her disarming twang. Both my hands curled around the phone. "Did I wake you?"

"As if I could bloody sleep."

I slid down the railing, my back to the city. Pulled out a cigarette. In the glass my lighter flared, an orange firefly. "Me either. Where are you?"

"In your room, reading your diary, learning all your secrets."

I laughed and tucked my legs beneath me. "You already know my secrets. Where are you really?"

"In your room," she said again, softer, and I shivered. "On your bed. Staring at the ceiling."

Quiet for a while. In the glass the city lights popped on and off, blinking like stars. The only stars you could see in Chicago were earthbound ones.

"Why'd you ring?" she said.

"To hear your voice." I lifted my face to the wet sky. "Tell me a bedtime story."

Even though it was Indian summer, the chill seeped into me with nothing but Armin's shirt to keep me warm. I closed my eyes and wrapped myself in the voice coming from the phone. She told me stories about being a kid, her dad taking her boating and how they'd see dolphins in the bay, sleek gray, those friendly, intelligent faces. Wind and salt in her hair, the sun bleaching the down on her arms and tinting her skin gold. Shrimp and beer lunches. The faces she'd make when he gave her a sip, his roaring laugh. At night she'd lie on the limestone cliffs and watch the moon floating like a sand dollar over an ocean of violet ink, feeling like she was at the edge of the world. It was silly, she said, but as a kid she half thought of it as a real sand dollar, and when she pictured the bottom of the sea it was covered with them, a carpet of bone-white coins giving off a pale, misty light, every full moon collected there.

"That's beautiful," I whispered. "You're beautiful."

A smile in her voice. "Sleepy yet?"

"No. But I guess I should go pretend."

"I'll pretend, too. And lie here thinking about how you should be in this bed with me."

My chest went tight. I felt like I'd swallowed a shoe. "Don't start."

"Why not?"

"Because you'll make me crazy."

"I'm crazy. Who are you? Are you crazy, too?"

Always the poetry nerd, riffing on Dickinson. "'Then there's a pair of us. Don't tell. They'd banish us, you know.'"

"Clever girl." The box spring creaked. She really was on my bed. "I keep holding my breath so I can catch your scent. It's in your sheets. Some kind of flower, I think. One that blooms at night, sips up the moonlight. I spent an hour in the bathroom sniffing your bottles like a bloody pervert. I lie on your pillow and catch the ghost of you. You're here but you're not here. It drives me mad. God, I miss you."

The balcony had dropped and I was just hanging there from my balloon heart.

"I miss you, too," I said. "'Missing someone is the whetstone that sharpens want.'"

She laughed. "And I make *you* crazy?"

That laugh felt like ribbons coming loose in my chest, a prettiness unraveling and somehow growing more beautiful. "It's mutual craziness. Look, I should go. I'll see you tomorrow."

"Tomorrow is so far away. Come see me now." Words rose slowly, thickly from her throat, drugging me like opium smoke. "Come see what I'm doing while I listen to your voice. Right on your fucking bed."

Holy shit. "I'll call a cab."

"You won't. You're teasing."

"I'll do that, too."

Another laugh, darker. "Do everything to me."

"I will," I breathed.

"It's past your bedtime. Good night, my little wolf."

Good night good night God why wasn't I there.

I sat on the balcony and smoked another cigarette, trying to stitch myself back together.

When I got up, my hair damp and netted with a thousand stars, I realized the sliding door was ajar. I hadn't left it open.

Inside, a faint blue glow.

Hiyam sat on the floor, knees propped up. She swept that richly knowing gaze over me and went back to her phone.

I sat beside her, pretending to be calm. "Enjoy eavesdropping?"

"Oh, you're staying the night."

As if I'd get fucked and kicked to the curb. Ice cold. My mind raced as I studied her, night-sky hair curling around that regal, expressionless face, the saffron in her skin, a tinge of desert sun.

"If this is weird, I can go home. I don't want to make things difficult for you and Armin."

"If you actually care about my brother, why are you cheating on him?"

I went very still and very blank.

"So naive," Hiyam said. "You think he won't figure it out?"

"Don't start drama over nothing. He told me your history." I didn't have to spell it out. *No one will believe you.*

"I know drama when I hear it, Keating." She scrolled the screen, disinterested. "The question is, who? I'm betting your door swings both ways. My money's on Miss Melbourne."

I'd never spoken a name out loud. "I don't know what you're talking about."

"You think you're different. It's sad. I've known Blythe longer than you have."

Something in me flared, coldly. "You were never friends with Blythe. She just got high with you."

Hiyam didn't flinch, but she scrolled faster, the screen blurring.

"It's been real." I stood. "I'm going to bed. With your brother."

"Don't get nasty. I'm just playing with you, Keating. We both love a good mindfuck." She stuck a hand out. "Help me up. And give me a cigarette."

I could've decked her, but my instincts said patience would be rewarded.

Back on the balcony the air had thickened into cottony fog, skyscraper lights burning pinholes in it like sparks eating through paper. I never took my eyes off Hiyam. She leaned on the railing, arms dangling over the hundred-foot drop, her phone held carelessly in one hand.

"Who's that girl?" I said. "You're always looking at her Facebook."

"How observant we are." She swirled her cigarette in the air, drawing smoke curlicues. "Just someone from high school."

"The one who got you thrown into rehab?"

"Been doing your research."

"So you miss her?"

"Could you not be so gay?" Hiyam ashed into the white sky. "I couldn't stand her. She's trailer trash, but she thought she was so much better than me."

"Then why are you stalking her?"

"Because she was better than me."

In the back of my mind I heard Zoeller saying, *Don't do it, Laney. You're better than this.*

"She's a scar to you," I said. "Don't pick at it. Let it fade."

Hiyam's face was empty, her eyes somewhere else. "I just wanted—I don't know."

"What?"

"I wanted to be friends, you know? I mean, once I got to know her. I'm sick of all this fakeness. All these people who only liked me when I had blow or cash or whatever. It actually felt good, being hated. It felt real."

"You wanted to be friends, so you blackmailed her."

"I was coked out of my mind. Nothing made sense."

"Then why'd you do it?"

"Jealousy," she said without hesitation. "It always comes

down to something crude. Don't kid yourself, Keating. It's human nature."

I blew smoke into the fog, a ghost thread merging into the larger haunting.

And then came my reward.

"Did she actually say that?" Hiyam stared into the tabula rasa sky, her phone hanging precariously. Mist on the screen. So easy to slip and shatter. "About only getting high with me."

"Blythe?"

"Yeah."

I flicked my cigarette into white space. "If you really knew her, you'd know."

I left Hiyam on the balcony, snaring herself in the web I'd strung there.

MARCH, THIS YEAR

It's one of us. The words hung in the air like gun smoke. They were violent, blasting holes in what we thought we knew about each other. One of us turned. One of us was going to destroy everything. In Armin's apartment there was a heaviness to the shadows, all that empty dark pressing down on us. We left the lights off.

He stopped pacing and looked at me sharply, as if I'd made a noise. "You already knew. That it was one of us."

"I had time to think. I've had all day to obsess." I grabbed my phone and flipped it end over end, like Blythe with her cigarettes.

"Does Blythe know?" he said.

"I showed her."

"Leaving a digital trail isn't smart."

"I showed her in person."

"*What?* Laney, we agreed no contact until graduation. You could ruin everything."

"Better than a digital trail, right? I was discreet." Not exactly true.

Armin frowned at me, some thought turning in his eyes. Then he snatched my phone before I could react. "This photo was sent yesterday afternoon."

"Yeah, so?"

"So you went to her first. You didn't come straight to me."

"I panicked, okay? I didn't know where you were."

"You could've called. Checked Umbra. Asked Hiyam. I'm a lot easier to find than Blythe."

"I wasn't thinking. I just acted." His eyes burned into me. "What?"

"Could Blythe have sent it?"

"Are you fucking serious?"

"We have to be thorough."

"But not irrational." I grabbed the phone back. "You always blame her first."

"With good reason."

"It's clouding your vision, Armin."

"She's clouding yours, too."

We stared at each other in silence. Then I said, "See? They're getting to us already."

He sighed. He'd stopped in a pool of red neon that drenched him like blood. "Fine. Let's analyze this rationally. We should consider everyone, starting with the most obvious."

"It's not Blythe."

"I agree. Too cunning. She's incapable of planning something five minutes ahead of doing it."

"She lives in the moment. But nice personality assessment when she's not here to defend herself." The tension in my hands spread through me like venom, hardening my limbs. "There's an elephant in the room you don't want to acknowledge."

"What?"

"No. Who."

He started shaking his head, more and more rapidly. "No."

"Only one of us has a history of blackmail."

"No, Laney."

"You said you wanted to 'analyze this rationally.' That we should 'consider everyone, starting with the most obvious.'"

His hands half curled into fists. He stood in that red blot, stained. "My sister is not a suspect. Do you fucking understand me?"

His words hit me like ice water. Awful, thrilling cold.

There it was. Where his real loyalties lay. A useful thing to know, to squirrel away in the back of my head, with all my other secrets.

Armin dropped onto a stool. "I'm sorry. You know the story. She lost everything. College, friends, my parents' trust. She'd never do it again."

"And she has nothing left to lose."

"What's her motivation? She's not jealous of us."

"No. Not us." I touched his shoulder. "Hiyam was jealous of me and Blythe."

He met my gaze and I didn't look away. Unspoken words echoed in the silence.

"I can't think clearly right now," he said.

"Okay."

"I need to—" He stood. "I'm going for a run."

"On the beach?"

No answer.

"I'll go with you."

"I need to be alone. To think."

"Armin," I murmured, pushing him gently back to the seat. "Please."

"Laney—"

"Don't you see what they're doing?" I ran a hand over the taut curve of his biceps, across his chest. Wedged myself between his knees and made him feel my smallness, my vulnerability. His eyes were closed yet somehow sad. His chest moved steadily against me but I felt the betrayal of his heart, pumping hard and wild. "They want us to doubt each other. They want to get between us. Remember what I said? Even the smallest crack will shatter us."

I'd said it in the kitchen the night the photo was taken. Blood on our hands. Hands on my skin.

"We're hard," I said, trailing down to his belt. "We're hard and unbreakable, as long as we're together."

He didn't stop me. He let me unbuckle it, let me shrug off my hoodie. Let my hands slide under his shirt, past chilled silk to the fiery skin beneath, the muscle that rippled against my fingers and made me giddy with power. My eyelids drooped, intoxication coming over me.

Armin put his mouth to my ear. "When you touch me," he breathed, "it feels so cold. As if you're touching a chess piece, thinking about your next move."

"I am," I said, pulling his belt from the loops. "You're the white knight."

His hand closed over mine, crushing. Bone grated against bone.

"Do you want me to stop?" I said through my teeth.

"No." He brought my hand between his legs. His voice was husky and raw. "Use me."

OCTOBER, LAST YEAR

U mbra went all out on Halloween. It was already a haunted house most of the year but tonight it was Dante's Inferno. Literally. You walked through the front door into the Malebolge, where demons stood on stone ledges and punished anyone who came close with candy whips and Silly String. Downstairs, the Oubliette had become the frozen lake of the Ninth Circle. For five bucks you could pose for a photo with Satan.

"No snark?" I said, ducking under Geryon as he blew a stream of soap bubbles.

Hiyam rolled her eyes in saintly tolerance. "I'm practicing positivity."

I kept a straight face. So to speak.

Hiyam hadn't dressed up for Halloween, but people constantly asked if she was so-and-so from such-and-such reality show, which flattered her at first, then made her suspicious, then sullen. She started saying, "I'm Hiyam Farhoudi," and raising her eyebrows as if her notoriety was self-explanatory.

As for me, I was one half of a duo. I wore an old-fashioned floral dress over a hoodie rimmed with felt fangs, and fingerless gloves with fur glued on. A name tag on my chest said HELLO MY NAME IS and in the name space was a blood stain.

"What are you?" Hiyam had said.

"The Little Bad Wolf."

"Where's Red Riding Hood?"

Blythe was in the Seventh Circle, dancing alone in a hearts-blood-red dress. Golden hair tucked into her hood, cheeks rouged. We hadn't seen each other for days and when our eyes met across the floor I felt my blood pulsing in my fingertips. Armin was deejaying the Cathedral tonight, doing a retro eighties set in my honor. As I stepped onto the dance floor he played "Hungry Like the Wolf."

"I'll get drinks," I said. "Keep Red company?"

Hiyam gave me a narrow look. Sometimes it seemed she knew exactly what I was up to. She joined Blythe and leaned close and the two of them laughed, their backs to me.

Whatever.

I grabbed sodas and a Red Bull from the bar. Instead of returning I detoured downstairs, descending through layers of dry ice like tulle. In the white haze everything was fuzzy and uncertain, uncommitted to form. Corridors branched off into sudden dead ends and spidery passages looped around and around until all sound and light died and you could not tell direction anymore—left or right, up or down, inside out. A schizophrenic mind modeled in architecture. Hidden rooms, turns that cut you off from existence. Long stretches where anything you said would be absorbed by stone, by a thousand cracks that each could hold a tiny part of a human scream.

I stopped in an alcove, put the cups on a ledge, and reached into my pocket.

How Poe-esque of me.

On my return, I was nearing the end of a corridor swirling with chalky fog when a sharp unease spasmed across my shoulder blades.

I glanced back. No one there.

I set off again, listening. My own footsteps barely echoed, as if the walls were eating them.

When I turned a corner I caught a streak of dark movement behind me.

Fear feeds on shadows. The monster we can't see is worse than the one that shows its face. Who was it, I wondered frantically, and how did they know, and *what* did they know? In panic I took several rapid turns, disorienting myself. Usually I was good at this, I was the minotaur at the center of my own labyrinth, but I hadn't expected to be discovered so easily, so prematurely.

I rounded another bend and collided with something red.

"Bloody hell," Blythe said, catching me. "Been looking everywhere for you. What're you doing down here?"

"I needed to get away."

It was even true.

She glimpsed the cups in my hands. "Let me help."

I tried to edge around her, but she took the Red Bull. I held on to it and our fingers interlaced. Mischief flickered in her eyes.

"My," she whispered, "what big claws you have."

"Let go."

Her grip tightened. She was going to crush it, spill everywhere. I released.

"Don't," I said despondently.

She raised the cup to her mouth, maintaining eye contact. Slow enough for me to stop her. But I didn't. I watched her drink it in one long swallow and toss the cup.

My heart pushed shards of ice through my veins.

Blythe's face was shadowed inside the red hood. She spoke with eerie sibilance. "It's inside me now. In my blood."

She had no idea. But she would soon.

"Come on, killer." She took my hand.

As we left I forced myself not to look back. It had probably just been Blythe, but I couldn't shake the feeling of something there, deeper in, that had watched me.

Still watched.

For a while we were normal clubbing college kids. Armin played Depeche Mode remixes, one hand on the faders and the other tapping beats in the air, bringing us higher, higher. We rode the wave of music until the crest couldn't hold us anymore and crashed in a glorious drop, all that energy bursting into brilliant foam and spray, so palpable the air sparkled with sweat. Then we did it again, again. Each time the euphoric rise, the ecstatic crash. Each time throwing ourselves willfully into blissful oblivion. Blythe was a blaze of blond and scarlet, an irresistible fire, and we danced together like we had that summer. Her arms curled around me from behind and I let her body hold mine. We moved in perfect sync, barely looking at each other. When we did, our faces were close enough to share a breath. My fingers trailed down her arms. Hers over my ribs. Armin played "Strangelove" and Hiyam stared at us, sulky.

"Why don't you two just fuck already?"

"Only if you'll join," Blythe said.

"That's so college."

When the song ended we disentangled ourselves and Hiyam stepped in, brushing Blythe's hair from her neck. Three red runnels marred her smooth buttercream skin.

"Did something scratch you?"

Blythe only smiled. I looked off into the crowd.

Hiyam let herself be coaxed into dancing and I became the wallflower again. Blythe flashed fuck-me eyes at a tall blond Slavic guy. Hiyam told an emo boy who disturbingly resembled Donnie to get on his knees and he did, and stayed there awaiting her command. We laughed. Mine was hollow. It was hard to look at Blythe, but the longer I watched her with

Hiyam the less bad I felt about the drink. Those two. Birds of a feather. Wrapping men around their fingers, toying with people's hearts. So fucking alpha. So cold. Why would she even want me around?

Hypocrite, I thought. How do you think she feels when you go home with Armin?

I felt sick.

Bathroom, I mouthed.

Hiyam flicked an eyebrow in acknowledgment. Blythe didn't even notice.

At the sink I braced my hands on the counter and breathed. Girls came and went, their voices a dim drone. Everything seemed flat and faraway. God, how it weighed on me, this fiction I was living.

A hand stroked my spine. I raised my eyes to the mirror.

Blythe stood behind me, face flushed, radiant. As rosy-cheeked and alive as a fairy-tale girl about to get eaten by the wolf.

"How do you feel?" I said.

"In-fucking-credible." Her hand slid to the small of my back. She smiled in that way that could blind you unknowingly, like the sun during eclipse.

There were people around us but all sorts of weirdness went down at Umbra. It was safer here than almost anywhere.

I turned and Blythe cupped my chin, her thumb on my bottom lip. She'd left little space between me and the sink. Fire surged from my toes to my fingertips, kindling every nerve ending.

"Get bored of that guy already?" I said.

"I was never interested."

"You sure you don't want to take him home and fuck him a bit?"

"I'd rather take you home."

A girl next to us held her lipstick motionless in midair.

Blythe leaned in. She tilted my face toward hers and brought her mouth close and my lips parted automatically.

"You dosed it," she said.

Fuck.

"I know what X feels like." Her hand tightened on my jaw. "You dosed the drink."

I spotted a stall opening and pulled Blythe inside, cutting in line. Slammed the door over someone's protest and herded her to the wall. "Could you be a bit more discreet?"

"Why did you dose our drinks?"

"Not yours."

She laughed disbelievingly. Then our positions reversed and she pinned me to the opposite wall. A garbage box jammed into my tailbone. "What the hell are you up to?"

"Artemis and Apollo."

She stared, unblinking. "What?"

"What do those names mean to you?"

"It's me and Armin."

I put my hands on her arms. It took a conscious effort not to clench. "Who else knows you by those names?"

"What does this have to do with—"

My nails poised atop her skin like ten tiny knives. "If you really care about me, be honest. Who knows?"

"Christ." She shrugged me off, slouched against the door. "Everyone knows DJ Apollo. No one knows me."

"No one?"

"No one who matters."

"So who knows? Blythe, *who*?"

Weirdly, she wouldn't meet my eyes. "A girl. Elle."

"Who is she?"

"Someone I used to know."

"When was the last time you saw her?"

"I don't remember. We drifted apart. It was all a long time ago."

"Where is she now?"

Blythe glared at me, suddenly and inexplicably furious. "She can drop off the face of the earth for all I care. What the fuck does it matter?"

"Okay." I took her wrists in either hand, my thumbs to her frenzied pulse. Made my tone gentler. "I believe you. I'll explain everything later. Not here. *It's not safe.*"

In her face was the same knowing as when I'd given her pills that first night, and all the nights we'd been bad together since. That dark electricity, the sinister spark between two girls who share a secret.

"Do you trust me?" I said.

"Yes."

"Good girl."

I brought her palms to my mouth and kissed them. Then put one to my chest, my heart. Pressed it there. Her eyes glimmered softly and she leaned in again, but I averted my face at the last second.

"Lipstick," I said.

"Who fucking cares?"

I gripped her hands harder. "The way you feel right now is how I feel all the time with you."

"It's agony."

"I know."

"Everything is agony. Every poem I write. Every song I hear. Every time I come. It's murder watching you fall in love with him."

A hot needle pricked my throat. "I'm not in love with him, Blythe."

"But in the end you'll go home with him. It'll always be him."

I struggled for something to assuage her, but nothing came. Her face twisted and she stormed out of the stall.

I inhaled, concentrating on the rush of oxygen in my blood, that free high. These things we do, I thought. What we need and what we want. Never the same.

When I left the stall I found Blythe at the sink, the hood cloaking her face. I touched her and she shook her head subtly. I started to speak and only then noticed what was wrong.

On the far side of the bathroom, watching us both, was Hiyam.

DECEMBER, LAST YEAR

Four of us sat in the truck, all in black save Blythe in her devil-red dress. December lay over Chicago like pieces of smashed-up jewelry, silver snowmelt dripping from branches, diamond shards floating down the river when the ice cracked. Donnie sat at the wheel. Armin and I were in the backseat. I rubbed a thumb over the aluminum bat balanced on my knees and stared out at the brilliant asterisks of streetlights, little smashed spots in the black glass sky.

"Last chance to change your mind," Armin said quietly.

I fingered the chain around my neck.

They all watched me. Each expression was so clear: Donnie's nervous innocence, Blythe's simmering determination, Armin's weary reluctance. All waiting for me. This was mine— my moment, patiently cultivated, buried in blood-rich soil and tended with loving madness until it came shooting up, lush and overripe, swollen with hate, so close to bursting. This was the seed that had been growing in me. Tonight it would flower.

I curled both hands around the bat. Leaned into the backseat and felt the hardness there, the steel at my spine.

"Phase one," I said, "starts now."

FEBRUARY, LAST YEAR

Friday night. My place. You'll be there.

The text echoed in my head all day. I got a pass to see the nurse and instead went to the Nest, the smokers' hideout near the track, and huddled inside a cocoon of evergreens, chain-smoking. Of course my reprieve from being school pariah didn't last. Zoeller had made it clear I was his new mindfuck toy. If I wanted it to stop, I'd have to take the fun out of it. Which left two options.

Kill myself.

Become him.

The third option—*kill him*—didn't occur to me for a long, long time.

At least he stayed true to his word. My coming-out video vanished. Not that it mattered—someone made a Facebook page in my name and filled it with lesbian porn. Facebook took that down; they started a Tumblr. *Ask the Fag.* Tumblr took that down and a still from the Kelsey vid became a meme, me handing her the rose. *Delusional Dyke.* It was actually kind of funny.

Upper text: WANNA COME OVER AND WATCH
   YOUTUBE?
Lower: I MADE A MUSIC VIDEO OF THE BEST
   L WORD KISSES

Upper: COULDN'T HELP NOTICING YOU SHOWED
    ME YOUR TITS IN THE GIRLS' LOCKER ROOM
Lower: SO WHEN ARE WE HAVING SEX?

No one can stop a meme once it's gone viral. The Internet
never forgets.

So when Zoeller texted me to show up at his place, I
thought, What do I have to lose?

I didn't tell Donnie where I was going that night. I parked
a few houses down, checking myself in the rearview. Coral-red
lipstick, guileless eyes ringed thickly with black. Wool coat
with a fur collar. Dead doll stare.

I looked small and lost.

Starlight speckled the asphalt, shimmering. It was pristinely
quiet, my footsteps ringing like clinking champagne flutes,
everything coated with a glassy dusting of frost. Zoeller lived
in one of those Naperville mansions typical of midwestern
gentry: cartoonishly oversized, glutted with emptiness. A
McDonald's Value Meal aesthetic. Big garage, big yard, big
fucking holes to fill. Those houses told a story. The bigger they
were, the emptier the people inside felt.

I walked in as Iggy Azalea's "Fancy" came on and felt ridiculously baller for a moment, but the glamour faded as I scanned
the crowd. So whitebread. Walking brochures for Invisalign
and Proactiv, future marathon runners and charity fund-raisers
talking about the college parties they'd throw, how they'd chase
drinking binges with Ritalin to maintain their GPAs, fuck an
entire frat, pay exchange students to write their papers while
they took X and *felt alive* for the first time. Trying so hard to
trash the emotional and financial stability their parents pro-
vided, to invent hang-ups and neuroses. Angels trying to scar
themselves, bored of perfection. Oh, let me, I thought. I'd

hurl the acid in their faces. There was no real ugliness in them. Their pain, like everything else they owned, was manufactured, manicured.

Happy little robots.

When Mom was right, she was so fucking right.

I skirted the crowd, looking for Brandt. My phone vibrated. *Backyard.*

Outside, my breath wrapped around me in smoky ribbons. Ice crystals hovered and swirled like winter fireflies. For a moment, somewhere between the glow of the house and the faint tremble of light far off, I floated in a peaceful darkness. I wanted to stay there forever, in that timeless twinkling place where there was no past and no future, no judgment or fear.

Xanax is fucking beautiful like that. I popped another, just in case.

The light in the distance was an RV. I tapped on the door. Voices inside, lowering. The door opened.

"Hello, Laney."

I followed Zoeller in.

The first thing I noticed was the smell. Sterile. Alcohol, or iodine. Like a clinic. Then I noticed the books stacked on every flat surface. All nonfiction: cosmology, anatomy, ethics. Stars and skin and sin.

Then I noticed Kelsey Klein.

I startled so hard I almost tumbled back outside.

"I take it you've met," Zoeller said, not smiling, though his voice curled at the edges.

He beckoned me to the couch. The Arcade Fire pulsed in the background, a sly lynx stalk of a bass line, sexy. On the glass coffee table were half a dozen neatly cut lines of coke.

Zoeller raised an eyebrow.

"No thanks." The couch wasn't wide. I pressed my legs to-gether to avoid touching Kelsey. First sign this was becoming another video, I was out.

"Kel, do a line."

She bent obediently, sealing one nostril and snorting hard. Coke sugared the peach-blond down on her upper lip and her pink tongue darted out to lap it, practiced. Zoeller watched me over her curved back. Her blouse was gossamer, thin and translucent as an insect wing. Black bra straps. I wrenched my eyes away.

"What do you want?" I asked Z.

"I want to know why you haven't come to me for help."

Kelsey thudded against the backrest, pop-eyed, neck cording. Her whole body hummed, electric. She exhaled in a loud girlish gasp that sounded incredibly rehearsed. And incredibly hot.

I never knew she was into blow. Never knew she touched drugs, period.

"Help with what?" This time I didn't look away. Kelsey was too high to notice.

"You have a PR problem." Zoeller's arm sprawled across the backrest, thick and pale as the underbelly of a snake. "I can fix it."

"You've fixed enough."

"Don't be like that." He smiled now. "You're a smart girl."

"Don't tell me what I am."

"Lesson number one: defensiveness is defeat. Never defend yourself."

Kelsey's palms lay on the couch, fingers kneading, seem-ingly unconscious of it. Her near hand brushed my knee.

"Spare me your pickup artist philosophy," I told Zoeller. "You're not going to mind-game me."

He stood and walked off as if suddenly bored. Grabbed a

random book, leafed through it. Kelsey moaned and rolled her head against the backrest.

"What do you really want?" I said. "You're the one who caused my PR problem. Now you want to fix it? That's like—" I tossed a hand out. "Machiavellian masturbation."

For the first time I'd ever seen, Zoeller laughed. A real laugh, his eyes shutting, that liquid baritone pouring out and filling his creepy serial killer wood-paneled RV. I watched his Adam's apple bob, imagining my small hands crushing it. When his laughter died he stared at me as if nothing else existed. Too intensely, but too-intense stares were my forte.

"I'm never wrong about people," he said.

We listened to the rest of that Arcade Fire album, watching Kelsey do lines and pace the trailer and scream joyously at the ceiling. Zoeller swigged from a bottle of warm schnapps. My mouth watered. I wanted a drink like crazy, but this was the last person in the world I'd trust not to date-rape-drug me. He told Kelsey to do things—*take your shirt off, pinch your nipples, put your hand inside your panties*—in a dispassionate monotone, and each time she did my face burned hotter. Still I refused to look away. He was testing me. This was some kind of initiation, like fraternities did. So I made myself watch. This wasn't the girl I'd crushed on. This was someone else, some beautiful falling star, her skin snow white, her heart trilling from coke and her breasts dewy with sweet-smelling sweat, so desperate for Z's dick that she'd debase herself in front of me. Anything for him.

Zoeller flicked me a liquor-glazed glance from the other end of the couch. "Kiss her," he said.

For a moment I was confused. No way was I taking orders.

Then Kelsey sat between us, turning to me.

"No," I said.

She didn't hesitate. She put a hand to my cheek.

If I were strong, I would've pulled back. Walked out. Gotten the hell away from Zoeller and his psycho sex circus. But part of me wanted to see where this would go, what exactly she'd do for him. Just how far under his spell she really was.

And part of me was dying to press my lips to that red satin mouth.

She kissed me softly, not with the raunchy abandon I'd expected. Even straight girls will kiss another girl softly. I knew it, I knew this was all some sick power trip, and I didn't care. Closed my eyes, opened my mouth. Her hand trembled against my face and I wasn't sure if it was a coke tremor or legit nerves but it sent ten thousand joules straight to my heart. There was a fragility, a preciousness to that kiss, two paper dolls meeting in the lightest, airiest touch. Even Z couldn't ruin that. I wasn't prepared for Kelsey to push me down to the couch, to kiss me harder. For her hands to move to my shoulders and pin me there. I let it happen out of sheer astonishment, only stopping when her tongue thrust into my mouth in a mechanical, dutiful way.

"What the fuck?" I gasped, twisting out from under her and stumbling to my feet. Hair disheveled, mouth slack and wet.

Zoeller watched me owlishly.

"God." I grabbed my coat off a chair, yanked out a cig. "You creeps. Both of you. Go fuck yourselves."

Kelsey blinked in confusion. "I thought you liked me."

"News flash, Kelsey. He's using you." I glared at Zoeller as I spoke, italicizing with little jerks of my coat. "Don't you get it? He doesn't give a shit about you. He wants to humiliate me, and he's using you to do it. He'll fuck you and throw you away like every other girl he's ever met."

"Or maybe she came to me after your confession," Z said, his words lazy, ponderous. "Because she couldn't stop thinking about you. Maybe she was scared to act on it after what happened. Maybe she knew she could meet you here, with me, in safety."

"Lying bastard," I said, fumbling at the door lock.

I'd made it outside and halfway across the lawn when the RV door banged open, a shadow looming over the snow. Kelsey caught me before I reached the gate. I shrugged her hand off violently.

"Laney."

"Don't call me that. You don't know me. We don't know each other. Look, I'm sorry about the rose, but this is so fucked-up—"

"I know." In the dark her face was a pale oval, that mouth I'd kissed a blood-red blur. I could still taste her, the tingle of coke and a whiff of peppermint schnapps. "I don't want to hurt you."

"Great. But Zoeller does."

She sighed, her breath clouding the space between us.

"How can you want a guy like that? Don't you see what he is?"

"You don't understand." She frowned at her shoes. Amazingly, she seemed angry. "I've been nobody my whole life. My sister has everything. She's the one my parents are proud of. I'm always runner-up, good effort, Kel, good try. When someone actually notices me, even if it's him, it's like finally—I'm somebody."

"The attention he's giving you is the worst kind of attention."

"I know. You think I should care, but I don't. I just want to feel wanted for once."

God, hadn't I done that? But she didn't want to be wanted by someone like me. She wanted some shitbag like Zoeller to get hard for her.

It was so sad. All of us were so sad.

I turned and she touched me again, softer.

"Delaney."

I winced, even though I didn't want to pretend we were friends. Because some pathetic twinge of hope still stirred in my chest. Some absurd idea that she'd see what an asshole Zoeller was and come running to me.

"I know what you want." Her hand remained on my arm. I didn't imagine the squeeze. "And he's right, I can't stop thinking about it. So I just want you to know . . . I'm open to trying. When you're high, everything feels good."

I walked back to Mom's car even hollower than I'd come.

DECEMBER, LAST YEAR

We moved fast, the bat light in my left hand. Somewhere behind me Armin's shoes whispered over the ice. We were shadows slipping through the alley, leaving ghost trails of breath. Despite the cold and our skimpy hoodies—we needed unrestricted movement—I didn't shiver. There was a fire in me colder than the winter blazing around us.

We reached the spot I'd scouted on Google Maps: a blind nestled between garages, blocked from the alley by a low brick wall. Armin vaulted over it fluidly, hoisted me up. I slung my bat and bag to the pavement and removed supplies: tubes of greasepaint, mini flashlights, gloves. As I unscrewed a cap he seized my arm.

"What?"

He just stared, his eyes glistening darkly.

"We don't have time for this." I pulled free and squeezed the tube.

Him first. I slathered thick paint onto his face: white base, silver streaks around his mouth, black teardrops over his eyes. The Snow Wolf. Kenosha Tech's mascot. Our rival school.

I showed Armin his face in my phone viewfinder. No expression.

When my turn came he hesitated. I bit the inside of my lip, sucked the thin thread of sweetness. The best way to control people is to not let on that you're controlling them. Set up the situation like dominoes, tip the first one, and lean back. Wait for it. Trust gravity.

Click clack crash.

He ran a fingertip down my cheek, as if drawing a tear.

When he finished painting I checked myself in the phone cam. I was actually cute, those big blue eyes wide and blank, empty of the evil inside me.

"How do I look?" I said.

"Like a stranger."

"Good."

I stashed everything in the bag and began to rise, but Armin had hold of my hand.

"You don't have to do this," he said, predictably.

"I do, though."

"The statute of limitations hasn't run out. You still have time. You can—"

I dragged the bat across the rough asphalt, a grinding metallic sound to match the churn in my gut. "Out of the question. We've discussed this."

"Tell me, Laney." His hand on mine was soft but enveloping. "Will this fix it? Will it really make you feel better, in the long run?"

"It'll make me feel better right now."

"That doesn't sound like you. That sounds like Blythe."

Our breath misted around us. I withdrew my hand.

"I'll do anything for you," Armin said, his voice rising and tightening like a note moving up a violin string. "You know that. But if you want to do this right, you have to tell. Violence won't solve anything, and it won't satisfy you."

Nothing satisfies me, I thought. My fingers flexed on the grip tape. I was a little high, warm white milk spreading through my veins, a steady-state buzz. Just for nerves.

"You know what telling means?" I said. "It means another Steubenville. No one cares. No one believes."

"What about the others?"

"Who?"

"Others it might happen to. Other girls."

I hefted the bat, spun it, smacked it into my palm. "I don't have the luxury of feeling sorry for others. I'm still trying to staunch my own bleeding."

Armin stared up at me, his face bathed in moonlight, on his knees like a saint. From the start he'd fought me on this. The good doctor, the man of compassion and morality. When he spoke he sounded far away.

" 'He who fights monsters should see to it that he himself does not become a monster.' "

"Get up, Nietzsche."

He stood. I gave him the bat.

"Better?"

He didn't look appeased. "Are you angry?"

"Do I seem angry?"

"You seem perfectly calm. That's what frightens me."

I looked him in the eyes, in our ridiculous painted wolf faces, and slung my bag over my shoulder. "Let's go."

Once, on a science blog, I read about the life cycle of a star.

When most stars die, they don't supernova. They aren't heavy enough. Instead they collapse, gas and metal condensing into a tight ball that burns ultrapure and ultrabright, a white dwarf. The rest of their body shivers off in clouds of luminous stardust and becomes a nebula, an echoing veil of grandeur. But the core is pure. The core burns superhot. And over billions and billions of years it cools off, the heaviest elements sinking into the center, condensing, hardening. Becoming diamond.

That's the fate of most stars. They burn away all their delicate parts and boil themselves down into diamonds.

Anger is like that. Runs on its own fumes, devours itself voraciously, explosively, until one day there is no fire left. Only pure, cold, unbreakable hardness.

Like the diamond core in me.

And the cold, hard object tucked against my spine.

FEBRUARY, LAST YEAR

Nice car," Zoeller said.

I had no idea if he was being sarcastic. I never did.

Despite the fact that he was richer than hell, Z didn't have a ride. His parents gave him a BMW for his sixteenth and he sold it to buy the RV parked permanently in his backyard. He didn't need to go anywhere. He was magnetic. Everything—and everyone—he wanted came to him.

Like me.

One foggy winter afternoon I picked him up after school in Mom's car.

He slid in, his crisp aftershave peppering the close air. That alcoholish smell, borderline formaldehyde, but a hint of smut in it, dirty sex. I fixed my eyes dead ahead, one hand on the gearshift.

"Where are we going?" I said.

"Hello."

I exhaled through my nose. Refused to look at him.

He fiddled with the glove box, the radio, the storage compartments. Finally I turned, teeth gritted. Dull sun slicked his brown leather jacket.

"What are you doing?"

"Music?"

My upper lip peaked. "Will you just tell me where we're going?"

"Don't be boorish." He flashed a smile. His hair was immaculately coiffed, gleaming. What light there was poured over him adoringly, as if it loved lavishing itself on him.

I shoved my phone into his hands, mostly so I wouldn't have to suffer his infuriating handsomeness a second longer.

Zoeller put on the Black Keys.

"That's better," he said.

Driving was a welcome distraction. His eyes slid over me the whole time like cold oil, but when he guided me onto the highway everything dissolved till it was just me and the smooth asphalt beneath my tires, my foot biting into the gas, the bluesy swagger of the music.

The address Zoeller gave me didn't exist.

I drove past the spot where it should've been twice. Had to make a U-ie in heavy traffic, cars zipping past, honking.

"You sure it's here?" I said.

Zoeller gave me a smugly amused look. Later I'd think of it as his liar's face. He always wore it.

I pulled into a parking lot and killed the engine.

"If you're seriously trolling me—" I began.

"Get back on the road."

I didn't move. He waited, patient.

"Get out of my car," I said.

Z laughed.

"Not kidding."

"I had to make sure you'd listen," he said. "Get on the road."

It was less of a hassle to do what he said than eject him from the vehicle. Dealing with Zoeller was a constant test of my threshold for violence. The only reason I'd even shown up was because Kelsey asked me personally, promising he just wanted to talk. When she gave me that lopsided smile, now a little knowing, a little teasing, that sullen teenage girl sexuality that ripped my heart up and dropped the shreds into my gut, I couldn't help myself. I wanted her. I'd do it for her. Didn't matter how fake this was—if fakeness was all I could have, I'd take it.

We drove west into the snowdrop sun. Z guided me out of Naperville, through rigidly perfect subdivisions into rough country. Lawns broadened into fields and fields turned fallow, the soil black and frozen. We were on a ragged highway slicing through farmland. When we hadn't passed another car for nearly a minute, he spoke.

"Let go of the wheel."

I looked over at him.

"Let go."

I laughed in his face and turned back to the road.

"Final warning," Zoeller said.

Strange word to use, *warning*. I understood why when I glanced at him again.

There was a very real-looking gun in his hand.

I jerked reflexively, swerving into the oncoming lane. A car a few hundred feet away laid on its horn. I straightened out.

"Are you fucking nuts?" I said.

"Take your hands off the wheel."

"What the hell is that, an air gun?"

"I'll fire it and show you."

My hands clenched desperately. I darted glances at the gun, his face, the road. "You're fucking insane. You'll kill us both."

Zoeller reached over and pressed the cruise control button, locking us to 50 mph.

"Let go of the wheel, Laney."

I lifted my palms, hovering an inch above it.

"Sit on your hands."

It was the same tone he'd used to tell Kelsey to take her clothes off and touch herself. Flat, clinical.

"Do you seriously want to do this?" I forced myself to match his calm. "We will die, Brandt. Me and you. Right here, right now."

He touched my ribs with the gun muzzle.

I held his gaze as I slid my hands beneath my thighs. It didn't matter if I looked at the road now. I was shaking hard, but felt detached from the shaking, from the body in my seat. Depersonalized.

Zoeller smiled with boyish glee and faced forward, relaxing into the heated leather.

My plan didn't work. I'd angled the wheel away from on-coming traffic, but some grade in the road thwarted me and we drifted left. I'd seen headlights a mile or so down. Less than half a minute before the ugliness.

I'd always envisioned my death as a small, self-inflicted thing. All I could think of now was Donnie, the sweetest boy I'd ever known, with the softest heart—a heart that poured un-conditional love. God, he'd cry. He'd be so alone in this world without me. I should've been there more for him, should've protected him from Mom.

From myself.

In my peripheral vision, I saw the semi coming. Heard the surreal Klaxon howl of its horn.

"Do you feel it?" Zoeller said reverently. I'd never heard such emotion in his voice.

"Feel what?"

"How free we are."

Then we were airborne.

A car crash is a flickering film reel of too-fast and too-slow moments, almost like when you come, simultaneously sus-pended in eternity and torn from it with terrifying speed. One second my arms and legs floated, weightless, tethered only by my seat belt, my hair hanging perfectly still in zero g. Even the down on my arms and the back of my neck rose, everything defying gravity. In that moment I was eternal and cut free from the heaviness of this life. Then my jaw slammed closed, a sweet burst of heat injecting my mouth, my skull snapping against the headrest and filling instantly with fog and rebounding just in time to meet the airbag punching me in the face. Then nothing.

It was a while before I realized the hands I was staring at were mine. The tiny puppet beneath me was my body. Alive. Sore but seemingly whole. The dashboard dinged politely, reminding us over and over: AIRBAG DEPLOYED, AIRBAG DEPLOYED.

I looked at the passenger seat.

Zoeller stared straight ahead, so still I feared—hoped, a little—he was dead. But he blinked, started to laugh in a weird high voice. Giddiness transfigured him, made him disturbingly childlike.

I opened my door and stumbled into the field.

It was dusk, the sky feathered in phoenix plumage, clouds in flame shades of violet and ocher. World on fire. More like Mars than Earth. For a second I couldn't find the road. Nothing around us, just the sunset and steam puffing from the tailpipe. We'd missed the semi by mere seconds. The hard bounce over a shallow ditch and into the field had triggered the impact sensors.

I walked around the car in disbelief. Not a single scratch.

Zoeller's door cranked open.

He took three steps before I tackled him. He'd left the gun in the car but I didn't care. It wouldn't have changed anything.

Despite my being a foot shorter, my momentum knocked him to the ground. I stayed on top, clinging to him with mon-keyish nimbleness, fending off his feeble throes. I hit his face with an open palm. The impact tolled through my body and jarred my bones and I hit him again, again.

"You fucking lunatic," I screamed. "What the fuck is wrong with you? What the actual fuck?"

Zoeller took the barrage without flinching. I didn't stop until I realized the sound gurgling out of him was a laugh.

I sat back on my haunches, breathless. I was numb all over, my fists raw.

He levered himself up. His lip was fat, crimson dripping over his chin and staining his shirt. His eyes had a fluorescent glow in the deepening twilight. Traffic swished on the road, far off as a dream.

"You are actually insane," I whispered.

"I'm so hard."

I got up, disgusted.

"Don't you get it, Laney?" His voice had a throaty nakedness that made me shiver involuntarily. "We are so alive right now."

I went back to the driver's side. By the time Zoeller caught up, I'd restarted the engine. The deflated airbag spilled into my lap, slithering between my legs. I didn't like it. I didn't like the way it made me aware of myself, of the tightness in my body, the hot arousal tensing my thighs.

Z got in before I managed to lock the doors.

"Get the fuck out."

"Stop being so conventional." He pulled his seat belt on. "Let's go."

My eyes rested on the gun at his feet.

"Think you can get to it first? Think you know how to use it?"

"I'll fire it and show you," I said, echoing him.

He smiled. "Feisty."

"I'll kill you. First opportunity I get, I will fucking kill you, Brandt."

"Good. But that's the future." He rolled his neck. "I think I strained something."

I relived a moment of bashing his face in with my hands. They throbbed now, the meat loose and spun out like candy floss. Adrenaline drained, I felt acidic and hollow.

"We're going to have a good night." Z beamed at me, red-toothed, the blood scrawling a switchback over his clean jaw, his muscular neck. "Me and you. Now let's go."

————

I let Brandt Zoeller into my head. Make no mistake, I let him in.

I could have called the cops. I could have told someone. I had a thousand chances.

That night I drove him around the town where I'd grown up, and it was a place I'd never seen before. Everything looked crooked, slightly askew, a painting knocked sideways, revealing something tender and secret beneath. Nothing had changed— the change was in me. We stopped at the Dairy Queen and the halogen bleaching our faces felt like a benediction. I tasted blood and leather in my burger. Every streetlight was a tiger's eye. I blazed through yellows, one hand on the wheel, just my fingertips, not really steering but feeling it steer itself. I thought of the way Mom drove, choking the wheel like a chicken neck.

Something was awakening in me. Something powerful.

I parked downtown near the Riverwalk. Zoeller followed me to the brick path along the bank and for a while we walked in silence save for the rush of our breath. The river was partly frozen, strewn with cracked ice, a mosaic of moonlight painted on glass shards. Against the moon the bare trees looked like nerve fibers, a dark brain spreading across the stars.

I sat down on the path's edge. Zoeller joined me and I offered him a smoke. He declined.

"What are you thinking about?" he said.

"The Shadow."

He studied me.

" 'Between the idea and the reality, between the motion and the act, falls the Shadow.' " No recognition on his face. "T. S. Eliot."

"I like it," Z said. "Unknown potential. Dark energy."

Not quite. Eliot was talking about hopelessness, a vast despair gathering and teeming in that moment between dream and doing. The futility of everything, the inevitable horror and sadness when anything was realized. How pointless it all was. How empty. Even when we got what we wanted, it was empty.

But I couldn't put any of that into words. I exhaled smoke into the winter night. In some symbolic way, it was closer to my thoughts than anything I could have said.

"Are you a dyke?" Zoeller said.

After the insanity of this day, nothing fazed me.

"It's complicated," I said wearily.

"You like girls more than guys."

Nod.

"When did you know?"

The last person on earth I wanted to talk to about this was Brandt fucking Zoeller.

Which was exactly the reason I did.

He meant nothing to me. He wasn't even human. I didn't give two shits about him, and in some strange way that made him safe. He already knew my worst secret, and I was already the most pathetic girl at school. Nothing to lose.

"My first and only boyfriend was Harlan Flynn. You know, that stoner kid with really long hair. Pretty obvious what attracted me to him."

Z snorted.

"I knew for years, I guess. I always had bizarrely intense friendships with girls. It felt weird when we touched. My heart would race and my skin would get tingly and if we stopped hanging out, it was like a breakup. I thought it was the same for everyone, but when I was twelve, my best friend—she was really touchy-feely, always hugging me, kissing my cheek. Saying how much she loved me. Girls are like that. It's confusing as hell. One night at a sleepover, we were telling secrets and she said she'd never kissed anyone, and what if she died before she did, and all this stuff, and she looked so sad and pretty that I just did it. I kissed her. On the mouth. It felt the same as when she'd kiss my cheek, but she freaked out and told her mom, and that was it. No more sleepovers. No more best friend."

I drank a lungful of smoke to smother the humiliation. You think those wounds are closed, but when you expose them to the air you learn otherwise.

"That was my first kiss. Sometimes I wished I was a boy so there'd be no ambiguity. When a boy kisses a boy, it's either stop or go. If he starts beating the shit out of you that's a pretty clear stop sign. But girls are a fucking mystery. Green light one second, red the next. And you have no idea how weirdly intimate it gets between us. Seriously. Spooning is a thing between besties. Like what the actual fuck. I spent so many nights agonizing over every gesture, every hug, every time our hands touched, every stupid thing that meant nothing to her and the world to me. I fucked up so many friendships by falling in love. I never knew where the line was. I still don't."

And I never will, I thought. I'd set my own heart up to be broken again, and again, and again.

"Anyway, I thought there was something wrong with me. I mean, emotionally. Like if I just stopped being such a freak and obsessing over girls, it'd happen. I'd fall for a boy."

"Was it Harlan Flynn?"

"No. But I was really horny, and really tired of being a virgin."

Zoeller laughed. He often looked at me like some strange

new specimen on a microscope slide. "We are so much alike, Laney. It's incredible."

I flicked my cig into the river. The water snuffed it with a tiny hiss.

"We are nothing alike. You're a monster."

"So are you."

In the car, he talked. He knew it was my mother's car, he said, because it was too cold, too clean. He knew I was terrified of her. He pulled out a silver money clip and peeled off half a dozen C-notes to pay for the airbags. I immediately threw them back in his lap. This made him laugh. "You're overcompensating," he said, and when I scoffed he snatched the keys from my hand and stabbed one into the plump leather seat. I stifled a shriek. "My mom's going to kill me, you idiot," I said, and he countered, "Do you see what I mean?"

I closed my mouth.

I did see.

"Stop living in fear," he said. "You're free."

On the way back Zoeller gave me "homework." This week I was going to start taking control of my life, beginning with her. When I dropped him off I seriously considered driving onto the lawn and running him over. This psycho had pulled a gun on me. He could've killed us both. For all I knew, he was planning to chop me into little pieces in that creeptastic RV.

You're a monster.

So are you.

Maybe I was trying to prove him wrong. Or maybe I wanted to be a monster on my own terms. If the world was going to constantly knock me down, I could at least choose the way I fell. Controlled descent.

Mom never mentioned the car. A couple days later, everything was good as new.

One morning I dallied in the driveway, my key jutting from

my fist like a claw, and dragged it slowly, deliciously across her flawless paint.

Still nothing.

But later that week when I woke and groped for my phone, the screen was hard to read. I sat up, blinking. A deep scratch ran across it, identical to the one on her car door.

So I began my homework.

NOVEMBER, LAST YEAR

The apartment was empty when I got home. Nothing moved inside but tree shadows, skeletal fingers crawling up the walls. I hadn't been home in days and the scent of blackberry perfume hit me like a drug. I dropped my bag, pressed my hands to my mouth. Tried not to breathe too much of it at once. Sweet summer musk mingling with warm vanilla. I ran through the shadows to her room. Stumbled into a nightstand, knocked something to the floor. Messy as always, her whirlwind presence everywhere, clothes crammed into the bookcase, books on the bed, crushed white stars littering the floor. Crumpled paper. A new poem taking shape. I ran my fingers down the groove carved in her pillow.

Still warm.

I found her on the roof. She sat on the ledge, earbuds in, legs dangling. Not yet full dark, the parfait sky banded with lemon, seafoam, cerulean. Her hair shone like one final sunburst against the twilight.

"Blythe," I said, standing behind her.

She couldn't hear me.

Something ineffably sad rose in my chest, a drowning feeling, as if my lungs were filling with water from the inside. My hand raised but not touching. My voice unheard. I'd spent all my life in moments like this.

"It's you." The breeze lifted a golden strand and spun it around my forefinger. "It'll always be you."

I untangled my hand and left, unnoticed.

Later that night I was in the kitchen, washing dishes, when she came down. Our gazes slid around each other.

"Armin's coming tonight," I said. "Will you be here?"

"Got plans."

"Stay anyway?"

She smiled unpleasantly at the table. "Heterosexual mating rituals bore me."

"We had an understanding."

"My understanding is you're a selfish cunt."

I dropped a fork, the jagged clang close to the feeling in my gut. Dried my hands, shored myself up to face her. She wore a challenging look halfway between smirk and sulk.

"Blythe, we talked about this."

"Talking about torture doesn't make it hurt less."

"It's temporary," I said, moving nearer, touching her forearm. "It won't be like this forever. Look at me."

"It hurts to look at your fucking face."

"Don't be like this."

"I hate it," she whispered. "And I hate you a little for making me feel this way."

She shouldered me aside and stalked out of the kitchen.

"Stay tonight," I called after her. "Please."

All I got was a cold, crystal laugh.

Mom used to say that if you listen, people will tell you exactly how to hurt them. Because part of us wants to be hurt. We want to know how strong we really are.

Blythe answered when Armin rang the bell. He carried a

paper bag fragrant with chilies and peanut sauce. She slung an arm around his shoulders, walked him to me as if presenting a gift. Kissed his cheek before letting go. Armin looked baffled but amused.

Don't fall for it, I thought. She's toying with her prey.

I didn't kiss him hello. Not with her eyes on us. He brushed my cheek, let his hand drop too soon. The air crackled like gunpowder right before the spark.

"This'll be a fun night," Blythe said.

Half a bottle of tequila later, it nearly was.

We ravaged the Thai noodles and lit candles and sprawled on the hardwood with the bottle between us, flames dancing through the glass, trembling over our faces in slow marmalade waves. We sat in a perfect triangle. A St. Vincent song played in the background, a rabid crank and snarl of guitars.

It's inevitable that three drunk friends with unresolved sexual tension will play truth or dare.

"Armin," Blythe said, "you know the drill."

He swept a hand through his hair. His cashmere sweater looked soft enough to melt in the candlelight. "Truth."

She smiled at him, not kindly, and I read her mind. *So predictable.*

"How do you feel about Hiyam being here?"

I'd expected nastiness. Something like, *Have you figured out how to make Laney come?* But somehow she still surprised me.

"I'm glad she's where I can keep an eye on her," Armin said. "But I'm disappointed, too."

"Why?"

He tilted his head back, flame playing over his neck. "Because I've made sacrifices for her, put my life on hold, and it wasn't enough. She threw it all away."

"You can't fix her. Just be there for her."

"I can't watch her fall apart."

"She wants a friend, not a bloody savior."

My eyes shifted between them. "Since when do you believe in saving people, anyway?"

"I answered the question." Armin faced Blythe. "Truth or dare?"

"Like you have to ask."

In her own way, Blythe was predictable because she always picked dare. *I never lie, so save your truths*, she said. *Dares tell you more about a person.* The challenge lay in trying to embarrass her. She stood on the back deck and belted out "The Star-Spangled Banner," deliberately butchering the lyrics while Armin and I collapsed against each other, laughing. She read us her worst poem, which described love and sex through over-the-top astronomy metaphors that made me bury my face in a pillow. She drank more than both of us combined yet seemed more sober, almost eerily lucid. Blythe was at her most charismatic tonight—witty, charged, burning bright.

When she went to the bathroom Armin said, "Did you notice the shadows around her eyes?"

I had, but I shrugged.

"Does she stay up all night?"

"We both do. We pull all-nighters to write papers."

"Does her behavior seem more grandiose than usual?"

I knew what he was getting at, and it disturbed me. " 'More than usual' is her modus operandi."

"What about sex? Has she been indiscriminate?"

My throat did not want to release words. "What?"

"Has she been sleeping around lately?"

"I'm not going to report her sex life to you." My hands were in fists. "And she's not indiscriminate. That was just a phase."

"It's a phase that repeats. Be careful, Laney. She makes poor decisions when she's like this."

"Poor decisions like what?"

"Like crossing the line with friends."

I lit a cigarette but immediately stubbed it out. "I don't like what you're implying."

"It's happened before." His brow furrowed. "If she starts acting strange with you, let me know."

"Want me to call if she gets a little gay when she's manic?"

"It's not a joke."

I should've shut up, but I couldn't help it. "What really bothers you? That she's bipolar, or that she's bisexual?"

"If I knew which one made her a cheater, I could answer that."

My mouth dropped but Blythe returned then, her expression blasé.

"Still here? Figured you two would've run off to the bedroom by now."

There was something nasty in her tone. She slammed a shot of tequila and banged the glass on the floor, shooting Armin a challenging stare.

I grabbed the bottle. "Here's to poor decisions," I said, and drank.

Things changed then. The liquor dilated our veins and our inhibitions and we got more personal. Dare you to take your shirt off. Truth you to tell me the hardest you ever came. We lounged half-dressed, gilded with sweat and candlelight, spilling confessions. Nerves loosened and we laughed and grew conspiratorial. Armin asked the best truths. Not too prying, but somehow I always ended up saying more than I'd intended. I told them about the night I jumped in Janelle's pool after a cocktail of vodka and codeine, half wanting to fall asleep forever, and how Donnie carried me home in his arms like a wet kitten. The time Mom had a breakdown at the pharmacy and screamed that she wasn't sick, she just had moods, the way other people got headaches or heartburn. Blythe dared Armin to undress and I stared at the feline svelteness of his limbs, the chevron of muscle dipping below his belt. He stripped to jeans. Then boxer-briefs. I dared Blythe in retaliation and she shrugged off her dress as if relieved to be rid of it. She stared at me defiantly, that eternal half smile slinking across her mouth.

"Truth or dare, Laney?" she said.

"Truth."

"How dull. I already know everything about you."

"You don't."

"Oh, but I do." She stretched one leg, a ring of amber light rippling over honey skin. Her hand trailed up the inside of her thigh. "I know exactly what you like. Exactly what you want."

"Fine. Dare."

"Good girl." She leaned forward, fire snapping in her eyes. "Show me how you get off."

The air sizzled. She'd dropped the spark into the powder.

"Blythe," Armin said, then addressed me. "She's not serious."

"She's dead serious."

Blythe's smile became full.

"Laney," Armin said, more nervously, "you don't have to do anything you're not comfortable with."

The tequila pumped my veins full of molten gold. "Do you want to see me do it?"

"It doesn't matter what I—"

"Simple yes or no question. Do you want to see me do it?"

A stitch climbed his throat, catching a burl of candlelight. "Yes," he breathed. "Yes. Everything you do is beautiful to me."

I stood on shaky legs.

Armin jumped to his feet and we swayed into each other. Blythe watched from the floor, eyes shining.

"Don't touch her," she said.

His hands fell.

I peered around the living room, my brain trailing a couple seconds behind my vision. Couch. Tumbled onto it, lank-limbed and warm. My skinny jeans were way too tight for this.

Armin and Blythe watched me like hawks on a rabbit, tracking every movement. The drag of my hand to my fly, the rose blush blooming in my cheeks, teeth meeting my lip. His expression was hazy and enchanted, hers fervent and sly. I operated on autopilot. Puppet girl. My skin just another costume, my face a mask. Someone else unbuttoned her fly, shrugged out of her jeans. Goose bumps flashed over her bare thighs. The chill was a shock.

"I feel like I'm on fucking stage," I said. "Come over here. Both of you."

They glanced at each other, approached together. Against the dancing candle flame they barely looked human—they were Artemis and Apollo in their burnished skins, hunter and healer. Blythe sat beside me but Armin hesitated. I called him closer with my eyes, the shyness gone. The cushions dipped toward him as he sat on my other side.

Nothing for it but to let the alcohol take control.

Everything was intense now: the scent of berry and pine, the tickle of tweed on the backs of my legs. The gravitational pull of these bodies so close to mine. My hand slid up my thigh and felt like it belonged to someone else. To Armin. To Blythe. I thought of the scrape of his stubble and the graze of her teeth and my hand slipped between my legs, the other tangling in my hair, as if fighting for control of this body. I sensed Armin tensing, Blythe uncoiling. Heard his breath coming fast while hers slowed. And I let go. Let my body do as it wanted, my fingers finding heat, my mouth opening in a desperate gasp. The agave on my breath smelled like sex. I arched against my hand, gritted my teeth. Pressed my finger hard against my panties, touching the wetness that seeped through, then under the hem to the wetness itself. Armin hovered at my side, his heat washing over me. I stiffened my finger and ran it along the inner edge of one lip and for a moment honestly believed it was his. Something cool and silky curled against my elbow, Blythe's hair, and seamlessly my mind switched over, imagining those slender fingers tracing me, her fingertip brushing my clit, teasing, maddening.

My left hand fell onto Armin's thigh and his muscle jumped under my palm. I gripped hard, kneaded the coarse-haired skin. Before he could react I cupped his erection through his briefs. Stroked my thumb along it, riding the ridgeline of a vein. He thrust involuntarily into my hand. As I held him I tossed my leg across Blythe's, settling it between hers, and her thighs tightened and she let out a soft gasp, eye-flutteringly girlish. If there was any inhibition left in me, that destroyed it. I was gone. I took my finger inside, just a little, not too much not too much control yourself, pulled out and circled my clit. Then again. Again. Each time a little firmer, deeper. Armin was thrusting into my hand, Blythe grinding against my leg, and where my skin touched theirs a current surged through me, two electric arcs meeting and colliding inside my body over and over, a fountain of sparks frothing higher, higher. I took my finger all the way inside. God, I wanted them. I wanted to fuck them both. I wanted his thick cock and her graceful fingers, his rough face and her warm tongue. I wanted to kiss her until I was light-headed and feel the weight of him crushing me to the ground. I cried out at the ceiling, not caring how animal I sounded, how raw. My head was a kaleidoscope of sensations and when I came there was no clarity, just a whirl of color and touch, fiery red and smoky blue overlapping and blending and blinding me with ultraviolet bliss.

I stared at the wall across from us, a watercolor painting of shadow and flame. My mouth hung dumbly. He was still hard and she was still tight. I pulled my hands into my lap, drew my knees together. Kept facing that wall.

"Holy fuck," Blythe whispered.

The candle at the center of the room pulsed like a heartbeat. There was something church-like about it—the throbbing light and hushed voices, the air heavy with sin.

Blythe broke the silence again. "That's the hottest thing I've ever seen in my bloody life."

I laughed self-consciously. My hand was still wet. God.

"You win," she said. "Forever."

Armin's gaze traveled the side of my face. "I've never seen you like this. I've never seen you so . . ."

"Confident?" Blythe said.

"Vulnerable."

Funny how they saw the same thing so differently. The hint of epiphany in his voice was troubling. I hopped to my feet, arms wrapped around my chest.

"What a tease." Blythe looked minxish, eyes half-lowered, lips red and fleshy as watermelon pulp. "Who do you think she was thinking of?"

Armin hesitated. "I don't know. Are you okay, Laney?"

"I'm fine."

"Come back here, then," Blythe murmured. "You look cold."

It was true. But I stood fast in my T-shirt and underwear, my shadow piercing the wall behind them. "It's my turn now, right? I truth myself. Who was that guy in the parking lot, Laney? The one you freaked out over?"

Armin straightened, suddenly alert, but Blythe sank into the couch, light touching her eyes like the flicker of a serpent's tongue.

"He—" I closed my mouth, opened it. "His name—" Curled my hands into fists, relaxed them.

"Laney," Armin said, "you don't have to do this now."

"Now is the only time I can." I stared at his long hands, the elegant lines of his bones. "I feel so close to you right now. Both of you."

"Come here, sweet girl," Blythe said.

I went and sat between them. Armin tucked a lock of hair behind my ear. Blythe's hand braceleted my wrist. I wished I could disappear, dissolve myself into their skin, their scent. My summer gods.

"His name," I said, my voice creaking, rusty, old, "is Brandt Zoeller."

And then I started to cry.

DECEMBER, LAST YEAR

I'd been crouching so long my knees had stopped burning and gone numb. Before us ice spread across the asphalt like ground-up glass, the cold so clear and sharp it hurt to breathe. All this poignancy was fitting. Very bad things were about to happen. At least the world knew when to wince.

I was reaching for another cigarette when the burner phone buzzed.

Armin and I glanced at each other, anxious. Even after hours of waiting, when it finally came it felt too soon. I pulled the phone out and we read the screen together.

Phase 2.

"Help me up," I said.

He gave me a hand. I almost fell, blood thawing my frozen veins too quickly, that awful hot lifestuff gushing through me. Nothing hurts more than being alive.

I strode down the alley, Armin trailing behind. He kept trying to drag it out, feeding me chances to second-guess myself, renege. If he really knew me, he wouldn't have bothered. There was no turning back.

I ducked into the lee of a Dumpster and signaled him to get in position across the alley. He paused in a long fang of moonlight, that white wolf face solemn, fixing me with an eye pure as a drop of liquid midnight.

"Armin . . ."

He stepped into the shadows.

This was it. God, this was it.

My high was gone. The tingle in my hands and feet was sheer adrenaline. I couldn't feel the cold. I was colder than anything in this world.

I heard her first: that Roman candle laugh, the snarky Aussie drawl. Before I could hear him, I saw him. Two blond heads above heavy wool coats. Blythe's dress shone in the streetlight, a slit of red running down her chest like a wound. She held her shoes by the straps and walked barefoot on the ice, impervious. Zoeller ambled beside her, listing, overcorrecting his steps. Drunk.

Good girl, I thought.

"Just up the lane here," she said, smiling. The closer they got, the more canine that smile looked.

Zoeller stumbled into a trash can and knocked it over.

"Come on, then. I drank more than you." Blythe hauled him up by the elbow and he leaned on her heavily.

His gaze brushed my hiding spot as they staggered past.

"You're fucking beautiful," Zoeller mumbled, and for a terrifying second I thought he was speaking to me. But his hand slid down Blythe's back, curving against her ass. "I'm gonna fuck you till you scream."

A small crack popped in the ice inside me.

"Hands off, mate," Blythe said, twisting free. "Let's get to the car first, yeah?"

Zoeller came to an abrupt halt. Something snapped through him like a whip. Then he straightened and took a few steps toward her, fast. His hands clamped onto her shoulders. Blythe spun, fist raised, and he caught it like a viper.

My heart went hard and still.

"Let go of me," she growled.

He wrenched her arm, forcing her to turn. "Where are your friends?" No slurring now.

"My friends are at the chapter house," she said loudly, "and if they don't hear from me in five minutes, they'll call the fucking cops."

Call the cops was the code we'd given her for *I need an escape.* My hand drifted toward the small of my back.

Zoeller beamed at something in the distance. "Call them. Then I can tell them how you tried to drug me."

I met Armin's eyes across the alley, two faint white rings. Shit.

"The fuck are you talking about?" Blythe said.

"GHB?" Z smiled. "Please. You're dealing with a master."

"You're crazy, arsehole. Get your fucking hands off me before you regret it."

He just kept smiling. Waiting.

My phone vibrated. Armin's text: *Abort?*

Rather than reply, I stepped out into the alley.

Zoeller released Blythe as soon as I appeared. Armin came to my side, the bat against his leg. We faced off in pairs. Blythe skirted us all warily, but Z slipped his hands into his trouser pockets and relaxed his stance.

"That's better," he said. "Now we can have some fun."

Blythe sized up the situation and improvised. "Oh, I see. You and your mates think you're gonna have a go at me. Cops are on their way, fuckwits."

I made my voice harsh. "Get out of here, bitch."

Even though she knew what I was doing, she blinked.

"I said get the fuck out."

Tell Donnie, I thought. *Be ready. This is about to go horribly wrong.*

Blythe turned and walked rapidly out of the alley.

As she left Armin and I moved toward Zoeller, positioning

ourselves to either side, rotating. Z pivoted, keeping us both in view. Mostly he focused on me. The speaker. The leader.

"The wolves are circling," he said, and chuckled.

In my peripheral vision I caught Armin's hands flexing on the bat.

"Little alpha wolf is bold." Z ignored Armin and turned with me. "She doesn't even carry a weapon."

"Shut the fuck up, faggot." The word passed my lips like a blade, slicing me on the way out. Laney Keating would never call anyone a fag. Laney Keating was terrified she was one, so Kenosha Tech girl had to say it. "Get on your knees."

Zoeller grinned. "Want me to suck your dick?"

"Drop him," I told Armin.

Armin hesitated. Of course he did. When it came to inflicting pain, his instincts were all wrong. I'd warned him not to hesitate. Zoeller had reptilian reflexes. Any softness, any exposure, and he'd strike.

"Now," I barked.

Armin winced and swung the bat at the backs of Zoeller's knees. Z dropped, but the grin stayed on his face. He'd sensed our disunity.

I slapped him as hard as I could.

He wasn't expecting it. His head jerked to one side and a jet of blood flew out. Where it hit the ice it congealed instantly, like red molasses.

My gloves retained a trace of paint and left a white stripe on his face. Blood marbled it, seeking fissures. I thought of the spiderweb cuts on my hand after I punched the window to reach Mom the morning she died and I hit him again, harder, as he looked up at me. Then once more. A nerve in my wrist sparked and burned like a fuse. That tiny fire worked toward my brain stem, toward the stack of dynamite piled at the back of my skull.

"Easy," Armin said.

The rage dispersed. I was cold and in control. "It's time someone taught you Corgan pussies a lesson," I said, reciting the script.

"What lesson is that?"

"How to keep your mouth shut, you stupid cunt."

"Misogyny *and* homophobia." Zoeller smiled with blood-stained teeth. "You are one messed-up little girl, aren't you?"

I almost hit him again. I almost said, *You're the one who was always spouting that shit.* I should have seen what he was doing.

"Big words," I said, maintaining the persona. "Your boy-friend teach you those?"

"I learned them from women."

"What else you learn from women? How to bend over and take it?"

"How to get inside their heads."

Armin stepped next to me. He didn't say a word, but his expression beneath the wolf paint was poised on the tense wire between dismay and acceptance. He pressed the bat into my hands.

Good boy, I thought.

Zoeller watched my hands on the grip tape, the way I stroked the barrel that would soon destroy his flesh. I ran a hand up and down the aluminum shaft deliberately.

"You're not from Ken Tech," he said.

I slipped the head of the bat beneath his chin and made him look up at me.

"This is something personal," he whispered. "I can see it in your eyes."

"Good guess."

I swung right through the cloud of my breath and con-nected full force with Zoeller's throwing shoulder. It sounded and felt like hitting a side of beef. He didn't scream, but an animal sound tore from his diaphragm. He fell forward, balancing on one palm, and I swung again at the same shoulder, overhand. This time something cracked and he collapsed to his elbow, coughing, and looked up at me.

"Again," he said hoarsely.

I obliged.

It felt softer, wetter, when I hit this time, and he screamed now, high-pitched. When it petered out his voice crumbled into rasping laughter.

I walked a circuit around him, the bat light as air in my hand. On a whim I slammed it into his elbow. He moaned. I aimed for a kidney and he doubled over, dry heaving. My feet moved faster. The bat was a silver blur. Each breath I took felt like a bump of meth.

"Fight," I said.

Zoeller wheezed. Blood drooled out of his mouth.

"Get the fuck up, pussy." I swung at his ear, the first head blow, and he toppled to one side. "You weak piece of shit. Get up. Take it like a man."

"Stop," Armin said.

I wedged the toe of my boot beneath Zoeller's chin. "Look at me, you pathetic fuck."

His eyes had closed. He grasped feebly at my foot.

I kicked him square in his perfect mouth. A tooth snapped and rolled across the ice like a loose pearl.

"*Stop*," Armin said again, grabbing my arm.

I almost swung at him. It was as if he interrupted me jerking off, that burst of hatred for ruining the purest pleasure.

"That's enough." Armin took the bat. Blood candy-striped the shaft. He knelt, feeling for Z's pulse, as I stood in a trance and watched him lift the coat, palpate the bones gently. Zoeller didn't even groan. His breath made a soft, moist sound. "I think you punctured a lung. He needs an ambulance."

I stared rapturously at my handiwork.

"Are you listening?"

Z peered up at me through a bruised eye. "Didn't work," he said haltingly. "Did it?"

I stepped closer.

"You're still. Hollow." He smiled, grotesque with blood and missing teeth. "The hollow girl. The stuffed girl."

T. S. Eliot.

"Get away from him," I said to Armin.

Armin shook his head. "Call 911."

" 'Between the motion and the act,' " Z said, " 'falls the Shadow.' "

My hand slipped into my waistband. That hard, cold weight shaped itself to my palm as if it had been made for me. To fill the hollowness. To complete me.

"Get away from him," I repeated, raising the gun.

It almost broke my heart, the way Armin reacted. Slow-dawning shock, his mouth falling, a glaze of distance filming his eyes. He kept his gaze trained on the muzzle as he stood.

"What are you doing?" he said sadly.

"Move." I flicked the safety off. "Now."

Zoeller laughed, which became a cough, spluttering blood. "Listen to her, Apollo. She's not. Fucking around."

Armin's stare bounced to Zoeller and back to the gun. He retreated, fumbling in his pocket. "I'm calling 911."

He faded from my consciousness. All I saw was the body laid on the ground before me like an offering. My prize. My prey. Even broken and mangled, Brandt was a beautiful boy. Those full cupid lips smiled at me tenderly.

"I've waited so long," he said. "For you. For this."

I cradled the grip in both hands. A .45 has a beastly kick, and I'm a small monster. " 'There will be time, there will be time to prepare a face to meet the faces that you meet. There will be time to murder and create.'"

He ruined that pretty smile by showing teeth.

"Did you get off thinking about this?" I pointed the muzzle unwaveringly at his forehead. "I did, too. You're the only boy who could make me come."

Zoeller didn't look at the gun. His eyes were fixed on mine.

"Do you know why?" I breathed slow and deep, filling my body with winter. Persephone in the underworld, her belly full of pomegranate seeds, her veins full of ice.

"Why?"

"Because you taught me how to let go."

I squeezed the trigger.

MARCH, LAST YEAR

The first Monday of March, someone replaced the front door of my high school with a portal to the Twilight Zone. When I stepped into the foyer, a rainbow banner fluttered in my face and Luke North, wearing his customary Chicago Blackhawks cap and a shirt that read LOVE IS LOVE, smiled and handed me a peanut butter cookie.

"Gay/straight, no hate," he said.

My mouth dropped.

The Rainbow Alliance was doing a baked goods sale, and not only had Luke tricked his way in, but so had Nolan, Gordon, and Quinn—the same hyenas who'd filmed my Valentine's debacle. I glanced around for Zoeller. This was exactly the kind of elaborate gaslighting scheme he'd cook up.

"We're having a rally Friday," Luke said, still smiling maniacally. "You should join us, Laney."

"You should kill yourself," I said.

His smile didn't crack. "This is a bullying-free zone. Have a great day."

I dropped the cookie in the trash before whatever he'd infected it with could seep into my blood.

The day got weirder.

When I slammed my locker closed after the last bell, Kelsey

was waiting behind the door. I made a surprised noise midway between shriek and sneeze.

"God bless you," she said. "Are you busy?"

The hall emptied, no one paying us attention. "What's up?"

That lopsided grin. "Brandt was going to give me a ride, but he canceled at the last second. Like usual."

A month ago, I would've died and gone to heaven if Kelsey Klein asked me for a ride home.

"I've got a ton of errands to run," I said, feigning regret.

"That's fine. I'm not doing anything."

"And the car's really dirty."

"You should see my room."

Oh my god. "Okay."

"You want to see my room?" she said, laughing.

"No. Yes. I mean, I can give you a ride."

She smiled, strawberry lips shining with gloss. I'd kissed that mouth, and I'd thought of kissing it again, pretty much every night.

"Okay." Her eyes held mine a beat, enigmatic.

We both looked away.

Kelsey insisted on errands first. Since I'd stupidly pluralized the lie, I had to invent at least two. At the library I prowled through the poetry section while she drifted in YA. That old-book smell blissed my senses, glue and gracefully rotting paper, a leafy decay, autumnal. I flipped open a thick omnibus and sank to the carpet. My head floated in words.

"What are you reading?"

Kelsey sat beside me, cross-legged.

She was the polar opposite of Zoeller: his soulless irreverence versus her wide-eyed sincerity. Naive but endearing. I started to tell her about the book, and then something took hold of me and changed the words in my mouth, and instead of saying *This is a collection of poems by T. S. Eliot,* I began to recite.

In my mind dark clouds pass over a garden. A shadow falls like a spell, every leaf and petal, every flutter of wing and air, every breath and green-blooded heartbeat going still. Eternity suffuses this moment. On a branch a bird flicks its wing once and looks at me, a stray sunbeam gliding off turquoise feathers, and when that wing

> *Has answered light to light, and is silent, the light is still*
> *At the still point of the turning world.*

I lowered my eyes to the page. Kelsey stared.

"You know that by heart?" she said.

Shrug.

"It's beautiful."

You're beautiful, I thought. But you don't love me.

I closed the book. "We can go."

In Walgreens we wandered the aisles, touching everything. Kelsey picked up a bottle of nail polish, asked what I thought of the color, set it down. "Don't you want it?" I said. She was broke. At the end of the aisle I spun her around, walked it again. A cool vial of violet polish slipped into my pocket. She smiled her crooked smile. We left wearing stolen sunglasses, laughing.

"Where's your house?" I said.

"Fuck my house. Fuck everyone. Let's get high."

I parked behind a Subway, sheltered in the blue shade of dirty snowdrifts. I'd saved two tabs of X in an Altoids tin because doing ecstasy by yourself is just depressing. We took them and split an Orange Crush and listened to the Silversun Pickups. I ran my hands over the heated leather seats and felt as if I were touching someone's body.

"Your car is sexy as hell," Kelsey said.

"It's my mom's."

"Your mom is sexy as hell."

I laughed, horrified.

"Drive," she said, tilting her head back.

There's something maddeningly beautiful about a girl baring her throat. The kind of beauty that makes you want to put your mouth to it, your teeth. The kind of beauty you want to destroy.

I drove out of the dollhouse suburbs into rural nowhere. We didn't talk, just let ourselves feel. The engine purred deep in my bones. I felt the grain of the asphalt as if I skimmed my bare feet over it, my skin a dense fabric of electrons buzzing euphorically at every collision with the world. Rolling on X feels like you're right about to kiss someone, constantly. As if you are endlessly coming up to the brink of something heart-shatteringly beautiful. It makes your lungs so big you can barely fill them and every breath is huge and warm and too much.

Dusk came on. The sun fizzled out in the snow like a snuffed cigarette and I kept driving till the tank ran dry. At the gas station Kelsey walked in wearing her ridiculous sunglasses and calmly placed a bottle of Grey Goose on the wooden counter. The clerk didn't blink.

"That's how it's done," she said in the car. The smile beneath those mirrored lenses made my belly tighten.

"I thought you were broke."

"It's not my money."

Zoeller had given it to her. I started the engine, wondering what she'd had to do to get paid.

Kelsey wouldn't tell me where she lived. She routed me from one edge of Naperville to the other like a broken GPS. I didn't mind. It got later and our X mellowed. The car was heady with the scent of nail polish and girl skin. I drove smoothly so she wouldn't spill and she flashed me a row of glitter-flecked nails. By tacit agreement we stopped in a forest preserve where the firs were still fleeced with snow. Found logs to sit on and cracked the vodka, sipping it raw. It was icy and it burned like nitrogen going down. Every time I spoke I felt as if I froze the world with my breath, reducing chaos to stillness, clarity.

"Did you fuck Zoeller?" I said.

Kelsey took a sip off the bottle. We weren't drinking to get drunk. We were drinking for courage.

"No."

"How come?"

"He doesn't want me."

I took the bottle back. The vodka had a sharp steel taste, like licking a razor blade. "He's a scumbag anyway."

"I know."

"You deserve better."

Kelsey looked at me. Mostly it was shadow and blur but here the moonlight cut through the trees, a clear arc showing half her face. "Why?"

Because I'm in love with you, obviously.

I drank.

When I passed her the vodka she took my gloveless hand instead. I let the bottle fall, not knowing if it landed upright.

"What are you doing?" I said.

"Do you still want me?"

Yes. God, a million times yes.

"This isn't a good idea," my traitor mouth said. "You're just high."

"I don't care." She brought my hand to her cheek. Her skin was chill but a red rush surged to the surface, meeting my palm. "You're the only one who actually wants me how I am."

"You're straight."

"That doesn't mean I'm not lonely."

Our eyes finally met then, and I saw myself reflected there, small and alone. For a moment I was like everyone else in this world: I wanted to be loved. Even selfishly, even just for a second.

I leaned in and kissed her.

It was soft this time, too, but sweeter. I'd done this in my head a hundred times and fell into it now like a familiar daydream, warm and numb, my skin scintillating somewhere between shiver and shimmer. When we'd kissed before I hadn't put my hands on her but now I cupped her face. She was different. Didn't try to lead. Let me control it, tilt her chin and open her mouth, twine my tongue with hers. Sensation whirled through my body but at the center I was the untouched eye, the still point. Paused in this perfect moment forever while the world spun on. This was what I'd wanted for so long.

And it was only happening because ecstasy made you love everyone. Anyone. I pulled away.

"What's wrong?" Kelsey said.

I stood too fast and sat back down in the snow.

She laughed, reaching for me. I scrambled to my feet. We hadn't parked far off but in the darkness and my drunkenness the forest expanded, becoming an eternal winter wood like something out of Dante, black trees twisting in impossible geometries, whispering of their suicides. Somehow I had snow in my mouth. I spit it out and the car wavered suddenly before me like a mirage. Right as I touched the door, Kelsey touched me.

"What—" I began, and she shoved me against the door and kissed me.

There's a difference in the kiss that comes before sex. It's less a desire than a devouring. She kissed me hungrily, meanly, and I stopped caring why because this felt better than any guilt could feel bad. I pulled her closer and took her lip in my teeth, slid my hands inside her coat, over her breasts. Pushed her against the car and held her down. I'd never done this with a girl but my hands knew what they wanted. They slipped beneath her shirt, touched the taut skin of her belly. So fucking soft.

"Is this okay?" I said, making a little cloud of breath.

She kissed me again and I tasted vodka and strawberry lip gloss. "You are so sweet."

I couldn't get enough of her. I could barely hold on—the incredibility of what was happening made everything ethereal, as if I gripped nothing but warm smoke. I kissed her harder, willing it to feel real. Her thigh slid between mine. Fingernails grazed the small of my back. The kiss became a rough brush of lips, too desperate to stop and focus. Our bodies pressed together and it felt so different than it had with boys, so supple, so fluid, no end to the ways we could melt and dissolve against each other. She made me high. I wanted more. I wanted to overdose on her.

I fumbled in my pocket for the keys. "Get in."

In the backseat our coats came off awkwardly, impatiently. She wrapped her legs around me. I undid her jeans with one hand while she took the other in her mouth and sucked my middle finger to the knuckle. Something ineffably strange happened inside me then. I didn't feel so much like a girl as both girl and boy, or neither. I wanted to fuck her and to be fucked, cycling rapidly between the two, relenting helplessly when she took my finger deep and bit the bone and growing fierce when I slid my hand between her legs and found her already wet. Her mouth opened plaintively. I touched her the way I touched myself when I got off to her, fingered that hot edge, raised gooseflesh over her skin, dipped into her wetness and stroked an oval until my palm was slick and she was grinding against my hand and saying, "God, fuck me, fuck me."

And I did.

———

Two girls sitting side by side, both facing forward, quiet. Too drunk to drive, waiting for Donnie to come pick us up. The silence made me want to claw off my skin.

"Smoke?" I offered.

Kelsey shook her head at the windshield.

Mom forbade me from smoking in her car, but she'd probably also have forbidden fucking girls in it if she knew that was a possibility, and now that it already smelled like pussy I figured what was the harm. I lit up and popped the moonroof. Burning tobacco grains crackled like little fireworks. The world was immersed in the icy licorice liqueur of midnight.

When I took a drag I smelled Kelsey on my hands. She'd made me come in my jeans with her leg between mine.

How the fuck were we ever going to go to school together again.

"Are you okay?" I said.

"Yeah. I think. I don't know."

"That means no."

She shifted in her seat.

"What are you feeling?" I said, not wanting to know.

And she proved me right by saying, "Nothing."

Nothing. It meant nothing to her.

Donnie's friend dropped him off and he drove us home, casting worried glances at me the whole time. "She's pissed" was all he said about Mom. Kelsey asked to be let out a block from her house. To freshen up. Scrub herself of me. We didn't say good-bye.

I thought of Plath: *I felt very still and very empty, the way the eye of a tornado must feel.* The opposite of Eliot's stillness. Not an illuminated clarity arrived at through beauty, but the void at the center of disaster.

I texted her in bed. Couldn't help myself.

Sorry if shit's weird now.

I know you're not like that. Like me.

It's not a big deal.

We can still be friends. Or not. Whatever you want.

Just let me know you're okay.

My texts went unanswered so long I thought she'd gone to sleep. But when I finally started to doze, my phone buzzed.

All she said was, *This never happened.*

––––––––

Back at school, Luke North appointed himself my new BF-fucking-F.

"Rally Friday," he reminded me on Tuesday.

I ashed on his shoe.

On Wednesday he slipped a Rainbow Alliance flyer into my locker. I wrote STOP PRETENDING TO BE HUMAN on it and stuffed it in his.

Thursday he paid someone to deliver a box of cookies to me in homeroom. Everyone stared. I gave them away. The attached card read UR ONE TOUGH COOKIE ♥.

No one died from eating them. I considered the possibility that Luke North had a brain tumor pressing on his empathy center, stimulating it for the first time in his life.

Then came Friday.

Let's get something straight. High school's not like musicals or the fucking CW. There are cliques, yeah, but in reality it's much less organized. People drift between groups, not quite fitting in fully, gravitating toward individuals and finding bits of their identity scattered in jumbled constellations, the ghostly lines between stars. My brother was emo but his best friend was a jock. Zoeller was a jock who hung out with weirdo loners like me. No one showed much solidarity.

Except when they had a common enemy.

Last period was canceled for assembly. I tried to ditch, but Mr. Radzen caught me in the hall and gave me a furrily meaningful look. His mustache hypnotized me.

"Very important message today," he said. "Not going to miss it, are we, Del?"

I mumbled something that appeased him.

"That's my girl."

I sat with Donnie up in the gym bleachers, as far from everyone else as we could get. His eyes had that baked glaze of mellowness. He smelled like weed.

"Bastard," I said.

We zoned out through the speeches. Blah blah cheerleading blah blah student government. No one cared about this shit. People only did it to pad out their résumés. It all fell beneath the Shadow—the meaningless mundanity, the paralysis of pointlessness. To my horror, when I tuned out their voices I heard my mother.

Let the sheep bleat. Their own noises soothe them.

I spotted Kelsey on the other side of the gym, next to Zoeller. Maybe it was my imagination but I swear she looked right at me.

I'd kissed the girl I was in love with. I'd slept with her. And she wanted to forget it ever happened.

"And now," the vice principal said, "a special message from the Rainbow Alliance."

You could tell what kind of message it was when Christina Aguilera's "Beautiful" started playing. The lights dimmed, a golden cone spotlighting Luke and company. I fingered the Xanax in my pocket.

"Bullying is a very serious problem at Naperville South," Luke began, devoid of all irony. "This school year alone, disciplinary warnings for bullying have almost doubled."

Christina said I was beautiful.

"Bullying is especially hard on students who identify as gay, lesbian, bi, or trans. Every year, we hear about teens who take their own lives because they can't stand the hate anymore. The Rainbow Alliance has pledged that we're not going to let one of our friends become the next statistic."

Christina said words couldn't bring me down.

"That's why we've joined forces with student government to make Naperville South a Hate-Free Zone. Starting now, any speech or behavior that discriminates against a student because of sexual orientation or gender identity will be evaluated by an arbitration team. Severe transgressions may count as an academic violation that will go on your transcript."

Gasps and murmurs. I sat up.

"To protect those who need support and safe spaces the most, we're taking it one step further. We're inviting all LGBT students to join the Rainbow Alliance. When you register, you'll get assigned to a special guidance counselor who'll be available for extracurricular counseling. Any incidences of bullying that you report will be escalated through the arbitration process. Alliance partners like me will be deputized with special monitoring status—so when we see bullying happen on campus, we'll stop it on the spot. Basically, you won't have to be afraid of being yourself anymore." Luke beamed righteously at the crowd. "We're saying no to the culture of fear here at NSHS. No more hiding. No more shame. But in order to make this work, we need your cooperation, too. It's time for our queer brothers and sisters to step forward and join the Alliance. Don't let the bullies keep you in the closet. Don't hide that rose in your bag anymore. Come out and stand proud."

Titters broke through the crowd. Kids side-eyed me.

"To show your support for this brave new initiative," Luke

said, ominously Huxleyan, "we've got some awesome T-shirts and buttons for sale . . ."

I climbed over legs to get out of the stands. Donnie followed, calling my name. People stared. I saw only Luke. Luke North standing like Jesus Christ in his heavenly ray of yellow gel light, soulful and sincere.

"Are you serious?" I reached the gym floor, wild with adrenaline. "Are you *fucking* serious?"

Heads turned. Mr. Radzen stood up from the guidance table.

I was already halfway to the mic in the center of the court. "Is this some massive joke, or are you all actually this clueless?"

The gym hushed. A thousand pairs of eyes on me. The same thousand that had watched "DYKE GET'S SHOT DOWN." The same kids who had laughed. Ignored. Isolated. Condoned.

"Does anyone believe a word he just said?" My voice surprised me with its volume. "He's the guy who made the video. You think he's going to 'protect' people with a registry of gay kids? Is this a George Orwell novel?"

Brian Sabano, Rainbow Alliance president, joined Luke in the spotlight. "We'll take questions from the audience after—"

"Shut the fuck up," I said, grabbing the mic. Brian Sabano was the darling of the cheerleading squad. The perfect straight-washed gay boy, clean-cut, urbane, witty. A cyborg, as Mom would say. Straight girls loved him because he was cute and they could flirt without threat. No one flirted with the creepy dyke. "You've never been discriminated against in your life, Brian. Just shut up."

Radzen looked at the VP. The VP looked at Radzen. They seemed confused as to which one should stop me.

"You fucking hypocrites," I said, turning to the crowd. My tiny voice coming out of the PA sounded surreal. I didn't see faces. I didn't see Donnie at my side, urging me to stop. I saw the blank smear of pale skin, the glassy eyes untroubled by pain. I saw the rest of my life, never relating to people, always outside, apart. Even my supposed allies had sided with the Gender Gestapo. "This doesn't 'protect' anyone. This registry is a hit list. It puts targets on people's backs. And you idiots made a bully your poster boy." I laughed but it came out a croak. "You don't really give a shit when bad stuff happens to people like me. You only care about *looking* tolerant. Buying a cookie, signing a petition. But all of you watched that video, and all of you would do it again. You pretend to care while you laugh behind my back. While you make my life a fucking nightmare. You're despicable. All of you. Someone should shoot this school up. You deserve it."

Radzen yanked the mic from my hand.

Time to run.

I crashed through the gym doors as a riot erupted behind me.

The hall was empty and dim, my footsteps slapping like someone beating at a face. I'd almost made it to the exit when hands caught me. I spun, crazed, clawing, and slashed Donnie's arm before I realized.

"Laney," he said in that soft, boyish voice.

I burst into tears.

He pulled me to his chest. "It's okay. It's going to be okay."

It was not going to be okay. My bullies had infiltrated the power structure. They were institutionalizing their terror.

"I love you," Donnie murmured into my hair. "And I've got your back, Rainbow Brite. No matter what."

I wrenched away from him. My hands made fists and my fists trembled, clutching air, wanting to warp it, twist it inside out. "This is all about me. Luke did this to get to me. Zoeller stopped them but they found another way."

"What?"

"I'm a fucking fag, okay? I fucked Kelsey."

Donnie's eyes widened.

"I fucked her and she doesn't want anything to do with me. She only did it because we were high. I'm so messed up, Donnie. I was lonely and so was she and now the entire school knows I'm a freak and I just want to know why she—"

"Lane, stop talking."

"No. I'm sick of pretending. I don't care what they—"

Donnie turned me around.

In the hall behind us stood Luke and company, Zoeller, and Kelsey. Of course. Because high school actually *is* the CW, and six of your closest enemies will appear spontaneously when you blurt out life-wrecking confessions in a seemingly empty hallway.

This video never got posted to YouTube. Zoeller prevented that. But Nolan managed to capture "I'm a fucking fag" onward, including everyone's reaction—Luke slapping a hand over his cap as if the hilarity would blow it off, and Kelsey covering her mouth, horrified, or sickened, turning away, and Zoeller watching it all with his vacant sociopath stare.

Then the camera turned back to me, and the last thing you can see is my small fist flying at the lens.

———

Takeout for dinner = emergency family meeting.

Fried chicken. Finger food. Mom didn't want me handling sharp implements.

Dad nibbled on a drumstick, worriedly watching Mom. Donnie rearranged his potato wedges, worriedly watching me. The Keatings: sweet nervous boys and cold crazy girls.

I didn't eat. I wanted an empty stomach to take oxy on. Mom, however, tore into a breast and let the grease run down her chin. She was an uptight elitist bitch who considered fast food unworthy of being fed to dogs, but when she did something she did it wholeheartedly, with perverse gusto, as if to show she was so far beyond irony she'd circled back to authenticity.

Before her illness progressed, she'd been executive chef at a glitzy restaurant downtown. Her mania worked to her advantage, then—she ran the kitchen tirelessly, flogging the lesser mortals who toiled under her. The *Sun-Times* food critic called her "a mad maestra," which pleased her. Sometimes she wouldn't come home for days, sleeping in hotels, living out of her car. While she was off cooking four-star dishes for foreign diplomats, we were scraping burned mac-'n'-cheese from a pot at home. She had affairs that Dad accepted in his quiet, resigned way as "the Illness." As if it excused everything. The Illness made her unable to resist impulses. The Illness was the bitch, not Caitlin.

Mania inevitably cycled to depression, and the depressions lasted longer and longer, and she lost her job. Now she was a lowly part-time sous chef at a "suburban feeding trough," as she called it. And she'd decided that if she was suffering, we were all going to suffer with her.

"How was school?" she said.

They'd made me sit in Guidance till she picked me up. Two-week suspension. They also barred me from joining any extracurricular clubs, including the Rainbow Alliance. I could no longer register to be "protected" by Luke North from . . . Luke North.

Mom knew, of course. She just wanted to make me say it.

"May I be excused?" I said.

"You may not." She ripped a strip of meat with her teeth. Her face had the pallor and tautness of skin pressed by a thumb, the blood squeezed to the margins. As if there was something too intense inside her, something that pushed everything in her to the edge.

Dad gave me a sympathetic, ineffectual look.

I smacked a palm on the table. "Let's get it over with, then."

Emergency family meeting = emergency Laney meeting.

"Delaney disrupted a school assembly," Mom told Dad.

"What happened, sweetheart?"

"Your daughter has taken a stance against sexual fascism," she said.

I gritted my teeth. "That's not what happened."

"That factory farm"—Mom always referred to school in terms of mass production—"has instituted some sort of sex offender registry for students who don't fit the heteronormative template."

"What?" Dad said.

"They want kids who aren't straight to register with the Rainbow Alliance," Donnie said. "For their own 'protection.'"

"It's supposed to stop bullying," I said, "by painting a huge target on someone's back."

Dad wore a small frown that made my insides curl. "Honey, what does that have to do with you?"

Everyone looked at me. I looked down at my plate.

"It's just wrong," Donnie piped up. "No one should have to. And the guys behind it are the biggest jerks at school. They're taking over."

"Not if I can help it." Mom dabbed languidly at her mouth with the linen. "I haven't been to a PTA meeting in years. What fun it'll be to see the breeding stock who produced these *enfants terribles.*"

A strange flare of warmth lit my chest. She was actually taking my side.

Dad's gaze never left my face. Troubling things were happening in it, things that looked like realizations. Not his little girl anymore, etc.

"Laney," he said in the voice that used to soothe me to sleep, "sweetheart, are you . . ."

I couldn't look at him.

"It's okay, Lane," Donnie said encouragingly.

I looked at my brother but he went blurry, a bunch of bokeh circles overlapping. So much for coldness. A tear rolled over my lip, salting my mouth.

"For Christ's sake," Mom said. "Our daughter is a lesbian."

"No I'm not," I blurted.

"Oh, honestly. As if I haven't known for years. Were you under the illusion this would come as a shock?"

"You don't know anything about me."

Her eyes burned. "I know everything about you. I made you."

I stood.

"Sit down," Mom said.

"Go to hell."

"Sit down or I'll call Dr. Patel."

She never raised her voice. I sat, cowed. Hateful.

"So." She ran a fingertip along the rim of her glass. "We have a daughter who denies her sexual identity crisis, a clueless father who is stunned, blindsided, et cetera, and a son who conspired to hide his sister's drug addiction."

Donnie's eyes bugged. Dad looked at my brother, then me, as if he'd never seen us before.

"What is going on, kids?"

"Mom," Donnie said, pleading, "it's not like that, I swear. They were my pills and they sucked. We'll never do it again. I'm sorry."

My baby brother, taking the blame.

Mom couldn't face him without softening, so she focused on me. "When you move out, you can self-medicate all you want. You can self-medicate yourself straight into oblivion if that's what you truly desire. Trust me, I understand the urge. But as long as you live under my roof, you will *not* abuse yourself this way. Do I make myself clear? This nonsense ends now."

My bones felt full of something black and awful, an ache that twisted deep into the marrow. I wanted an oxy so badly my teeth ground.

"Answer me, Delaney."

"Or what?" I couldn't meet her stare, so I spoke to the table. "You won't ship me off to Dr. Patel. You're scared she'll put me on something that'll mess my head up even more. I should do it. I should go become a robot."

Dad shoved his chair back, rattling the glass and silverware. We all looked at him, startled.

"You hear that, Caitlin? That's your bullshit coming out of her mouth. You've brainwashed her into thinking getting help will make her worse."

Wonder flitted across Mom's expression. "Are you finally growing a spine?"

"I raised them. I'm the one who took care of them while you were off wining and dining. While you were enjoying the fun parts of your illness. And I'm putting my foot down now. It's time for you to take a step back. She needs help that you can't give her."

Donnie and I exchanged shocked glances. Dad never talked like this.

"You didn't raise them," Mom said, snorting. "The Internet raised them. You don't know anything about them."

"I know my little girl is in pain, and needs help."

A weird hiccup went through me. Don't cry.

"Your little girl had her heart broken by another girl. It's teenage melodrama. It'll pass."

Wait. There was no way she could know about that, unless—

"Did you read my stuff?" I said.

Mom looked at me sedately. Took a sip of wine.

"I can't believe you." I grabbed the table's edge. "You snooped through my private journals."

"I paid for those journals. I paid for the therapy. I even pay for the drugs you're trying to kill yourself with. Nothing of yours is private to me."

My nails gouged wood. I imagined it as her face.

"What did you expect, Delaney? You refuse to tell me what's going on. I have to learn about it somehow, and I'd rather it not be in your suicide note."

"You don't deserve to know what's going on." The words came out screechier than I'd hoped, but I couldn't stop. "You're never here when I need you. You spend all your good days with other people. You only spend the bad ones with us."

She peered into her wine.

"Did you ever realize that not taking your meds is selfish, Mom? That they're not just for you, but for *us*? So you can act halfway human when you decide to actually grace us with your company?"

Dad stood up. "Sweetheart. Kids. Let's take a break, let's cool down—"

"And don't even talk about melodrama," I cut in. "You're the biggest drama whore in this house. You never let anyone else feel bad. It's always you, you, you."

This piqued her at last. "Oh, is that it? Angry that mommy dearest is hogging the spotlight? Did you think sticking your face between a girl's legs was going to shock and awe me?"

"I'm not doing this for attention. I hate what I am."

"Lesbianism." She imbued the word with the same disdain she'd used to order a twelve-piece bucket of extra crispy. "How passé. If you wanted to impress me with your bourgeois depravity, why not fuck your brother?"

"Caitlin," Dad said.

"Benjamin," she said, "for God's sake, shut up. People are speaking honestly for once."

Dad's face drained.

"It's not about you," I spat. "You are so egotistical, Mom. I don't care what you think about anything. I have my own problems. Everyone at school hates me. Luke hates me, Kelsey hates me. I hate me. I'm a total freak and they all know."

"And I suppose you blame me for that, too? You know, your great-aunt Rebecca is a lesbian. Perhaps I passed the gay gene along to you."

"Stop saying that. I'm not—that." God, I still could not fucking say it. It had been easier to call myself a fag than to say the inoffensive word. Easier to hate myself for it than to accept it.

"Or perhaps my cells conspired against you," she went on. "Perhaps they poisoned you with too much androgen while you were in utero. Now you'll never fit in with the popular crowd. How tragic. Whatever it comes down to, you can always blame Mommy."

You'll feel it, the moment you snap. It's like working out a kink in your neck but deeper, its roots snaking down not just your spine but your whole life, every humiliation, every indignity, every lunch spent crying in a bathroom stall, every clenched fist, every granule of ground-up tooth enamel. Every Zoeller, Luke, and Kelsey. Every night you desperately jacked off to her and loathed yourself for it. Every fantasy of bringing the gun to school. It goes through everything and finally reaches the core of you.

I rose. Barely five feet but rage made me a titan, limbs like Roman columns, teeth like guillotine blades. Mom stood too but somehow I was looking down on her.

"It *is* your fault. You made me this way. You're ruining our family."

"Yes, I'm certainly the biggest drama whore in this house," she said dryly.

I played into it, uncaring. "I wish I wasn't your daughter."

"Isn't that sad? I'll be your mother as long as I live."

"As long as you live."

The silverware jingled. She'd grabbed the corkscrew. "You could be motherless right now. Shall I?"

Then Dad's hands were on me, ushering me from the room. Donnie was crying. My eyes were wet, too, but it was from fury, not pain.

"Do it," I yelled over my shoulder. "You're a fucking cancer."

"I've tried," she called back. "Oh, how I've tried."

Dad put me to bed. He talked for a long time but I didn't hear a word. I only heard her, over and over, filling the hollow channels of my heart with her mother's-milk venom.

She was right about one thing.

I was her daughter.

In every hateful, destructive, murderous way.

———

It stood at the foot of the bed so still and so long I was certain it wasn't real. Nothing watched you like that but the demons in your head.

Then it sighed and said, "Delaney June."

I was too tired to tell her to leave. I'd cried myself raw. All I could muster was a sluggish roll to one side, blinking crystals from my eyelashes like a mermaid sloughing away sea salt. Mom moved soundlessly but I tracked her smell, rosewater sweat, cabernet breath. She sat and the bed bowed toward her. My body tensed.

"When you were a little girl," she said, "you were fascinated by me."

Incredibly, she began reminiscing. Told me how I'd watch her paint on makeup like liquid magic. How I'd stare when she spoke, imitate her expressions. How I'd follow and watch, unnervingly quiet, a silent doll with blue glass eyes.

"You were so serious. Always observing, absorbing. Some-

times I hardly saw you as a child. You were my little protégée."
Her voice floated to the ceiling. "I never wanted children. You
were a concession for Ben. Ben was good to me, good for me,
and he wanted this, the full house, the sitcom fantasy. Two-
point-three children, two-point-three-car garage. Two-point-
three orgasms a month. He kept me from hurling myself off
the ledge, so I gave him what he wanted. What harm could
there be in more anchors to this world?"

I listened. Deep down I'd known all this but she'd never
confessed it so baldly.

"I never wanted you until I had you." She looked at me
now, her breath ruffling my hair. "And then I couldn't imagine
my life without you. You're the dark thing that was in me. I
set you free."

"No mother on earth talks like this."

"I'm no mother. I'm a creator."

I didn't know what she meant, but it sounded apologetic.

"What dark thing?"

She touched my head. "There are two parts of me. The
night and the day. One part went to you, one to your brother."

"You think I'm the bad part of you?"

Her hand twisted in my hair, painful. "Darkness isn't bad.
It's only darkness." Those fingers relaxed. "All it means is you
don't see the world as they do. You see what's really there. They
see what they wish was there."

I didn't speak. I was a little afraid of hearing more.

Her hand ran down my face, fell. "It unsettles me to see so
much of myself in you."

"What do you want, Mom?"

"To release you."

A shiver scuttled over my shoulders. "From what?"

But she didn't respond. She gazed across my room, lost in
herself.

I didn't buy it. She'd accused me of doing all this for attention. Fuck her.

"You can't treat me the way you do," I said, bolstered by the shadows. "It's emotional abuse."

"I know."

"I'm sick of being your punching bag."

She looked at me.

"I'm sick of your mood swings. Sick of never knowing if you'll be sweet or a total bitch. I'm sick of walking on eggshells all the time. And I'm sick of the way you treat Dad. He deserves better. The only one you actually love is Donnie, and you're warping him."

"I'll stop drinking."

"It's not the drinking. Being bipolar isn't a license to be a bitch, Mom. You said you could handle it without meds, but you were wrong. And we're all paying the price."

She looked away. Moonlight scalloped over her throat. "I can't take medication."

"Why?"

"It makes me feel dead inside."

This was like some biblical moment when the scales fell from my eyes. I stopped seeing the Gorgon and saw a human being in pain.

"How?"

"Everything is the same. No more highs or lows. I'm inside a glass box with the air pumped out. I can see, but can't taste or smell. Can't get enraged or aroused. Can't hear myself scream." She leaned closer but her voice sounded farther away. "It's awful, Delaney. I start thinking, What if I'm already dead? Isn't that what being dead is, the inability to feel? What if I stepped in front of a train? Would there be any difference?"

"Mom," I said, getting freaked-out.

"I need the highs *and* the lows. It's who I am. I need them both, but they're killing me. There's no way for me to be at peace."

"You're scaring me, Mom."

"It scares me, too," she whispered.

I was clenching her hand. Since when? "They can change your meds. You don't have to take lithium. You can take something else."

She stared at my hand on hers as if she couldn't comprehend it.

"Please. Say you'll try something else."

"I've tried so many ways to be normal. I just want to be myself for a little while."

Something tiny and sharp cracked in my chest. We are the same, I thought. I could have said those words.

"You should go to bed." I pulled away. "Talk to Dad. Tell him all of this."

"There's no one to tell. No one understands. Only you."

For the first time she had given me control of something, and it was her life.

"Go to bed," I said, baffled by possibilities.

And she did.

———

I paced up and down the street outside the house, shadow to lamplight to shadow again. Twice already I'd let my finger float over the doorbell. This time I pressed. No electrocution. That'd be letting me off too easy.

Warm gingery light glowed from the inset window. A ponytail bobbed in silhouette. The door opened, and a girl I didn't recognize—pretty and put-together—said, "Yes?"

"Is Kelsey here?"

The girl blinked. Then she turned and said, "Dad."

That's when I should have left.

Idiot me waited on the doorstep until Mr. Klein eclipsed the light with his Hummer-wide physique and crew cut and faint odor of beer and onion rings.

"What do you want?"

"I'm Delaney. I'm Kelsey's friend."

"I know who you are."

Run, my mind said. My mouth said, "Can I talk to her?"

Mr. Klein glanced into the house. Then he stepped onto the porch, pulling the door closed.

Neither of us spoke. My neck ached from craning to look up at him.

Finally I said, "I want to apologize."

"Apologize."

"Yeah. I—" God, what did he know? "I embarrassed her at school. I feel bad."

"Embarrassed."

This echoing shit creeped me out. "I understand if she doesn't want to talk, but I want to tell her I'm sorry for—"

Mr. Klein advanced until he nearly touched me. I retreated to the railing.

"You want to tell her you're sorry," he said in that frighteningly calm voice. "For what you did to her. To her body."

"No." I edged toward the stairs. "This was a mistake. I'll just—"

A massive arm seized the railing, cutting me off. Instinctively I lunged the opposite way and the other arm came down, bracketing me. I looked up at that slab stone face.

His voice remained calm.

"If you ever touch my daughter again, I will beat the living daylights out of you. I don't care what you are, girl, boy, alien. You stay away from her, you sick freak."

I stared at the miniature gold cross gleaming against his throat.

"She's a good girl. Not like you."

In all my life I had never felt this small. Maybe small enough to get away if I ducked under his arm.

"She's my little girl." Beer fumes bathed my face. He was actually teary-eyed. "My goddamn little girl. You keep your faggot hands off her."

I raised my eyes.

The wolf raised its head.

My breath was thick as smoke in the cold. I exhaled into his face. When the pall cleared I saw the muscle tremor in his jaw, his forearms. Smelled the acrid yellow fear coming off him. Fear of this tiny trembling person who could ruin something he loved. So afraid of what I could do with soft words and small hands that it took every bit of testosterone and menace in him to fight back.

The wolf did not cower from the sheep.

"There's something you should know," I said.

I thought of all the things he wanted to hear. *Nothing happened. We just kissed. She felt guilty and guilt blows sin out of proportion. She can still go to heaven with the other good girls.*

I told him the truth.

"She wanted it," I said. "She begged me to make her come."

Somewhere in the night a bell tolled. Oddly, I was on the ground, my cheek pressed to something icy and rough. Pine plank. The porch.

Mr. Klein knelt beside me, frowning. "You all right?"

My mouth tasted like melted copper. It took a while to process that he'd hit me.

In my head was a haze of confusion and pain and a poem. One of my favorites, "Invictus."

> *In the fell clutch of circumstance*
> *I have not winced nor cried aloud . . .*

His lips moved but I only heard bleating. Everything was black-and-white save the red stain on the wood and my hands. I touched it with wonder. My blood.

> *Under the bludgeonings of chance*
> *My head is bloody, but unbowed.*

I stood up and walked home, dizzy, aching, exultant. Alive.

———

Monday morning, first day of my suspension, I woke late to an empty house.

I showered, dressed. White pants, white hoodie. White beanie over wet hair. My lip was still puffy but I didn't put makeup on. I wanted everything to show. Every glorious spot of color. Especially the reds.

I dumped out my book bag and took it into my parents' bedroom.

Mom had driven her car that morning. Didn't matter.

Before I left I eyeballed myself in the foyer mirror. Aside from the dark petal of hair slipping over an ear I was pale as death. Ghost flower with see-through skin, my veins blue roots. A black iris blooming in snow.

I didn't smoke on the walk to school but did when I got there. Once more for old times' sake. A dozen drags before fire reaches your fingers, the closure of that final crush against pavement, the cherry bursting into a hundred sparks.

I entered through the backstage theater door that was always propped open. Thanks, smokers. No metal detector.

Precisely six minutes until homeroom ended.

Nearest girls' bathroom. A cheerleader eyed me in the mirror. I swung my bag onto the sink with a heavy clank.

She capped her lip gloss and hurried out.

I didn't bother barricading the door. Didn't matter.

Dad never wanted a gun. It was Mom's doing. She couldn't get it in her name because of her mental health history, so she convinced him: recent burglaries in the area, home invasions, what about *the children*. Dad caved but kept it in a safe. He gave me and Donnie the combination. Mom raged that she'd never kill herself but he had another fear: that she'd turn it on one of us.

Funny, how he'd always worried about the wrong person.

I walked down the hall two minutes before the bell, bag on hip, hand inside. Head clear. Just a touch of oxy to stop the shaking. I was surefooted as if I walked on four legs, not two. I passed classrooms where dull-eyed sheep baaed in their pens. When I walked into room 211 Luke would be standing up, torso exposed. Bells and locker slams would drown out the sounds.

Zoeller was right. Letting go was control.

Thirty seconds. Fifteen steps.

I flicked off the safety and drew my hand from the bag.

Something heavy and python-strong clamped around my chest. At first I thought it was a panic attack.

Then it dragged backward, pinning my arms, and a voice in my ear that sounded uncannily like Zoeller said, "Put it in the bag. Quick, before the bell."

I aimed at his foot.

"Don't do it, Laney. You're better than this."

"Give me one good reason not to."

His massive hand covered mine on the .45. "Because I'd miss you."

The bell rang.

Zoeller's arm uncoiled. His hand lingered a moment, released.

I stood there holding a gun as kids spilled from doorways.

This was it. Let go or keep holding on. Give in to the hate or swallow it for one more day.

The world was full of people like Luke and Mr. Klein. I could take out one or two and billions more would line up to spit, mock, hurt me. Humiliate me. Hate me. Because I had the audacity to exist.

It was full of girls like Kelsey, too. Girls who'd toy with my heart. Break it. And I'd let them.

What was the point of it all? Why not kill one asshole and then myself? Why stick around for a lifetime of this shit?

Because of my brother.

And because of the psychotic boy behind me who seemed to almost care.

Maybe all you need to pull you back from the ledge is to know someone would miss you if you fell.

I put the gun in the bag. My heart beat like Plath's heart: *I am, I am, I am.*

Zoeller's hands were on me again.

"One foot. Then the other. There you go."

He walked me out into the sweetest sunlight that had ever touched my face.

NOVEMBER, LAST YEAR

It's easier to tell truths in darkness. We let the candle die, let the apartment fill with a sea of shadows. Blythe and Armin sat on either side of me. I lay against his chest, one leg in her lap. Briefs, bras, panties, skin. Their hands were gentle.

"Would you have done it if he hadn't stopped you?" Armin said.

"Yes."

Neither of them recoiled. Armin took a deep breath and my body rose and fell against his chest.

"I'm glad you didn't," he said finally.

There was a silence where I was supposed to say *Me too*.

"You can tell us anything. We'll never judge you."

It sounded like he had something specific in mind for me to tell. I gazed over my shoulder at Blythe, streetlight falling through leaves in urban camo patterns on her skin. The only tat I could make out was the new one: a girl's red-nailed hand clawing across her collarbone. Below the wrist the skin became black fur that was actually, if you looked closely, iris petals.

She called that one Little Wolf.

Our truth or dare game had become my life story. I'd been telling them about senior year, ramping up to the grand finale of Mom's death, but I danced around certain things because, as you've already guessed, I'm an Unreliable Narrator.

Armin sensed my reticence.

"Laney, I found something on my laptop I've been meaning to ask you about."

I said nothing. In my mind I twisted the air into a rope and strung it through my fingers like a cat's cradle.

"There are searches in my browser history I didn't make. 'PTSD' and 'suicide.'" His next words were thin. "'Sexual assault symptoms.' 'Rape survivor.'"

"So ask," I said.

Shadows shifted over the wall, Rorschach monsters.

"Was it you?" he said.

"Yes."

He touched my face. Pulled me in delicately, fragile as a paper doll. I let him hold me. Blythe's fingernails dug at my thigh and I tensed the leg, making it hurt more.

"Poor thing," she said in a low voice.

I buried my face in Armin's neck and breathed in balsam and winter.

"I'm sorry," he said. "I'm so sorry. I should have known. The signs were all there."

Blythe's fingers carved into the gracilis, the slim ribbon of muscle on my innermost thigh. She'd taught me their names, traced each one with the scalpel of a nail so I'd remember. *Anatomy is poetry*, she'd said. Then she showed me.

"You don't have to talk about this now," Armin said.

"I'm not."

"Does anyone else know?"

"I thought I didn't have to talk about it."

An incision of pain cut across his face. I watched him struggle with the need to know more versus respect for my boundaries versus clinical professionalism versus love.

Blythe had no such inhibitions. "Brandt Zoeller," she said,

curling the name on her tongue and holding it like a razor blade. "I'll fucking kill him."

Adrenaline jabbed my heart, a burst of intense aliveness. When she got wild it made me wild, too.

Armin looked fretful.

"If you have any empathy you'll agree," Blythe said.

He said nothing.

"Zoeller deserves it," she said.

Still nothing.

"Christ, this isn't the time for Hippocratic bullshit. Do you love her or not?"

The big arm around my shoulders flexed. "Of course I do." Then he touched my cheek, gazed into my eyes. "You know that, right? I love you, Laney."

In a typical college romance novel, this was the moment I would've been waiting for. The validation of all my shame and suffering at the hands of other men: a beautiful boy loved me. What had been done to my body didn't ruin me for Mr. Right. Zippity-fucking-doo-dah.

I looked back into those sweet brown eyes and said, "I love you, too."

He kissed me, and despite myself the core of me tightened, rose toward him. Blythe's hand slid off my leg, raking skin as it went.

"Well," she said. "That's that."

We kissed a moment longer. He pressed his forehead to mine. We both looked back at her.

"What?" Armin said.

"We kill him."

"Blythe." He reached past me to touch her. His body felt both like shield and shackle. "Everyone's emotional right now, but talking like that doesn't help."

"We have to do something. He's a fucking frat boy on an athletics scholarship. Blokes like that never pay for what they take. The world is their playground."

"Let's calm down."

"I can't calm down. If someone hurts her, then we hurt him."

This time Armin didn't argue. We let the words hang, settle, coat our skin in a fine electrostatic dust. It thrummed between us, crackling. Our codependence. Our potential for violence. Our love.

"Then we hurt him," I said.

DECEMBER, LAST YEAR

When I pulled the trigger Armin crashed into me, sending my shot into the asphalt.

We toppled to the pavement and the gun spun out of my hands and skittered over the ice. I lunged for it but he held me down. I screamed and so did he, neither coherent. My elbow met his jaw. Spit flew and froze midair. He pinned my arms to the ground.

"Are you insane?" he yelled into my face.

"Get off me."

"I won't let you throw your life away."

"He already took it," I screamed back.

Tires screeched. A car door popped open.

Armin restrained me until Blythe reached us. She'd changed into a hoodie and jeans and knelt beside me, wide-eyed.

"What happened?"

"She brought a fucking gun. Hold her."

He let go and I sat up. Deep breaths. My necklace had tangled around my throat and I almost twisted it tighter, wanting to hurt something, anything. My body buzzed with unspent violence. Blythe pulled me to my feet, fetched the bat. Armin carried the .45 as if it might explode.

"Put the safety on," I said.

He grimaced helplessly.

I pointed to the side and mimed flicking the switch.

"Bloody hell," Blythe said, seeing Zoeller.

Z had lost interest in our drama and closed his eyes, breathing shallowly, slowly. His throwing arm was twisted beneath his body at an angle that would have hurt if not for massive nerve damage.

"Bloody *hell*," she said again.

I bent to pick up the wasted bullet. When a hollow-point impacts a target, something beautiful happens. The tip splits into petals that peel back from the center and it becomes a metal flower. It was almost lovely, the thought of filling Z's body with a garden of them.

Down the alley, Donnie honked. Time.

"Got everything?" Blythe said.

Armin was still hung up on the gun. He looked at it in his hands, his eyes far away.

"There's a problem," I said. "He's not that drunk. He'll remember this."

"You hit him in the head pretty hard," Armin said.

"That's not a guarantee."

"You want to fucking kill him? Is that what you want?"

Armin rarely swore or raised his voice. Blythe moved to my side.

"He identified you, *Apollo*," I said. "You don't want him to remember that." I eyed them each in turn. "We all need his blood on our hands. We have to be in this equally."

The implication was obvious:

In case he died.

Blythe didn't hesitate. She moved to Z, lifted the bat, swung viciously at his flank. Ribs crinkled like paper. His lungs emptied. I felt nothing.

She held the bat out to Armin.

"Now you," I said.

"No."

"I'm not asking."

He still cradled the gun as if it were the delicate thing, not the thing that destroyed delicacy. "This is not what we talked about. This isn't justice, it's sadism. This is not okay."

"Let's discuss what's okay." I scraped the bat on the ground, the jaw-grinding brux of metal on stone. "Is what he did to me okay? Is the way I am okay? You said you'd never judge me."

Donnie honked again, two sharp blasts.

"I'm not judging you," Armin said.

"You are. You don't think this is right, but it's what I need."

"His mind's made up," Blythe said. "Let's fucking go."

I looked at her, then back at him. "If you really loved me, you'd do it."

Jealousy is the rust that eats away at morality's hard steel. It's cancerous, and once it starts it spreads, and spreads. At first it lets small concessions through. He watched me drink, do drugs. He looked the other way when we stole things. He was in love. He never realized all these lapses were weakening him, that a moment would come when I'd push harder than before and the entire structure would crumble into red powder.

Armin gave me the gun. Took the bat. Closed his eyes and inhaled. Opened them and swung and exhaled.

He'd gone for the head.

———

My hoodie was soaked with blood straight through to the shirt beneath. I didn't notice till we were in the car and Blythe touched me and her hand came away red. Surreal, that this stuff that had been inside Z's body now belonged to me. I sat with her in the backseat, restless, feeding on her energy. She took a wet cloth to my face and scrubbed the paint off. In the front seats Donnie and Armin were silent.

Armin had put the gun in the glove box. Donnie's eyes rolled to it occasionally, frightened.

"He's alive" was all I had said about Zoeller.

We'd called 911 from a burner phone, used a voice changer app to report the beating, smashed the battery. Donnie had thrown a brick through the picture window of the Pi Tau chapter house. The note wrapped around it read, simply, *LOSERS*.

Star quarterback beaten to within an inch of his life by thugs in Ken Tech face paint. Pretty clear how it'd all play out.

If only Zoeller forgot who we were.

If only he lived.

I took Blythe's hand, chained my fingers with hers. I needed to touch someone. I needed to expel this wildness inside me.

Every time I'd hit his body it had felt like fucking him. Like being inside him, torching his nerves, igniting his blood, making him feel exactly how alive he was by destroying him one piece at a time. Violence is a violation of the body. I had violated him.

I shivered, not with cold.

In the passenger seat Armin sat with his head bowed.

Donnie dropped us off a block from my and Blythe's apartment. I couldn't hug him because of the blood but I kissed his cheek.

"Everything will be okay," I said.

His face said he wanted that to be true.

I took the stairs two at a time. Flung the door open and stalked through the apartment from one end to the other, pacing, no destination. My hands twitched. The three of us met in the kitchen and insanely I imagined I could smell their emotions, the animal reek of revulsion and lust.

"Are you all right?" Blythe said.

"I'm a fucking werewolf."

Armin flipped the switch and blood-orange light tinted the

room. We were filthy, caked with paint and sweat and frozen fluid.

"Come here," I told him, moving to the sink.

I soaked a towel and ran it over his face. His eyes were solemn. Blythe leaned on the counter, watching.

I wiped away the last vestiges of white and said, " 'I will show you fear in a handful of dust.' "

Armin blinked at me, startled.

"Are you afraid Brandt will die?" I said.

"I'm afraid of who we really are."

Something dark coursed between the three of us. It was not a new thing, but it was new that it was this palpable. A black flicker at the edge of vision. A skulking, shadowy presence.

"We're in this together now," I said. "No doubts. No regrets. Even the smallest crack will shatter us. We have to be hard. Unbreakable."

Blythe laid her hand on Armin's back, the first time I'd ever seen her so tender toward him. There was history in that touch. His breathing changed, a different energy flowing through him. When he looked at me his eyes were full of shadows.

"The blood," he said.

Blythe unzipped my hoodie and pulled it off. Armin peeled the shirt over my head. He washed my body and she washed my face. Oh, the symbolism. How fucking literary. I wished I were filthy everywhere so I could feel their hands all over me, so I could be touched again and again, cleansed of my sins, stained with new ones. His hand stroking my belly drove me crazy. When Blythe finished she eyed me a moment, then grabbed the discarded hoodie and bloodied her fingertips and smeared them over my mouth.

I took her face in my hands and kissed her.

In a heartbeat the beast in me came loose. We were wolf

girls, kissing wildly with teeth and nails. Our hair fell in our faces and our fingers drew blood and we didn't care. We'd always been savage with each other. My hand found Armin's and I pulled him close and tore my mouth from hers and kissed him. He was slower, stunned. Blythe kissed like she wanted to tear me apart and Armin kissed like he wanted to make me whole again. Her teeth grazed my throat and his lips moved over mine and our limbs intertwined, mine with hers with his. I pulled away from them, breathless.

"I want you both," I said.

It was a floodgate opening. This had been in us all from the start, this mutual wanting. It had just been waiting for one of us to release it.

He brushed his knuckles across my cheek. She kissed my palm. When they looked at each other my heart stuttered. Knowingness brewed in her eyes, the way she'd size up men at Umbra. In his the old flame smoldered. The thought of them fucking each other was as intense as the thought of them fucking me.

Blythe seized my face and we kissed again, brutish and raw. I bit her lip so hard it bled, hers and Zoeller's mixing in my mouth. I ripped at the zipper of her hoodie. She knotted my hair in a fist. We were feral and we wanted to ravish each other. I drove her toward the wall and Armin enclosed me from behind, those iron arms enveloping me, around my waist, between my legs. Then we shifted and Blythe slammed me against the wall and unclasped my bra and put her mouth to my breast. My spine curved, my hands finding her face. I swore and begged for more, more. Armin slipped off her hoodie, inhaled the scent of her hair, strangely tender in the midst of our ferocity.

I don't know how we got to my bedroom. It was madness, all skin and mouths and hands. They undressed me first. Her touch was furious and rough while his was gentle, soothing. My wild girl and my sweet boy. She hurled me to the bed and held me down, her knee between my bare legs, and I rode her thigh and made her jeans wet. Then another shift and Armin and I were over her, and he took her clothes off while I dipped my tongue into her navel. Then us girls on him, our small hands on the cascade of muscle pouring over his body. She grabbed his erect dick unflinchingly, stroked it. God, that made me so hot. So hard. So wet. So I-didn't-know-what-the-fuck except turned on like all hell. The wolf in me surged and she was the one I wanted to devour. The monster always eats the pretty girl, right? I pinned her to the mattress and we wrapped ourselves around each other, hands between legs, lips fused. With girls I lost myself, all the softness and fluidity enough to drown in. I couldn't stop kissing her. Even when all I was doing was gasping into her mouth, I couldn't stop. But Armin's presence changed things, and when he clutched my hips and jerked me back against that hard cock I cried out, let go, let him take me. His hands moved over my back, my breasts. He fucked me hard but without making me feel used, fucked me like it wasn't for his pleasure but only mine, and I gave it to her like he gave it to me, obsessively, relentlessly. I took his dick so deep my whole body ached with fullness, ran my fingers along her lips until she was so wet I slipped inside like water. I don't know which got me off more. I wanted to fuck that sweet tightness out of her and I wanted him to fuck it out of me. At some point I stopped noting whose hand or mouth was whose. Identity was irrelevant. Feeling was everything. Only the slick silk thickening around my fingers, the steady strokes thrusting into the core of me. Our bodies blurred into one animal. Kissing was too overwhelming now but Blythe held my face, our eyes locked. When she got close to coming a dreamy lostness stole over her that broke me up inside, and I breathed her name and she arched against my hand, her mouth a dark half-moon tilting upward, the slender cord of her throat stretching taut. There is nothing more beautiful in this world than a girl when she comes. It's everything, our delicacy and our fierceness made one. I came then, watching her, and Armin with me. Ours was bestial, graceless. The crudeness of boy and girl. It twisted through every cell in me like some paranormal transformation, a monster briefly emerging, pushing from behind my face, shredding the inside of my skin. My blood boiled and every bone snapped and nothing was left of the girl whose skin I had worn.

Then silence, stillness. The fouled bodies of beasts inexplicably intertwined, him inside me, me inside her.

We parted. I pulled Blythe to my chest, our limbs fitting together perfectly. Small as I was, I could hold all of her in my arms. My face nestled against her cheek, softness to softness, and Armin curled up behind me and put his arms around us both. The solidity of him against my spine was the boulder at the edge of the cliff, a place I could not fall from.

The three of us had held each other like this before in the sand at the lake at dawn. We'd been in love then, too, but it had taken blood and violence to make us admit it.

"I love you," I whispered. I didn't attach a name. It didn't need one.

Armin said it back. Blythe didn't. Her hair obscured her face and I couldn't read the emotion there. Maybe there was none.

After a while we became three again, our separate, secretive selves.

"We should check on Donnie," Armin said.

"In a bit. I don't want this to end yet."

After this came darkness. Subterfuge, paranoia. Eventually the police would connect me to Z (*Did he have any enemies,*

Mrs. Zoeller?). I'd leave this apartment for the new one Armin leased. I'd pretend I didn't know the girl in the red dress Zoeller was last seen with. For so long all I'd focused on was tonight, reaching him, ruining him, and now it was done and I was hollow and all I could think was how this would end, this closeness between us. I slipped my hand through Blythe's messy hair. Those heavy-lidded eyes were drowsy with ecstasy, pure pale blue.

"You know what really got me off?" she said. "Watching you being fucked."

Armin stiffened against my back. I traced Blythe's cheekbone with a finger. Her face had a chiseled quality, the bones sharp and fine as diamond facets, her mouth chipped garnet. Indestructible.

"You got everything you wanted." Armin couldn't see her, the layered meaning in her gaze. "You got your revenge. You won."

If he was the last thing to hold on to at the cliff's edge, she was the drop. The exhilarating free fall into annihilation.

"Is it worth it?" she said.

"Laney." Armin breathed against the nape of my neck, a warm pulse down my spine. "So much has happened tonight. We're all emotional right now. Don't try to process it yet."

"We still have work to do," Blythe said, heavy with irony.

I felt strange. I'd beaten the life out of someone, fired the gun, fucked my two best friends. I was supposed to be hard and cold. Instead I fought down a rising panic like a swarm of butterfly wings stirring in my lungs. Tonight was it. Tomorrow we became strangers. It could take weeks of waiting before suspicion died down. Days upon days that I wouldn't spend with her, mocking our professors and the bad books they taught, reading each other's writing and getting high off it, getting drunk and dancing like lovers at Umbra, lying in bed with our legs tangled and quoting poetry. Nights she'd spend with Hiyam and faceless pretty boys. I turned away, burying myself against Armin's broad chest.

Days and nights of this. Me and him.

He stroked my hair and it wasn't until he said, "Don't cry, Laney," that I realized I was.

MARCH, LAST YEAR

I left the front door ajar. Zoeller followed me in but I was too out of it to care. I headed for my parents' bedroom, hand in my bag, holding the gun. Once I returned it to the safe this entire day would disappear like a bad dream.

My father sat on the bed, his shoulders concave.

I must have made a noise. He looked up.

"Sweetheart."

"Dad."

The closet was open, the safe in plain view. Clothes strewn on the floor. Things pulled off shelves. Oh, fuck.

"I thought you were at work."

"I thought you were with friends."

We smiled weakly at each other.

"Bad day?" he said.

All I could manage was a deer-in-headlights stare.

"Sweetheart," he said again, and I ran to the bed, threw myself into his arms, the bag between us. I was crying and I didn't know why. It just came over me, a seizure of grief. My limbs twisted so hard it felt like they'd pop out of my body.

"I'm sorry," I mumbled into his chest. "I'm sorry, Dad."

He patted my hair.

"I didn't do it. He stopped me. God, I'm sorry."

"Sweetie, what's wrong?"

I pulled back, wiping a hand over my face. When my eyes worked again I noticed the suitcase on the bed behind him.

Oh.

Oh.

I had lied to my father many times over the years. They were lies to spare him, things he couldn't have changed anyway. Kissing girls. Losing my virginity. Drinking at twelve, drugs at thirteen. The first time I did X. Oxy. Morphine. Heroin. Coke. Meth. The first time I speedballed. The hesitation marks on my wrists. The personal pharmacy I used to treat the rotten decayed thing inside me that made me so sick. The ways I'd tried to bleed it out, choke it, drown it, overdose it. It was un-killable, this dark seed my mother had planted.

The lie flowed smoothly from my lips.

"I was with some kids who had drugs. Needles. They wanted me to try."

Dad blinked, dewy-eyed.

"But my friend stopped me. I'm so sorry. I didn't mean to scare you."

He took me in his arms again, his .45 in my bag on his lap. For a while we just held each other.

"Please don't go," I whispered. "Don't leave us here with her."

"You know I don't want to."

"So why are you packing?"

"Your mother and I—" He sighed. "We haven't been in love for a long time. That's no surprise to you. But we stayed together for you and your brother. And you're almost grown-up now, sweetie. You're ready for college, for leaving home. It's time for both of us to set out on our own."

He trembled in my arms, crying. I stared over his shoulder at the wall.

My eyes were dry now.

He thought he could just walk away. So easy for a grown man. He wasn't bound to her by blood. He wasn't dependent. I'd be in college soon but Donnie was stuck here two more years. And this man thought he could leave my brother in the hands of a lunatic.

Over my dead body.

———

Zoeller made me stop at Jewel. It was surreal watching him push a cart down the aisles as I followed with a gun in my book bag. Like a serial killer couple going grocery shopping. In the pop section he filled the basket with bottles of strawberry Fanta.

"Do I even want to know?" I said.

He smiled.

I drove out to the boonies again, past the place where I'd run off the road, then farther, farther, till he told me to turn onto a dirt lane through a field of snow-cowled grass. A weatherworn farmhouse lay at the end. There was no visible sun but a watery blue mist of light. Z left me in the car and returned with a rusting wheelbarrow. I watched as he loaded it with pop bottles.

"Are you going to waterboard me with Fanta?" I said.

"Little help?"

It took both of us to push it up a frozen footpath to a deadwood fence. Zoeller dumped the wheelbarrow unceremoniously on the ground.

"Get your gun," he said.

When I returned he'd placed the bottles on fence posts. My heart chilled.

"Don't be a pussy."

He had his own pistol, the black Smith & Wesson he'd once pulled on me. Smaller than mine, .40 cal. He checked the mag, slapped it back in, racked it.

We could kill each other right here, I realized.

Zoeller spun and, seemingly without aiming, fired twice. Two bottles exploded, one after the other, in brilliant red bursts like liquid poinsettias. Droplets hit my sleeve, fizzing. The air turned sweet.

"Bang bang, we're dead," he said.

I stared at him, afraid to blink.

"Who'd you talk to at home?"

"My dad."

"What did he say?"

A noose of muscle tightened around my throat. "Nothing. He was packing his stuff. He's leaving us."

"Why?"

"My mom." The tightness coiled around my whole body. It felt good to be holding a gun while saying this. "She's fucking crazy."

"Actually crazy or just a bitch?"

"Bipolar. And an alcoholic. And a cunt. And I fucking hate her."

Zoeller looked at the fence. "She's the one on the left."

In a smooth series of motions I flicked the safety, racked, raised, aimed, fired. My body jolted. The bottle burst with a deeply satisfying *pop*.

"Not bad," he said.

I didn't drop my arms. I swiveled to the next bottle, correcting the recoil. "This is Dad."

Bang.

"Luke."

The sensations came so close together they were one. The kick through my body and the red bloom. The power was intoxicating: press a tiny lever and destroy a piece of the universe.

I did them all. Quinn, Nolan, Gordon. Mr. Radzen. Dr. Patel. Mr. Klein. Dead center. No misses.

Z grinned. "You do know how to use that thing."

Two left. I took aim but glanced at Zoeller.

"This is Brandt," I said.

Bang.

His eyes were bright and insane. "And then there was one."

I smiled. He thought he knew me. He thought he was always a step ahead.

I sighted on the last bottle.

Then I put the hot barrel beneath my chin.

"No." Zoeller lurched toward me, eyes wide. "No, Laney."

I curled my finger around the trigger and he froze. I could see his white sclera. I'd never seen him frightened. I was only half-serious but his fear made it feel suddenly real.

"Don't," he said.

"This is all I want. It's all I can think about."

"It's defeat. You're too strong for this."

"No I'm not." I laughed, the muzzle digging into the soft meat beneath my jaw. "I'm weak, like you said."

"You're better than me. I'm broken, Laney. I'm a sociopath."

"If you're a sociopath, you can't feel compassion. You don't care whether I live or die."

"I do. I need you. I've never met anyone like you."

I rolled my eyes. "Spare me the suicide hotline bullshit. I've heard it all before. You know what the definition of insanity is? Doing the same thing over and over and expecting different results. Well, I'm sick of this. Things are going to change."

"Don't leave me," he said.

The parallel of my words to Dad startled me. That gleam in his eyes wasn't madness. It was tears.

Was this really happening?

Look at every terrible thing he's done to me.

Look at every good thing he didn't have to do, but did.

I could've ended my life today. Killed Luke North and fired

at the police, suicide by cop. Or blown a forty-five-millimeter hole through my skull just now. I could be a cloud of cooling molecules drifting apart, losing information density, the thing known as Delaney June Keating gone back to the oblivion she was once conjured from. I was still here because of Brandt.

Maybe it wasn't so crazy. Maybe the only person who could understand a villain was another villain.

I lowered the gun.

Z tackled me, smashing me to the ground. I lost hold of the grip. He's going to kill me, I thought. Never lower your guard around a psycho. Didn't Mom teach you anything?

But he simply held me down. And after a minute, I realized he was doing just that.

Holding me.

———

Dad gave Mom an ultimatum that night:

Meds or divorce.

Divorce meant a custody battle. Her mental health history would be put on trial.

She's going back on meds, I texted Zoeller. *But it won't last. She hates it. Says it makes her feel dead inside.*

I know the feeling, he replied.

I wondered what they'd made him take. Had his parents put him through therapy and prescriptions, too? Chemical fire and sword?

So do I, I said.

What's your diagnosis?

Borderline personality disorder.

He didn't respond immediately. Then: *Antisocial personality disorder.*

Nice to meet you, I wrote, and imagined his sardonic smile. *We should have a talk show.*

You're too emotional and I don't have a heart. We make a great pair.

I thought about that for a while. *Emotion doesn't make me weak.*

Don't be defensive, he said. *You are better than you think. A-one, a-two, a-three.*

Vonnegut.

Goddammit, Brandt. Goddamn you for making it harder and harder to hate you.

Where are you going to college? he said.

Corgan. You?

Same. You'll never get rid of me now.

I stared at his text. Impossible to tell his tone.

Maybe I don't want to get rid of you, I typed, but mercifully backspaced before I hit SEND. What are you thinking, dumbass? He's still the enemy.

As I was falling asleep, he texted again.

What meds are they giving her?

Lithium.

Pause. *She doesn't have to take it.*

Dad will leave if she doesn't.

She doesn't have to take lithium.

My turn to hesitate. *What do you mean?*

You know exactly what I mean.

SEPTEMBER, LAST YEAR

She was here. I could smell her. She'd come in from the garden but I couldn't find her anywhere in the house. I ran through rooms calling for her, aware of strange tension in the walls. The house was holding a secret. Shadows pulled away from my footsteps. Halls tilted upward or sloped down or ended in walls that weren't supposed to be there. It was diverting me from something. I searched the first floor, the second. Warm and sunny and open. A game was running on Donnie's computer, showing a pause screen. A cup of coffee, still steaming, sat on the kitchen counter beside Dad's tablet. I called for them but no answer. They'd just been here. Where was everyone?

When I found myself on the second floor again I realized the house was trying to keep me out of the basement.

I came into the kitchen, my eye fixed on the basement door.

It was stuck shut. I banged on it, yelled, left the kitchen and made for the foyer to go around to the cellar, but the front door was stuck, too.

Back in the kitchen the basement was open, a rectangle of pure black.

Mom? I said.

The scent of roses led downstairs.

I went slowly. It wasn't just dark; the blackness below

seemed to eat anything that entered it, and I had a sense that what went inside didn't come back.

I put my foot on the first step. The second. Every other, I called her name.

Caitlin. Caitlin, where are you?

The cold below was bone-cracking, deep as midwinter. I felt along the wall for the light switch, groping uselessly until I was stricken by the thought that another hand would close over mine.

Flashlights somewhere. Dad's tools.

The floor buckled in a way I didn't remember and I stumbled. I found the workbench, shook a flashlight till it pissed out a weak beam.

The concrete was cracked. In places where smashed stone revealed open earth I spied roots, thick and black and gnarled. Something was growing beneath the house. Roots running wild, destroying the foundation. Dad was a construction contractor. This was the kind of thing he knew. Why had he let this happen?

As I stared at a root, it slithered back toward the depths of the basement, the lightless room with the furnace.

My feet started toward it involuntarily.

I fought my body. Please, no. Please please please.

Whatever was growing in there was big. The furnace roared but did nothing to alleviate the chill. The closer I got, the colder it felt.

Please don't go inside. Please don't look.

I stepped into the doorway.

Roots raced to the corner, scaling the wall in a fat braid. The fibers were a waxy black but here and there were odd bits of debris, glints of pearl, shiny strips of red velvet.

Delaney.

I ran the light up the trunk. The voice came from the corner.

Little one.

Oh my god.

Not pearls and velvet.

Come here, darling.

The white bits were teeth. The red ones were meat.

Come here and let me hold you.

Skin and hair. Her hair, all around me.

I screamed and turned to run and the doorway was filled with writhing blackness. I backed away, beginning to cry. Something moved in the shadows. Part of a hand, the first three fingers. The rest melted into that dark mass.

Mom, please, I said. *I'm sorry.*

Roots curled around my feet. Pulled me toward the corner.

What do you want? I cried.

Closer and closer to a whorl of teeth, a glistening bloody hole. God, no. Wake the fuck up. Now.

What do you want? I screamed.

Set me free, it said in my mother's voice. *Let me go let me go let me go.*

———

I sat up in bed, gasping. Unfamiliar room. Walls too far away, my bed an island in a frozen sea of moonlight.

Blythe's apartment. Safe. Awake.

Alone.

I collapsed onto the pillow. My camisole stuck to my sweaty skin like cellophane. Just a nightmare. Over now. I inhaled deeply, flooding my body with cold air, and something familiar tickled my nose. A cloying, coppery sweetness.

Blood and roses.

I turned my head.

The hall beyond my room was dark, but a milky haze of moonlight lay on the hardwood, broken by the thing in the doorway. By the shadow I'd know anywhere.

This isn't real, I told myself. You're still asleep.

I closed my eyes and breathed. Chills scurried up my bare arms like things with too many legs. Wake up now, Laney. Wake up.

I opened my eyes. The shadow stood beside the bed.

"Blythe," I screamed, rolling away. "Blythe. Help. Please."

I kept screaming as I ripped the sheets off and crashed to the floor. My palms slapped icy wood. I scrambled blindly, one leg caught in the sheet, snared. I hadn't even realized the room light was on and Blythe was calling my name until she grabbed me.

"Christ," she said. "Are you okay?"

In seconds it all became ridiculous. Me tangled in a sheet, shrieking like a child, her with an aluminum bat in one hand and a glare that said she wanted to use it.

I slumped against the wall. "She was here."

"You were having a nightmare."

"How do I know I'm awake now?"

Blythe's voice softened. "It's okay, Laney. I'm here. It's over."

This had happened before. I rarely remembered calling for her, but one night I woke panicking and found her asleep on the floor beside my bed, a mane of wild gold hair and splayed lion limbs, guarding my dreams. I watched her until I drowsed off again. We didn't talk about it. We were still technically not on speaking terms since I'd moved in, because of the kiss, and all that weirdness.

"Sorry," I said. "I shouldn't have disturbed you."

"I'm already disturbed."

Blythe dropped the bat and popped the window above us. Cold air shrilled in. She wore only a T-shirt and underwear and I looked away when she looked at me. She sat at my side, snatching my American Spirits from the nightstand. We lit up off one match.

"Tell me your dream."

It was too personal, too grotesque. But I never held anything back from her, so I told.

She didn't speak till I'd finished. Then all she said was "That's bloody fucked."

I missed that about her. Armin would analyze and interpret and prescribe. Blythe merely absorbed, accepted. She knew I was crazy. She was crazy, too. All writers are.

Around us the calligraphy of our smoke stroked the air, scrawling ghost secrets.

"What was your mum like?"

How to explain someone so beautiful, intelligent, and cruel? Mom was right about us inheriting separate sides of her nature. Donnie got sweetness and sunshine, I got venom and darkness. In her they were one. Sugar-tongued snake.

"Like Lady Lazarus," I said. " 'Out of the ash I rise with my red hair.' "

" 'And I eat men like air.' "

Goose bumps.

Without prompting Blythe dragged the blanket from the bed onto our legs. We looked at each other. Streetlight fell over her shoulder in a chiffon scarf, illuminating one side of her face.

"I miss you," I whispered. "I miss this."

"What is this?" she said just as softly.

I didn't answer. I drew figure eights with my cigarette cherry.

"Why don't you ever talk about your mom?" I asked.

"Nothing to say."

"She hurt you."

Blythe sniffed. "I hurt her. Told her what an ignorant cunt she is." She tipped her head against the windowsill, blowing smoke into the lemon light. "Lovely world where your own mum calls you a filthy slut who'll burn in hell."

"Wow."

"I'd fuck anything with a pulse, according to her. Maybe a few things without a pulse, too."

"Did you love any of them?"

"Just one."

I swallowed. I wished I could swallow the words as well, but I had to know. "Was it Armin?"

She glanced at me. "No."

A shiver racked me again, but it was relief.

"How long were you with him?"

"A year."

It seemed an eternity. I hadn't even known them that long and they'd had an entire year together. Sleeping with each other, sharing everything.

And she hadn't loved him. But he'd loved her.

"Why did it end?"

"I tore his heart out." She flicked her cig out the window, exhaling smoke through her nostrils in blue tusks. "Let's not talk about this. It makes me sick."

"How come?"

"Because I'm a fucking arsehole, okay? I hurt him. I hurt him so badly he's never gotten over it."

"I hurt someone, too. In the worst possible way. I'm a bad person, Blythe."

"That makes two of us."

Cool autumn air swept in, prickling our bare arms. Beneath the blanket her warmth seeped into my bones.

"Why did you kiss me?" I said.

It was impossible to catch her off guard. She was excruciatingly honest. Even a white lie was anathema to her. Her voice was calm, almost wistful.

"I'd wanted to since the night we met."

All the weight went out of my chest. It was an empty cage full of the memory of wings.

"You don't know what you do to me, Laney. You have this dark energy, nocturnal and intense. It touched something inside me that I've been holding back. My essential fucked-up-ness. My own darkness." I heard the smile in her words. "When you quoted Dickinson I knew we'd be friends. I never knew we'd get this close."

"Don't try to sound romantic. Not when you bring guys home every night. Not when I have to go to sleep listening to you fuck them."

"You really don't get it, do you?"

"Apparently not."

"You know why I fuck boys?" Her fist balled in the blanket between us. "Because I can't fall in love with them. It's just sex. I don't have to feel, I don't have to think. It's safe."

She can't fall in love, Armin had said, *and I can't fall out.*

"I hate that you do it," I said.

"Good. I'm glad you hate it."

"Do you even care how much it hurts me?"

"Hurts you?" She grabbed the cigarettes, tried to draw one with shaking hands. It broke and spilled tobacco everywhere and she flung the pack into the shadows. "You ever fucking consider how I feel, seeing you with him?"

"It's complicated. It's not what you think."

Blythe kicked the blanket off and started to stand. I grabbed her wrist and she fought, raked red down my arm. Blood for blood. But when she broke free she just knelt there, her hair in her face.

"It was never him." My throat stung, my breath merely burnt fumes. It was a fire inside me, eating me away. "I only wanted you, Blythe."

Her hands ran through her hair, viciously. Like she wanted to tear herself apart.

"I can't do this again."

Then she was up, leaving. I sat alone on the freezing floor, incredibly small.

This was never supposed to happen.

I had a plan going in.

You stick to the fucking plan.

The cold, rational part of me said let her go. It was becoming too messy, too unpredictable. She'd ruin everything. Stay cold, Laney. Stay hard. Show them all.

But a fire had awoken in me that could not be put out. And I wanted to give myself to it. Even if it destroyed me.

I ran through the shadows. Halfway down the hall I collided with something warm. For a moment it was a jumble of limbs and resistance and then hands found my face.

"I can't lose you," she said in a fierce whisper.

"Then don't let go."

I touched her cheek, her lips. We were both shivering.

"I promised myself," she said, her mouth moving against my fingertips. "I promised I wouldn't do this again."

"Do what, Blythe?"

"Fall in love."

I cupped both hands to her face and kissed her.

The first time it happens, it can be explained. Accident. Experiment. Fluke. Everything was confusing. The lines blurred.

The second time is when it really happens for the first time.

I kissed Blythe the way I'd wanted to from the very beginning. Unrepentantly, unremittingly. Nothing held back. Our teeth tapped together, those charming canines scoring my tongue. Her mouth tasted like smoke and mint and I wanted every part of it to taste like me. I sucked her lower lip till I couldn't resist the urge to bite, and she bit back. I wasn't sure if it hurt or felt good or if maybe the hurting itself was what felt good. Each time one of us backed out for breath the other interrupted, needing to be connected as intensely as possible every single second. Not so much a kiss as a consumption. No girlish coyness now. We were wolves, wild and mean. Voracious.

She shoved me against the wall, dominating with her height. I raised my face to the ceiling and she bit my neck, kissed a trail across the flute of my collarbone, bit me again. Her hands were hard on my breasts. God, this feeling. Giving myself up to boys had always felt like some kind of defeat, but when I gave myself to her, it felt completely right. I traced the sine curve of her spine, her ass, slid my thumbs inside the hem of her underwear to the velvet crease at the top of each thigh. She gasped and my head went fever white.

"Talk to me," I said.

Hot breath on my ear. "I'm going to fuck you, sweet girl. Like I've wanted to since that first night."

Her voice. Pure heroin. The most beautiful warmth I'd ever felt inside me, her whisper turning liquid, rolling through my veins.

"Why didn't you? I wanted it, too."

"You were all over *him*." One hand slipped under my shirt, cupping my breast. As she spoke her fingers tightened on the nipple. "Do you know how hard it was, holding back? How many nights I fucked some bloke on the other side of this wall and imagined it was you?"

I closed my eyes, bit my lip in pain and want.

"You are so pretty." Her mouth grazed the corner of mine. So different, a girl's face. Impossibly smooth. No friction, nothing to slow us down. "I want to be gentle, but you make me an animal."

"Don't be gentle."

She kissed me again, deeply, made me take her tongue as she manacled my wrists to the wall. Her bare leg slid between mine. I was crazy fucking wet and she knew it. Made me feel my own wetness against her thigh, made every nerve fire, electricity webbing beneath my skin. Made me. Dominated me. Hers. I was all hers.

We stumbled from the hall into a bedroom. Wasn't sure whose. She pulled the camisole over my head and when she kissed my breasts I cried out. Blythe grasped my face in one hand.

"You are the most perfect little thing. Let me hear that lovely voice again."

"Make me," I said.

She did. She took my breast in her mouth, that kiss undoing me, a line of muscle unlacing down my belly and all my limbs coming unraveled, and I thrust my hands into her hair and cried like she wanted, gave her my voice, my body, my control. I'd have given her anything she asked for.

We collapsed onto the bed. She pulled my lounge pants off and I her shirt and we rejoined, craving the opiate heat of each other. A second was too long a withdrawal. She lay between my legs, her hair a gold blur in my eyes.

"How do you want to be fucked?"

Those words unknit something in me.

"Use your hands." I circled her waist, pulled her hips to mine. "I want to see your face."

In a prism of streetlight I caught the edge of her smile.

But Blythe was never good at following rules. She used her mouth first.

Her lips marked every delicate place. Behind my ears, beneath my jaw, inside my elbows and wrists. My small breasts, the harpsichord of my ribs. I stared at the ceiling, at lilac shadows dappling the plaster. A jet passed and shook the sky like sheet metal. Her mouth moved down the hollow of my belly, over the yoke of my hips. Leaves drifted from a tree. Everything was coming undone, tearing itself into little piles of red and gold. The slow disintegration of summer. The slow disintegration of my body as she pushed my legs apart, exhaled against me. I closed my eyes. For a while I felt only heat, liquid fire pouring through my belly, and then through the heat her tongue, running down one side of me slowly, so maddeningly slowly I felt every little grain in it, every flat stroke up the center, every brush of her lips as they met over my clit and her warm breath washed through me. Then the other side, lazily, unhurriedly. Torture. Her hair tumbled between my legs and I buried my hands in it. My tension was volcanic, rising higher, higher. I made some kind of noise and shaped it into words. Easy things at first, things like "Fuck me, Blythe, please, fuck me." My voice could be so sweet sometimes, so girlish. I wondered how far I could push it. Wondered what it was doing to her. "God, I'm so fucking wet. Make me come in your mouth. Make me taste myself."

She rose above me, breathless. "Dirty girl."

I pulled her face down and kissed her. Smoke and a hint of something mineral, like saltpeter, or gunpowder. The taste of something about to explode.

Her thigh nestled between mine, one hand sliding down beside it. I could have come against that satin skin, but she slipped a finger inside and then another and my desire rose and kept rising. This. This was what I'd longed for. This fusion of soft bodies, this gorgeous sameness. These breathy voices merging in the darkness. This pretty girl all tangled up with me, our legs linked, breasts pressed together, my hands on her slim back pulling her closer, closer. "You're so fucking tight," she said in my ear. "You won't let go." Her fingers moved with murderous slowness and every time she stroked in deep I wanted to scream. Girls could fuck like this forever, hard and steady, never worrying about coming too soon, about going soft. We fucked like boys better than boys did. Her hair was in my face, smothering me, and I was so close to coming it was agony, everything too intense, every shift of the sheet against my back a mauling, every skim of hair against my throat like being choked. When her thumb brushed my clit I shuddered, but she wouldn't let me come. I fought for it, riding her hand harder. Put mine inside her panties. She grimaced. The inked shoulders above me heaved. Still she was brutally steady, slow. Misery and ecstasy at once.

"Beg me," she said, her voice rough.

I pushed her hair out of her face and looked up at her. "Make me come. Please, make me come."

We stayed like that, never breaking eye contact. She gave it to me all the way inside, her thumb hard on my clit, finally, finally letting the fire loose, letting it surge and spill through me. I fucked her with my fingers and she was already close herself and we both lost it, tangled up and frenzied and delirious, crying out one after another as our bodies twisted together, hair snarled, hands wet, hearts pounding violently as if to break through bone and reach each other.

In the aftermath I felt only warmth. Condensed heat. A wavelength of light temporarily coalescing into a girl.

We lay entwined and let our blood cool, our sweat dry. After a while Blythe put her arms all the way around me. She held so tightly I could barely move. I felt something building in her, a gathering of breath, and laid my head between her breasts to feel the words. My seashell ear filled with the tides of her heart.

"You are mine," she said.

JANUARY, THIS YEAR

CORGAN QUARTERBACK BRUTALLY BEATEN. RISING STAR SNUFFED?

I aced my first semester at CU. Straight A's, special permission to sit Professor Frawley's Advanced Fiction course second term. Each day I had a breakfast smoothie of oxy, vodka, and OJ and then staggered onto the L. Each night I went home to my condo in the South Loop, a beautifully furnished prison cell overlooking the blue eternity of the lake. Life always provides apt emotional metaphors. I wrote alcohol-fueled essays I didn't recognize in the morning. Adopted a ginger tabby and rechristened him Orion. I needed to feel another presence in the shadows, something to scare away my nightmares. To confirm whether the visions I saw were real or in my head. Each night I opened the Word document that contained half a crazed cat's cradle of a novel, the story you're reading now, and stared at the heartbeat of the cursor on a blank page, that small dark impulse against blinding white. The black seed struggling to sprout in snow. Each night I went to bed alone.

Orion gazed at me from the windowsill in my moments of sodden self-pity, my body numb, brain blown, and he looked so droll and wise it made me laugh. Everything is absurd, that face said. Stop being so serious.

He was so much like her.

VICTIM SPEAKS: DOESN'T REMEMBER ATTACK. RIVAL FANS SUSPECTED IN VICIOUS ASSAULT.

The news loved Zoeller. Nothing like a glowing golden boy torn from his Manifest Destiny to get their dicks hard.

The police interview was surprisingly mundane. Part of me had looked forward to it, misleading the cops, vibrating with expertly suppressed sins, but the reality was two hours in a drab waiting room with bad coffee and depressing celeb mags, then ten minutes at a table where real murderers and rapists had sat. I made my eyes big and said *No, Detective* and *Yes, Detective*, and the woman smiled sympathetically as if I were the victim.

I stumbled out of the station, sucking in sweet winter air. When I lit my cigarette I tasted hot saline. Depression checklist: inexplicable crying, realizing you've been awake for eight hours but can't remember a thing, talking to cats.

(*I'll tell you a love story in ten words*, I said to Orion.)

Some days I didn't eat. I confused the gnawing in my belly for hunger and fed it, but it only made me sick. Strange how much missing someone feels like hunger. How the hole they leave behind is so much larger than they were. How it grows even bigger, feeding on you.

(*Girl meets girl.*)

Once, as I cleaned out my book bag, a fragment of paper fluttered to the floor like a lost fairy wing. On it, her manic handwriting: *If the moon smiled, she would resemble you. Something beautiful but annihilating.* Her beloved Sylvia. I pressed the paper to my mouth, imagining the motions of her hand.

(*Girl falls for girl.*)

I had a short story due in Advanced Fiction but I opened and saved and closed a blank document for weeks. When I finally wrote, it was this:

I miss you. I miss you. I miss you. I miss you.

All the way down the page.

(*Girl loses girl.*)

I swallowed another pill. Before it had time to kick in, another.

Another. Another. Another. Another.

All the way down the bottle.

———

Armin and I met at a coffee shop in Evanston. Somewhere we didn't know anybody, busy and anonymous. He wrapped me in his arms and for a moment it actually felt real.

"I've missed you," he breathed against my hair, and kissed my ear.

His wool coat scratched my face. I sat down at the table.

"Are you all right?"

I gazed through the window at gray people on a gray street. Valentine's was coming, everything festooned with hearts in panty pink and *Scarlet Letter* red, and I thought, What if they were real? What if they'd been ripped beating and raw from a thousand chests? Would you show them then?

"Laney."

I looked at him.

"Are you high?"

"No."

A hundred and twenty milligrams of oxycodone purred in my blood.

He leaned across the table, that handsome face creased with worry. "Sleeping poorly? You've got dark circles under your eyes."

"Can you be my boyfriend for a minute and not my fucking doctor?"

Armin sat back as if he'd been punched.

"I'm sorry," I said.

The shrieking and caterwauling of espresso machines seemed the perfect soundtrack to this moment. I closed my eyes, summoned my softness. Reached across the table and tried to look small and needy.

"It's been really hard, not seeing you."

He covered both my hands with one of his. "We're together now."

"Yes, we are. Together."

He eyed me strangely. Maybe there was something in my voice.

"You look exhausted," he said. "How are you really?"

He looked pretty scruffy himself. His stubble had become a light beard, that artful bedhead now unstyled, legit bedhead. He wore a dress shirt that was done up one button off. It warmed the ice around my heart a little.

"I'm the same old messed-up freak," I said. "Have you seen the news?"

His eyes swept across the coffeehouse. We were well isolated by noise and space. "They bought the Kenosha story."

"He's lying to the cops. I know he remembers."

Armin lifted his hand. Both of mine had become fists.

"Why would he lie?" he said.

"Because he's Zoeller. He manipulates people because he can. He doesn't need a reason—he gets off on control."

Armin didn't say, *Like you*, but I saw it in his eyes.

"All we can do is remain vigilant," he said. "And go on with our lives. Because that's what looks normal."

"We fake it." The way I've been faking with you.

He eyed me oddly again and I wondered if I'd said it out loud.

Get a fucking grip, Laney.

"How's Blythe?" I said.

Armin glanced at the coffee bar. "Want something to drink?"

It was all I could do not to ask again while they prepped our order. I shifted weight from one foot to the other, paced a small circuit, bared my teeth at the Valentine's mugs. When Armin asked about school I growled. Finally he said, "Why don't you go for a cigarette or something?"

Because it reminds me of her. Because everything fucking reminds me of her.

"Sorry." I put a hand on his chest, rested my head on him experimentally. "I'm so wound up. I shouldn't take it out on you."

He sighed into my hair. The heat made me aware of how cold I was. I shivered and his arms circled me, big and strong and supportive.

Everything a girl could want.

I watched him pay for our coffee, pulling out that silver money clip with the familiar symbol. Two discs. Eclipse.

Falls the Shadow.

At the table I cupped my hands around the mug, bathing my face in steam.

"Blythe's scared," Armin said finally. "The cops have been questioning her. A lot." He spun his mug, frowning. "Zoeller won't ID her but it doesn't matter. She's got a record. All petty stuff, misdemeanors, but it establishes a history of violence."

"History of violence? What, they think she went from punching assholes at clubs to almost killing someone?"

"All I know is she's a 'person of interest.'"

My hands clenched scalding ceramic. The burn felt good. First real thing I'd felt in a while.

"They canvassed the neighborhood," Armin went on. "Witnesses confirmed a gunshot. Blythe says the cops are pressing her for names, asking about 'others.' Seems their theory is that it was two unrelated crimes: vandalism and attempted robbery."

"Shit."

"And it gets worse. They keep mentioning her visa."

My spine went straight as if a blade touched it. "They can't."

"I don't know what they can do, exactly. But we need to be very cautious. We can't do anything that links her to Zoeller, or you. I think it's best if you refrain from contact with her until she graduates."

It hit me in the chest like a Mack truck. "What?"

"It's just a few more months."

"It's half a year." It's eternity. "This makes no sense. Why go after her if Z's not pressing charges?"

"I don't know. Maybe she's a link between you and him."

"But they don't consider me a person of interest."

"I don't have all the answers, Laney."

If I wasn't gripping something I might've throttled him. "I can't do it. I can't wait that long."

That strange look again. "Wait for what?"

Stay calm. Maintain eye contact. "She's my best friend. I haven't seen her in weeks. Now you're saying I have to abandon her, after all of this? I can't."

"Well, you fucking dragged her into it," he snapped, twisting his mug so hard hot coffee slopped over the rim.

We stared at each other.

"I'm sorry." He rested his head in his palm. "I'm freaking out a bit, too."

You're freaking out, I thought. You're telling me I have to cut contact with the girl I love for six months.

"I won't let anything bad happen to her," he said. "I'll fight this. I'll retain the best immigration lawyer money can buy. I'll even marry her, if she wants. We talked about it a long time ago. A green card marriage. As a joke."

Steam drifted into my mouth. I was gaping.

Joke. Right.

He touched my hand on the mug. "I love her like a friend, Laney. Like you do. Neither of us wants to lose her."

You have no idea.

I didn't know who I hated more at that moment: myself or him.

There was only one way to make myself feel better right now. To combat the powerlessness I felt. To feel closer to her, in some sick way.

"Armin." I curled my fingers around his hand. "I hate when we're apart. The three of us."

"I do, too."

"We need each other. I need you. I'm not whole without you."

He looked into my eyes and spoke in that rasping voice. "Come home with me, Laney."

Something dark in me smiled.

"Yes," I said.

And I did.

OCTOBER, LAST YEAR

No matter how high I turned up my headphones I could still hear Blythe swearing. At first I'd found her seemingly endless conjugations of *fuck* amusing, but now it was after midnight and I'd written two hundred words of a two-thousand-word essay on feminism in Woolf and I wasn't so enamored. A room of one's fucking own indeed.

I found her in the kitchen. Jameson on the counter, Bacardi on the stove. Stacks of plates on the floor. What appeared to be smashed green grapes or ectoplasm on the table.

"What are you up to?" I said warily.

She looked at me as if I'd asked why kids did drugs. "Writing a poem."

There was, in fact, a notebook lurking amid the chaos. The open page was so scratched out the paper had pulped. On the intact part, a disturbing red stain that was probably, hopefully, just wine.

"How's it going?" I said.

"Bloody fucking fuck."

I stifled a laugh. "Come here, you psycho."

Her wildness mellowed, and she came with that jack-o'-lantern grin that so enchanted me. Both of us in tanks, skinny-boned and slight, her hair pinned in a messy chignon, mine loose. She circled my waist and I traced the inkless apricot skin over her collarbone.

"You should get one here."

"Of what?"

"Of me."

She moved my hand lower, to her sternum, her beating heart. "You're already here."

Now I laughed. "I bet your poem is great, full of cheesy platitudes like that."

"Bite your tongue, you Philistine."

"Why don't you?"

She kissed me.

Weeks of this would not dull me to it. Nothing would. Each time we kissed, every atom in my body floated in dazed pause, every nerve fiber separating from the rooty tangle and firing in slow motion. I felt like a cross-section of a girl being kissed, an anatomical diagram. I'd grown familiar with her ways and still she surprised me, her canines digging into my lower lip, pain piercing the sweetness. The way she'd stop and hold her mouth millimeters from mine as we traded breath, peering through the gauze of our eyelashes. The way she'd complete it, lip running against lip, teeth on tongue. Always a little too intense, too rough, and always it made me want more, more intensity, more roughness. Every kiss felt as if we returned to it from a long, unwilling parting and were desperate not to be parted again but knew we would be. Every kiss was the first and the last one.

We stopped only to look at each other.

"I adore you," she said. " 'I love you as certain dark things are to be loved, in secret, between the shadow and the soul.' "

"Neruda is for Hallmark cards. What's next, Rilke?"

Still, my heart betrayed me by going haywire. Even if she'd used another poet's words, they'd come from her mouth. Those magic three.

Blythe merely laughed and kissed me again.

We got high together, got drunk, got off on saliva and skin, and still found no way to capture this feeling. It was so much bigger than us, so brutal. Even when we fucked as savagely as we could bear, it was only the shadow of this thing between us. Killing each other would hint at a fraction of it. I couldn't fuck it out of her, couldn't bleed it out of myself, couldn't purge, drug, numb it away. Like the dark seed in me, this was a drive so deep it was embedded in my core. I had never loved a girl like this. I had never loved.

"I feel crazy," she said, running fingertips down my cheeks like tears. "I need to get out of here."

I thought she meant the apartment, into the night air, but part of me also thought she meant here, this body. This life.

Unease stirred in me.

On the roof Chicago sprawled around us in a billion blinking lights, but nothing was brighter than her. Any second she might run off over the treetops into the forest of steel and stone, hunt the moon, make arrows from animal bones and dip them in blood and shoot it out of the sky. She screamed at nothing and her voice echoed off the bricks.

"You *are* crazy," I said, laughing, but my uneasiness grew.

Blythe climbed onto the roof's edge.

"Hey." I hovered near. "Be careful."

She stood boldly, not looking down, unafraid.

"Blythe?"

"I'm so fucking alive."

"You're freaking me out. Come down."

She closed her eyes, her face raised to invisible stars. "I wish you could feel this," she whispered.

I had seen one too many suicides in my life. I was not going to watch another.

As I reached for her she tumbled. I screamed something

inchoate, not the brilliant last words I'd planned but more like *Oh fuck God no*, and her hands came down on stone, and with frightening grace she turned a cartwheel on the ledge, her all-too-breakable body balancing fifty feet above merciless asphalt.

I realized shutting up was my best chance at not getting her killed and watched her snap to a perfect landing. She crowed at the sky, palms upheld as if waiting for something to fall into them, then hopped down and grabbed me, flitting like a hummingbird. Even when I touched her skin it seemed more a dense vibration than something solid.

"This is amazing," she said. "I feel like I'm on X. Everything's so bright, so vivid, so beautiful. You're so beautiful. Kiss me."

I did, and her kiss was exhilarating and insane, but I stopped after a second. "Blythe."

She pressed her cheek to mine and it was so hard not to lose myself in the bliss of her skin on my skin.

"You're acting manic," I said.

She laughed it off, but when I looked at her soberly the laughter faded.

"I'm in love." She took my face in both hands. "It's you. You're like a drug."

I wanted to believe it. I wanted to think I had this kind of effect on her. But there was a too-bright, too-sharp glint in those blue eyes, a knife's edge twisting, honing itself.

"Come over here," I said.

I led her to a wooden bench far from the ledge, piled with pillows and quilts. Shook out a blanket that smelled like weed and cloves. Beneath it, the two of us nestling together, all I smelled was her.

"I don't want to sound like Armin," I said, "but you've barely slept the past few days."

"I'm trying to write a bloody poem."

"You've written a dozen this week."

"All rubbish."

"Okay, I totally get that. But you've also been drinking like crazy tonight. And now you just did a cartwheel. On the edge. Of the fucking roof. Blythe, seriously."

She wore her usual wry expression, but it dropped at that. "Christ." Her brow furrowed. She looked off into the night for a while. "Did Armin put you up to this?"

I slinked an arm around her waist. So strange, to feel how slight she really was. "No. I've suspected since we met. There's a spark of madness in you. Most people don't have it, but you burn."

Wisps of hair had come loose from her chignon as if some electricity in her pushed them out. "Maybe it's just who I am."

"It *is* who you are. Doctors talk about it like it's this separate thing, like a cold or flu. Something that can be cured without curing your personality, your uniqueness, your spirit. They don't understand. It shapes us so much that it's more like a scar, a deformity, on the inside where they can't see." I twirled a loop of gold hair around my finger. "I'm not Armin. I don't want you to change to fit someone else's definition of normal. Besides, it's part of what I love about you. 'She's mad but she's magic. There's no lie in her fire.'"

"I don't know that one."

"Bukowski."

"No-name American," she said airily.

I tugged her hair, and she smirked.

"Just don't leave me." My voice was small. "Not when I've finally found you after so long."

All the humor went out of her face. She was so pretty like this, when the cockiness dissolved and something girlish and dreamy replaced it, a soft wonder. The way she'd look after I kissed her breathless, after I made her come. I wanted to say something dramatic and meaningful but there was a strange intensity inside me, a fullness in my chest that made my lungs ache, so heavy it was paralyzing.

We both looked out at the city. Her shoulder peeked from the spill of her hair, the screaming mouth that was also a blossoming flower, open, yearning.

"Your mum had it, too," she said.

"Yeah."

"Tell me what it was like."

"By the time I was old enough to understand, it was full-blown rapid cycling. She was horrible to my dad. They always argued about money. She worked all the time, made tons of cash, but then she'd blow it on stuff she didn't even want. Rented expensive hotel rooms, slept with random men. Drank constantly. My dad threatened to leave, so she went on heavy meds. But the person on drugs wasn't my mom. It was a shell."

"The person off drugs was a monster."

"She said she was at war with herself, and no matter which side won, she'd lose."

Blythe tensed in my arms and I held on gently, but inescapably.

"They had kids as a last resort. I guess according to some fucked-up adult logic, becoming a mother would stabilize her and save their marriage. Instead it screwed up four lives instead of two."

Blythe frowned at something far off. "I'd never do that to you. I'd walk away first."

"Don't walk away. No matter what."

"Your mum was terrible to you, Laney."

"Sometimes we're terrible to each other. It's human nature."

She looked down into my face. After a moment she pressed her forehead to mine, eyes half-shut.

"It's not just mania," she said, her breath warm on my skin.

"And it's not some drug. This is how I feel about you, always. I'm in love with you."

That pressure in my chest felt like it was going to burst. "You're not in love with me."

"Except when I'm in love with you."

I was barely in control of myself, in possession of this body that climbed onto her lap, locked its knees around her waist. "Say it again."

"I'm in—"

My head bent over hers and I kissed her. Again, and again, and again.

Soon it was too much and I had to stop, curl up around her, and simply hold on. The blanket had slipped off and when I shivered she pulled it back over us. Her voice seemed to come from somewhere distant.

"It's cold here, Lane. This city is so cold."

My arms tightened but I knew she meant something metaphysical, not physical.

"I miss the sun. I miss the ocean. I miss my dad." Her last words were barely audible.

This was the truth of it. No matter how tightly I held, I couldn't make her feel like she was home. Couldn't make her stay. Girls touched with madness are like that, rare birds that alight in the hand, dazzle, depart.

"I'll take you there someday." A trace of her usual mischief returned. "To Melbourne. Get you tan on the beach. Get you drunk on real beer."

"Get me eaten by wild animals in the outback."

"I'm a wild animal from the outback."

"Oh my god." I shoved her away. "Go write horrible poetry."

Blythe laughed, pulling me in again. "It's all about you. You can suffer it."

We giggled stupidly, uncaringly, then like in movies there was that sudden seriousness when I stopped, looking into her face.

"My wild girl." I kissed her cool cheek. "My mad girl." I kissed her temple, her brow, her closed eyes. "I don't need anything in this world except you." But no matter how many times I said it, no matter how many times I showed her with my hands and my mouth, it would never add up to what I felt inside. It would never be enough to hold her here with me.

FEBRUARY, THIS YEAR

It was late, the white arterial corridors running cold and silent through the hospital. Nothing human stirred. Only beeping machines and arcane whirrs, MRIs scanning for mutations, centrifuges spinning tubes to isolate diseases. A vast settling of fates by computers. When they'd brought Mom to the ER it was more human: hands prodding her flesh, stabbing with syringes, shocking with paddles, but even when they restarted her heart the faces remained grim. No brain activity. That's the real death. The heart can stop and start again many times throughout a life—and it will, when you fall in love, when you fall out—but erase enough neurons and it's over.

The quiet was unsettling, the well-wishers gone home. All that remained were the desperate and devoted. I guess I was one of each.

I ducked beneath the nurses' station and into a private room, whipped the curtain across the glass.

He seemed asleep, but when my eyes adjusted I saw two faint whites amid a firefly scatter of LEDs.

"Hello, Laney," he said hoarsely.

"Hello, Brandt."

I rested my gifts on his lap. Too dark to see his face but the proportions seemed wrong, bloated. They'd done total reconstructive surgery on his jaw. Not handsome anymore.

"You look good," I said.

Zoeller laughed. It sounded as if he were choking.

His right arm was encased in plaster. Bandages encircled his neck and chest. A catheter ran beneath the sheet. He watched my eyes notice each of these.

" 'My name is Ozymandias, King of Kings,' " he said in that reedy voice. " 'Look on my Works, ye Mighty, and despair.' "

I slid the book off his lap and laid it on the bedside table. "I brought you some Plath. You'll like her. She gets inside the ugly and mundane and makes it sound biblical."

He might've smiled, but it was hard to tell with that new face.

"And I brought you a treat."

I unwrapped the box. Chocolates, expensive. From Armin. I left it there, the weight of it on Z's groin, and plucked one. His mouth opened obediently, his eyes locked on mine.

"Good boy."

I let him kiss my fingertips with dry, cracked lips.

"Happy Valentine's," I whispered.

He sucked at the chocolate, moaning softly. I watched his bobbing throat with fascination.

"I figured it out." My fingertip touched his abs and drew two circles through the bedsheet, one smaller, eating the other. "I know everything."

Zoeller grinned, something shiny between his teeth. A candied cherry.

"Very mature." I hopped onto his bed, my hands roving over the box, selecting another. He refused to swallow the cherry. "You going to eat that?"

"Only yours."

I removed it from his mouth and replaced it with a fresh chocolate.

"I'll talk. You listen." I ate one, minty. "I've got the video, too. All the dominoes are lined up, ready to be pushed. I can bring the whole thing down whenever I want."

"So what are you waiting for?"

"I'm setting up the last domino. I want it to fall hard."

"Cold feet."

I considered slapping him, but I'd done enough damage to that pretty face. Plus I didn't want the nurse to come check his racing vitals when he inevitably got a hard-on.

"I'm not the monster you thought, Brandt. I'm much worse."

"Did you fuck her?"

I picked another chocolate. "Who?"

"Artemis."

"Why, you want jerk-off material?"

He shrugged feebly. His weakness was entrancing. Even my small hands could have strangled him right now. "Can't jerk off. Hurts too much."

"How sad. Pity you can't find anyone to help." I leaned in, running a hand up his thigh. "Yeah, I fucked her. I fucked the hell out of her."

"How was it? Heard she gives a killer blowjob."

It's a good thing I didn't have a gun right then. Strangling is personal. You've got to feel it. A gun lets you make a mistake faster, before you can feel.

Besides, I enjoy visceral pleasures.

"This isn't all I can do to you," I said. "I can make things much worse."

"I'm too interesting to get rid of."

"Oh, we're not done yet. We'll meet again someday. When you're whole, and strong. And I'll tear you apart then, too."

He seemed to relish this idea.

My hand tightened on his thigh. It was thin now, wasting. We both were. "You know the difference between us? Besides the fact that I can throw a football and you can't anymore."

"Tell me."

"I'm hard." I squeezed his flaccid dick, and his eyes brightened with pain. "I will take this as far as I can. I'll hurt everyone who's hurt me. I'll make it as nasty and as awful as possible. But you—you're soft, Brandt. At the last moment, you bitched out. You could have destroyed me but you didn't. That was your biggest mistake."

I felt the stirring of an erection and let him go.

"I miss you," he said huskily.

"You miss getting beat up, you sadomasochistic creep."

He laughed. "You're the only girl who does it for me, Laney."

"Let's not get into our respective Stockholm syndromes. This is my game now."

"So how did you get the video?"

"Please. That was easy." I fed him the chocolate, let him lick the melt from my fingers. Like a dog. "I found someone as lonely as me."

JULY, LAST YEAR

I sat in a Barnes & Noble café half the afternoon reading about Arya Stark, girl assassin. My favorite George R. R. Martin character. Small, unassuming-looking, kills more people than most of the men. A girl who does bad things for a good reason. I'd been loitering there all afternoon because Chicago summers are vile. Solid objects become sponge. Every breath comes through a wet towel. The upshot is that geeky college kids will gravitate toward free sources of central air, like bookstores.

Halfway through an assassination, a voice said, "Laney?"

I looked up. Heavyset boy in a polo. Beard and glasses.

"You don't remember me, do you?" he said. "Your friendly neighborhood neckbeard? From the Pi/Phi party?"

I closed my copy of *A Dance with Dragons*. "Josh?"

The boy who'd seen me naked. The boy I'd nearly fucked.

Nearly being the operative word. I wouldn't have, because I knew Josh Winters, junior, age twenty, had broken up with his first serious girlfriend that summer and was desperate for female companionship, even more than for sex. I knew a quote from his favorite author would score major brownie points. I knew my body would linger in his mind all those lonely nights while he jerked off to tasteful soft-core porn of nerdy bookish girls. I knew he'd look for my face around town.

Because this was all in my plan.

He flushed such an enthusiastic pink I almost felt bad. "Yeah. You remembered. How are you?"

"Good." I rotated the book so he could see the title. "Just reading over lunch."

"Oh, hey. I love that series. Want some company?"

I tried not to show too many teeth in my smile. "Sure."

NOVEMBER, LAST YEAR

Blythe was disturbingly quiet in the cab. Early morning after Halloween night we'd ditched our friends, claiming she was sick, and I watched her run her hands through her hair and down her dress and over the lamb-soft leather seats, rolling hard on ecstasy. Her movements were anxious, erratic. I paid the fare and chased her upstairs but she locked me out. "This is stupid, Blythe," I said through the door. "I have a key."

She made me use it to get in.

I tracked her to the bathroom, also locked. Sat on the floor. In the knife slit of light beneath the door I saw a red shadow, her dress.

"Talk to me," I said.

No immediate answer. Then, in a compressed, angry burst as if we'd been arguing, "I don't even know you."

"Come out here."

"Fuck off."

"If you want to know me, come out here and I'll show you everything."

Rush of water, things slamming. Long pause. Then she flung the door open. She'd changed into pajamas and scrubbed off her makeup, but her cheeks were flushed from the X, lit up the way blood glows when you hold a light behind flesh, her skin blooming from within. I stood slowly.

"You've been dosing him," she said.

"Yes."

"Just him?"

"Yes."

She snorted as if she wouldn't get an honest answer anyway. "You know he'd rather be caught dead than high. Or does he know? Is this some fucked-up thing between you two?"

"Before you say anything else, come with me."

I led her to my bedroom. Left the lights off. Removed my silly granny dress and wolf hoodie and retrieved the Moleskine from my book bag.

"Blythe," I said, then realized I'd have to list a million disclaimers and qualifiers and simply handed her the notebook.

She took it to the window to read by streetlight. I watched her face.

First her scowl smoothed away, becoming blankness.

Then blankness became a small frown.

Then the frown became a gape and she paged rapidly, flipping back and forth.

"Oh my fucking god," she said.

I stood in a neutral position near neither the window nor the door. Kept my hands in plain sight.

"This is us," she said wonderingly. "Me. Everything. It's some kind of dossier."

"Yes. A dossier."

Her head rose and I couldn't make out her face in the darkness.

"Why?" she said.

I didn't answer.

She skimmed through, fingers bookmarking pages. "Fucking Christ. You knew the whole time."

She meant the photos. Herself and another girl, a redhead, skinny and nerdy, cute. Their faces at oblique angles, never quite looking at each other. But even in still photos something resonated between them. A shy smile, a longing gaze. Armin was in those pictures, his arms around Blythe, oblivious.

That girl was Elle.

"How did you find her?" Blythe whispered.

"I've been looking for you for a long time."

She dropped the notebook on the windowsill as if it had caught fire.

"You stalked me. Before we met. This is serial killer shit, Laney."

"Don't be melodramatic."

"Who the fuck are you? What is this?"

"We've both done bad things, Blythe."

"I've never done something this fucked-up."

"You have. You and her." I took a step closer, another. Blythe didn't back away. "I know what happened between you two. That's why I trusted you. That's why I'm showing you everything. Because it proves you couldn't have been involved."

"With what?" she said, bewildered.

"What Apollo did to me."

APRIL, LAST YEAR

Prescription for Keating."

I walked out of the pharmacy feeling shady as hell. Zoeller laughed as I got in the car.

"Relax. You look like a narc."

Back at his place, in the freezing RV—he said the cold helped him focus—I dumped the pills in the trash and set the empty bottle on a table. Zoeller tossed me a Ziploc full of new pills. With nail files we smoothed off all identifying marks. A pile of colored dust formed, baby blue.

"Where'd you get these?" I said, scrutinizing one. ZOLOFT.

"I've got a hookup."

"If it's actually cyanide or something—"

"It's real. My friend's a doctor."

"Right. Your 'friend' the doctor. Like your 'friend' the night club owner and your 'friend' the arms dealer. All these mysterious 'friends' who owe you favors. What are you, in some kind of cult?"

"Yes," Z said.

I rolled my eyes and filed the pill smooth.

———

Dad was on the back deck with a six-pack. Beer in one hand, but it looked forgotten. He stared across the lawn as if it were an ocean, vast and unknowable.

"I picked up Mom's prescription." I could feel the bag pulsing on the kitchen counter in nervous sympathy with my heart. "They only had generic."

"Thanks, sweetheart."

Instinct told me to leave. The less time you spend near the lie, the less chance you'll give it away. But his demeanor made me uneasy.

I dropped beside him and grabbed a can of Coors. When I popped it he blinked, then smiled.

For a while we sat silently in the cold. Often it would still be snowing on Mom's birthday. She used to say it was because she was an ice witch, and if it snowed her powers would be strong that year. It would kill the early flowers, all but the hardiest. When I was little she took me into the garden once and showed me a frozen rose, the petals an opaque red like sculpted cake frosting, furred with a thousand tiny spines of ice. It looked like something out of a fairy tale. She cupped it in her hands and told me to breathe, and for a second as it melted it bloomed bright as blood.

"Dad."

He took a sip from his flat beer. "Yeah, sweetie?"

"If she doesn't get better this time, what are we going to do?"

He didn't answer. He never could. Mom had all the answers, and they were dark, hateful ones.

I drained my can and threw it into the rosebushes. Dad grimaced. When I went inside he'd fetch it in his quiet, fastidious way, careful not to disturb the garden, to anger the demon.

"Why did you marry her?" I said suddenly.

It was more personal than anything I'd asked him in years. Mom was right about that—we hadn't known each other for a long time.

Maybe he was drunker than I thought, because he actually answered.

"I loved her fire," he said from far away. "I didn't know that I would burn."

JULY, LAST YEAR

After the set Armin was exhausted but wired. I met him as he came down from the DJ booth, handing him a red cup. Umbra was packed, mostly college kids going crazy before fall semester started, thick-necked bros in collared shirts and sorority girls flawless as walking Photoshop pics. Enough fakeness to choke on.

"I thought taking drinks from strangers was bad," Armin said, smiling that phosphorescent white smile.

"Only when the stranger is a boy."

"Oh, I see. Selective sexism." He drank, a rivulet of sweat streaking down his throat. His abs painted faint shadows through a skintight Henley. From certain angles I could not tell the difference between him and a romance novel cover.

"Where's the midnight pumpkin?" I said.

"Speak of the devil, and she appears."

Blythe flung an arm around each of us and flashed that Cheshire grin. Tonight she wore a navy dress that made her ink pop, the tats on her arms a living scarf. Her fingernails dug into my bare shoulder. She didn't seem aware of it.

"What've you been up to?" Armin asked her.

"The usual. Drinking, carousing. Rousing the local rabble."

"Hit anyone yet?"

"No, but the night is young."

He smiled. "I need to change. I'm going to run to the car. Keep an eye on this troublemaker, Laney?"

As if I could keep a comet like Blythe in check.

"I'll try," I said, and they both laughed, making me feel silly.

"Brave girl," she said.

When we were alone she shot me a sly, meaningful look. This was a language I understood. I popped the locket on my bracelet and produced two oxy pills. Gave her one and said, "I like your accent."

"I like your face."

That face went warm. "What do your tats mean?"

"You'll have to be more specific."

I touched her shoulder, the pink flower that looked like a lily but hauntingly human, mouthlike. Her skin was softer than I expected. "This one."

Blythe didn't glance down. Her eyes remained on me. "That's a secret I couldn't tell."

"What secret?"

"It's called a secret for a reason." She ran a finger under my chin and I shivered. In one slick motion, she raised that hand to her mouth and swallowed the pill.

"Armin says you can't fall in love," I said. "Is it true?"

"Armin says that because I can't fall in love with Armin."

"Who can you fall in love with?"

"Someone with whom I can share my secrets."

"Good grammar," I said appreciatively.

"It's one of my secrets."

"One down, then." My heart beat hard. "I'm already ahead of him."

Blythe switched on that electric smile. "You are fucking adorable. Do you want to dance?"

Our chemistry was crazy. I'd never met someone who got under my skin like this, made me feel I was about to touch a live wire. Kelsey didn't come close. A song I liked came on, that Digitalism/Youngblood track "Wolves," the kick drumming in my pulse, and I wanted to seize this moment, grab the wire in both hands and light my body up, but you stick to the plan. You stick to the plan.

"I should wait for Armin," I said.

Disappointment dimmed her smile. "Right."

Her midnight dress slipped into the crowd, and I thought, longingly, *There will be time to wonder, "Do I dare?" and, "Do I dare?" Time to turn back and descend the stair.*

Armin returned in a button-up, smelling like green bark and winter sky. "She give you any trouble?"

I shook my head. I could still feel her fingertip running beneath my chin.

I said I needed a smoke and we went up to a private balcony off the Aerie. Summer heat dampened the air, soaking up city lights and transforming them into hazy bokeh, shimmering amber and violet dots.

I'd tried to get him a beer earlier but he declined. He only acccpted a Red Bull after I nagged about hydration. There was nothing in it yet. Not until I had proof.

But for now, I could condition him to trust me.

"So you're a DJ who doesn't even drink," I said.

He breathed fresh air away from my smoke. "It's not for me."

"Have you ever tried anything?"

"I don't need to try poison to know I won't like it."

I shook my head. "Brainwashed."

"Trust me, I deal with enough mind-altering substances on any given day. I'm not missing out on anything in the illicit drug domain."

"That's hypocritical." I pointed at him with my cigarette. "You're fine with putting stuff in people's heads and screwing up their neurochemistry when half the time you don't even know the mechanism of action. How's that any better than weed or ecstasy? We know more about how those work than psych meds."

"People have died on ecstasy."

"People have died on Zoloft."

"We use them for a clinical purpose—"

"So do I."

Armin frowned.

"And some of your stuff is worse than mine." I exhaled into the night. "Some of it actually makes people sicker. You know how many depressed people end up killing themselves on antidepressants?"

"I've seen the studies."

"Doesn't it bother you that someone might die because of something you said would make them better?"

"You can never know that."

"But what if you did? How would you feel?"

He put a warm hand on my shoulder. "Laney, this seems very personal to you."

I stubbed my cigarette in an ash can. "Sorry. I've been watching too much news lately."

His hand fell and he rolled his shoulders, as if shaking off a troubling thought.

It was quiet for a while.

"Blythe is strange," I said.

"She can be eccentric."

"I think she was flirting with me."

He looked at me sharply. "Why do you say that?"

Because I was flirting back.

"I don't know, just a vibe. Is she, like . . ."

"Who knows what she is." He sighed, leaning against the railing. "I've asked myself that so many times. I wish she'd just decide."

You're still in love with her, I realized. It all made sense. The brotherly way he acted toward me, how he wouldn't kiss me, wouldn't respond to my frank advances. He still wanted her. And she didn't want him.

She wanted me.

"She's really pretty," I said vaguely.

"What about you?"

"Am I pretty?" I said, laughing.

"You're beautiful." His voice was sincere, but it didn't move me. "But I mean, are you into girls?"

"You asked me that before, remember? The first night I met you."

"You didn't answer."

"Is it that important?"

"Yeah, actually, it is." His face clouded. "I've been hurt before by someone who wasn't honest. So I need to know where things stand. Where you stand."

The lie came easily, like a boy.

"I'm straight, Armin."

It didn't assuage him.

"Be careful around Blythe," he said.

"Why?"

"She's ruthless."

And I thought, Perfect.

NOVEMBER, LAST YEAR

We faced each other across the bedroom, me in the shadows and her in the light, like always. I could not see her face and she could not see mine.

"Why didn't you tell me this before?" Blythe said.

"Would you have believed me?"

"Christ."

She walked away from the window and then back. Cast a mournful glance at me, a word forming and dying in her mouth. I took a step closer. My room smelled like her now. There was no more division between us.

"That first night," she said. "You knew."

"Yes."

"You weren't looking for Zoeller."

"I was looking for you and Armin. Artemis and Apollo."

I heard the breath she released. I took another step.

"You used me, Laney. Manipulated me into becoming your fucking roommate, your 'best friend,' your—whatever I am to you now."

"Yes."

She cringed like she'd taken a blow and I did, too.

"I don't know you at all," she said.

"I could've kept you in the dark. You never needed to be part of this."

"Why didn't you?"

Another step toward the light. "Because something changed."
I put a hand on her shoulder, soft as breath, and she didn't
flinch. Unbearable, being this close with a chasm between us.

"What?"

"I fell in love with you."

She let me touch her face, my fingertips tracing the wish-
bone of her jaw, her slim throat. I lay my lips on the carotid,
felt it beat against me. All the life in her gathered there against
my vampire mouth.

She pulled my face up to hers. "Was he really the one you
wanted to dose tonight, or was it me?"

"I never did it to you. I never had to."

"You used me."

"You wanted me from the start. Like I wanted you." I
brushed her hair aside, cupped her cheek. "It was always different between us. We were never just friends."

She watched my mouth move. "How do I know any of this
was real?"

"You don't know. You feel it."

Blue eyes met blue. Two hunters in the night, circling.

"What do you want from me?" she said.

"Everything." My hands moved over her shoulders, down
her chest. To her breasts, the caged heartbeat thrashing between them. "I want you. I want the badness in you. I want
the craziness, the animal. I'm going to hurt them all, Blythe.
Every single person who's hurt me. And you'll be there at my
side."

"You drugged me."

"I didn't, I promise."

"You drugged me," she repeated, her fingers wrapping
around my neck, "with your skin, and your hands, and your
mouth. You're in my veins. My blood." Her lips were a breath's

width from mine, her wolf teeth bright. We teetered on the delirious brink of a kiss. "You poisoned me, and it feels so fucking good. I want more."

My breath came fast. "Will you do it with me?"

"Yeah, I will. I'll fuck this world up with you."

"Good girl," I said. "Let's be bad."

I tore off her clothes. I tore off every shred of resistance she still held. And I fucked her, wild and rough, animal, like the monsters we were.

———

A couple stumbled out of the bar, arm-in-arm. Drunk. It was a dive in Aurora called O'Malley's, a low building at the edge of the woods. Winter peeled the trees clean and left them looking like charred bones. I huddled in the truck bed beneath a blanket. The text ten minutes ago had said, *Soon*.

The couple passed into a circle of streetlight and she tossed her head. He said something in a deep voice; she laughed.

My hands tightened on the rubber grip.

Blythe danced a few steps forward, coyly. "You're trying to take advantage of me."

"I'm a perfect gentleman." He followed, a massive lumbering shadow.

"A perfect gentleman with a wife."

When he caught up she disappeared into his silhouette. He murmured something I couldn't hear. Blythe gasped and shoved him away, and he laughed and came after her.

The chase was on.

She retreated to the truck, leaned up against the bed. I kept my face swathed in the blanket, peeking through an eye slit.

"I shouldn't do this," she said, slurring. "I don't fuck married men."

"What *do* you do with married men?"

She laughed. Pushed him away playfully. He came back with force, crushed her to the truck and swallowed her face in his huge hands. Kissed her. So hard the chassis rocked and I gathered my legs to jump out, but then I noticed her hand on the rim of the bed, one finger raised.

Wait.

The longest eight seconds of my life.

Blythe tore her mouth away, moaned like a porn star. "You drive me wild, baby."

I watched that raised finger as if it were a sword over his head.

"Get down on your knees," she said.

He laughed, gravelly. Blythe didn't. After a moment his mirth died.

"I want to show you something," she said, opening her coat.

"Let's go to my car."

"I need to show you now, baby. I'm so fucking wet."

He sank to the ground, staring up at her.

I would have, too.

"Good boy." She touched his face. "Oh, almost forgot."

The finger fell. I shook the blanket off, put the grip into her open palm.

"This is for hitting my girlfriend," Blythe said.

She smashed the butt of the baseball bat into his face.

He dropped onto all fours on the asphalt. I vaulted out of the truck, landing lightly. My legs tingled from euphoria and lack of circulation. In the harsh light his blood looked oil black, a violent stripe on the ground, a dark web in his beard.

"Mr. Klein," I said.

He looked up at me, watery-eyed, stunned.

I spat in his face.

Blythe tossed the bat in the truck and wiped her mouth.

Lifted his chin, surveyed the damage, and ripped the gold chain from his bull neck.

"Early birthday present," she said, tossing it to me.

"You're so sweet."

We got in the truck, laughing cold, glassy laughs, hard as ice, high as fuck on what we'd done.

Blythe turned to me with bright eyes. "Who's next?"

———

I'd only been gone half a year but already Naperville South looked aged and quaint, like a yellowing photo. We climbed through a window to the indoor track. Shadows stretched over the turf. I stuck to the moonlight. At night all schools are haunted. Blythe wandered from me and it was ineffably strange, her being here, where my mythologies began. We took up position in the outside lanes of the track.

"Race you," she said.

I knew better than to hesitate. I darted off.

"Bloody cheat," she yelled after me.

I'd run track in school before I decided my best sport was drugs. I was faster but Blythe was taller. She caught up, grabbed my shirt, spun me out, and we tumbled to the floor, loose-limbed and flushed. She held me down, her hair in my face.

"Bloody cheat," I said.

She kissed me.

My heart seized, conditioned with fear. This was where I'd learned to hate myself. To survive in a cage. I closed my eyes and thought, Fuck you, Naperville, and lost myself in her kiss. Two girls, cherry-mouthed, glitter-lashed, our skin luminous with moonlight and sweat, making out beneath pennants that still shivered with the afternoon's boy bravado.

If only you bastards could see me now.

"Show me what it was like," Blythe whispered in my ear.

Our phones lit the halls spooky spectral blue. We climbed the catwalk above the auditorium, where I'd smoked weed with Donnie and colored my shoes with Sharpies and dreamed of places I'd escape to someday. Then into the underground disaster shelter where our lights fell on crumbling concrete that looked torn up with claws, rust-stained pools of water smelling weirdly like blood. I used to tell Donnie ghost stories down there, before Mom died.

"It wasn't all bad, yeah?" Blythe said.

It felt weird being in the guidance office again, even though it was empty. They stamp that fear of authority in you with permanent ink. Blythe marched straight to the door marked J. RADZEN.

She burst into laughter at his selfies. "Christ, no wonder you're so warped."

After a dozen tries we couldn't guess his computer password.

"It must be something simple," I said. "He's a dumb pedo. Look at that mustache."

"Try something in the room."

"This isn't TV, Blythe. It's not going to be right in front of our—"

We both glanced at the ceramic fish on the desk.

She typed BIGFISH. Access granted.

"Oh my god." I shouldered in. "Let me do the honors."

Insert thumb drive. Copy-paste. Mr. Radzen, please enjoy ten gigs of the finest Barely Legal Boys. Blowjobs, handjobs, anal, bondage—a fine mix. Plenty of servicemen for your pleasure.

Blythe blew a kiss at the fighter jet photo.

When the upload finished I sent an email from Jeff's account to the entire school board (*FWD: SUPER HOT!!!!!*)

and attached a JPEG of the youngest-looking boy we'd found deep-throating a massive veiny dick.

"You are evil." Blythe slid her hands up my ribs, cupped my breasts. "It turns me on."

I tucked the ceramic fish into my bag. A souvenir, like the necklace I now wore.

"Ever fucked anyone in school?" she said.

"No."

She grazed my ear with her teeth. Her hands were unzipping my hoodie. "Shame."

I had one more memory to make there. The one where I sat on my guidance counselor's desk, my bare ass on the blotter and her face between my legs.

———

The final night of our spree was so cold it felt like the sky would crack open. We huddled together in an alley behind the bar, our faces and fingers numb. The hardest part had been finding the opportunity. Until I remembered the Blackhawks hat.

The game had ended hours ago. We'd tailed him from the stadium to the Billy Goat Tavern, watched him shove cheeseburgers into his face and laugh with his meathead bros while we shivered on the street. At midnight his friends split and he continued on to the Cobra Lounge, alone.

Chicago had a quiet grandeur at night, the streetlights gold sequins pinned to a vast blackness, redbrick warehouses marching up Ashland Avenue. This late the streets were dead. Every now and then people stumbled into or out of cabs and the Green Line screeched on the elevated track, grinding sparks, filling the air with ozone.

Blythe hadn't wanted to know details beforehand. "Surprise me," she'd said.

I would.

No weapon this time. Nothing but this great old city to do my bidding.

"There he is," I said.

Jeans, parka, hockey cap. Indistinguishable from a dozen other guys who'd left the bar, but you never forget someone who's hurt you.

We rose, worked the pins and needles from our legs, watched him meander and stare at his phone. When he paused near a taxi, I swore, but he moved on. Blythe and I pulled our hoods low and followed, our shadows sliding down the street like stilettos.

He walked beneath the baroque wrought-iron lamps to the Green Line station. It was a throwback, Queen Anne style, lacy metalwork and bay windows. We waited half a minute and then padded up the steps after him. I stopped Blythe before the top.

"Borrow his phone," I said. "Act drunk. Drop it on the tracks."

Those cool polar-blue eyes didn't blink.

"No fingerprints."

She stared a moment longer and went up.

Winter air washed over the platform. Far away a siren screamed, a thin ribbon of agony fringing the edge of the night. Here it was quiet. I lurked behind the turnstile and watched.

Blythe bent to tie her shoe, her hair spilling from her hood and dangling over the tracks. No missing her tight ass in those skinny jeans.

Blackhawks Hat glanced at her, at his phone. Back at her.

I smiled.

She looked around as if only just realizing where she was. I couldn't see her face but pictured her biting her lip, the same way she'd bite it when my fingertips slid down the hot velvet of her belly.

"What's up, girl?" Blackhawks Hat said.

Blythe sauntered toward him and began explaining, between flights of giggles, how she'd lost her phone at a bar.

As she closed in I mirrored her, clicking quietly through the turnstile, staying behind him. Just like Umbra. Wolves circling, moving in perfect sync.

"I only need it a minute," she said. "I'll give it right back."

Blythe touched his phone, her sleeve covering her hand.

Something spooked him. He jerked away. She followed, caressing his chest, but he fended her off.

"You trying to rob me?"

"What's your problem, mate?"

"Get your hands off."

Blythe caught my gaze over his shoulder. I shook my head. Abort.

Something jagged glinted in her eyes.

No, I mouthed.

She drove him backward, her hands on his coat, angling him toward the platform's edge. At the last second he sensed it and seized her.

"Cut it out, crazy bitch."

"Fuck you," she said, giving him a slight shove.

He shoved her back. Hard.

I bolted forward, shouldering him aside and reaching for her, but her heel caught the edge and she tumbled onto the tracks, boneless as a rag doll.

I jumped down without a second thought.

Bare rusting rails. A shape lay in the shadows, a scrawl of dull gold.

God no.

Six hundred volts of raw electricity coursed through the

third rail. If someone touched it, there was nothing you could do. Nothing. Not unless you wanted to die, too. In the darkness I couldn't tell if she touched it and I couldn't touch her and I was about to fucking scream.

"Bloody hell," she groaned.

I grabbed her under the arms, euphoric with relief. "Get up. Come on. You are so fucking crazy."

The guy's shadow loomed over us. "Worst thieves ever."

Blythe's hand closed on my wrist. Her eyes touched something above me. The security cam.

It couldn't see us down on the tracks.

"I saw you push her," I said, glaring up at the silhouette.

"Still trying to run your scam?"

"You're on camera. Help me get her up before a train comes."

He hesitated. His head turned, the cap pointing toward the exit.

"If you leave her here, they'll find you. You'll rot in jail the rest of your life, asshole."

He climbed down, muttering.

I kept my hood low and face averted as we lifted her onto the platform. Blythe hammed up the drunkenness, cursing, smacking at him. She swung blindly and knocked his cap onto the tracks.

"Shit," he said, bending over.

Our eyes met.

"Luke," I said.

He froze, fingers outstretched between the second and third rails, where his hat had fallen. "Holy shit. I thought you looked familiar."

"I'm one tough cookie."

And I pushed.

There was no sound. That was the strangest thing. Six hundred volts going through a body should sound like *something*, but all I heard was the weird stuttering moan he made, the drum of shoes on wood. No flash, nothing to tell what had happened except the silent convulsion tearing through him.

You can't touch someone on the third rail. Not unless you want to die, too.

But I'd pushed with enough force to carry him backward, and his hand lost contact with the rail after a few seconds. He sprawled motionless between the inbound and outbound tracks, facedown. Wisps of steam rose from his jacket. I heard the faint hiss of heat escaping into the cold.

"Jesus fucking Christ," Blythe said behind me.

It registered that I might be looking at a corpse.

I turned to climb up and she thrust out a hand without another word.

"A man fell on the tracks," I told the station attendant in a bizarrely calm voice. "I think he was electrocuted."

In the same way I'd lost time on the morning of Mom's death, I lost slices of reality here and there. Suddenly we were in a cab and I was staring down at my hands, which held a cap that they turned over, and over, and over.

Killer's hands.

Earlier I'd spent hours researching third rail deaths. It wasn't just the voltage but the duration of contact that killed. As when being shocked with defibrillator paddles, touching the third rail could stop a heart. Flatline. Whether that heart started beating again depended on various things.

Like whether the Norths had a family history of heart problems.

Like how fast someone could administer CPR.

I sat in the taxi holding his hat and thought, How poetic.

I literally broke his heart.

———

We stayed up all night watching the news. The story aired at dawn. *Loyola student in serious but stable condition after Green Line fall. Police ask witnesses captured on camera to come forward. Tonight: The Dangers of Underage Drinking.*

"And then there were two," I said.

Blythe's arms wrapped around me. I kissed the inside of her wrist, felt the fury of her pulse.

"Are you going to kill him?" she said.

"Who?"

She wouldn't say. But we both knew.

———

I told you what I was when we began. I'm the black iris watered by poison. The wolf that raised its head among sheep and devoured its way, ruthless and bloody, to freedom. I never forgave, never forgot.

I didn't feel sorry. I felt bad. As in *bad girl*, not guilty. And feeling bad made me feel so fucking good.

"What are we doing?" Blythe said, tugging at the chain around my neck.

"Going over the edge."

She put her mouth on mine and kissed me as if nothing mattered except this kiss. When I began to lose myself in it she withdrew, her lips wet and wine red, drunk on me.

"I knew you'd love falling," she said.

I pushed her down to my bed and kissed her temple, cheekbone, throat. Pulled her shirt over her head, pinned her wrists to the mattress and pressed my lips to every inch of that smooth fawn-gold skin. Kissed her breasts and made her body ripple beneath me like a sheet of silk. Her hand snared in my hair, plucked every nerve in my spine. Greedy girl. Nothing was ever enough for either of us. I kissed a trail down the lee of her arm, up the inside of her thigh, across her belly. Felt the ribbons of muscle furl tighter. Left my saliva all over her, my clear venom.

"'What did my fingers do before they held you?'" I murmured, changing Plath's words slightly. "'What did my heart do, with its love?'"

"You're becoming very good at this."

"At what?"

"Making me fall for you."

Her mouth drove me crazy. I kissed it and bit her lip and wished I could gash it open, bleed out that vivid redness. Laced my arms with hers, blank skin against inked. God, she was so pretty.

"Who are you really?" she said.

"You know all my secrets. I've shown you everything."

"Not everything."

I held her hands down. "You know the darkest parts of me. That's who I really am."

"Her little black iris."

Something unpleasant coiled in my belly.

"Why did she call you that?"

"I don't want to talk about it."

"You never do."

"My skin," I said, staring at the sheets twisted beneath our hands. "The scent reminded her of irises. I don't know why. I never gardened."

I could still smell it, rain on petals, and that dark luscious air rising from the earth, a perfume swarthy with secrets and shadows.

"What did she grow in her garden?"

Me.

"Roses. Deep red, with thorns like talons. Things that were beautiful, that could hurt you with their beauty. But her favorite was the black iris. It's the darkest purple, so dark it's black unless the sun hits it just right, and it has these folded, sensuous petals that look like—well, like a girl, you know, the inside, both pretty and obscene, like—"

"Like this." Her thigh slid between mine.

"God. Yes. Fuck. Do you want to hear this or not?" Blythe laughed, stopped. Wrapped her arms around me. "When I was small she'd brush my hair and say, 'My little black iris is growing.' When I got older she'd catch me curled up in a corner in a mood and say I was wilting. And at the end, before she died, she called me that so I'd know she was sorry for making me this way. This dark thing. Fucked-up, innately flawed."

"You really think she saw you like that?"

"She saw her darkness in me. I think she wanted me to find a way to live with it, the way she never could. My entire life, I've felt infected by her. Like she made me into something that can only produce more darkness."

"That's not who you are," Blythe said.

"Who am I?"

"My little wolf." She traced my jaw, the ridge of my knuckles. "All teeth and claws. Cunning, and fierce, and insatiable."

My blood warmed.

I leaned in to kiss her and she grasped my head, put her mouth to my ear. Her voice was thick, almost drunk.

"I love you," she said. "Whoever you are, whatever you are, I love you."

I kissed her crazily. Her mouth. Her skin. The blade groove between her ribs, the soft stretch of her belly. The sheen of blond down shimmering over her skin. Slid my hands between her legs and spread them apart like a reverse prayer. The gold cross dangled from my neck, a cool brand against the heat of her thighs.

"I want you inside me," she breathed.

She raked her fingers through my hair, held my head.

When I gave her my tongue she cried at the ceiling. Fucking a girl is heaven. All the lines blur. It's pure softness, darkness, warmth. Her thighs against my face, her clit between my lips like a cherry stone. Her wetness all over my mouth. *Tell me what I taste like*, she'd said once, and I couldn't. What word is there for the way summer tastes, that accumulation of sunlight in the air like a head of sweet foam, the snap and fizz of fireworks, heat that never relents? *I'm not a poet*, I'd said. *I don't have your silver tongue.* She'd laughed and said, *You do when you stop talking with it.* God, it was crazy. Us. This. This girl was mine. She let go of me and grabbed the pillow beneath her head, the bed frame, seeking some anchor to the real world, and I ran my tongue from the hot core of her up to her clit and back again. Hands on her thighs, holding her open. The movement of her body was a second language. I read every semantic shift of muscle, knew when to flutter my tongue, when to slow and suck. When to give it to her hard and when to brush softly, girlishly. When to slip my fingers inside. Her voice above me was a spell. As she got close every thread in her tightened, her legs tensing around me, nails shredding the sheet, and I stayed steady and she arched against my tongue, crying out, her heat filling my mouth. She gave herself to me, completely undone. Nothing else was this beautiful. Nothing.

I would do anything for you, I thought.

Blythe grasped my face and kissed me. Clutched me to her chest, clawed a hand down my back. We were a mess of wild hair and wet mouths and slick skin.

"Fuck," she said, and began laughing, deep in her throat. "Fuck, fuck, fuck."

She threw me to one side of the bed and held me down. She was charged, electric.

"Let's go get him," she said. "Right now."

"Zoeller?"

"Yes."

"You're crazy," I said, gazing up at her with wonder, and slight apprehension. "We have a plan."

"I am crazy. There's a demon inside me. I could kill someone tonight."

My nails framed either side of her face like wolf claws. "Hold on to this. What you feel now." I scraped them down her skin, lightly. "Zoeller's easy. But the one after him won't be."

Our friend. Our sweet, sensitive boy. The one we'd both fucked.

The one I was still fucking. Pulling him in deeper.

"It drives me mad," Blythe said, "seeing his hands on you."

"Good."

"That's how you want me, isn't it?" Her fingers knotted in my hair. "Desperate and jealous. Willing to kill for you."

I kept quiet.

"How does it feel," she said, "fucking someone you don't love?"

"You know how it feels. You fucked him when you loved Elle."

Her grip eased. "Are you really going to hurt him?"

"Are you?" I raised an eyebrow. "Remember what you said? 'If someone hurts her, then we hurt him.'"

"We have a history, Lane. I can't. But I won't stop you."

"Watch the video."

"I don't want to see it. I'm already fucked-up about this."

"So you're taking it all on faith." I tucked a lock of hair behind her ear. "Faith is dangerous."

"I've been known to live dangerously. Impulsively. Recklessly." She shackled my wrists with her hands. "That's what you love about me."

I love everything about you, I thought. My beautiful mad girl.

"What would you do for me?" I said.

"Anything but that."

"Show me."

Blythe held me down, her bare legs tangling with mine, hair obscuring her face. All I saw was that blood-bright mouth.

She smiled.

MARCH, THIS YEAR

We stayed in the Chinese restaurant till closing, drinking cup after cup of green tea. The walls rippled with red silk, spotlights flaring along the pleats like lit-up muscle. I forced down a few spoonfuls of egg drop soup. My body was too wired with adrenaline and heartache to eat more. In the warm glow Blythe's face looked angelic, fallen. Had it always been so thin, ligaments moving beneath the skin when she gave a weak smile, like puppet strings?

I tipped our server a twenty and he left us alone with a polite nod.

Blythe eyed the crisp bill. Her voice was sad. "Armin taking good care of you?"

"Of us both."

Looking at her was unbearable. I tore my napkin into small squares, then smaller, smaller.

At first she'd been the usual blast of TNT, freaking out in the bathroom, vowing seven types of revenge, *I'll find whoever it is, I'll bloody kill them*, etc., until I grabbed her and made her calm down. My touch always focused her, honed her scatter-shot energy into a laser. Before things got too intense we sat at the table to talk.

"You know who it is," I said. "It has to be Hiyam. She's behind this."

"Why would she blackmail again?"

"People never change." I dug the tines of my fork into my thumb. "We commit the same sins over and over."

Like you with Armin, I didn't say. Breaking his heart twice. Once with another girl, once with me.

"What about the blokes we hurt?"

"Klein wouldn't. Not after hitting me. Radzen is clueless. And Luke's brain is too fried. He's lucky he's still got any short-term memory."

"Zoeller."

"I saw him last month. It's not him."

"His mates?"

"He doesn't have any real friends."

Bluntly, she said, "Your brother."

"Donnie has no motive. He adores me, and you, and even Hiyam. He doesn't have a bad bone in his body." I shook my head. "It's her. She's had a raging girl crush on you since forever. She always resented me for taking her place."

"You didn't take her place," Blythe said, and our eyes struck for a second, explosively.

I took no one's place. There was only me, in the cavern I'd hewn with my bare hands, in the deepest reach of her heart.

"She saw us," I said. "When I moved in, and on Homecoming, and Halloween. She's known the whole time. She might even know about the X."

"We weren't exactly covert."

"I couldn't be." Ten inches between our fingertips on the tabletop. I felt each one. "I couldn't control myself with you."

Blythe bared her teeth. It was not a smile. "You could've just texted, you know. Found some other way to tell me."

"I had to see you. To see that you're okay."

She laughed, still showing teeth. "Do I look okay?"

Neither of us did. I counted the bones through my skin,

heard my own voice like an echo of someone else's. I couldn't sleep without a head full of oxy and even then I couldn't sleep, drifting in and out of daydreams. Her hands. Her half smile. Sometimes I woke in Armin's embrace, panicking, for a moment smelling blackberries until he stroked my hair and it went away, and I was alone. The tighter he held me, the more alone. My body was a thin sheet of paper I could crumple and tear from my bones.

Blythe wasn't herself, either. She clutched her teacup with scarecrow hands. Her eyes were bruised with shadow, the irises pale platinum, all color washed out. The furor and glee that once animated her face were gone. Armin said she hadn't written in months, turned in a poem for class that simply read, *Fuck this*, said something awful to Hiyam that actually made Hiyam cry but which he wouldn't repeat. One morning he found Blythe drunk in her backyard in a blanket and she chased him to his car, screaming. Her depression was the angry, destructive kind. The Mom kind.

The downstroke of the bipolar pendulum.

I never wanted this. I wanted to keep her safe, but not like this.

The restaurant lights dimmed. An anxious face peered at us from the kitchen door.

"Let me walk you to the train," I said.

It was still raining, misty, the sky sighing a cool breath over us. We'd nearly killed a boy on the Green Line when we were cold and hard as diamonds, but it was a lifetime ago. All I felt when I took her to the turnstile was every hairline crack in my body.

"Come with me," she said. "We'll leave all this behind."

"I can't."

The rising roar of the L in the distance.

"You can. Just take my hand."

"I can't, Blythe. I've worked so hard for this. I have to see it through."

"I read your manuscript." Her eyes were bright now, but glassy. "You left it behind when you moved. I wanted to chuck it but I read it instead, a little bit every day, like a psalm. As long as I read, I could still hear your voice. And in my mind you still felt the things you wrote."

"I still feel them now."

Did I actually say that? She didn't seem to hear.

"You left it unfinished. That's the agony. I have to know, how does it end?"

I took a step closer, my hands outstretched. "I don't know."

"Is this a love story or a hate story? Is it about me, or your bloody revenge?"

"I don't know." I crashed to my knees, clutching at her wrists, her fingers.

"Answer me, goddamn you."

Rewind.

I hadn't moved, hadn't spoken. I stood paralyzed and silent several feet away. My mind had gone off to a fantasy world, the line between real and not-real blurring with fuzzy eraser strokes of oxy.

"That's your answer, then," Blythe said. "Revenge is what makes you happy."

"It's not about happiness. It's about getting the poison out."

I'll never forget the way she looked that moment in the fluorescent light, her face haunted with shadows, the arriving train stirring eddies of cold air that lifted her hair and curled it around her throat. Never more beautiful, or more alone.

"Do you still love me, Laney?"

With all my bitter heart.

But if I said it this would end here. If I said it she'd make

:3

me stop before I hurt him. Before I put the last drop of poison into his veins. So I stood there, wordless, watching something fracture in her face, watching her push through the turnstile and run up the steps without me.

I am the hollow girl.

Down on the street I slumped against a concrete pillar beneath the L and lit a cig. A cab idled at the curb. My eyes met the driver's, both of us blowing smoke dragons into the rain.

"Where to?" he said when I got in.

In the romance-novel version of our lives, I go to her apartment. Throw myself on her doorstep, tell her I've realized the folly of my vengeful ways, we are meant to be, let's run away tonight, I love you, I love you, I love you.

In real life I went home and crushed four random pills into a lowball of Stoli.

I drank it leaning on the wet balcony railing. The tumbler slipped from my fingers, a glass bullet firing down at the ground. I heard it smash a windshield, the whoop of a car alarm. Armin would pay for it. Armin would take care of everything. Armin would make sure Blythe was okay, because money, not love, is what saves.

My phone buzzed.

I pulled it out with tingling fingers, relieved. Her. Unable to let go. I'd call another cab. I'd be there in mere—

Unknown number.

The photo was of us at the Red Line station as we parted, her hand half-raised. Both faces clear. Skeleton girls. Emaciated and raw, shorn down to bones.

The message was the same as the first.

I SAW YOU.

But this time it kept coming. Or maybe I was hallucinating, my head heavy, tipping woozily over the rail.

I SAW YOU.

I SAW YOU.
I SAW YOU.
I SAW YOU.
My phone buzzed endlessly, demonically, until I ripped the battery out.

———

This is what addiction looks like.

Alone in a suicide forest, trees with screaming faces, rain that burns like salt. So high I don't even feel high anymore. I feel detached, totally outside my body. Depersonalized. Like I always wanted.

No feeling. No body. Nobody.

I'm Nobody! Who are you?

If you finesse it you can ride the edge. Vomit the initial badness out, then take some Dramamine and chase it with more oxycodone. Wash it down with a shot of Patrón. Up you go again, back to the beautiful numb plateau. Consciousness without feeling.

I know what you were searching for, Mom. The same thing I want.

To live without pain.

But the only way to live without pain is to live without feeling. Or to not live.

I don't know why they call it a downward spiral when you're rising up, up, up.

This was everything I'd dreamed of for so long. Get to him. Get inside him. Dig my fingernails into his soul and rip him inside out. And I was in there now, my claws wet with heart pulp, my fangs sunk gum-deep into hot meat. The wolf mid-feed, drenched in gore. As soon as I whipped my neck he'd tear in half. I had him. I was ready for the kill.

But I already knew it wouldn't be enough.

I became addicted to everything I tried. Drugs, girls, violence.

For a while, hurting them helped. Klein's fat face spitting blood. Luke's surprise as he fell backward onto a lightning bolt. Zoeller's bones breaking into a thousand pieces inside that pretty skin.

Temporary fixes. Nothing satisfied me.

And it wasn't really the hurting that I loved. It was after. The audacious realization that *we got away with it*. We took revenge. We walked away unscathed. Me and her.

All I'd really loved was her.

And all I had now was drugs that were making me sort of crazy.

There was a shadow in the apartment. It followed me from room to room, folded into corners, slithered into tile cracks. Orion would sit and gaze at it sometimes, untroubled. It wouldn't hurt him. It was there for me.

I saw things. Things that were there, but not as they really were. A pile of clothes on a chair was a crouching human shape. The hat on the counter was a head peering at me. I got so jumpy that Orion left the room when I came in. Going out didn't help. On the train, in class, I saw faces in the corner of my eye, twisted and snarling, gnashing teeth. When I turned it was just a girl scrolling her phone, a man reading a book.

I couldn't look at anything.

"This building is filthy," I told Armin when he came to see me. "It's full of bugs."

Spiders in every shadowy nook. Sometimes a centipede, horrifying, huge, running across a blank wall.

"I can't live here."

"I'll take care of it," he said, combing his fingers through my hair.

Orion and I stayed in a hotel while they fumigated. Unbelievably, the hotel was full of bugs, too. A wolf spider crawled onto the sheet when I let a careless hand sprawl. I didn't sleep.

It was a relief to go back to the condo.

"Laney," Armin said as we carried suitcases back in, "what exactly did you see?"

"Things with too many fucking legs."

He paused, backlit by the hall light, face obscured. "They didn't spray. They couldn't find anything."

In the corner of my eye, a black squiggle skittered up the wall.

Don't look. It's not really there, you fucking psycho.

"Laney," Armin said again, more carefully, "what are you on right now?"

"Can you stay here tonight?" My voice sounded small. "Please?"

He scooped me up in his arms and carried me to bed.

We lay with the lamps on, me atop him. Made out for a while with a doomed urgency, a sense of things accelerating toward an end, leaving marks with teeth and stubble, but when he took my shirt off I started shivering and the shivering became crying and he just held me, which was what I'd wanted to begin with.

Why didn't this feel good anymore? I used to love it with a nasty satisfaction. I used to feel so powerful, knowing what was in my hands. That I could crush it anytime I wanted.

Come with me. We'll leave all this behind.

Armin stayed the night. As I dozed, my head filled with silly memories, things that used to make me happy. The time the three of us were walking to the beach and stumbled into an alley with amazing acoustics, and Armin sang backup while Blythe and I belted our lungs out to "Total Eclipse of the Heart." Or that drunken night I told her, "Talk Australian to me," and she rattled off every clichéd phrase she could think of from *fair dinkum* to *no worries, mate* while I feigned a swoon and Armin caught me in his arms, laughing. Or when he taught me how to greet someone in Persian, ever patient, and I tripped over my tongue and Blythe fell on the couch in hysterics and Hiyam listened appraisingly, giving unexpected encouragement.

Fake. All fucking fake.

We were never happy together. We were liars, all of us.

Why couldn't I get high enough to block it out? You can only go so high before cardiac arrest.

On lonely nights I sat on the beach by myself, the sand cold as ice dust. No hands to hold me. Alone with my incipient victory. Alone with my hate and my hollow white-shelled pill of a heart.

Forgiveness is weakness, Mom said. *The weak forgive because they have no power to do anything else.*

Don't be weak, Laney. Don't be a fag. Pussy. Coward. Don't be what you really are. Look what happened before when you opened your heart. When you loved.

I was hard and brittle when Armin texted.

They sent me one, he said.

Sent what?

You know. Her too.

Blythe. Those two, talking. Discussing this without me.

Paranoia swelled. How would I know if you're both lying to me? What if she told you what's coming, what I'm going to do?

Would she?

We all need to meet, he wrote. *You know where.*

The three of us back at Umbra. Where everything began.

When?

Tonight.

I stood, a cloak of pale sand falling from my legs like snow. Shook my shoulders, felt the sharp kiss of winter on my skin.

A ghost-eye moon stared down at me, unblinking. I raised my head.

Did I howl? I'll never tell.

———

Umbra had an Ides of March theme going on. Dancers in slashed, bloody togas swept through the halls, sipping goblets of wine. Every hour they reenacted the murder of Caesar in the Cathedral.

The irony was not lost on us.

They were there first, Armin in a V-neck, clean-shaven, impeccably handsome, Blythe in snug leggings and a loose sleeveless top, gorgeously sulky. I wore my usual nerdy skinnies and plaid. Nothing special. This could've been any night.

Just like old times.

They were talking when I arrived, but broke off and stepped apart. I joined them in a cone of hot cherry light. We looked like characters in film noir, all shadows and lurid red highlights.

The last time the three of us were together in one place was the night we'd hurt Zoeller. The night we'd fucked each other.

That same dark energy sizzled between us now.

"We need somewhere to talk," I yelled over the bone-jolting bass. "Private."

Armin seemed to sigh. His eyes closed for a second. "Follow me."

Down to the Oubliette, where I'd danced to his music, her touch. Where the three of us had been careless and free. I trailed a hand along the brick wall, remembering. Things would never be like that again.

I knew the room before I stepped in. After a series of abrupt turns and seeming dead ends we came to a hidden door that opened onto a long, rectangular chamber. Armin pulled the chain on the single bare bulb. It looked exactly how I remembered: an old wooden bar at the far end, taps rusted shut. Tarnished mirrors leaning behind fat fresh candles. Ladder-back chairs arranged in a circle.

I dropped my bag and locked the door behind us. On the inside panel, the Umbra eclipse logo was sketched in chalk.

Armin retrieved a box of matches and we all lit candles. Light flickered weirdly through the room, casting skewed, startling shadows, as if there were more people here than merely the three of us.

We took up positions at triangle points in the circle, like in truth or dare.

No one spoke.

Dust in the air suspended marks the place where a story ended.

I saw it in both of their eyes. They knew that once this began, it wouldn't stop until we'd all been torn apart.

Armin sighed again. "We each got one, Laney."

They held up their phones. On Blythe's was a pic of me and Armin getting out of a cab, his hand on my waist, possessive. That day we met for coffee. I'd spent the rest of it in his bed while he kept me warm. On Armin's phone Blythe and I were walking home together, hands linked, heads tilted close. Autumn, the leaves a tessellation of fire. We'd begun kissing in the stairwell and barely made it to her bed before we'd fully undressed.

"Huh," I said.

Armin looked at me a long moment. Then at Blythe. Then he said, "I got more."

He scrolled through pics. I didn't need to see. The blond and brunette blur. Me and her, together. Damningly.

"I got more, too," Blythe said, flashing her phone at us. Me and him going into apartments, coming out, hair tousled, mouths swollen. Post-Zoeller.

"Huh," I repeated, mesmerized.

"Care to explain, Laney?" Armin said in a tight voice.

Blythe was angry about something. "I'm the one owed a bloody explanation."

"You?" he said.

"Me, yeah. You told me it was over."

"That's hardly the issue. Because what I see here is that you did it to me again. *Again.* After you promised it was nothing."

"You arsehole. *You* promised *me*. You promised you wouldn't touch her."

"So you could do this behind my back? Fuck you."

"No, fuck you, Armin. *Fuck you.*"

I stared at them, dazed. Perfect, I thought. Hiyam set us up perfectly.

I'd never given her enough credit.

Blythe leapt to her feet, paced through dappling shadows. "I can't fucking believe this, you lying bastard."

Armin gazed at me. His eyes were dark and full of knowing. "How long has it been going on?"

"Has what?" I said, at the same moment that Blythe spat, "September."

We looked at each other, me and her.

"September," Armin echoed.

"Yes," I said.

My hands tingled. I'd done some oxy but not my usual dose, and this wasn't a chemical high. This was . . . *feeling*. Fear. Anxiety. Exhilaration.

"I've been fucking her since September," I said in an even tone. "I lied to your face. I never loved you."

The first domino teetered. I held my fingertip against it, giddy.

Armin sank into the chair as if all his bones had melted. He exhaled, not a sigh but a sound of release, long and mournful.

Blythe moved toward him, amped. "That's right. The whole bloody time."

"You did it to me again."

"I didn't plan to, but it happened."

"You fucking did it to me again."

She loomed above him. "You always hung it over my head. You never forgave me. What did you want from me?"

He sat up and gripped her forearms, bronze on gold. "I wanted you to give a shit. About what you did to me. To us."

"Christ's sake, I've apologized a million times."

"You never meant it once. And here's the proof, Blythe. You didn't care, so you did it again."

She reversed his grip, dug her nails into his skin. "You don't want me to apologize. You want me to lie."

"I want you to be a human being who feels remorse."

"You want me to pretend I love you."

Armin sat back, his face contorted with pain. "How could I have been so blind? How could this happen twice?" That smoky voice wavered in a haunting way. I'd never heard him cry before. "It was right there in my face, but you convinced me I was imagining it. Convinced me so well, Blythe. So well."

Except Blythe was a terrible liar.

"What is he talking about?" I said.

She spun toward me, her eyes shining. Tears. "Fuck this. Fuck him. Let's just go."

"Not yet."

I turned my phone in my hands. Armin eyed it with a distant expression. He did not seem quite present, as if part of him had receded from the moment and floated in an empty, remote space. I knew the feeling.

"Apollo," I said.

The feeling inside me was incredible. Like petals opening up, a dark place receiving light for the first time.

This was the real moment I'd been waiting for.

"You know what's on here, don't you?" I said.

"No."

"Yes, you do. You've known this was coming for a long time."

That handsome face looked weary. "Show me, Laney. Go ahead."

It's crazy, that the defining moment of your life can be nothing to someone else. Like an infatuation, an unrequited love, every bit of you is drawn to it, orbits that heaviness at the center of your universe, everything you think and feel revolving around it and yet, nobody knows. Even the one who caused it. Especially the one who caused it.

I fetched my bag. Inside, two objects, one glass and one metal.

"First we're going to play a game," I said, in the grand tradition of every villain ever. "You'll like it. It's called truth or dare."

I set the bottle down carefully and turned. And like every villain ever, I raised the gun.

APRIL, LAST YEAR

It rained all day. April was wanton and cruel like that, mixing dull roots with spring rain. Which is an apt antidepressant metaphor.

"She's getting twitchy," I said, kicking a stone into the river. Raindrops dotted the surface, a million needles pricking silver skin.

"That means it's working."

Zoeller walked beside me. Our breath fogged in the chill. Ever since the pill switch we'd been watching her like a science experiment: Mom, cooking in a petri dish full of Zoloft. Nothing happened the first few weeks, but as we neared her birthday the tics began. Footsteps pacing the halls. Overtime at work, then awake all night at home. Once she was up till dawn working furiously in the garden. In the morning I found the early irises plucked bare, gathered into a neat heap of indigo petals.

"I'm pretty sure she's manic," I said.

This was the danger with bipolar people: the depression was soul-crushing, the blackest black, more intense than "normal" depression, but if you gave them antidepressants it could swing back the other way into mania.

Which was precisely what we aimed for.

"She'll snap," Zoeller said. "Wait for it."

I had my phone ready at all times to film one of her episodes. Some night she'd drink too much, pick a fight, put me in a chokehold or try to throw me out again, and I'd capture it in glorious HD. Insurance. If she and Dad split, she'd never win custody. She'd be kicked out of the house and Donnie wouldn't be alone with the Gorgon while I went to college.

The perfect plan, all tied up with a little bow.

Except something nagged at me.

"What if she does something really fucked-up?" I said, ducking under a branch. Rain dripped off the trees in sterling bracelets and crystal charms, piling on the ground, melting into mirrors.

"Then get your dad's gun."

The idea of pulling it on her seemed absurd. She was too big, too mythical.

Zoeller saw it in my face. "You're still afraid of her."

"I'm not afraid for myself. I'm afraid for Donnie." Z offered a hand to pull me over a pool but I ignored him. "She'll keep making excuses to refuse treatment. She's selfish and likes her mania too much to give it up. Besides, she never wanted us. She only had us as some kind of life insurance policy for herself."

"Your mom is too vain to destroy something she created."

Harsh, but possibly true. "So just cross my fingers and hope she doesn't kill her darlings."

"Or control her breakdown."

I paused, quicksilver rippling around my feet. "What do you mean?"

He wouldn't say more till we reached a bank of black mud where the cobblestones ended. Spring threw the river into a frenzy, tearing dead leaves and branches loose, all the clotted, brooding thoughts of winter sweeping away. Z crouched at the waterline.

"Come here."

I approached warily. His lessons tended to involve attempted murder.

"Give me your hand."

I snorted.

Z waited, patient.

I gave him my damn hand.

His was brutishly huge but the skin was smooth, surprisingly so. He pried my fingers open, rubbed the cold out. I jerked away.

"Stop being such a dyke."

Not even worth a response.

Zoeller placed a stiff, ice-crusted leaf in my palm.

"Land it on that," he said, nodding at a boulder jutting midstream.

"How?"

"Figure it out."

"It's impossible."

He rocked back on his haunches, bored.

This was a Zoeller puzzle. There was some trick.

My first thought: lesson in humiliation. He wanted me to wade in and place it by hand. But ever since we'd confessed our personality disorders he'd softened toward me a little, no longer so casually cruel. He showed legit interest in my life. In his deranged way, he was helping me deal with Mom.

If this kept up, I might actually start thinking of him as a friend.

God.

For the next fifteen minutes I made a complete ass of myself.

I threw leaves like a child, and the wind blew them back into my face. I rigged them on sticks that snapped in the current. I found a loose string and made some kind of fail slingshot that nearly took my eye out. I slipped in the water twice. By then I was too incensed to feel the cold.

"How do I fucking do it?" I said.

Zoeller beckoned me back to the shore. When he took my hand this time, I didn't balk. He placed the frail stem of a frozen leaf between two fingers and pinched them closed.

"How?" I said again.

Our faces were unsettlingly close. I could feel his breath when he spoke. "Let go."

I looked at the rushing water, then back at him. "You are a total waste of time."

"I'm serious."

"This is another dumb thought exercise in how you can't control anything and life is meaningless, random pain. I never should've read you Eliot." I started to stand.

His hand contracted. "You control when you let go."

We both looked at the water. It was chaos, wild and elemental, madness. But if you looked long enough you could discern threads, slick silver, jet black, splitting and merging and weaving in a living loom. There were patterns, if fleeting, ephemeral ones.

His thumb pressed down, opening my fingers. The leaf whisked away and rode a fat black swell and slapped itself onto the side of the rock.

You're fucking kidding, I thought.

When I looked at Zoeller he was still uncomfortably close, and my heart sped up. Anxiety. He was, after all, a sociopath.

The rain that had been weak and skittish all day thickened.

"Shit," I said, standing. I felt weirded out, off-kilter.

We headed for the car, silent, but halfway there the rain became a downpour and we ran, splashing through puddles and throwing ourselves, soaked, onto Mom's spotless leather.

My hands shook. It took three tries to get the key in the ignition.

"What are you feeling?" Zoeller said.

"I don't know."

It wasn't the cold, or not just the cold. Something was out of balance inside me. Something moving fast, accelerating. Skewing my center of gravity.

I'd always thought the way to get free of Mom was to become stronger than her, but it wasn't that at all. The way to win was to let go. Stop caring. Stop trying to control everything. Let it flow. Look for the opportunity, the current that could carry me where I wanted to go.

Let it happen, Laney.

This thing you want.

I drove to his house.

The mansion was lit up like a church, dazzling rays of gold piercing the pewter haze. We walked through the rain to the dismal RV in back.

Freezing inside, like always. That cold chemical smell. The creepiness of it all, the least safe place I'd ever been.

Zoeller glanced at me and stripped off his sopping hoodie. Then his shirt. Milk-white skin, molded by muscle. A faint trail of blond hair disappeared below his belt.

When he reached for the zipper of my hoodie I didn't move.

"No kissing," I said as he took it off. "Just fuck me."

"All right."

That was the last thing either of us said that night.

———

In the morning I walked home in runny makeup with a depressing taste in my mouth and my head full of weirdness and found my mother hanging in the garage.

I knew. I knew how unstable and dangerous she was. I smoked a cigarette and thought, Is this the only way I can hurt her back?

The only way I can free us from her?

So I watched Lady Lazarus writhe on that cord. Filled my lungs with smoke while hers starved for oxygen. But she didn't come back, not then, not one year in every ten, not with flaming hair to eat men like air. Her throat cinched shut, pulled tight by ten feet of braided nylon and the infinite heaviness of the dark seed inside her.

I could've saved her. Saved us both.

But I let it happen.

I let her go.

———

At the hospital they fed me Xanax to calm the panic. Which was good, because the highest risk of confession lay in those first few hours.

Whirling lights. Flashing chrome. White sheets.

A frantic burst of activity in the ER, paddles to her heart.

The grim faces, the shaking heads.

Time of death: 6:36 a.m.

At 6:36 in the morning she'd be walking through the garden with her coffee, trailing fingertips over the rose leaves, sucking the sweet dew, the bead of blood from a hidden thorn. Smiling mysteriously at some wry internal observation she'd never share. Lifting her face to the pink sun, caffeine singing in her veins. Beautiful and terrible. Alive.

Her face was so still. More consummate than sleep, a stillness that would never change, the still point of the turning world. I stood at the glass ER doors, screaming, beating with my fists until red smeared the clear and they dragged me away and gave me more Xanax and a white blank space opened in my head.

By afternoon I was totally unhinged. I hadn't eaten or slept in two days. Everything blurred—Zoeller, Mom, Donnie sobbing his heart out, Dad crying, everyone so sad, so fucking sad because I took her away.

Autopsy, a white coat said. *Toxicology report.*

Confess before they figure it out. Before they accuse me of a cover-up.

Jesus God. This was real. This was a real thing that had happened, was happening. Would keep happening for the rest of my life.

A thousand times I opened my mouth, and they stuffed drugs in it. The one time in my fucking life when I didn't want to be high, and everyone kept getting me stoned.

They marveled when the initial dose didn't work. They put in more until I stopped grabbing their coats, their collars.

Send me a fucking priest. Someone take my confession.

Go home, Dad said. *Both of you.* He had to stay and fill out paperwork. The dead generate a lot of paperwork.

His eyes looked through everything like X-rays. He did not see me trying to spit out the truth.

Donnie never stopped crying. Not once. When the energy left him it was just water, leaking endlessly down his face.

And me, Laney Keating, the killer, driving him home.

No one had taken down the noose. I found that out when I pulled into the garage.

———

I pounded on the thin metal door until it began to dent under my fist.

Zoeller opened it, blinking. Naked except for boxers, hair mussed. His eyes cleared when he saw me.

"Laney."

I stood in the cold, my hands hanging uselessly, staring up at him.

"What's going on?" he said.

I couldn't get words out. What words were there for this?

I stood there, mute and limp, until he drew me inside and

sat me on the couch. Just because we'd fucked last night—a lot—didn't mean there was any tenderness between us. He sat on the armrest, watching me curiously. Emotions fascinated him. Things we can't experience personally are always fascinating.

"Do you have anything?" I said.

He rummaged in a cupboard and handed me two pills. I didn't even care what they were. I swallowed them dry.

"We did it."

His head tilted, almost avian.

"We killed her." The words fit strangely in my mouth. "She's dead."

"Who?"

I spoke in a slow, dull voice. "My mother is dead. She hanged herself."

Compression of the carotids. Rapid unconsciousness. Night sweeps in from the edges, sound blurring into an ocean roar. The world shrinks smaller and smaller to a pinhole of light, to the diameter of the last artery still feeding blood to the brain, to a singularity where all you have ever dreamed and felt condenses into one bright, trembling speck, then closes.

My palms smacked the coffee table, bracing me from a fall. Zoeller's arms wrapped around me. Too woozy to fend him off.

"I'm fine," I said.

As soon as he let go I collapsed to the floor in a dead faint.

I woke on the couch. Z sat in an armchair nearby, watching. He'd put on sweatpants but no shirt. His body was meat. I felt nothing, not even revulsion.

"When was the last time you ate?" he said.

I tried to sit up. Something invisible pushed me back down.

"You're dehydrated. At least drink something."

Water bottle on the table, and a peanut butter and jelly sandwich.

I chugged the water. When I put it down I wanted to puke.

"What happened?" Zoeller said, his voice hushed.

"We triggered her mania and she killed herself."

If I just said it enough, maybe it would stop sounding so real. It would become a fact, a thing in a book, not my real life.

"Tell me about it."

So I told him. How I'd watched unwittingly. Found the note with my name. The sick realization, when it was over, that this was not what I had wanted at all, at all.

"What did the note say?"

"I couldn't read it."

He seemed to understand. "What did she look like? The body."

I straightened, suddenly awake. "You sick fuck. You're getting off on this."

"Tell me, Laney. I know you want to tell me."

"Her face was fucking white. There was no blood in her head. It pooled around her throat in a necklace the color of a deep bruise. The vessels in her eyes burst. Is that what you want?"

I stood, forcing the tears down. My hands raked through my hair.

"We have to tell them. It was an accident. It wasn't supposed to go this far. We can explain."

"Did you know?"

I looked at him askance, fearfully. "Know what?"

"Was she still alive when you got home? Did you let her die?"

This was the question I couldn't answer.

I didn't know. I didn't know if it was intentional. I didn't know if I fully understood what was happening, if keeping my feet on the porch and finishing the cigarette was an act of murder, or innocent apathy.

I knew I hated her that morning. I knew that much.

"It was an accident," I whispered again.

Zoeller eyed me with dispassion. "We're not telling any-one."

"They'll find out we switched her meds."

"They won't find out anything. Your mom had a prescription for Zoloft."

Even in my fugue, this struck me as odd. "What?"

"My friend the doctor took care of it. He called in a favor."

I gaped. "You covered your ass. You anticipated this."

Z said nothing.

"Don't you feel the least bit sorry? A human being is dead because of us. My fucking mother."

"You don't see the gift I've given you, Laney. You're free."

I stared a moment longer. Then I flew at him.

It was pointless. He was twice my size. I was weak and crazed. He spun me around, crushed me to his chest, his hard body. I recoiled.

"You sick fuck. You actually think this was a good thing."

"I set you free. You don't see it now, but you will."

I bit his hand, hot red salt. He let me go.

"Is this what you wanted all along?" I screamed. "To make me kill her? Was this all some sick game? Pretending to like me, messing with my head?"

Only once did I ever see Zoeller look regretful, and it was then. His bloodied hand hung at his side, forgotten. There was something almost rueful in those dead green eyes.

"Smart girl."

A chill went through me.

"Look back, Laney. Think hard. Did you really believe Luke could organize that anti-bullying shit? Did you believe Kelsey actually wanted to fuck you? That she'd ever tell her asshole dad?"

An ax lodged in my chest, snapping through me rib by rib.

"Did you believe I was starting to care?" He moved closer, gazing down at me. "Letting you in, trusting you? Sharing my thoughts and feelings?" His face was too close to mine, his breath cold and scentless. "Did you believe I fucked you because I felt something?"

I couldn't speak.

"I don't give a shit about you. I just wanted to see how far you'd go." Zoeller laughed. "You killed your mom. For me. Because of me. What a psycho."

I looked around the trailer for something sharp. "You are dead. I'll fucking kill *you*."

His hands shot out, clamping onto my shoulders, and I fought but there was no point. He put me on the couch where he wanted, under him. This is not even happening, I thought. This is some nightmare. Not real.

"Look at me," he said. I looked. "Now say it. Say, 'You ruined my life.'"

I didn't want to be here anymore. In this sad little scene. In my body, in this universe.

"Laney."

His voice was a hiss. He put his mouth near my ear.

"Say it. For the camera."

Another chill. Deeper.

"You ruined my life," I said, robotically.

Zoeller's arms flexed, drawing me closer. "If you want to know why, find Artemis and Apollo." He pressed a finger into the hollow of my throat and traced something. Two circles. One big, one small, eating the other. "Figure it out. You're a smart girl."

I stared at the fluorescent tube overhead. His body lifted, his shadow sliding over me. Then he left the trailer, left me alone in the light.

JULY, LAST YEAR

I handed Josh the flask of Jack, grinning. "C'mon, you wimp. I'm like one-quarter your size. You can't quit already."

He made a sour face and sipped. "I'm gonna puke, Laney."

"Not on me." I rolled to the other side of the mattress.

I was in Josh's room at the Lincoln Park house, sprawling on his bed, watching *Game of Thrones*. Every time we saw tits, we took a drink.

Fifteen minutes into this ep and we were sloshed.

"You remind me of Varys," Josh said.

"Are you calling me a eunuch?"

"No, you just—you know things. You're like the spider at the center of the web, pulling all the threads."

I raised an eyebrow enigmatically.

When Josh no longer resembled the next stop on the Vomit Comet I slung my leg across his, nonchalant. Then an arm. Then I was atop him. He bit his lip, put his hands on my breasts.

"I don't think you really like this," he said.

"Shut up. Let's make out."

He held me, but tentatively. "Can I ask you something? I apologize in advance if it offends you."

Oh god. Here we go.

"Are you gay?"

I flung myself off him. Pressed my face into the mattress.

"I'm sorry," Josh said. "I didn't mean to—"

"Offend me. I know. You haven't." I raised my head. "You're a good guy, Josh."

He eyed me cautiously, that broad face kind, open.

"I'm not gay," I said. "I wish I was."

"Why?"

I flipped over, air puffing out of me. "I wish there was one word for what I am. That would be so much easier. People would still hate me, but at least I could say, 'You hate me because I'm gay,' not, 'You hate me because I'm a five on the Kinsey scale, and sometimes I fuck guys but I've only fallen in love with girls.'"

Josh paused the TV, the screen dimming.

"If I was gay," I told the ceiling, "I wouldn't need an asterisk beside my name. I could stop worrying if the girl I like will bounce when she finds out I also like dick. I could have a coming-out party without people thinking I just want attention. I wouldn't have to explain that I fall in love with minds, not genders or body parts. People wouldn't say I'm 'just a slut' or 'faking it' or 'undecided' or 'confused.' I'm not confused. I don't categorize people by who I'm allowed to like and who I'm allowed to love. Love doesn't fit into boxes like that. It's blurry, slippery, quantum. It's only limited by our perceptions and before we slap a label on it and cram it into some category, everything is possible." I glanced at Josh. "That's me. I'm not gay, not bi. I'm something quantum. I can't define it."

"You're just human."

I started to laugh. "Thank you. Seriously, thank you. You are the first guy I've met who gets it."

What a bitch I was, using him.

But as the girl I was falling in love with would tell me someday: a bitch is a woman who gets what she wants.

"My turn." I sat up, cross-legged. "Explain why you're in

a frat when you're way too intelligent and open-minded for these assholes."

We talked late into the night, lying together on his bed, and it never felt awkward. It was like chilling with my brother. I turned it in my hands, the invisible Rubik's cube Z had left me with. Pieces were beginning to line up. I wandered around Josh's room, scanning his bookshelves. Lots of YA, surprisingly. Lots of John Green, unsurprisingly. The literature of sensitive nerds nursing crushes on manic pixie dream girls. I grabbed a money clip from the bureau with his ID.

"Let's see your school photo."

"Oh god. Laney, please."

My thumb brushed the eclipse symbol on the clip. "I've seen this before. This is from Umbra."

"You go to Umbra?"

"I'm friends with DJ Apollo."

Instantly his demeanor changed. He came to my side, frowning, tense. "Apollo? Are you serious?"

I flipped the clip back onto the dresser. "What, is he like some major douchebag?"

Josh's eyes darted after that silver gleam.

I watched him struggle. That's the hardest part, letting them fall on their own. Not pushing. His reservations buckled under the bond we'd built.

"Come sit down," he said.

We sat.

"I'm going to tell you something you can't tell anyone else. Anyone. It could get me in massive trouble, but I think it's right for you to know. You're not safe with him."

"Who?"

"Apollo."

"What? Why?"

"Laney, do you know what Eclipse is?"

I glanced again at the money clip.

"It's a secret society at Corgan. Most of them are members of Pi Tau. You know, rich kids, all-star athletes. It's very prestigious. They recruit guys still in high school, groom them to become masters of the universe. If you're tapped your life is pretty much set." Josh sighed. "My dad was a member, so I am, too, but I hate it. A lot of them are bigots. They talk shit about gays, women, people of color. It's like a locker room. Anyway, you make connections. Business, politics. Nothing outright evil, just sort of unethical. You scratch my back, I scratch yours. But they do some really messed up stuff, too. Hazing. Stuff that ends up hurting people. Innocent people."

"Okay," I said. "What does any of this have to do with me?"

"Apollo is the leader. And he hates girls like you."

"Girls like what?"

"Girls who like other girls."

MARCH, THIS YEAR

I found a dusty glass at the bar and brought it back to the circle. It felt like we were in the center of the Earth, far from the din of Umbra above.

Long ago I'd decided my villainy would not extend to things like tying people to chairs, remote detonators, final countdowns, etc. Our feelings for each other were the only tools I needed to make this hurt.

Well, and the gun. Just to make sure.

"Armin," I said, settling the .45 in my lap.

"Truth."

"Good boy. When did you first meet Brandt Zoeller?"

His teeth flashed in a grimace. "We don't have to do it like this, Laney."

"But this is more fun. Don't you agree, Blythe?"

She looked troubled. It was rare to see her wrestling with something inwardly, something that didn't simply explode from her in a burst of truth. What was I missing?

"You already know," Armin said.

"But I want to hear you say it."

His teeth ground harder.

"You seem tense. You need a drink." I unscrewed the bottle, poured a finger of tequila into the glass. "Bottoms up, Apollo."

He downed it without hesitation.

"Never take drinks from strangers," I chided.

"What's in it?"

"That's not the drink you should've worried about."

He frowned at me, then at Blythe. She averted her face.

"So," I said. "We were discussing Zoeller."

"Laney, I didn't know."

"Didn't know what?"

Veins bulged in his neck. An ugly pain kept twisting up his throat, creeping into his jaw, but he fought it back. "It was a mistake. I wasn't myself. I'm sorry. I am so—"

I stomped my foot, startling them both. "Give it a rest. This isn't drama club. It's AV club. Let's watch a short film, boys and girls."

I played a video on my phone and tossed it onto the floor between us. It spun, tiny voices whirling from the tiny speaker. I'd seen it a hundred times.

On the screen, a gangly teenage boy knelt before a man in a black robe. Candles, flickering shadows. This very same room we were in. The man in the robe wore a deep hood, his face a hole. He spoke in a familiar rasping voice. *Initiate, your brothers charge you to swear a sacred oath . . .*

"Christ," Blythe said, leaning closer.

Armin didn't look at the phone. His gaze locked with mine. "Turn it off. Let's talk. I didn't—"

"Shhh. No spoilers."

The first boy was charged to score a blowjob from Blythe.

The second boy was charged to have anal sex with Elle.

The third boy was Zoeller.

Blythe watched the screen, her eyes apocalyptic. Armin looked like a cornered animal.

Initiate, the man in the robe said, *your brothers charge you to swear a sacred oath of fealty beneath the umbra that darkens the sun. Will you pledge your shadow to us, brother?*

Zoeller looked up. *Yes, my lord. How may I serve?*

The robed man paused. With the others his words had been stylized, scripted, but now a spasm of emotion racked him. Maybe he was responding to the zeal in Brandt's eyes. He shed the formality.

You're young, initiate.

Yes, my lord.

Your father sent you to us early. He fears you are on a wayward path. The robed man shook his head. *But I don't see callowness. I see virility. I see strength.*

Zoeller bowed his head humbly.

Show me that I'm not wrong, initiate. You will demonstrate what befalls liars and deceivers. Find a girl. Find one of those fucking dykes, one who denies it. Seduce her. Fuck her. Ruin her. Take everything from her, everything she cares about. Make her regret what she is. Do you understand?

Zoeller's eyes shone. *Yes, my lord.*

Initiate, the robed man said.

My lord?

Make it hurt.

The video ended.

For a second none of us looked at each other. It was too much, this undoing.

I made myself meet Armin's eyes.

His face was no different. Still the gentle, handsome boy I'd always known. But there were tears in those eyes now, a film of gold gel in the candlelight.

"Armin," Blythe said, then clenched her fists on her knees, shuddering, as if holding in a terrible violence.

"When did you realize it was me?" I said. "The girl he found."

"Last year." His words were thin and torn, falling apart in the air like cobwebs. He was a ghost of the man in the video. "Truth or dare. When you said his name."

"Did you suspect before then?"

"Yes. But it could have been coincidence. I wanted it to be coincidence. More than anything I've ever wanted in my life, Laney."

"All of this was because of *you*," Blythe snarled.

"Because of *you*," Armin shot back. "Because of what you did to me, Blythe. For an entire year. Behind my back, in front of my face."

"It was a fucking mistake. I can't keep apologizing my whole fucking life."

"Who was the mistake, me or Elle?"

"Bloody both of you. It doesn't matter. It didn't give you the right to do this."

"No, it made me crazy with pain. It made me do something I regret with all my heart."

"You don't know what craziness is."

"I do. It's love. I fucking loved you."

They were screaming at each other. I'd never heard Armin raise his voice like this.

"Do you realize you told him to violate her?"

"I was violated, Blythe. What you did to me, that was a violation. You betrayed me. Physically. Emotionally. With that lying snake, that disgusting—" He bit his tongue.

She stared at him coldly. "So you told a bloody sociopath to hurt some random girl. This girl. *My* girl."

"Laney," Armin said, his sudden quiet contrasting against Blythe's fury, "what did Zoeller do to you?"

Showed me I'm a monster.

"Exactly what you told him to. Seduced me, fucked me." I laughed. "He didn't ruin me, though. I ruined myself."

They both grimaced, her indignant, him elegiac.

"I'll go to the police," Armin said. "I'll tell them everything. He can still be put away."

"For what?" I rocked back on my chair. "He never hurt me."

"The searches on my computer. Your symptoms—"

"Come on, Armin. The Internet is a how-to guide for faking anything." I balanced one shoe atop the other, jauntily. "It's such a cliché. The damaged girl must have sexual trauma in her past, right? Give me a break. Plot twist: there was no rape. I fucked Zoeller because I wanted to. I'm not sexually traumatized, I'm just messed up."

I scooted my chair closer with a screech. He jumped.

"But you. You're pretty messed up, too, aren't you? You told a psycho to go after a queer. They have a legal term for that." I pointed the gun at him like a blaming finger. "You made him target me because of what I am, not who I am. That's a hate crime."

Blythe was breathing so hard I could hear it. A candle nearby stirred, lashing her with light.

"I was out of my mind. It seemed like the whole world went crazy." Armin's voice was ruminative, the anger gone. He spoke now to Blythe. "Everyone sympathized with you. They called you brave. Your cheating was 'brave' because it was with a girl. It was okay that you hurt me because you were discovering yourself, and I was just a man, no one to take seriously. Another notch on your belt. I felt subhuman. Like you thought I deserved to be hurt because of what I am." He met my eyes soberly. "So I made someone hurt you because of what you are. I couldn't break the cycle."

Blythe snared her hands in her hair, ready to snap.

"Jeez," I said, my tone light. "Everyone looks so depressed. Let's have a drink."

I filled the glass and took a long slug. Blythe next. When it came to Armin he stared at it.

"What did you mean about not taking drinks from strangers?"

"Smart boy. You're learning."

"What is it you want me to do? Tell me, Laney. Anything."

"I don't want you to do anything. I want you to feel." I reached out, grazing his hand. "It's going to hurt. I've been through it. Withdrawal feels like the worst depression you've ever known."

Armin frowned.

"They call the comedown 'Suicide Tuesday.' My mother died on a Tuesday. It's sort of fitting."

"What are you talking about?"

"I'm talking about chronic MDMA abuse and what happens when you quit cold turkey."

He stared at me, expressionless.

I gestured with the gun. "Let's review, class. Ecstasy unleashes a shit ton of serotonin, dopamine, and norepinephrine into the brain. It makes you feel amazing. Awake, sensitive, turned on. In love with the whole world and everyone in it. Those neurotransmitters trigger the release of testosterone and oxytocin. Sex and love hormones, basically. You'll say, 'You make me feel high, Laney.' Intoxicated. Pure, dizzying bliss. Like we're some Adam and Eve in a dangerous paradise. Remember? You'll drink anything I give you, because I'm the broken little doll who needs a big strong boy to fix her, and that feels so fucking good after Blythe dumped you for a girl. Sometimes when you fuck me, you'll really be fucking her in your head. But that's okay. I am, too."

Armin leaned away from me, the tension in his body slackening, becoming shock.

"I got you up to three doses a week. MDMA dissolves in liquid, but leaves a bitter aftertaste. Red Bull isn't really that nasty." I shrugged. "Withdrawal is different for everyone, but your serotonin has been continually depleted for months. You've been growing more agitated, anxious, depressed between doses. You thought it was because of this secret guilt you've been nursing, but actually it's science. Your neurochemistry is severely fucked, Armin. And it will be for a long, long time."

He was totally still. Only his chest moved. Shallow breaths. "Is this some kind of sick joke?"

"It's sick, but it's no joke." Every time I pointed at him with the gun, he flinched. "I wanted you to feel what it's like when someone screws up your brain. I wanted you to feel the highs and the lows. Especially the lows. She's dead because of you and Zoeller. You gave him the poison to put in her head. Now you have a literal taste of your own medicine."

"I didn't know what he would do."

"You gave him the fucking pills. What did you think he'd do?"

"I had no choice." Armin looked at the glass trembling in his hands. "Zoeller threatened to tell Blythe everything. He would've hurt her, too. He doesn't care who he hurts. He's a rabid dog. I thought it'd be harmless. For most people, anti-depressants are harmless."

I sat back in my chair. "So you got my mom killed so your ex-girlfriend wouldn't find out you're a homophobe. Un-fucking-believable."

"I'm not responsible for your mother's death. It was tragic, and I'm deeply sorry, but she committed the act."

"I bet a court would see it differently."

"Do you want to take it there? Put us all on trial, including yourself?"

I ignored his question. "You shoved a loaded gun in some-one's hands and said, 'I'm not responsible if she pulls the trigger.'"

"No one forced her. She needed serious help. She—"

I knocked the glass from his hand with the gun. It burst on the floor, filling the air with honeyed musk. "You don't get to say that. You don't get to say what she needed. You don't fucking know what it was like."

"I do know, Laney. I've seen Blythe when she's rapid cycling. I bet she didn't talk about that much. How many times I coaxed her down from the ledge, how many 'doctor's notes' I wrote that could've cost my career if anyone questioned them. I know what it's like to care for someone who isn't always herself."

Blythe wasn't looking at either of us. She held one fist to her mouth and bit her knuckles.

"She's always herself," I said. "The illness is part of her. Part of us both. You will never understand that."

"I won't argue with you. But in the end, it was your mother's choice. Words and care can only do so much. That's why you did this to me with chemicals, with God knows what. Laney, *you* could have killed *me*."

"Isn't it beautiful when things come full circle?"

"Why did you sleep with me?" His voice roughened. "You could have drugged me without any fake romance."

His pain made me feel strange. It made my pulse race, but not in the pleasurable way I'd hoped. It was the sick acceleration of nausea. "Seduce him," I said doggedly. "Fuck him. Ruin him. Make it hurt."

Armin looked from me to Blythe, another wave of pain crashing through his face, breaking.

"Blythe," he whispered.

She wouldn't look at him.

"Blythe, did you know she drugged me? Were you in on it?"

"Don't blame her," I said. "No matter how she hurt you, it doesn't excuse what you did."

"Did you plan it together? Get me high and fuck me so you could both break my heart?"

"Shut up," she snapped.

"What?" I said, and Armin said, "Tell her."

Blythe's face twisted, her fingers clawing at her knees.

"Tell her."

"Tell me," I said, softly.

She turned her head. I knew her so well. She didn't have to say it.

"Blythe." Keep breathing. Steady, even. "Truth or dare?"

"Don't."

"Truth or fucking dare."

"It didn't mean anything. It was just—"

"Fucking pick."

"Truth. Blythe, did you fuck him. Yes, Laney, I fucked him." She hurled it at me like handfuls of broken glass. "Christ, I fucked him, okay?"

"When?" My voice was oddly calm.

"After you and me."

"When?"

"Valentine's."

Something tore in me, a tight, neat rip, deep inside.

"How many times?"

"Once. Once, I swear to God. It didn't mean anything. I did it for you." She laughed, gruesome. "I know how it sounds, but I hated it. I hated that you were with him instead of me. It made me sick, like swallowing poison every day, black and vile. He's so bloody infatuated with me he promised he'd stop seeing you if I slept with him. I was going mad. I could smell you on him. On his clothes, his skin. I wanted to kill you both."

"But you fucked him instead."

"Because I wanted *you*. That part of you that was in him. That part of you that belongs to me."

My mouth stayed shut but a door opened in my mind, and I went inside, closed it, and screamed.

"And for what?" Blythe said, rounding on Armin. "You never stopped with her, you goddamn liar."

"I was in love with you both," he said. "And you betrayed me. You're the liars."

"Take a good look in the mirror, mate. Then go fuck yourself."

"Go fuck yourself, Blythe. You wonder why men become this way. Look what you did to me, after all I did for you."

"You never accepted that I couldn't love you the way you loved me."

"I could've accepted it if you were honest. But you cheated, and lied, and twisted my mind into knots, and now I'm just as fucked-up as you two."

She stood and kicked her chair into the shadows.

My insides were all mixed up. I felt queasy.

"It's over, Lane," Blythe said. "Let's just go."

I fixed my stare on a candle flame. "This is why you wouldn't hurt him."

"I didn't want to hurt him because we have a history, and it's messy. It was just sex. It meant nothing."

"Your words mean nothing, you fucking cheater."

That torn place inside me burned, alcohol seeping into the wound. Valentine's. After I'd gone home with him, because I missed her. Because I wanted to feel some tenuous connection to her through him.

I should have known. No one really changes.

"All that stuff about the police," I said to Armin. "How I had to cut contact or she'd lose her visa. All lies. You wanted her for yourself."

"Exaggerations, not lies. And it was for her sake, not mine. I didn't want her dragged deeper into our situation with Zoeller."

"You made me believe I was protecting her by giving her up, you selfish fuck."

Armin shook his head. "Do you realize how hypocritical this is, when you two were cheating on me?"

"You're the hypocrite," I growled. "You cheated, too. God, both of you make me sick. Go fuck each other forever. You're disgusting."

Blythe flung her hands up. "Christ, everyone here has fucked everyone else. It's a bit absurd to freak out over it now."

"Then why did you hide it?" I said. "Because you knew it'd hurt me."

"You hurt me, too. The only thing that mattered was your bloody revenge. Not me."

My hair hung in my eyes. I must have torn at it unaware. "Is that why you did it? To hurt me back?"

"Maybe I did, yeah. Maybe hurting you felt good." Her voice lowered. "Maybe I loved you so much I couldn't stand seeing you with anyone else."

"You don't know shit about love. You'll fuck anyone and throw them away. You're a total cliché, Blythe. The bi slut who cheats on everybody. Maybe your mom was right."

Her eyes were furious, but she didn't rise to the bait.

"Let me tell you what I know about love, little wolf. It's craziness, like he said." She grabbed the back of a chair, knuckles white. Her tone was fervent. "It's a dream. It's a drug. I craved you more and more and no matter how much you gave me, it was never enough. I don't know who I am anymore without you. I don't know which day it is, which planet I'm on. Every hour feels like three a.m. and the night never ends. There's only darkness, and you. You're the last bright thing left in this world."

Something thudded dully in my chest, like a fist hitting a bruise, over and over.

"Love is mania, Laney. It's ecstasy. It's everything. And I may be a fucking cliché, but I know I love you."

I needed more tequila. A lot more.

"What have we done to each other?" Armin said quietly.

I pushed my chair back. My fingers wouldn't hold the gun right. "None of this matters anymore. It's over. It's done. Which one of you is it?"

They were both silent. Armin looked exhausted, that bone weariness, an ache in the deepest, darkest parts of the body. Depression. A black lethargy that oozes from your marrow, your DNA. But Blythe brimmed with pain, her body wound tight, her face fearful, hopeful, hurt. It was torture to look at.

"Which one of you is blackmailing us?" I said.

I'd gone into this thinking it had to be Hiyam. But now it was clear we each had a motive.

Armin knew this was coming. Blackmail could be his bargaining chip. Drive a wedge between me and Blythe, turn us against each other. I could nail him with a hate crime and ethics violations but he could retaliate against both of us with the revenge spree.

Blythe, as always, was harder to decode. She sounded sincere, but she always sounded sincere. Maybe she wasn't a bad liar—maybe love blinded me to her lies. I couldn't trust myself with her. Blackmail could be a way to prevent me from hurting Armin, whom she still cared about, *and* keep me for herself. Tie both of our hands.

Of course, there was another possibility: the two of them, together . . .

"I know what you're thinking," she said, reading my face. "It's not like that. I swear."

"Why should I believe a word you say?"

"Because you hid things from me, too, you bloody hypocrite. It doesn't mean this wasn't real."

"For all we know," Armin said, "it's you, Laney."

"What?"

"Is this another part of your elaborate revenge? Make us doubt each other, question everything we ever said, or felt?"

"I'm doing that myself right now," I said.

Blythe kicked another chair.

"I won't fight you." Armin sighed heavily. "Do what you need to do. Turn me in, tell the police. I'll take full responsibility. I don't want to hurt you anymore. I don't want you to ever be hurt again. You didn't deserve this." His head turned partway, those sooty eyelashes lowering. "Just don't hurt Blythe. Please."

"I'd never hurt her. No matter how much she hurts me."

"Goddammit," she said, and made a tiny sound of rage, a half scream.

The cool calm in me was long gone, shattered like glass. I was emotional and it's dangerous to make irrevocable decisions when you're emotional. But I didn't have a choice.

"Blythe," I said.

I tossed her the gun, safety on. She caught it nimbly.

"Keep him here. I'll be back in a few hours."

Armin rose, alarmed. "No. Laney, please, no."

I went to the door. Pulled my keys from my pocket, crushed them into my palm till it felt like they'd break skin.

"She's going after Hiyam," Armin said. "Don't let her do this, Blythe. Laney, my sister had nothing to do with it. I'm the one you should hate."

"Oh, I do. But now we play process of elimination." I glanced at Blythe. "Show me if you still deserve my trust."

I thought of the first night in the cab, the furtive thrill in her eyes when I passed her the oxy. She'd sensed it, instinctively. Us versus him. He was my prey. And she'd been with me every step. In a nasty way, her fucking him made this even sweeter. Made it hurt him more.

She wrapped both hands around the gun.

"Sit down, Armin. I know where the safety is on this thing."

Relief flooded my veins, powerful as a drug.

Good girl, I mouthed.

I turned my back to them and opened the lock.

"I'm sure you two have a lot to talk about. Just try to refrain from fucking him again, Blythe."

And I left them there, in that room filled with their shadows and our shared past.

———

Driving always cleared my head.

I got on a westbound expressway so I could go fast, followed the trails of taillights, a rush of neon blood streaming out of the city. No new plan yet. I'd been sure one of them would crack and confess, but their reactions and my intuition said otherwise. He'd been blindsided by the ecstasy. Like I'd been blindsided by Blythe and him—God. Every time I thought of it my mind filled with images, the way they'd touched during the threesome, so knowing, so tender.

She was faking it, I thought. The way I'd faked with him.

I was in love with you both.

Not true. He didn't love me. And we didn't love him, either.

How the fuck could I love someone who'd hurt me so much?

The speedometer crept over 80 mph. I took the next exit for Naperville.

One way or another, I had to eliminate Hiyam as a suspect, and for that I'd need a weapon. Zoeller's gun. It'd be good to see him again, let him know I'd taken down his old master.

I parked in the lane behind his RV.

He was out of the hospital but not back in school. Still needed assistance bathing and getting dressed and resisting the siren song of suicide. I climbed the ladder to the sunroof he'd leave unlocked for me. Open.

No one inside.

The trailer was cold, as always. Walls lined with books. The place on the shag rug where I'd gone down on hands and knees and let him fuck me. My fingers curled into my palms.

No gun.

I searched everywhere. Found the spare keys to his safe but it didn't contain anything useful. Drugs, notebooks. Zoeller's serial killer diaries. The poem I'd written for Kelsey, which I set on fire and dropped in the sink. Burned discs and thumb drives, probably full of videos. His treasure trove of blackmail fodder.

Hmmm.

I hunted through the trailer again and found a messenger bag, reopened the safe and swept all the discs and drives inside.

Always plan ahead.

Where the hell was that gun?

I couldn't go up to the mansion. Parents, witnesses. Screw it. Get the baseball bat and head back to the city.

We'd stowed it in the crawl space at my old house. It was going on one a.m. Dad and Donnie would probably be asleep.

I started the car.

Our house was dark and still. Good.

I crept into my room, into the crawl space I knew so well, sized just right for a small monster. But the bat wasn't there.

Shit. Maybe Donnie had to move it. Dad talked lately about selling the house. He might've gone poking around, cleaning things up for a real estate agent.

If Donnie wanted to hide something, he'd hide it in the garage. Dad never went in there anymore.

I backed out, a fine layer of dust glimmering on my coat.

Since Mom died no one had touched the garden. It was wild now, weeds and predatory flowers killing everything delicate and uncertain. No irises this year.

No irises ever again.

I slipped the spare key from the top of the doorjamb and fit it to the lock, but it was already open.

Sometimes my dreams were like this. Walking into the garage unassumingly. A shadow turning, looming. Her screaming white face.

I froze in the doorway. "Mom," I said as quietly as I could.

"Laney," came the answering whisper.

I almost ran. My overstimulated brain took a second to process it. Then I stepped in, squinting. "Donnie?"

I fumbled at the wall. The light sputtered on.

He was sitting on the workbench in jeans and a jacket. His shoulders slumped, face flushed beneath a tumble of hair. He'd been crying.

My heart softened. "What are you doing out here?" I said, moving closer.

No answer.

This is how much I love my brother:

I didn't notice the glint of metal to either side of him till I was two feet away, arms raised, ready to embrace.

I looked at the bat. I looked at the black shine of Zoeller's gun. Then I looked at his face.

"Oh my god," I said. "Please don't."

I didn't move. Someone who's suicidal can startle easily.

"I love you," I said. "More than the world. Please don't leave me."

His eyes glassed over. "I saw you, Laney."

And I loved him so much it took another delayed moment to really hear what he'd said.

I saw you.

All the tension went out of my body in an instant.

When we'd come home from the hospital we'd climbed into the rafters together to cut down the noose. We didn't speak, and for a while I didn't think of it as the thing that had killed Mom but only rope, rope that was hard to cut with my right hand stiff and bandaged. Her presence was still there. Removal of the body doesn't change that. Any second she'd peep in the window, lift an eyebrow. Everything else was still the same. Motor oil on cement, the cool, spooky scent of rain and raw wood. My brother with his sinewy adult body and baby face, his hair always in his eyes. The round earth beneath us, tilting, turning slowly, taking a dose of sun. It was all still the same so why wasn't she here? If she was really dead there would have been some outward proof. Apocalypse, disaster. The world would change. My hands stopped working then and I dropped the blade. I let myself dangle and fall to the garage floor, crumpling where I landed. Donnie came to sit with me on the cold concrete, our arms wrapping around each other, and we cried for a long, long time.

I stood now in the same place we'd sat, where the noose had hung, and lowered myself to the floor. I was so tired, suddenly. So tired. Of all of this.

"What did you see?" I said.

"Everything."

I thought of the morning she died. Me texting him with no response.

"The pills," I said.

Donnie nodded.

In my typical way, I thought: How can I control this? What can I lie about? But part of me, knocked loose by Blythe and Armin, thought also: Confess. Get the truth out.

That's the real poison, truth. Keep that shit inside and you'll see. You'll wither and die.

I pressed my palms to the gritty cement. Felt the faint white scars lacing the back of my hand, the dimple inside my lip where Kelsey's dad had hit me. A tiny arrowhead on my shoulder where Blythe had bitten too hard. I felt so old. Nineteen going on a thousand.

Scars tell a story. My whole life was written on my body.

How are you supposed to leave the past behind when you carry it with you in your skin?

My mother never believed in forgiveness. Hold it all in as hard as you can. Hate what you can't control. Rage at the world, at this endlessly disappointing life.

How exhausting it was to hate.

I didn't ask, *What do you know? When did you find out?* I didn't look for ways to hedge around the truth, shield myself.

Instead I said, "It was my fault, Donnie."

The words were hot smoke in my mouth, a fire in my lungs eating all air, but I made myself go on.

"Remember how they said she shouldn't have been on antidepressants? She wasn't supposed to be. I switched out her meds."

"Why?"

My whole chest ached. "To make her manic. To destabilize her."

This was so much harder than I thought. Not saying it, the mechanics of it, but taking the blame.

"I knew," I started, and had to gather myself and start over. "Bipolar people who go on antidepressants have a high risk of becoming manic. And if you go straight from depression to mania, there's a danger of violent behavior. Of self-harm."

"You made her do it," he said.

"Yes." It was strange. Confession almost felt good. A justified ache. A deserved one. "Yes, I did. Dad was going to leave us. He was going to leave you alone with her. I had to do something."

His shoulders shook. The brightness in his eyes made its way down his face.

"I'm so sorry," I said, hugging my knees to my chest. I wanted to press on the place that hurt, close the wound, but it ached, and ached, and wouldn't stop. "I didn't want her to die. I just didn't want her to get custody."

"That's what she said," he mumbled through tears.

"What?"

"She didn't want Dad to leave, either. She was scared of being alone with me. She said weird stuff about driving off a bridge, or parking on train tracks. That I was too pure, that it would be better if I died before something ruined me. It freaked me out. I don't think Mom would hurt me, but I don't think she realized we would both die, you know? Like I was just part of her, like a hand or foot."

Her son, her figurative sun. The good part of herself, the part she wanted to preserve, even as her thinking got more unstable, deranged. We'd become a living metaphor for her illness.

"When did she say this?"

"The night before she did it. She came to talk to me."

"What else did she say?"

He wiped a sleeve across his nose. "That she was sorry. That she saw herself spiraling down, but couldn't stop. There was no one to catch her. We slowed her fall for a while, but then she dragged us down, too."

"Donnie, why didn't you tell me this?"

"I tried." A sob lurched from his throat. "I called you a million times. You didn't answer. I went looking for you at Zoeller's and saw you there, with him."

In his trailer. Fucking him. While my mother wrote me a suicide note.

"It's not what you—"

"You said he was your enemy. You said you liked girls. You made me feel so bad for you."

"He was. Is. And I do."

"Well, I thought you lied. I was so mad I turned off my phone. I wanted Mom to catch you sneaking back in. And now I think, If I wasn't mad, if I got your texts, everything would've been different. I would've gone downstairs and seen her and we could have saved her. We could have saved her, Laney."

My hands covered my mouth, tears spilling over in warm threads.

"It was never your fault," I said. "It was mine. I just wanted to keep you safe."

For a while we simply cried, separately, miserably. When a lull came, I spoke.

"Why were you following us? The pics, the blackmail. What did you want?"

"I don't know. I didn't really plan it out." His leg swung, nervous. "I wanted you to tell me about the meds. If you were trying to help her. I kept hoping you'd been trying to help. But you never told me the truth, and then you got obsessed with this revenge plan. You're scary when you're obsessed."

I looked again at the gun and bat lying beside him.

"You didn't bring those to hurt yourself," I said slowly. "You brought them to protect yourself. From me."

He lowered his head.

"God, Donnie. How'd you know I'd come here?"

"I texted Blythe, to apologize for the pics. She told me everything. I knew you'd come home eventually." He sighed. "I'm sorry for what I did, but you wouldn't stop. You took revenge on everyone to cover up your guilt about Mom. If you'd just told me, I would've forgiven you. You could have let all this bad stuff go."

"I can't let anything go. I'm a bad person."

"No you're not."

"I am. I'm full of hate. I hate everything. Myself, and everyone who's hurt me. The way I am. Borderline and queer and all of it. I never asked to be this way, and if I could change it I—"

I stopped. For so many years I'd wished, desperately: Make me normal. Make me the cheerleader, the Homecoming

Queen, the girly girl who falls in love with square-jawed boys. Make me a happy little robot. Anything would be better.

But if I was normal, I'd never have met Blythe. Never fallen into this crazy, all-consuming love. Never plunged to the depths of myself and found something hard and enduring there, an unwillingness to die. The grit that Mom was missing.

"When did you start following me?" I said.

"Summer. I saw you with Blythe. Me and Hiyam figured it out, but she never told anyone. She talked to me. She's a lot nicer than you think. And she said sometimes people do bad things, but you can't intervene. You have to let them see the wrongness on their own. Otherwise they won't learn and they won't change." He fidgeted, shoulders hunched. "I should have listened to her. But all you cared about was hurting people. You didn't want to feel better, you just wanted everyone else to feel worse. You hated Zoeller but then you became just like him. You forgot he was the enemy."

"I still hate him. He pretended to be my friend, but he was screwing with me the whole time. He hurt—" I changed what I was going to say. "He made my life hell."

"Lane, it's okay. I get it now. Sometimes you love and hate the same person at the same time."

Armin.

Mom.

"Is that how you feel me about me?"

"I never hated you, Rainbow Brite. You're my big sister. I always looked up to you, even when you were down."

My throat burned. "You are so much better than me."

This had all started as a means to protect my little brother, and I ended up becoming the thing he needed protection from. Just like her.

I was just like her.

"I hate myself," I said again.

"Don't say that."

"I'm worse than she ever was. I'm a monster, Donnie. You shouldn't be around me."

"What?"

"I need to go away." I tried to stand, made it to my knees. "You're almost in college. Once you have a job, your own life—you're the only thing I stayed for. I don't want to be on this fucking planet anymore. I hate it. All I feel anymore is hate."

"Stop it." He sat forward, fists balled. "I still love you, Dad loves you. And Mom loved you, too." He was crying openly, struggling to get the words out. "You didn't even ask. The very last thing she said."

"What was it?"

"She said, 'Let go of pain, not people.' She had to let go, but she wanted us to hold on. And I will, Laney. I'll never let you go."

You'll feel it, the moment you crack. When the brittle hardness finally shatters. When the anger, hatred, resentment, loathing, everything crumbles, and all that's left standing is the little girl who'd built those walls, wide-eyed, covered in dust.

I tried to rise but I was too tear-blind. Donnie slipped off the table and knelt with me, a watery shadow. He put his arms around me the way he had that morning. I held him as tight as I could and cried, *I'm sorry, I'm sorry, I'm sorry*, to him, to her, the ghost inside both of us. And I know I didn't imagine this part. I was lucid. It was real. He said the words but somehow I heard her voice inside his, an echo of her.

I forgive you, they said.

APRIL, THIS YEAR

No rain that anniversary morning. I drove east toward the Chicago skyline, the buildings tinted pink-gold from a sun still rising. Donnie and I sat side by side in silence.

Navy Pier wasn't open yet. I parked nearby and we walked to the Ohio Street Beach, pulling our shoes off, barefoot in cold sand. Skyscrapers reflected on the lake in smudged pastel sticks of color. In another lifetime I'd come here with Armin and Blythe. Some of the footprints chiseled in the sand might still be ours.

"Do you remember that day?" Donnie said.

He meant the photo, the one in the Moleskine he gave me. Me and him on the pier. I was fifteen. Mom had decided to be maternal that weekend and insisted on photographing us everywhere, riding the Ferris wheel, eating hot dogs, glaring at her with teenage superiority. We made goofy faces. We photobombed each other. At the end of the day, exhausted from our brattiness, we slouched on the dock sharing a pop and she snapped us covertly.

"Mustard mustache," I said, and we both grinned. Mom didn't even notice till she had the prints done: Donnie lurking in the background of my portraits, a neon yellow squiggle over his lip. In contrast I looked way too intense, quietly volatile, already harboring the pain of realizing who I was, who I loved, how the world would hurt me for it. Mom took so many photos of me that day. What was she searching for?

Donnie had his camera, too, but he only got one shot of Mom, gazing at the lake while waiting for us to return from some ride. He caught just the right angle so you could see the sun reflected in her eyes, a distant fire.

If only I'd seen you that way, Mom. If only I could have looked past my own pain to yours.

Our grins faded into solemnity. I blinked away tears.

I'd become a lot more emotional these days. It was unsettling.

"Are you ready?" he said.

"No."

Like I'd ever be. But I took the paper from my pocket anyway.

We walked to the shore and dropped our shoes. I shivered, but it came from inside. I pulled out my lighter.

"I don't have to read it," I said. "I can let go without knowing what it says."

"It's the last thing she ever wrote, Lane."

I owed her that, I guess. Someone should bear witness.

I gave Donnie the lighter. My hands shook so hard the name on the front blurred. *Delaney.*

She always knew it would be me.

I unfolded it with exaggerated care, afraid I might tear it accidentally, or purposely. I'd carried this for a year, her final words to me. Right there against my skin. Whispering to my blood. I held the paper so we could both see. In my head I heard her voice reading.

You set me free. Now let me go.

I grew you well, my little black iris.

Only those two lines. I reread them, confused, but Donnie pulled away from me, inhaling sharply.

"Laney."

"That's it?" I shook the paper, as if I could force more meaning out. "That's it?"

"Don't you get it? She knew."

I stared at him.

"She knew what you did. The pills." Relief suffused his voice. "She knew."

I looked back at the words in bewilderment. I wanted an essay, an explanation. Why did you treat us this way, Caitlin? What did you want me to become?

Why couldn't we save you?

Only those sixteen words, insubstantial as air.

I was trembling uncontrollably. Donnie took the paper.

"Laney, it's okay." He pulled me into a hug. "She forgave you."

I stared past him to the white disc rising above the horizon. Some massive force seized either side of my ribs, cracking me in two.

I'd wanted, needed more.

But this was it. All she'd left me with.

We both put our hands on the paper, and Donnie touched the lighter to it, and we held as long as we could, till the orange tongues licked our skin. Then we let go, watching it tear itself apart and fly on the breeze like flaming feathers, vanishing into ash, water, wind.

My hand stretched out vainly, grasping nothing. Just a kiss of smoke on my fingertips.

———

Umbra without Armin was a strange place.

It was the first time I'd been back since the truth came out, and I felt a million years older. I walked through stone halls filled with black lights and ghoul grins, dry ice, monster shadows, skewed echoes, and it all seemed so small, so quaint, like going back to high school. I wandered through the Oubliette and never lost my way or felt afraid. No shadow followed. I still didn't know if it'd been Blythe or Donnie or my own drugged-out imagination, and I didn't want to know. All that mattered was that it was gone.

I wasn't sober. You don't quit a bad habit in a few weeks. But I'd cut back. I could sleep now with a clear head, though I didn't sleep much. Most nights I lay awake, stroking Orion's ginger fur, staring at the constellations of city lights on the ceiling and remembering. Remembering all of it.

Me, and him, and her.

"Everything is so fucked-up," Hiyam said, lifting her soda. We sat on a divan in the Aerie. The disco ball galaxy spun slowly above us. In a twist I found morbidly amusing, we were actually becoming friends. "Like, in what universe am I the straight arrow?"

The official story was that Armin got into X while deejaying, got hooked, broke up with me when I refused to swan-dive headfirst to the bottom with him. He'd withdrawn from grad school, checked into outpatient rehab. Resigned from Eclipse, which was in recess now while they reorganized. And his sister, the ex-junkie, was taking care of him.

It unsettled me. Some nights I lurked in the alley outside his building, my hood up against the rain, watching little pills of neon light scatter and roll on the wet streets, wondering what we'd say if we saw each other. Wondering what it was I even felt.

Did you really love me once, Armin? The way you loved her?

Did I ever really love you?

I recalled those moments when, in the thick of my revenge, my lies and machinations, he'd reached through it all in his gentle, precise way and touched some raw red place in my chest. Made me feel things I should not have. Made me feel.

Like Zoeller.

I had told Armin I wanted to break his mind and his heart, but I wasn't so sure anymore about the latter. Not sure it was entirely vengeance that drove me to let him close. Or that his was the only heart broken.

All three of us. We'd broken each other. Me. Him. Her.

At the thought of Blythe, my lungs tightened till every breath was an effort.

She'd never been gentle. She'd flipped my life over, destroyed my self-control and complicated everything, terrified me and intoxicated me and thrilled me, and I missed it like hell. Girls get under each other's skin. We get too close, too attached, too crazy, and then we can't let go. Our claws sink too deep. When we separate, we tear each other apart.

I missed it. The blood under my nails. The wildness. The highs and lows.

I missed her.

"He needs you right now," I told Hiyam. "More than he ever has. You have to be there for him, like he was for you. I can't believe I'm saying this, but you're good for him."

For a second something passed through her face, not her usual superior knowing but a flash of wisdom, of burgeoning adulthood. "I know, Keating."

It was the closest she'd ever get to *thank you*.

"Know what's scary?" I said. "We're more alike than you think."

Her eyebrows rose. "You're not really my type, but if that's an attempt at flirting, I'll play."

"You're the last person on earth I'd flirt with, Hiyam."

"You're a total freak."

"You're a complete bitch."

"Hate to break it to you, Keating, but I think we're actually flirting."

I laughed. So did she.

God.

I didn't want to ask the question that had burned on my tongue all night, but the drunker I got, the less likely it seemed I'd stay in control. Before I got too ripped, I decided: fuck it.

"How's Blythe?"

"Ask her yourself."

Hiyam stood to hug somebody and the world went still. Seeing someone you once loved is like falling in love for the first time all over again. Those bare shoulders vibrant with ink, the sweeping grace of her movements. The low, easy laugh at some exchange I didn't even process. I felt drugged. Hiyam left us with a look that uncannily resembled her brother's *be good*.

"Anyone sitting here?" Blythe said.

"You are."

That impish smile. She sat. Closer than Hiyam but still a good two feet off, far enough that those things I craved, the blackberry perfume, the warmth of her breath, were beyond me. I wore a tee and jeans; she was in a sleek black dress like that first night, eons ago. I'd always known she was beautiful, but it's something you don't fully appreciate when someone is yours. Even miracles become routine. It hit me hard now, the lazy way she flicked those piercing blue eyes at me, a girl toying with an infinitely sharp knife that could carve your heart out.

In my head I'd rehearsed a million things to say. Bits of brilliance. Quotes about love and loss. A whole fucking Tumblr post. Instead I stared awkwardly, then drank.

You are so close and so far away, I thought. Is this how it is now, forever?

"Do you want to dance?" she said.

I nodded.

It was better like this. We could say so much without speaking.

When we stepped together on the floor there was a moment of electric proximity, a buzz between our skin, uncertain how to touch but needing to. Her arms slid around my waist, mine around her neck. I laid my cheek on her shoulder, my mouth beside the lily.

I didn't know what the song was. I didn't know what anything was. I closed my eyes and felt nothing but the body against mine.

"How I missed you, little wolf."

I was just drunk enough to touch my teeth to her skin, lightly.

Blythe laughed. Her arms went tighter, pulling me close.

We'd danced like this a hundred times before but always hid what we really felt, really were. Afraid of Armin. Of the world's judgment. Afraid of unraveling the tangled web we'd spun around ourselves, these lies we told to manipulate, destroy. To survive. It still kicked fear into my heart, but some of that fear was really exhilaration. No more hiding. We could be anything we wanted, now.

I just wasn't sure what that was anymore.

As we danced I was acutely aware of the people around us, boy-girl pairs. Stubbled jaws and lipstick smiles. Newness shining in their eyes. Unbrokenness. Blythe felt me stiffen and put her mouth near my ear. Her voice was low.

"I still feel the same about you."

"I'm still hurt, Blythe."

"I am, too. We're very good at hurting people. Especially each other." She ran a finger under my chin. None of her usual mischief. She looked tired, longing, like someone who misses home. "'Pain has an element of blank; it cannot recollect—'"

" '—When it began, or if there were a day when it was not.' "

"But it doesn't hurt now. This moment."

"It will again," I said.

"Does that mean there's an again?"

I didn't know. "I wish we'd met in another life," I said, wistful.

She winced, but in a second it was gone. "This is another life. We're strangers. Brilliant writers who meet by chance, dancing at a club."

"Who are you?" I meant it half-seriously.

"Blythe Spencer McKinley." Her old wryness ghosted over her lips. "Nice to meet you. I like your accent."

"Delaney June Keating. And I like your face."

She started to laugh, but the tremor of sincerity in my voice made it too real.

Blythe laid a hand on my cheek. We had slowed, stilled, while the world revolved around us, voices and flashes moving at light speed as this moment between us crystallized.

"I don't want to be strangers," I said.

"Neither do I."

"This is who we are." My fingers curled in the filmy silk of her dress. "Even the worst parts. Especially those."

"You know, when I met you I had this crazy idea that I'd be the one to save you, not Armin. That I'd show you how beautiful life is. Make you feel alive, the way you made me feel."

I took a strand of her hair and drew it between two fingers.

"You did," I said.

Our eyes met.

"I never wanted to be saved. I wanted someone to follow me down into the darkness. To hold my hand as I fell." I wrapped that lock of hair tighter, pulling ever so gently. "I didn't need you to hold me back from the edge. I needed you to take the leap with me."

"We fell bloody hard."

"And it felt amazing. Even when we hit the ground."

Something stormy shifted in her expression. "Will you trust me like that again?"

"I could ask you the same thing." I let the lock uncoil. "There's something I've always wanted to know. How did things end with you and Elle?"

This time she didn't avert her face. She held my gaze, showed me the hurt in her smile. "She broke my heart."

"How?"

"There was someone else in her life. I was a rebound, a stop on the road. Poetic justice, really." Blythe looked so much older than me then, so haunted. "It's rare enough to find someone in this world you can love with all your heart. To have it recip- rocated is a bloody miracle. And we throw it away, because it's not perfect. Because we make mistakes."

My chest felt weird. All twisted up inside.

She leaned closer, spoke softly. "Do you remember the night you came to me on the roof and said, 'It'll always be you'?"

I blinked.

A smile flitted over her face. "I heard. And I held on to that. No matter what happened, I knew it would always be you."

I had to laugh, because otherwise I was going to cry. "I meant it. I meant everything."

"Me too."

"God, we're ridiculous. You're bipolar and I'm borderline. We're fire and oil. Who could stand us without getting burned?"

Armin couldn't. I wonder if he always knew that.

"We were good together," Blythe said.

"We were bad together."

"That's what I mean."

Her grin was slow, and sly, and it did dark, crazy things to my heart.

EPILOGUE

NOVEMBER, THIS YEAR

The sun was every bit as fever-pure as I imagined, in a sky so blue and infinite it seemed the only real thing, the land below a hallucination, rough brushstrokes of sand and gorse sketching out to the horizon. We'd been driving along the Great Ocean Road, stopping at dusk in a tiny town called Apollo Bay, because of the name. I turned twenty today, in Australia—tomorrow, in Chicago—and for my birthday dinner we bought fish and chips wrapped in butcher paper from a shack near the beach. We walked down to the shore, the grease tinting the paper clear. Salt spray whipped off the water, scooping up the smell of sunbaked sand, like heated glass.

"I could breathe this forever," I said.

Blythe glanced at me over her sunglasses, smiling.

Back home she became even more like Artemis, her skin tanning and hair lightening, barefoot and bare-limbed, a wild thing stalking through the long grass. Her eyes were a shock of winter in a summer-kissed face.

We sat near the tideline, picking apart hot fish with stinging fingers. When I yelped she laughed and fed me a piece by hand. I feigned further helplessness and she kept feeding me, and eventually we set the food aside to lick the salt from each other's fingers and tumbled into the sand in a burst of gold glitter and kissed, hair tangling in our mouths, fiery-skinned and fierce. But the sun was coming down and she didn't want to miss it.

"You only turn twenty once," Blythe said, straightening my shirt.

"You only love like this once."

She gave me a no-nonsense look. "Watch the bloody sunset."

I laughed.

This girl.

The sun came down slow. For a while I watched with her, arms around each other's waists, heads on shoulders, the perfect Instagram snapshot, but I was itching to check the news. I pulled my phone out over Blythe's disgusted protests. She stood and kicked sand at me. When I remained undaunted, she left to wander down to the water. But soon enough she was back, sprawling on my thighs and giving me an evil eye.

"So?" she said.

I showed her the screen.

DEPAUL SOPHOMORE NOLAN HART INDICTED AS MASTER-MIND OF GRADE-HACKING SCANDAL.

Her face lit up. "That leaves Gordon and Quinn."

I scrolled the screen breezily. A small smile kept playing over my lips.

Nolan was a mastermind of nothing, but that wasn't a problem for my computer-genius friend Josh. One night over drunken book chat, I told him my life story. By the end he'd appointed himself to my "team" and pitched a plan to nail Nolan.

Team Laney. I liked the sound of that.

Remember what I said, back at the beginning? I told you. No forgiveness. No redemption. No fucking character arc where I make a one-eighty and decide vengeance isn't worth it.

What, you thought all that stuff with Armin and Donnie

would change the core of me? That I'd realize this cycle of hurting and revenge has to end, that I should be the bigger person, let the buck stop with me?

Fuck forgiveness.

That's what *they* want me to do. Make it easy for them. Clear their consciences. Let them get away with what they've done.

The powerful. The strong. The privileged.

Not a fucking chance.

Armin wasn't a bad guy, but he made a very bad mistake. He hurt me because of what I am. And I made him pay for it. Like I made Zoeller pay. And Luke, and all the others.

This is what helps me sleep at night. Knowing that one of us stood up and refused to take it. One of us said, *Fuck you*, and struck back.

One of us became the wolf and bloodied her jaws so that others can live without fear.

Change isn't peaceful. Change is violent, savage, cruel. I won't be the heroine remembered for her good deeds, but I can guarantee Luke North and Brandt Zoeller and Armin Farhoudi will think twice before they fuck with another girl's life. Before they hurt someone they think is weaker. Before they judge someone based on *what* and not *whom*.

I won. Because I survived. And I made sure they'll never forget it.

My head is bloody, but unbowed.

"What about Armin?" Blythe said.

"No word yet."

We'd met up before we left the country. He was guarded, withdrawn, wincing every time he glanced at the two of us together. He eyed us like we were wild animals that could maul him at any moment. And we were. But when I dumped Zoeller's blackmail trove on the table he sat down and, like his old self, helped us work out logistics. There were others I hadn't gotten to yet. Gordon and Quinn. Eclipse was still full of bullies like Zoeller, guys who drugged and drank their way into dubious consent, beat up queer kids, made the Walk of Shame a celebrated ritual, made college hell for so many of us. The fraternities were complicit. The sororities, too. If we really wanted to shake things up, we needed to get inside and take them apart. Bring down the baddies. Expose them. Shine a light on all that nastiness.

Zoeller included. Someday I'd finish what I'd started with him.

And what we'd started. The three of us.

We'll always be tied to each other, I had told Armin when we were alone. *Me and you and her.*

He'd looked at me a long time. There was pain in his eyes now that came from a deep place, and part of me felt sad about it, and part of me thought, Now you have a dark seed inside, too. What will you do with it? How will you let it grow?

Promise me, he'd said. *When she gets bad—and she will, Laney—then you'll be there for her. Get her on meds. Therapy. Whatever you have to do. Just don't let her go.*

Blythe looked up into my face. The light was failing, bluing. "We're vigilantes."

The word felt good. I smiled. Then my smile turned inward, fading, and she eyed me suspiciously.

"I know that scheming glint, Lane."

"We *could* be vigilantes. For real."

She sat up, smoothing the sand with her palm. "More than just personal vendettas, you mean."

"Why not? We're good at it. We've got a shitload of practice."

"Convenient lack of moral fiber, bloody good looks . . ."

I tried to contain my excitement. "It could be my birthday present."

"Your present," she said, tossing my phone aside and pressing me down, her legs between mine, "is waiting back at the hotel. In the bed. Not wearing any clothes." She buried my hands in the sand. "Spoiler alert: it's me in like fifteen minutes."

I laughed, giddily. "I'm serious. We could do it." I wrestled a hand free and seized her wrist. "Think about it. Eclipse must have started the same way. They had principles, values. Ideals. Over time they became lost and corrupt. That's why new societies rise up to take their place."

"Our own secret society, full of bad-girl vigilantes." I flicked sand at her with my fingers, but her face grew serious. "Everything starts with a name."

"You're the poet."

She drew the Eclipse symbol in the sand. "Corona. The light behind the darkness."

"Not bad. But that's a beer."

"Halo."

"Video game."

"Bloody hell."

She scowled, and then our eyes widened, and we spoke at the same time.

"Black Iris."

She grinned. So did I. Then she leaned in and kissed me delirious, her skin against my skin, her hair flecked with sea salt and catching in my mouth, her leg between mine making me almost forget the name. When she stopped, the horizon tilted, unsteady.

"Get me the bag," I gasped.

She dragged it over and I dug inside till I found a pocket-knife. Snicked the silver blade open. Ran it across my palm, a bright sting.

"Give me your hand."

Blythe didn't flinch when I cut. I dropped the knife and

pressed my palm to hers, blood to blood. We mashed it together and locked our fingers.

"Black Iris is hereby founded," I whispered, "by Laney Keating and Blythe McKinley."

She had that no-good smirk on her face. "Oh, this is going to be fun."

This time I was the one who pushed her down and kissed her. For a while I forgot the world, forgot everything, till she grasped my face and looked past me, a fine slash of red light in her eyes.

"It's almost gone," she said.

We sat up hastily, breathless. Sun poured like magma over the water. Out here at the edge of the world it was surreal, oil colors spilling over molten blue. When I glanced at Blythe her eyes reflected it, catching and holding a distant fire. I thought of Caitlin on the pier. The mad girl gone down alone into darkness.

But not you, Blythe.

I'll never let you go.

She grabbed my arm, pulling me close. The sun scattered off the waves and filled her eyes with a thousand tiny lights.

"You're not looking," she said.

But I was.

ACKNOWLEDGMENTS

This book is something I never thought I'd have the guts to write. *Unteachable* was much easier; it was all fiction. *Black Iris* isn't. Some of it, I lived.

I've struggled with my sexuality my whole life. As a teen I openly identified as lesbian, and at my first high school most people were tolerant. Being in drama club helped. All of us were kinda weird. But I hid my sexuality from my family because it was a "sin," and never truly came out. Never joined the Rainbow Alliance. Never found the support I needed. Liking girls was this shadowy part of me that I shoved to the back of my head and tried not to think about too much. Except for when I fell in love.

With straight girls, usually. Isn't that always how it goes?

Sophomore year, I transferred to a new school. The kids there weren't so tolerant. I was teased and bullied. It got bad. I dropped out.

They won.

I can still see their faces, the nasty smirks and ugly leers, and sometimes I wonder if they remember me. Probably not. The people who had the biggest impact on you rarely know it.

Some part of me hopes it works the other way, too. That people I don't know will be impacted by this book in a positive way. That a teenager who's struggling with her identity, who feels like no one understands, reads this and realizes: she's not alone. I went through it, too. I was bullied and beaten down, but I survived.

Ellen Page's coming out speech on Valentine's 2014 inspired me to finally have my own pseudo-coming-out. I'm not exactly lesbian, but a 5.8 or so on the Kinsey scale is pretty damn close. And I'm in a long-term relationship with a man, which makes things even more complicated. "Lesbian" and "gay" aren't the right words for me. Neither is "bi." Like Laney says, it's quantum. You can't pin it down. If I have to claim a label, I prefer "queer," but human sexuality is far more complex than choosing one inadequate label, or any label at all.

I am who I am. It's taken me three decades to reach a state of okayness with it. It shouldn't take anyone that long, and that's part of why I wrote this book.

I hope *Black Iris* (with its ironic acronym—I swear, not deliberate!) shows the fluidity and quantumness of human sexuality. I hope it speaks to others who know what it's like to not fit the default template. And I hope it lets the bastards who've made me feel subhuman for the way I was born know:

You haven't silenced me. You haven't won.

My head is bloody, but unbowed.

———

Righteous indignation aside, some thanks are in order.

Writing this book took guts, but so did publishing it. For that, my endless admiration, respect, and love for Sarah Cantin, my incredible editor at Atria. Sarah, thank you for being so damn smart and savvy and open-minded. Thanks for pushing back and challenging me to be a better writer. And thanks for being proud of me. Ditto, lady. Against All Odds, you saw my True Colors shining through. (PHIL COLLINS 4EVA.)

Thank you to my agent, the fabulous Jane Dystel, and to everyone at both Atria and Dystel & Goderich for making my life feel like a fairy tale come true. It's a privilege to work with all of you.

My deepest love to the sweetest boy I know, my partner, Alexander. Thanks for weathering my little storms of madness, buddy.

Mad ♥ to these writers: Dahlia Adler, Bethany Frenette, Ellen Goodlett, Abby McDonald, and Lindsay Smith. You're all inspirations to me.

Thank you to these kick-ass book bloggers: Natasha at *Natasha is a Book Junkie*, Aestas at *Aestas Book Blog*, Jenny and Gitte at *Totally Booked Blog*, Lisa and Milasy at *The Rock Stars of Romance*, Wendy Darling at *The Midnight Garden*, Steph and Meg at *Cuddlebuggery Book Blog*, Emily at *The Book Geek*, and all the fine citizens of Goodreads.

Gross amounts of love to my Facebook fan group, the Raeder Readers: Allen, Cam, Jaime, Jen, Louisse, Michele, Ramona, Sara, Sheri, and everyone I can't list here for space reasons. You guys make me smile every damn day. Heart you all, hard.

And finally, to all the queer, gay, lesbian, bisexual, trans*, intersex, genderqueer, pansexual, asexual, questioning, and other gender/sexuality-diverse kids out there:

This book is for you.

You are beautiful human beings. You inspire me. You make me proud. I hope that stories like mine and Laney's and those of people who've been hurt for being born different will some-day be just that: only stories. Not realities for us anymore.

Keep your heads up. Be strong. Be proud.

Never be afraid or ashamed to reach out for help.

You're not alone.

All my love,
Leah Raeder
Chicago, November 2014